This book is dedicated to all of my friends that never let me give up. The ones that periodically checked in to make sure I was still writing and planning to get published one day. No need to call you out. You know who you are.

TCG

CHAPTER 1

ORDINARY PEOPLE

BENAE

The sounds of the city were sweeter than usual to Benae. The energy from the bustling New York City traffic and the bright sunshine beaming down formed a happy harmony that matched her mood. She moved through the crowded streets with confidence that caught the attention of both men and women. It was more than her natural brown hued hair that flowed and bounced just below her shoulders, her matching chestnut complexion that was mostly hidden behind a large pair of Gucci sunglasses, or the simple Tahari dress and pumps that exuded class, nor was it her lips that were glossed to perfection, the French manicure or the latest Louis Vuitton bag she carried. What made everyone take notice was the ebullient smile and random outbursts of laughter she just could not contain, despite the fact that people were looking at her like she was crazy.

A passing bike messenger yelled out, "Damn, baby whatever it is that's that good, let me get some."

Without hesitation, Benae responded, "What I got is just that good, but I'm selfish and I'm not sharing."

"I heard that." The biker put on the brakes. "Hey wait a minute sexy, let me get your number."

Benae continued walking down the street, her mind back on her private thoughts. Just before she left her office she had received the news that she had been waiting for. The condo that she had made an offer on was hers. Her offer was accepted, and she was now the proud owner of a condo in a renovated Brownstone in the tony Brooklyn Heights area of Brooklyn. The best part was that she would finally get away from Max.

Benae had ended her four-year relationship with Max when she discovered that he was a pathological liar. During their time together she caught him in numerous lies but overlooked them as a character flaw because she loved him. She looked at them as small lies that did not take away from the fact that he very clearly loved her. In fact, he adored her. He bought her anything she wanted and took her on the luxurious trips abroad that she was accustomed to from traveling over the years with her parents.

Benae thought life could not get any better and unfortunately, it didn't. Max's little lies, like working late when he really wasn't or that he was spending time with his mom, when she was really home alone were the kind of lies that Benae could not overlook anymore. He started spending nights out and coming home with tired excuses. Benae drove herself crazy trying to figure out what to do. She could not understand how someone who seemed to love her so much, lied just as much. She was thirty-two-years old and desperately wanted to get married and start a family, but she could not marry a man that she no longer trusted.

Her parents never cared for him anyway, especially her father. Even though Max was the owner of his own company and could take care of his daughter in the manner in which she was accustomed, he never liked him. Reed was a successful businessman in his own right and had lived most of his life enjoying his financial success with his debutant wife and only daughter, but Reed knew a man that was full of shit when he saw him. Max may think all he saw in him was the man that he was trying to be today. However, as the saying goes, game recognizes game and Reed knew Max wasn't on the up and up on many levels. If this was the final straw for Benae she had his full support.

It had been nine months since she ended their relationship, during which time they stayed under the same roof, but led separate lives. Intermittently, Max begged Benae to forgive him all the while still doing his own thing. She couldn't care less because now it was truly over. She was moving into her own place and would not even inform Max of her new address.

The smell of barbequed salmon wafted from the doorway as she entered the apartment. Her sniff was confirmed when she walked into the kitchen to see two plates of salmon, broccoli, and white rice on the table, along with a bottle of her favorite Chardonnay. She shook her head at Max's attempt to please her. She already made plans to go out and celebrate her new apartment with her best friend Chrissy.

Silently she stepped out of her shoes, wiggled her toes, and was sorting through the day's mail when the bedroom door swung open and Max stepped out wearing nothing but a freshly shaved face and a towel. In spite of herself, Benae sucked in her breath a little. Max's eight pack, bronzed skin, and his bald head was such a turn-on. He knew it and smiled seductively at her reaction. His white teeth and deep dimples were too much. She shook off the lustful thoughts invading her mind and recalled his disgusting ways.

This is why his ass can't be faithful, she thought, *Too many women see the same thing I see when they look at him.* She looked him up and down with disdain. "Max," she said with attitude, "You know the rules. The bedroom is mine.

Why were you in there?"

"Why are you being like this, baby?" he asked in his lilting Bajan accent. "Don't you see I made your favorite fish? Just the way you like it. I got the wine and flowers," he said moving closer to her.

"Max, you didn't answer the question," she said, hardening her stance.

"Baby come here. Let's stop this war. We have so much love between us still. Let me show you how I feel." He pulled off the towel to expose his engorged member. Unbeknownst to her, her left hand fluttered to her throat and her lips parted.

None of her actions went unnoticed by Max. Deftly, he dropped to the floor and placed himself under her dress. He slid the thin fabric of her thong to the side and slid his tongue into her folds.

"Oh, my God!" she gasped and held onto the doorknob for balance. It had been months since they had exchanged any type of intimacy and even though she knew she should stop him the pleasure could not be denied. Through no willful act of her own, her legs parted to allow Max more access. He licked and sucked her expertly while she wondered who would pass out first, her from the pleasure or him from sheer lack of oxygen under her dress. He brought her right to the brink of satisfaction and stopped. He stood up, unzipped the back of her dress and lifted it over her head. He turned her around and looked into her eyes, seeing the familiar look of desire that he loved. Removing her bra, he sucked each breast as he backed her into the bedroom. Once again, he turned her around so that she could climb up onto the bed, onto all fours. She moaned as his penis filled her tight walls. She loved doggie style and Max stroked long and slow while circling her nipples with his fingertips.

"I know how you like it, baby," he said letting his wet lips brush her earlobe.

She felt the waves of pleasure building until she could no longer contain herself. She slid back and forth with increasing speed along his shaft and gave into a powerful, long overdue orgasm. Her senses slowly returned, and she heard the sounds that signaled Max was reaching his peak. He held her hips tightly and pumped into her ferociously.

"No, Max!" she yelled, remembering that there was no protective barrier between them.

She pinched both his hands and scampered across the bed away from him. Not able to give chase, Max took his penis into his own hands and smiled at her as he gave himself the release he needed. Disgusted, Benae threw his towel at him, grabbed her outfit from the closet, and locked herself in the bathroom.

"You are so weak," she said aloud to her reflection in the mirror.

Tears beckoned but she refused to let them fall. Instead, she stepped into the shower and washed all traces of Max away from her body. Her mood picked up as she decided that was their *goodbye fuck* and there was no need to feel bad about it. She put on her sexy little black halter dress, pulled her hair into a loose ponytail, applied eyeliner, mascara, and lip gloss, and was ready to go. She scurried through the kitchen and into her bedroom and stepped into a pair of strappy, black Jimmy Choo sandals. Grabbing her keys, her wristlet containing cash, cards, and license she ignored Max who was lounging on the sofa eating the dinner he had prepared and walked through the door leaving the scent of DKNY's *Be Delicious* in the air behind her.

"Congratulations!" Chrissy yelled from the doorway of her house as Benae pulled into the driveway. "Girl, I am so proud of you. Now you're a New York homeowner, too!" Chrissy grabbed her in a bear hug. "Girl, let me live to see it again." They both laughed. "I'm sorry but I am just so happy for you. You've been through so much and you deserve this".

"Thanks, Chrissy," Benae said finally stepping inside the house.

Chrissy walked over to the stairs and yelled up to her husband, "Greg, come down and have a drink with us before we leave!" Benae sat at the dining room table and took a good look at Chrissy's outfit for the evening.

"Look at you." Benae looked Chrissy up and down. "Greg is letting you go out like that?"

Chrissy posed sexily and said, "Hell yeah, he knows when I get back all of this is for him." She ran her hands along her curvy hips and very ample bottom. She was wearing shiny, black, pleather pants with a matching bodice, sky-high platform pumps, and a long fake ponytail that trailed down to the middle of her butt.

"That's right," Greg said as he came down the stairs and grabbed Chrissy from behind. "I know all of this is coming home to me." He let his wife go and headed over to Benae to give her a hug and a quick kiss on the cheek. "So, I hear congratulations are in order."

"Thank you, I am so excited," Benae gushed.

"Alright, time for a toast." Chrissy handed Greg the bottle of Korbel champagne she had purchased for the occasion.

Over the next hour, they drank two bottles and polished off a small ice cream cake Chrissy also bought.

"Well ladies," Greg said while getting up from his seat. "I've had more than enough to drink. If you two are still heading out, I suggest you get started it's almost midnight."

"Perfect time," Benae and Chrissy said in unison.

The two had been friends since Junior High School. Everyone knew Christmas Birch and Benae Givens were inseparable. They never argued and never competed, both respected the other's life choices though they were very different. Benae chose to follow in her mother's footsteps and attended Spelman, and after receiving her MBA was hired as a Management Associate at a top 100 financial firm where she now held a prestigious position in Accounting. Chrissy chose to marry Greg right out of High School and maintained a job at Bloomingdale's as a make-up consultant. All they ever wanted was what was best for the other, real true-blues.

They hopped in a cab since they were both slightly intoxicated. Benae rested her head on the back of the seat, rolled down the window and inhaled the hot July air that held the undeniable scent of summer.

"What are you over there thinking about? You're too quiet," Chrissy inquired.

"I had sex with Max today," Benae blurted out.

"What!"

"I don't know. I just gave in. It's been months since I had any."

"Well, was it good?"

"Hell yeah, you know that was never a problem."

"Well, then that's all that matters. Just don't let it be the start of something. Let it be the end."

"That's why you're my girl. We're always right here." She motioned with her fingers pointing them back and forth from her eyes to Chrissy's. "I had already called it our goodbye fuck."

"Then that's what it is then," Chrissy confirmed. "Now once we get inside we have another reason to celebrate. Whoop, whoop", she said flailing her arms in the air.

As usual, The Lounge was packed. The spot was unique in that it had live music and lite fare upstairs while downstairs was more of a lounge area with big sofas and chairs taking up most of the room. Heavy damask drapery curtained off a small dance floor where most of the patrons were dancing to the latest mix of hip-hop, reggae, and R&B. The two friends ordered Bellini's and headed to the dance floor.

Along the way they flirted and responded to the various, "Hellos!" "What's ups?" and "Damn, girl!" from admiring males.

Chrissy was married but her radar was always on point. She often had to clue in Benae who never seemed to notice when a guy was checking her out. This was one of those times. While Chrissy led them across the floor, she noticed a tall, fine, brother looking past her and at Benae.

Just as she thought, *He's going for my girl.*

He stepped between them and took Benae by the hand. She looked up and into the eyes that she would become lost in. She let him lead her to a seating area.

Chrissy followed them with her eyes and when Benae looked her way, she mouthed, "You betta get that."

Benae turned her attention to the handsome stranger and left her friend to her own devices.

"So, what you drinking?" the cutie asked her.

"Bellini!"

"Bellini? What's in that?" he asked, clearly unfamiliar with the cocktail.

"It's champagne and Peach Schnapps'."

"Oh, okay, I'll be right back."

Benae noticed all the women checking him out and decided to accompany him to the bar. "Hey, I'll come with you."

He held out his hand for her to hold onto as she stood up. Benae smiled to herself as his *fans* stepped back and out of the way. She was sure they thought he was her man and she didn't even know his name. He ordered her drink and a beer for himself.

She clinked her glass against his bottle, "Here's to Friday night".

He smiled a sexy smile and said, "So, when are you gonna tell me your name?"

"I'll tell you when you ask."

He bent down and lowered his face next to her ear. "What's your name?"

"Benae," she answered feeling a little flushed.

"Benae? That's different. Nice to meet you. My name is Sincere."

"Really, and you said my name is different. Is that what your mama calls you?"

"Most of the time, but sometimes she calls me Sin," he said flashing the bad boy smile most women couldn't resist.

"Okay," Benae said, but she thought he couldn't be more aptly named. He was sincerely fine.

"Want to go upstairs and listen to the band?" he asked,

"Sure, can you find us seats? I want to tell my friend where I'll be."

After letting Chrissy know things were going well with Sincere, she met him upstairs. They spent the rest of the night listening to the band, having drinks, and getting to know each other. A girl's night out turned into a first date.

SINCERE

Sincere drove the ambulance recklessly. He couldn't get back to the hospital soon enough. It had been a long day that started at 5:00 a.m. He was scheduled to work from 7-4, but it was now going on 7:00 p.m. and he was exhausted. It was his first week back to work after an eight-week hiatus. A couple of months ago he fractured his ankle while playing basketball and had to take time off for the injury to heal. He also decided to parlay the time off into some much-needed vacation time as well as take care of a little business under the table. He sped into the parking lot and expertly maneuvered the truck into its assigned space. Some of his co-workers waved and yelled goodnight as some headed to their personal vehicles to go home, while others were walking from their cars to start their shift.

"Have a good night," Sincere said to no one in particular as he opened the door to his ten-year-old Lexus coupe.

Although he had some money stashed for a new car, he loved his car. It was hooked up just the way he wanted it with 24-inch chrome rims, new deck, Bose stereo system, and black leather interior. As he pulled onto the Bruckner Expressway, he noticed that the traffic was light.

That's one good thing about working late, he thought to himself.

Once he got home and stepped into the small, two-bedroom apartment he shared with his brother and his pitbull puppy, Meth. The little dog was all over him. "I know, I know it's late," Sincere spoke to the exuberant pup. "I know you have to go but let me go first." He shuffled into the bathroom and relieved himself.

As he washed his hands, he caught a glimpse of himself in the mirror. His light-brown skin glistened under a thin sheet of sweat. He cocked his head to the side to check out the sharp edges of his hairline even though he knew it looked good. He had just got a fresh cut yesterday so his thin mustache and light beard were all on point.

"Damn, I look tired though," he said stretching his eyes open wide. Meth yelped and it sounded like he agreed. "Yeah, you agree, huh?" He kneeled down and held the little pup's face between his hands. "Let me tell you something, I still look good. I'm Sincere, baby." Meth reacting to his tone, started jumping around and barking. Sincere grabbed the leash from behind the bathroom door. "Come on boy." He attached the choke collar around Meth's neck. Although the puppy was playful his energy scared people. The choke collar was part of his obedience training.

The two ran down the six flights of stairs at top speed out into the warm evening air. The streets were busy. It was Saturday night in the Bronx and the driving base of reggaeton blared from an apartment nearby. Kids were hanging out and having fun. Some were still wet from the johnny pump that was just shut down for the night. As they walked passed Cuchifritos the scent of the fried chicharrones filled his nostrils and Sincere decided he would pick up dinner from there on the way back.

"Oh, my God, he's so cute!" Out of nowhere a young lady dropped down in front of him and started petting Meth. "What's his name?"

"Meth and he steals all the pretty ladies," Sincere joked.

"Meth for Method Man, right?" she asked still petting the puppy.

"You know it. One of my favorite rappers," he answered. As if on cue, Meth sat and wagged his tail, giving the pretty stranger his undivided attention.

"So, where you two off to?" the friendly dog lover asked.

"Just taking a walk. You know, let him run around a bit and do his business." He watched her put her pinky in her mouth as she scanned his upper body and saw how his large muscled form tapered down to his slim 36-inch waist.

When her eyes met his again, his conceited smirk revealed that he knew her dirty thoughts. He wanted her to know that she presented no challenge and he knew it. He was getting tired of easy pussy. He'd take it, but he could certainly afford to turn some down. He just winked at the girl and returned to walking his dog. Her angry cries after him blended with the sounds of the city and were lost. He continued his stroll and thought about the fine shawty he met last night, Benae.

He wanted to call her all day but didn't want to seem thirsty. He was already impressed with the fact that she hadn't called him. There hadn't been a woman that he wanted to hit it with so bad in a long time, the way she moved her body turned him on. It wasn't a slutty bump and grind, it was cool and sexy, yet, totally captivating. He particularly enjoyed it when she glanced over her shoulder at him while shaking her ass like a pro to the band's beat. Oh, yeah, Ms. Benae Givens was definitely going to get a call. The loud honking of a horn and someone yelling his name snapped him out of his reverie. He turned to see his younger brother Tru rolling up beside him.

"Yo' Sin check it out." Tru bopped his head and rapped along to the latest *Drake* braggadocious hit, stopping only to invite his brother to admire his brand-new black Yukon Denali. "Straight cash man, copped it with the extras."

"Why you go and get something so flashy? Man, we told you to keep it simple stupid. You never fuckin' listen."

"That's right. I don't listen to nobody. You already know that brother. I got this. Ain't nobody checking for me. Chill the fuck out. There ain't nothing to worry about," Tru defended.

Sincere glanced at the face that was almost identical to his, except Tru's eyes were a hazel hue and his face was a rounder less-chiseled shape. Tru was reckless and crazy. Sincere both appreciated and resented these traits in his brother. The recklessness could put them in danger, but it was the crazy that had kept them safe too many times to count. Coming up in the South Bronx the brothers learned at an early age that they had to be there for one another. Their dad, Leon now a recovered drug-addict was a functioning addict during their younger years. Their mom, Vivian worked hard to keep her fledgling family together.

During the day she worked at their school as a *lunch lady* and at night as a waitress at a diner a couple of blocks away from their apartment building. She knew leaving her young sons home alone was a risk but she needed to provide for them and because the diner was so close she knew she could get back home quickly if they needed her. What she didn't know was that her boys were sneaking out of the house at night after she left. Sincere was twelve and Tru was ten when they started working for an up and coming drug dealer in their building. He used the young boys as lookouts and runners. Sincere was often the lookout standing on the corner to alert the crew if the cops were coming or if the block was hot for any other reason. Tru would deliver drugs and take payment.

He was ten but he was a big ten and already had a reputation for beating up dudes twice his age. When the word on the street got back to Vivian that her boys were part of a newly formed drug ring in her building, she was determined to not only get her son's out of the game but to get them on the right track. It broke her heart when she came home early from work to an empty apartment when both of her boys should have been in bed. She questioned other young boys that were outside past their bedtimes until she found Sincere. She snatched him from the corner and marched him to the basement of their building to pick up Tru, where he and a group of other little boys were waiting for instructions.

Vivian brought her two sons into their modest apartment and tried her best to appeal to their sense of logic, pride, and love for her. If nothing else she knew they loved her. After hearing her plea both boys promised to stay off the street and focus on their schoolwork. She knew that was only half the battle. The other half was keeping the drug dealers away from her sons. She used some of the guys in the building that knew her since she was young and looked out for her and her boys. Over the years Sincere dipped in and out but managed to maintain decent grades in school and graduated on time.

Tru on the other hand found a love for the streets and never applied himself in school. He was kicked out and transferred too many times to count. By this time, Vivian divorced Leon, remarried, and moved to Florida. She wanted to take her sons with her but both declined stating that they needed to stay to keep an eye on their dad. They also didn't want to leave the Bronx for what would surely be a boring life in Florida. Fortunately, with the departure of his wife and the demands of his sons, Leon was admitted into rehab and had remained clean ever since. That was over ten years ago and the father and son trio was rock solid.

No one and nothing came between the Law men, except Vivian. She was still the Queen of the family no matter how far away she was. All of a sudden the tiredness of the past couple of days hit Sincere and he reluctantly walked around to the passenger side of the car and climbed in.

"Yo man, you look tired," Tru observed.

"I'm tired as hell."

"From what, you been home chilling for months. You just went back to work."

"I know. I have to get back in the groove. You'd be surprised how tired you get doing nothing," Sincere said.

"Alright. In that case, we gonna take a ride up the Grand Concourse to Giovanni's, get you some chicken parm and a beer then go straight home so you can chill."

"Sounds good brother," Sincere said while adjusting Meth so that he could look out of the window.

"I told you, I got you," Tru said, turning Drake up to full blast and cruising slowly through the streets.

After a while, the loud music and smooth ride calmed Sincere down. He reflected on the job they pulled. His take was $50,000. Back in the day, he used to hustle and sell drugs like Tru but he completely left that life behind seven years ago when he moved back to New York from a short stay in Chicago. He studied to be an Emergency Medical Technician, got his certification, got the job, and had been legit ever since. Well, not exactly legit, but he was out of the game. He felt his phone vibrating in his pocket and he pulled it out to see who was calling him. He scowled slightly at the name on the screen and put his phone back in his pocket without answering. He knew she would be calling again.

BONITA

"I can't believe this man ain't answering my calls." Bonita sat her phone down, her face expression was puzzled.

She and Sincere had been together for two years in April. She sensed something was wrong when he chose to recover from his surgery in Chicago instead of here with her so that she could take care of him. She never imagined he would come back to New York still acting distant. The least he could do was talk to her about whatever it was that was going on with him. She picked up her phone again and this time she called her best friend Shakirra.

Shakirra and Bonita were friends since first grade. They were both third-generation project girls. Bonita's mother Lillian had taken over the small two-bedroom apartment when both of her parents passed on. She married Bonita's father and vowed not to raise her children here, but her husband though a good man, had a gambling addiction that made it impossible for them to afford to move anywhere else. When he died, she looked forward to using his life insurance to finally get herself and her daughter out of the projects.

She was devastated when she found out that her husband had let the policy lapse and not only would she not be receiving any money she had to beg and borrow just to cover his final arrangements. Fortunately, Bonita was oblivious to her mother's struggles at the time. All she'd ever known were the PJs and she loved it. She'd grown up here, knew everyone here and the best thing about it is her BFF Shakirra was here. She was good here.

"What?" Shakirra said rudely.

"Shakirra, you really need to stop answering the phone like that," Bonita scolded her friend.

"Don't tell me how to answer my phone. You don't pay no bills up in here."

"Well, you don't either. I guess the state can tell you how to answer your phone then."

"I know you not tryin' to throw shade," Shakirra said mockingly.

"No, I actually need you to be serious for a minute," Bonita said softening her voice.

"Okay, sounds like a Sincere issue is coming," Shakirra said with attitude.

"Yeah, I still didn't hear from him and he ain't picking up my calls."

"I told you, you better tell him that you're pregnant. He trying to leave you alone as it is."

"Nah, it's not like that. He's' gonna take care of his. He went out of town to get some money together for our family so stop trippin'."

"You the one trippin'," Shakirra shot back. "If he went to get money for y'all, where the hell he at then, huh? Where the money at?"

Bonita had no reply.

"Listen, Nita, I am not trying to hurt you. You know I love you like a sister, but he was backing off before you got pregnant. Trapping him is not gonna keep him."

"Know what Shakirra?"

"What?"

"Shut up! You got three kids *and* you got Joseph. He was nowhere near staying with you until you had Joe Jr. So quit it."

"That's right." Shakirra laughed. "But that's me and Joe. Don't nobody want Joe 5'5" ass but me. Sincere is fine, 6'2' built, and did I say fine. He's a whole other story. I don't know how you got him anyway."

"So, what you tryna say?" Bonita wanted to know.

"I ain't tryna say nothing, I said it."

"You better act like you know. I look good. Dudes be trying to get with me wherever I go and you know it's true. So, you need to quit it," Bonita defended.

As if she needed to confirm her statement, Bonita stood up and peered into the mirror that was poised above her dresser. Her flawless, butter pecan complexion set the backdrop for large brown eyes that always seems to be smiling. She smiled at her reflection and turned sideways to admire herself from all angles. Happy with her appearance she let her weaved in red ringlets fall from the ponytail and frame her face.

She pursed her succulent pink lips and thought, *Sincere is lucky to have me. Shakirra doesn't know what she's talking about.*

"Whatever, Nita, let me go feed my kids."

"Feed your kids? It's almost nine o'clock."

"It's a Saturday night in the summer, ain't no dinner time. My kids are happy as hell to be going to McDonald's. I can't wait for you to have that baby so I can criticize your ass and how you parent," Shakirra teased.

"Bye Shakirra." Bonita dismissed her life-long friend. She loved her, but she didn't agree with some of her ways, especially the way she took care of her kids.

Still looking in the mirror, Bonita pushed a pile of clothes to the right and the pile of paper, books, and makeup to the left to clear out a spot in the center of the dresser. She examined her profile and smiled at the slight bump in her abdomen. Lovingly she caressed her belly with both hands. She was only two months pregnant but already in love with her unborn child.

"God," she prayed silently, "Let Sincere love our child, too."

She laid across the cluttered bed and surveyed the messy room. Her full-sized bed took up most of the space. The two colorless nightstands held a lamp and mounds of clutter. On each side of the bed were bins of clothing, shoes, and anything that didn't officially have a place. She was not the neatest person, but this mess was extra. It was due to an inner sadness. Since Sincere left for Chicago over two months ago she had sunk into a depression. She missed him so much. She thought back to the beginning of their two-year relationship when things had been wonderful. They met outside her building while he was riding with his brother. The two of them had locked eyes as she walked past his truck and neither broke the stare. Bonita smiled brightly but kept walking giving him an unobstructed view of her wide ass in her red daisy dukes and matching top.

"Yo." She kept walking

"Yo', you know you hear me, girl!" Sincere yelled to her.

"Me?" She turned around innocently.

He looked her up and down with an appreciative smirk on his face. She strolled over to where he stood in front of the car and they exchanged numbers. They talked on the phone late into the night and by the weekend they were inseparable. The lovemaking they shared was passionate and loving, unlike anything she had ever experienced.

Bonita knew she had found the man she wanted to spend her life with. The boys before Sincere were selfish lovers who only used her body for their own pleasure. Sincere made sure she was pleased and made her feel beautiful while doing it. He was there for her when her mother fell sick. He held her and her mother together and earned Bonita's deepest love and respect. She became used to him taking care of her and her needs and fought to take care of him.

By the time she realized her error, he had already become distant and spent less and less time with her. He came back from Chicago days before their two-year anniversary. She invited him over for dinner and made his favorite dish – chicken parmigiana, bought a bottle of wine, and prepared to revive their relationship. Fortunately, the anniversary coincided with her ovulation cycle. Her dinner did not get her the response she wanted from him, since she hadn't seen him since and barely heard from him, but what they did for dessert would surely secure her, her man.

CHAPTER 2

LOVE CHANGES

BENAE

"You want me to come down?" Benae smiled into the phone.

"Yeah, come down. I want to holla at you for a minute," Sincere said.

"Okay, I'm coming, but I'm going to get in trouble if I keep sneaking out to see you," Benae said as she slipped her ID into her suit jacket pocket and headed for the elevator.

She had already taken an hour lunch but knew she could hang out with Sincere for another 30-45 minutes without being missed. When she reached the lobby, she saw Sincere waiting for her. He looked damn good, even in his EMT uniform. He turned and smiled as he watched her approach. She noticed him do the quick once over that included a head to toe inspection in a two second glance.

His smile must mean I pass, Benae thought and smiled as she reached him. They pecked on the lips, held hands and walked the two blocks to the South Street Seaport.

They had been talking many times a day for the past two weeks. They found that they worked in the same downtown Manhattan area. Sincere got off at 3:00 and started stopping by to see Benae before heading home.

"You are going to get me fired," Benae joked as they sat down on a bench facing the East River.

"I'm not trying to do that, I just want to see you for a minute," Sincere said looking down at her.

"I know, I like seeing you, too," she said looking directly into his eyes.

Slowly, he reached up and held her face then leaned down and kissed her softly on the lips. She wasn't expecting the kiss but responded by parting her lips and slightly tilting her head. Gently, he slid his tongue between her lips while still maintaining his hold on her face. When he released her, they looked at each other and smiled.

"Our first kiss." Benae breathed.

"Yeah, it was," Sincere replied grinning boyishly. He put his arm around her, and they made plans to go out to dinner on Friday. Then he walked her back to her building.

"Now you know I don't want to go back to work now, right?" Benae said.

He reached down and kissed Benae on her nose and then her forehead. "I'll call you later, alright."

"Okay." She waved goodbye and headed back upstairs.

She barely did any work the remainder of the afternoon. She daydreamed and reflected on the past two weeks. Just the thought of him made her smile and get a little moist. He called the Monday night after they met, making her wait for three days. They were both happy that neither had kids. She told him about Max and that she would be moving into her own place at the end of the month. He told her that he was in a similar situation with his ex-girlfriend as far as breaking things off, but that they didn't live together. He made her feel completely comfortable, maybe it was because he called or texted at least 2-3 times a day. When her schedule allowed, he stopped by after she finished working and they hung out at the Seaport and sometimes in her office. During these times they would laugh and joke like teenagers. There were no awkward silences or tension. Everything just flowed.

When she got home, she finished packing everything except the essentials that she needed for the upcoming week. That was all the time she had to wait before moving into her own place. Thoughts of decorating her apartment filled her mind. She quickly took a shower and put on a pair of shorts and a long T-shirt. She didn't want any reason to give Max the wrong idea. Since she had told him she was moving out, he seemed to back off with the niceties, purely relying on the sexual energy that still existed between them. He was supposed to sleep on the sofa but lately she woke up to find him in bed with her. Often times she had to remove his arms from around her waist and scoot out of his spooning embrace. This bothered her even more now that she was spending time with Sincere. Max irritated the hell out of her, and she was glad he wasn't home. She poured herself a glass of Moscato and dialed Chrissy's number while settling on her bed under the AC.

"Hey girl, what's up?" Chrissy answered.

"Guess what?"

"What?"

"He finally kissed me," Benae gushed.

"And you are already this excited! Not good."

"Anyway." Benae ignored her friend. "I'm excited because of the way things are going. He's so attentive and so smooth and cool with it."

"I get all that, but the deal was for you to get out and date, not rush into another relationship. It sounds like you are ready to make him yours," Chrissy cautioned. "All I'm saying is take it slow. You fall in love way to fast."

"I didn't say anything about being in love. He's a nice guy and I like him. There's nothing wrong with that."

"Well, it depends on who you ask," Max interrupted.

He was standing in the doorway staring down at Benae. She jumped at the sound of his voice. Between the effect of the wine and the hum of the air conditioner she didn't hear him come in.

"Oh, shit! Is that Max?" Chrissy whispered through the phone.

"Yeah. Let me go. I'll call you tomorrow," Benae said hanging up the phone.

"So, you talking about the dude you leaving me for and moving in with?" Max loosened his tie and removed his jacket never taking his eyes off her.

In an attempt to appear nonchalant, she casually turned on the TV. "Max get out and close the door, you're letting the air out."

"I can't believe that you already met someone."

"If I did, it's none of your business."

Max looked at her so deeply, she could barely meet his gaze. It felt like he was trying to peer into her soul. Taking a big gulp of wine, she turned her attention to whatever reality TV show was on the screen. Silently, Max turned and walked out of the room, closing the door behind him. Benae shivered and prayed that he would stay on the sofa for the rest of her time here.

SINCERE

"Yo man, I think it's about time for you to get up. It's 3:00 in the afternoon!" Tru yelled to his brother.

"I'm up, I'm up!" Sincere yelled back. He reached over to the nightstand and picked up his cell phone.

There were six messages and 12 missed calls. They were all from Bonita. He felt a bit guilty thinking about her. He knew Bonita wasn't wife material, but her sexy body and sweet disposition eventually won him over. Now that he was going on 30, he needed more than that from the woman in his life. A big butt and a smile just wasn't enough anymore. He chuckled at that thought.

Instead of rushing to return her calls, he turned on the TV and caught the latest sports news on ESPN and whipped up a quick breakfast. Before he could call her, she called him again.

"Yeah, what's up?" he asked.

"What's up? That's how you talk to me now?" Bonita asked.

"Nah, I'm still a little tired. I just got up."

"Well, I've been trying to reach you. I miss you and I thought we could spend some time together," she said, her voice loaded with sweetness. "Today is a bright, sunny day maybe we can go out to eat and sit outside."

"I'll have to see," Sincere sighed. "I didn't really plan my day out yet."

"Sincere, you really need to come through."

"I don't know about eating out, though."

"We can do whatever. I just want to see you. It's been two months. Don't you miss me?"

"I'll call you back later. There's someone on my other line," he said clicking over.

"Yo', what's up man?" Sincere was happy to hear from his homie Rick.

"Not much dog," Rick answered. "You gonna hit the gym today?"

"Yeah, I'm about to get dressed and head out."

"A'ight, I'll see you there. Bring a change of clothes, Kendra changed the suits for the wedding. We have to get re-fitted and everything."

"Today?" Sincere asked aggravated. Kendra was already getting on his nerves with this wedding.

"Today, it's the only day we can get everyone together. My bad for not telling you earlier, but I figured you'd be with me after we work out anyway. You got to come through for me or else Kendra is gonna be in my ass."

Sincere laughed. He understood far too well what his homeboy would have to endure if he didn't show up. "No problem, man, I got you."

After lifting weights, and running they hit the showers. "Yo' man, I went to The Lounge a couple of weeks ago and I met this bad chick. She's smart, got a good job like Kendra and she just bought a condo in Brooklyn Heights.

"Word?" Rick asked. "Kendra doing alright, but she ain't got no Brooklyn Heights condo money."

"Yeah, man. I been talking to her ever since. I'm taking her out to dinner tonight.

"What about Nita?"

"I'm sliding out of that. She ain't doing nothing with herself. She was supposed to be going back to school six months ago and nothing yet. I am looking for more in a woman, someone that's more of a go getter like me."

"I feel you on that. That's why I'm wifing up mine. Kendra is the total package. Beauty and brains," Rick boasted.

"You forgot Balls. Beauty, brains and balls."

While they were laughing at Sincere's joke, Rick's cell phone rang. He replied, "yes" and "okay" a few times and hung up. "That's Kendra. She's waiting for us at the suit shop."

The suits Kendra chose were basic black suits. They were of much better style and fabric than the suits she originally picked out and much more expensive.

"Eight-hundred dollars!" Sincere exclaimed loudly.

"Yes, seven-ninety-five is the retail price but we are getting the suits at a forty percent discount so the out of pocket cost to you will be less than five-hundred," Kendra said proudly holding the suit up in front of Sincere. "Look at it this way, you'll have a good quality suit for future occasions. You know you can't wear J's and jeans everywhere," she said glancing at his attire.

Kendra was a brown skinned beauty. She was 5'11 and taller in her heels. She had a very narrow waist and wide hips with a huge ass. She carried it all very classy. Today she wore a black and white Torrid dress with Tori Burch sandals and bag. She had a full weave identical to Kenya Moore, who she idolized.

She sauntered over to Rick who was looking at her intently. "What?" she asked innocently while putting her arms around Rick's neck.

As much woman as she was, Rick was more than enough man for her. He was 6'4' and 250 pounds of solid muscle. He had a deep chocolate complexion, piercing eyes, and beautiful smile which he bestowed upon Kendra as she embraced him.

Sincere took in the scene and knew his argument was futile. Kendra had Rick in the palm of her hand. "A'ight, no debate from me," Sincere declared. "I'll put it on my card. Okay, Kendra?"

"Thank you." She sauntered over to him and swiped his credit card from his hand and headed to the front of the store to make the purchase herself. Sincere was about to protest but changed his mind once he caught the stressed out look on Rick's face. "I'm doing this for you man," he whispered.

"I heard that," Kenya said stopping in her tracks and snapping her neck to look back at them.

She looked Sincere over with disdain and continued to the front of the store to pay for the suit. The wedding was in two weeks and she was not to be played with at this point. On top of that, Kendra couldn't stand him, and he knew it. She felt he was full of himself and disrespectful toward women. More importantly, she didn't think his partying and non-committal ways were a good influence on Rick. She had overheard Rick asking him to be his best man and instead of just answering the question, Sincere asked Rick if he was sure he wanted to get married. He proceeded to provide a barrage of reasons why he might want to wait. It was bad enough he was in the wedding, but she was not about to deal with his nonsense.

Sincere threw Rick a look that let him know he was trying his best to keep his cool with Kendra. He didn't know how his man put up with her. True she was a good-looking chick with a good job, but her attitude overshadowed all of that in his opinion.

"See it all worked out. The hardest part is over," she said returning his card to him. "Now who is next?" She turned to the rest of the guys in the bridal party.

As the other guys took turns trying on and purchasing their suits, Sincere realized Kendra really had love for his friend and felt the first twinges of happiness for them. In fact, he wouldn't mind a little of that for himself. A good, smart, successful woman who loved him there's nothing wrong with that.

BONITA

The numbers on the digital clock beside her bed glowed a bright red 8:30 p.m. It meant that Sincere wasn't coming and he didn't even call. As much as it hurt, Bonita held back the tears. She didn't want her mother to see her crying again and be forced to defend Sincere when right now he didn't deserve her support.

Earlier in the day she had taken extra care getting ready. Taking her time, she applied her make-up and popped in her contacts even though she found them to be extremely uncomfortable. Her favorite denim, miniskirt did not disappoint. It hugged her curvaceous backside just right and she knew Sincere loved her ass. The red tank top served double duty as the vivid color accentuated her tanned skin as well as enhanced her sized D cups. She was ready hours ago but refused to believe he would pull a no-show. She didn't call because he said he would, and she had already called enough.

Since she was dressed, she decided to take a walk and treat herself, and the baby to some ice-cream. "Ma, you want some ice cream? I'm going downstairs to wait for the ice cream truck."

"No, Nita, I'm fine," her mom replied.

"Okay, I'll be right back."

The dingy walls, dirty floor and pissy elevator did not please her. She was born and raised in these projects and sometimes the familiarity comforted her. Other times she was disgusted and couldn't understand why some of her neighbors didn't care more about where they lived. If people wouldn't pee in the elevators and stairwells and was mindful of litter, things would be a whole lot better. Just because we were poor was no reason to live like animals. Knowing that her thoughts were useless, she turned them to Sincere as she strolled towards the double-parked Mr. Softee ice-cream truck.

"Let me get a vanilla cone with sprinkles."

"Anything for you sexy." The monster serving the ice cream smiled flashing big yellow teeth.

Bonita made her purchase and walked around until she had finished her cone. She was surprised that she didn't see anyone she knew out and about. People sat on the benches that were strategically placed around the massive complex. When she reached Myrtle Avenue, she thought about going to the Liquor Store on the corner and picking up a bottle of Alize' then she remembered the baby. She hadn't taken a test yet, but she had missed her period the past two months and she was sure she was pregnant. All she needed was the blood test at the doctors to confirm it.

"Little baby, your mommy already loves you. She will not take a single drink of alcohol while she's carrying you," she said aloud.

Feeling better as her thoughts turned to the new life, she was carrying she pulled her phone from her skirt pocket hopeful that she has missed a call or text from Sincere. A blank screen stared back at her. Sadly, she started the walk back home intermittently wiping tears from her cheeks. She couldn't deny it any longer, the man she loved was no longer loving her. Just the thought of Sincere not being in her life hurt so bad. All she could do once she got back in the house was undress and get in the bed. The full face of make-up would just have to wait until the morning to be washed off. Instead she listened to *Keyshia Cole's Love I Thought You Had My Back* until sleep rescued her from her sorrow.

CHAPTER 3

TENDER LOVER

BENAE

After getting caught on the phone talking about Sincere, Benae was being extra careful to keep the peace with Max. She knew she didn't owe him anything after all the crap he had put her through, but she figured it would be an easier transition if he wasn't concerned about her personal life. Thankfully, he had just gone to sleep that night. Today was a different story. She was very excited about her date with Sincere and didn't think she would be able to contain it. So, she left the house and told Max she was going shopping.

She dressed casually in shorts and a tank top and headed out to the boutiques that lined Montague Street. Once she found what she liked, she bought an entire outfit for her date – dress, shoes, jewelry, a bag, even new underwear. She went to the NY Sports Club to shower and get dressed. From there she went to the hair salon for a wash and set. Her mani/pedi was still fresh so she didn't need that. She told Sincere she would meet him at the restaurant after he offered to pick her up. He had chosen an Italian restaurant in her new neighborhood. She never told him where she currently lived. She clearly didn't need that drama, and thankfully, he hadn't pressed.

The restaurant received great reviews and some of the items she'd seen on the online menu looked delicious. She arrived promptly at 8:00 and looked for his shiny black Lexus on the street. She didn't see it, so she found parking and headed inside.

"Good evening, pretty lady," a tall, slender gentleman greeted her at the door.

"Good evening," Benae responded.

"Dining alone?" the gentleman inquired.

"No, I am waiting for my date. Our first." She beamed.

"Well, you made a great choice. Our restaurant is famous for romance." He gestured around the elegantly appointed dining room.

"It was actually his choice. This is my first time here."

"Hey, sorry I'm late," Sincere bellowed from the doorway.

He walked over to Benae and grabbed her in his arms. She enjoyed his exuberance and blatant display of public affection.

"Come let me show you to your table." Once they were seated. "The lady says this is a first date?"

Sincere looked over at Benae and smiled. "Yes, it is."

"In that case, I will bring over a bottle of champagne...on the house."

"Thanks Sal. Good looking out," Sincere said.

"Wow, you must be a good customer," Benae teased.

"Yeah, I've been here a few times. It's my favorite Italian restaurant. The food is always on point and the prices are decent. And if I'm really being honest my Dad's a distributor. He's been in the industry for years. Over the years he's got to know some of the owners and managers really well. He puts me on to some of the best restaurants in all the boroughs.

Benae opened her menu, "Well in that case, let me see what the most expensive entrée is on the menu. I don't want to be decent tonight," she teased.

"Go for it," Sincere offered. "But there are other ways you can be indecent if that's how you're feeling."

"I'm aware of that, but I'll stick to the pricey food." They both laughed.

Benae actually ordered Caesar salad and linguini and clam sauce. They finished the bottle of champagne and Sal insisted Benae try the Tiramisu. She tried it with a cappuccino while Sincere polished off his Zeppoles with ice cream and Courvoisier.

"Oh, my God this is so good," Benae said after trying the Tiramisu. "Definitely the best I've ever had. She dug her fork in for another bite. She licked her lips and looked up at Sincere. He had a smirk on his face and his eyes were locked on her lips.

"What are you thinking about?" she asked.

He licked his lips. "You really want to know?" She smiled and raised her eyebrows. Sincere reached across the table and lightly held Benae's hand. "So, what you want to do now? It's only ten-thirty."

She knew what he wanted to do, but she wasn't ready for that just yet. "I don't know. I'll probably just go home and call it a night so I can get up early and run."

"Oh, okay, I can't compete with a good workout especially if the payoff is the way you look in that dress," he said, eyeing her appreciatively. "Speaking of dresses, I meant to tell you my homie is getting married in two weeks. That's what made me a little late today. I'm in the wedding and we had a last-minute fitting tonight. Anyway, I want to know if you would come with me to the wedding. Like I said, I am in the wedding, but I will make time for you." He smiled.

OMG, he is killing me, Benae thought. *This is a great date. He's holding my hand across the table, that smile and now an invitation to accompany him to a wedding. Girl, be cool.* "Sure, I love weddings. I'd love to go."

"Good, good. I won't be able to pick you up or anything since I'll be with the bridal party, but I'll email you the details."

"Okay, I'm looking forward to it," she said removing her napkin from her lap and sitting it on the table.

"Did you enjoy your dinner?" Sal asked.

"Yes, everything was delicious," Benae said. "I'll definitely be back."

"That's what I want to hear. We aim to please," Sal said with a slight bow.

Sincere and Benae held hands while walking through the busy streets. Benae noticed a lot of the traffic was headed to the Haagen Dazs located on the corner. They stopped at Benae's car. "Thank you for a wonderful evening. I really enjoyed dinner and being with you tonight," Benae said while resting her backside against her car.

Sincere read her queue correctly, he stepped into her ready embrace and kissed her deeply. Benae could feel his manhood against her belly and had to really try to calm herself down. Before she could do so, Sincere turned them around so that he was against the car and she was against him. He reached down and caressed the curves of her ass and pulled her into him. Benae felt her juices flowing and wanted him more than she realized. She had never been handled so personally in public and it excited her. Sincere ended the kiss by trailing light kisses along the side of her neck. She moaned softly as she inhaled the tantalizing scent of his cologne. Sincere pulled away from her and pressed the car fob that she held in her hand, unlocking her car. She was a little confused as he held her hand and walked around to open her driver's side door. Following his lead, she got in and sat down.

He leaned in and kissed her gently on the lips. "Goodnight beautiful. Call me when you get home."

"Damn," she whispered to herself. "Chrissy is right. I am falling for him already." She rolled down the windows letting the warm summer air in and turned to WBLS broadcasting live from the Shadow Night Club, so she wouldn't hear any love songs or continue to smell the lingering scent of his cologne.

SINCERE

The sun beat down on the city streets showing no mercy. The temperature hovered in the mid 90's and the humidity was just as high. Either the dog days of summer came late or this was Indian Summer, whichever it was it was hot for mid-September in New York. It didn't faze Sincere. He parked the ambulance, punched out and strolled toward his car. In the car he rolled down the windows instead of putting on the air conditioner enjoying Summer's last blast. He pulled up his Jay-Z play list full blast and navigated through the heavy lower Manhattan traffic headed for the Bronx.

He felt the vibration from his cell as he transferred from the FDR to the Willis Avenue Bridge. He smiled when he saw Benae's pic pop up and he purposely let it go to voicemail. He would be seeing Benae in about an hour so no need to return the call when he would be seeing the real thing in a few. She had taken off a couple of days to move and he promised he would stop by and help her get settled. Once he got home, he scooped up Meth for a quicker walk than usual and returned to tend to the three S's – shit, shower and shave. He threw on a pair of jeans, a Yankee cap and a white tee. He hopped back in the car and headed to Brooklyn Heights.

This was his first time at Benae's new apartment. The pristine brownstone building looked sophisticated and expensive. Sincere was more than impressed. He knew that Benae was doing alright for herself, but not this alright. Amazingly, he found a parking space on her street. He walked up the stairs and rang the intercom to her second-floor apartment.

Benae peeked out of the window. "Who is it?" she asked while looking down to at him.

"Come open this door, girl,"

Within seconds he heard the buzzer unlocking the front door. "Hello there," she purred extending her arms to embrace him at her door.

"Hello to you." He engulfed her in a big bear hug. Sincere looked around the spacious layout with awe. He had never been in an apartment so huge. The hardwood floors shone brightly and looked as though they had no idea what dust was. From where he stood all the walls were freshly painted and everything was new. There was a foyer and sitting rooms to the right and left of the spacious living room, a cream-colored leather sectional looked feminine and comfortable, but the heavy mahogany accents gave the room the proper balance. There was also a six-seat dining room table in a cream color with gold accents, complete with a matching gold tone chandelier. *Hmm. This girl has taste.*

"So, what do you think of my place?"

"It's a'ight so far," Sincere replied. "Let me see the rest."

She showed him around. "Here's the kitchen. I bought all the stainless-steel appliances myself. My dad is going to be so proud of me." The walls were a rich burnt orange hue. "My favorite part is wine fridge," she said opening the door to what seemed to be a smaller refrigerator that only held wine bottles.

"Now that's some fly shit," he said somewhat in awe.

They walked down the long hallway a bit and stepped into a room on the right. "This is going to be the guest room, but I don't have anything to put in here yet."

On the other side of the hall she clicked on the lights to show him the bathroom. It was all-natural toned marble with a tub and separate shower stall. They walked to the end of the hall. "And this is my bedroom."

Sincere was taken aback by all the turquoise. The carpeting was a deep turquoise, the bed coverings folded on the turquoise chair were striped turquoise and white, the sheer drapes were a turquoise tone and there were turquoise picture frames stacked on the dresser along with turquoise figurines and turquoise candles.

"I see you like turquoise."

"Yes, I feel it brings peace and tranquility. That's why I have it in the bedroom. Look up." She pointed up at the ceiling. "I had a celestial theme painted on the ceiling. I love it. It makes me comfortable and helps me sleep."

"It's a very nice place. Very nice," Sincere said nodding his head.

"And you haven't even seen my walk-in closet," she said, opening the closet door, "or the bathroom. I love the double sinks, perfect for two." She smiled at him.

"Where are all your boxes. I thought you needed help?"

"I do. I need you to help set my bed up, hook up the TV, the wireless printer, Bluetooth, you know stuff like that. I emptied all the boxes and the maintenance man took them for me."

"No problem. You only have one TV?" he asked eyeing the 55" inch flat screen sitting on the floor.

"Yeah, I didn't get around to getting another one yet," she lied. Max actually kept the other one, but she wasn't getting into that right now.

Sincere busied himself hooking up the electronics while Benae made some calls. He saved the bed for last. Once he was finished putting the four-poster cherry wood bed together, he laid across it. "Come here," he said reaching out to her.

"No, you come here," she said heading for the doorway.

Sincere appraised her round tight butt in the low rider cargo pants. He could see hints of a black lace thong underneath and made up his mind that he would get the full view before the day was over. He got up and followed Benae as she sashayed down the hall and into the living room.

"My cable's not connected yet, but we can watch Netflix. I can use my tablet as a hotspot."

"What you need to get is a Firestick," he said.

"What's that?" she asked turning to look at him.

"Never mind." He shook his head, amazed at how out of loop she was at times.

"How about The Five Heartbeats?" she suggested while scrolling through the movie titles.

"Yo, that's my favorite movie," Sincere exclaimed.

"Really? Mine too."

Neither said anything, but both made a mental note that it was another little thing that they had in common. They cuddled on the couch and watched the movie they had both seen many times.

As the credits rolled Benae's stomach growled. "I'm hungry. Want to go get something to eat? I don't really know what's around, but I can pull up Grub Hub."

"Nah, I'm comfortable in here. I can whip something up." He prayed she would go for it because he was broke. All the money he laid out for Rick's bachelor party, the suit and incidentals left him strapped this week.

"Oh, okay," Benae said excitedly. "Women like a man who can cook, but I don't have much in here." Sincere checked out the freezer and found a package of ground turkey. "Do you have any spaghetti?" Benae, opened the cabinet and looked around. "Yes, I do." She sat the box of Ronzoni spaghetti #8 on the counter. Sincere thawed the ground turkey in the microwave and made spaghetti and meat sauce. Benae made lemonade and a cucumber salad.

"I'm impressed," Benae said after her second forkful. "This is good."

"Told you I know my way around the kitchen, but I don't have nothing on my brother Tru. Now he can throw down."

"Well, so can you."

They ate heartily and shared funny stories of cooking disasters they created and experienced at the hands of others. Afterward, they cleaned up the kitchen together.

"Whew, I think I have Itis," Benae said flopping down on the couch.

"I know, me too. We need to work it off," Sincere said slyly.

"We can take a walk, but I thought you didn't want to go out."

"We don't have to go out to get a workout." He slid down on the sofa next to Benae and ran his hand across her breast. Her nipples hardened as they immediately responded to his touch. "Baby, I want to see you in that thong," he said looking at her with desire.

Without a word, Benae stood up with her back to him and obliged him his view. He reached up and stroked her brown sugar cheeks. He turned her around to face him and pulled her down to kiss him. They kissed furiously. Desire showed in their eyes and neither attempted to hide it. Sincere closed his eyes as Benae's tongue flicked up and down the sensitive spot on his neck. He lifted her tank top and exposed her braless breast. He held them both and sucked them one at a time sending Benae into a grinding frenzy.

"Ohhh," Benae moaned, "Let's go in the bedroom. You have a condom, right?"

"Nah, I didn't bring one." *Damn,* Sincere cursed inside. He purposely didn't bring a condom because he didn't want her to think sex was all he was after. Plus, she was so independent he sort of thought she would have some of her own.

Benae retrieved her tank top and slipped it over her head. "Well, we are going to have to continue this some other time, as the saying goes, no glove, no love."

"That's okay, we have all the time in the world. I ain't going nowhere." He stood up and started kissing her.

They held each other and kissed for a while. Benae pulled away. "I can't believe you don't have a condom," she whispered.

I don't believe it either, he thought. "Listen, I didn't want you to think that's what I came here for. Any other time, with any other woman, I would have been ready because that would have been my goal. I'm doing things different for you."

"Oh, Sincere, you are so sweet." She planted a lingering kiss on his lips. "But next time, come prepared."

"Shit, you don't have to tell me twice," he said adjusting his hard dick in his boxers.

"So, you want to watch another movie?" Benae asked while trying to keep her eyes away from the bulge in his pants.

"Yeah, why not," he said. He thought about leaving but realized sex or not, he really wanted to stay.

BONITA

"Gary, you are *not* the father," exclaimed Maury from the screen of Bonita's 19 in Daewoo TV. Bonita and Shakirra rolled with laughter.

"I don't believe how these girls come on TV playing they selves like that." Shakirra laughed. "Ain't no way I'm bringing someone on national TV to be tested to be my baby daddy unless he was the only dick I had that year."

"Now, you know you ain't sure if Josie is Joe's daughter," Bonita quipped.

"Yeah, and you don't see me on no damn Maury either." They slapped a high five and continued laughing.

"Bonita moved their breakfast dishes from the table to the sink. She and Shakirra had a routine. A couple of times each week they would trade off eating breakfast at each other's house. Bonita lived in 16E and Shakirra lived 17F. Both girls lived with their mother's in the same apartment they had grown up in. Bonita made the third generation of Griffin's in the projects. She often thought things would have been better for her and her family if her father wasn't shot and killed for his armful of Christmas gifts on a Christmas Eve when Bonita was ten years old. The shock and pain changed Bonita and her mother, Lucille. Her mother once full of life and a natural beauty faded into someone unrecognizable by those who knew her. She wore clothes that were decades old and looked even older draped over her extremely frail body. She was what guys referred to as thick, but no one could imagine that looking at her now. Bonita was her only child as she was to her parents. She did what she had to do to raise her daughter and that was it. She had a job as a housing assistant and paid very little rent. She bought food on pay day and made sure Bonita went to school. She loved her daughter but her reason for living died with her husband Bernard.

"It's nice out. What you wanna do after I get my kids dressed?" Shakirra asked while feeding her 6-month old baby, JJ, a bottle of formula.

"I don't know. I'm tired, I think I'm gonna lay back down."

"What's the matter with you?" Shakirra asked. "Pregnancy getting to you?"

"Yeah, I think so. Sometimes I feel like I can sleep all day."

"Well, get all the rest you can now because once the baby gets here, you can kiss sleep goodbye," Shakirra said heading for the door.

"It can't be that bad. You had four of them!" Bonita yelled from her bedroom. As she laid down her cell phone rang. It was Sincere. "Hello?"

"Hey, Nita, what's going on?"

"Nothing, what's up with you?"

"I'm on my way over there. I should be there in about fifteen minutes. I have some downtime and I'm gonna stop by real quick.

"That's fine. I need to talk to you," she said seriously.

"About what? I was coming to talk to you."

"We'll talk when you get here." She hung up and hurried to make herself presentable.

She hadn't even showered yet. By the time Sincere arrived 25 minutes later, she was showered and dressed in a pair of blue leggings and a flowing white top. It was low cut enough to highlight her boobs and loose enough to camouflage her growing belly. She didn't want him to notice her belly before she had a chance to tell him. He walked in and headed straight for her bedroom. She walked over to him and gave him a hug. He hugged her back.

"I missed you so much," she whispered near his ear while still holding him tightly.

"Listen Nita," Sincere began, removing his arms from around her waist. "I need to tell you something."

"No, you listen," Bonita interrupted, "I'm pregnant, you gonna be a daddy."

"*Pregnant!*" I ain't seen you in months. You trying to say it's mine?

"What?" Bonita said incredulously.

"I'm just asking," Sincere said looking at her. "It seems like a valid question."

"Not to me it isn't. I haven't been with anyone else but you since we met. How can you even ask me that?"

"Come on now. I wasn't even around. I've been out of town and I been by here once since I got back. The last time we got down, I wore a condom. So, I'm just asking how you can be so sure."

43

"I can't believe you're sitting here saying this to me," Bonita said, tears welling in her eyes. "Sincere this is your baby and we didn't use a condom. It was our anniversary remember?"

"We talked about this before and I told you I don't want no kids. We don't even get along and now you come at me with this? Having a baby is not gonna save our relationship. That's what I wanted to come here and talk about."

"You know what, I'm not even gonna trip," Bonita said standing up and looking down at him. "When the baby comes you will see."

"How far along are you?"

"Almost four months."

"*Four months!* Why you just telling me now?"

"Maybe because I just found out myself not too long ago," she lied. She had known for three months but didn't want to tell him until it was too late to do anything about it. She was not getting an abortion. "You know my periods are irregular. Plus, you not answering your phone didn't help," she said loudly. He sat quietly inspecting her stomach. "Look," she said wrapping her hands around her stomach emphasizing her small belly. "I'm carrying small."

"So, you plan on keeping it?" he asked sounding defeated.

"Of course, *we* are keeping it. You know I don't believe in abortion. We made this baby and we're going to keep it."

"You need to really think about that." Sincere eyed Bonita coldly. He walked past her towards the door. "I'm gone."

Bonita sat stunned. This was not the reaction she was expecting at all. She knew he was going to be upset because he had told her many times that he didn't want kids. She was sure that he would come around once he found out she was carrying his child. This was not the Sincere she knew and loved. He seemed like a different person. Something was definitely up, and she was going to find out what.

CHAPTER 4

THAT'S THE WAY LOVE GOES

BENAE

"I have to find a hot dress," Benae said to Chrissy as they pulled into the parking lot around the corner from Bloomingdales. "I cannot show up on the arm of this fine man looking just okay. I have to work it."

"I still can't believe he asked you to go with him to his best friend's wedding," Chrissy said. "That's pretty major."

"I know," Benae said. She stomped her feet and spun around in a tiny circle. "He makes me so happy. He's doing everything right. He took me to a nicer Italian restaurant than I expected. Best of all he doesn't seem to be intimidated by my career. And did I mention he cooks. He may not have the best occupation, but those corporate types bore me anyway."

"Yes, you've mentioned it all quite a few times. The only thing I haven't heard about yet is sex. He still hasn't' tried?"

"Oh, I forgot to tell you about that. We were all ready and he got it started but he didn't bring a condom. So, we stopped."

"*Stopped!* What's up with that? Couldn't he just go to the store?"

"I guess he could have, but neither of us thought of it."

"Well, I guess that's a good thing," Chrissy said. "It'll happen when the time is right. Now focus on your dress shopping. Do you like this one? It was a wine colored, chiffon Donna Karan dress with light beading around the trim. The top was cut just low enough to show-off what Benae considered her best asset her toned shoulders and firm breasts.

"Ohhh, I love it," Benae said as she grabbed the dress and held it up against her body.

"All you need with that is a chiffon wrap and the right shoes. I know a wrap that should work," Chrissy said as she headed toward the Bloomingdale's accessories department. Benae followed without hesitation, having a friend with the fashion experience Chrissy had from her years at Bloomingdales was just as much of a perk as using her discount.

"Well, I guess it's decided. I'm getting the dress."

"Girl, that's you all day. I can't help it if I have an eye for the right dress for the right occasion. To be honest, I have the whole outfit picked out down to the nail polish color and hairstyle," Chrissy said as she snapped her fingers as punctuation.

After an extensive shoe search Chrissy chose a pair of Jimmy Choo T-strap sandals with crystals up the center strap. She also found the matching chiffon wrap, a sterling silver choker, and a sexy black bodice to wear underneath. Chrissy also picked up some items for her boys and hubby. When they were done, they walked the few blocks up Third Avenue to Hillstone. It was their favorite eatery after a day of shopping. They both appreciated the dim lighting, live jazz band and large selection of wines. They shared the spinach artichoke dip followed by the Classic Caesar salad. Benae signaled for the waiter when Chrissy stopped talking to take a call on her cell.

"Oh, that's Greg, he's here to pick me up."

"That was quick."

"You know how he is." Chrissy shrugged. "Well, what's my share of the damage?"

"I got it, don't worry about. Go ahead and get in the car. He's probably double parked and getting honked at by cab drivers," Benae joked.

"Okay girl. I'll see you soon." Chrissy reached down and gave Benae a big hug. "Call or text me when you get home"

"Will do, tell Greg, I said hello.

"I will," Chrissy said as she grabbed her bags and headed for the door.

Benae smiled as the blinking light on her answering machine greeted her. Yes, she had a cell phone, but she still used her land line often and gave out the number. She pressed the play button and her living room was filled with the voice that warmed her heart when she heard it.

"Hey, it's me. Call me when you get this." She loved that he spoke with a little bit of attitude.

He was so different from the guys she was used to dating, including Max. She put away her purchases and poured herself a glass of wine. It was the third one today.

"Whoo!" she exhaled, sank onto the bed and plopped her feet up on a pillow. She called Sincere back and got his voice mail, she was disappointed but decided to leave a message.

"Hey it's me. You've been on my mind all day. I bought a nice dress for the wedding and I can't wait for you to see me in it. I'm in for the night, so *holla* back when you get the chance." She giggled as she hung up because he always laughed at her attempts to talk slang and sound cool. He said she just didn't sound right.

Bored but not in the mood for TV, she turned on the light on the nightstand and picked up Gabrielle Union's book she was reading. She got up and headed to the kitchen for a refill and a snack when her cell phone rang. She ran back to her bedroom fully expecting to hear Sincere on the other end.

"Hello."

"You forgot about me already," a male voice stated bluntly.

"Max?"

"Yes, you have so many men calling that you don't know my voice?" Benae was seriously contemplating hanging up when Max continued, "Just because I don't know where you live, doesn't mean I've forgotten about you. I still know where you work, I still got your number. To me that means there is still a chance," he said. His lilting accent made the devil sound like an angel.

"Max we are done. You have to move on. What we had is over," Benae said. "Goodbye Max." Benae hung up the phone and felt uncomfortable all of a sudden.

She double checked her locked door and armed the alarm. Maybe Max was right, she should get a new phone number if she really wanted him out of her life and she did.

SINCERE

"Wake up, wake up! Today's my day and y'all drunk ass mofo's better rise up and represent!" Rick yelled while walking through the spacious house his boys rented for this bachelor party.

They had already had their fill of laughing at the overuse of Bears and Deer in the décor, but Rick still thought it was funny. The only thing that was sort of cool was the bear skin rug, but that was old school as hell. The wedding was 30 minutes away in the Pocono Mountains. Sincere and Rick's brother, Randy selected the secluded area to ensure they were nowhere near Kendra and her minions. They wanted to make sure Rick enjoyed his last night of freedom without worrying about his wife-to-be. The villa was perfect. It comfortably slept ten but only the six guys in the bridal party were able to attend. The night started with a round of toasts and wishing Rick all the best as he took this monumental step in a man's life. As the guys sat and reminisced about the girls they dated back in the day and the myriad sexcapades they encountered over the years, the caterer arrived with the buffet style food setup and with bottles of Courvoisier, Hennessey and Ciroc.

"This is nice man," Rick said with two plates piled high in front of him and two drinks to wash it down with. "I really appreciate what y'all did for me."

"You ain't seen nothing yet," Randy said from his seat next to his big brother. "We didn't even get it started."

"That's right," Sincere chimed in, "It's time for the pornos," Sincere clicked on the 75-inch TV and the sounds of cheesy porn music filled the room.

"Yo, this chick right here is the best." Randy pointed at the screen. "That's my fantasy girl."

"Man shut up. Ain't nobody trying to hear you with that shit!" one of the guys yelled out. They all got a good laugh at Randy's expense.

"He got a good point, though," Rick said. "What's the point in watching this and sitting around a bunch of dudes, we going out later or something?"

"Just chill, I got this," Sincere said. He walked over to Rick and patted him on the shoulder. "Come on man, won't you go on and relax in the Jacuzzi?"

Rick grinned slyly and headed outside to the 12 person Jacuzzi, while Randy blasted *Drake's For Free*" on the sound system throughout the house.

"Alright!" Sincere yelled. "Time to get the party started."

He danced over to the door, feeling no pain and enjoying the buzz he got from drinking Ciroc neat. He opened the door and three strippers entered the room. The appreciative stares and licking of lips was the only indication the girls received that let them know they did not disappoint. No words could be heard over the blaring music anyway. Sincere waved for the girls to follow him through the sliding glass doors and out to the Jacuzzi. Once out there, Isis the lead dancer, closed the glass doors to drown out Drake and put her own music on courtesy of a small but powerful speaker. Soon the heavy beat of *Beyoncé's Partition* filled the small back yard. Each girl presented Rick with a raunchy dance that ended with her joining him in the hot tub. Sincere and the rest of the Groomsmen were dying to get a piece of the action but let Rick take center stage. Isis stood up and showed off her magnificent body that was dripping wet and covered only in a bright pink G-string. She put her globes in Rick's face and he could not resist running his hands over them. She turned around and shook her large ass in his face and once again Rick latched on to her assets.

Unexpectedly, she seductively turned to face Rick, "Are you sure you want to get married, baby?"

Sincere smiled wickedly from the doorway. The girls were executing their roles exactly as instructed. When the excitement became too much, Rick stood up to climb out of the hot tub. No matter how good his intentions were, there was no way he could resist the attention of three sexy women in a hot tub shaking T&A in his face while he was inebriated. The best thing he could think to do was abandon ship.

Sincere and the rest of the crew couldn't help but laugh at Rick. "Yo, he running from the pussy," Randy called out, still laughing.

"Nah, it's not that," Rick defended. He sat back down as Isis approached him again.

"Hell, yes, it is. Drunk or not he got Kendra on the brain. Time to go inside anyway," Sincere commanded.

Everyone headed into the great room where the girls played their sultry music and started their show. The guys were going crazy, whooping and urging the girls to do more and take off more. No one else noticed that Rick and Isis were still in the hot tub together. Sincere watched as Isis moved her sexy body and performed a skillful lap dance that left Rick wanting more. Sincere turned his attention back to the strippers in the room as he saw Rick stand up and get out of the hot tub.

Damn, Sincere thought. *He's going to hold to that no sexual contact with strippers rule Kendra enforced.*

"Man, you hooked me up," Rick said, shaking Sincere's hand.

"I told you not to worry. I just want you to be happy my man." They exchanged dap.

Rick looked at Sincere, "Yeah, I am. I love Kendra and look forward to a good life ahead with her and our daughter."

Sincere thought about telling him about the news he received from Bonita but thought it was neither the time, or place.

"You know I act like an ass about marriage and stuff like that, but I really am happy for you man. I'm happy you found a woman like Kendra. I may not like her but she's good for you and she loves you. That's what's important." He gave Rick a partial hug and a hard slap on his wet back. "Man go towel off and enjoy the rest of the show. We still planning to go out later and get our gambling on. FYI, I paid Isis a little something extra. She can come back later if you want to hit that on the low. No one would know. Not even me. She'll give you her number before she leaves if you're interested." Sincere joined the rest of the fellas and watched the show, satisfied that Rick would take the bait and prove that Kendra didn't have him by the balls.

The wedding was at 3:00 pm and it was now noon. The partying didn't end until about four in the morning. The groom, the best man and the four groomsmen discussed the night's events as they got dressed for the wedding. Rick took a moment to pull Sincere to the side and thank him for Isis. She'd come back while the guys were still at the casino. She pleased Rick in every way possible and left before the groomsmen returned. In fact, she dropped Rick off at the casino to join his friends on her way out. They were all still slightly hung-over and needed some breakfast to sober them up. Fortunately, Randy had breakfast delivered even though it was lunchtime. By the time the videographer arrived at 1:30 they were dressed and ready for filming.

"Time to go, the limo is here," Randy bellowed. "Let's go.

"We're on time, right?" Rick asked nervously.

"Yeah, we good. We have to stop by the Hilton and pick up mom and dad. We'll be on our way from there."

As soon as the limo pulled up in front of the church, the wedding planner started giving orders and rushing the guys into place. As Sincere stepped out to stand beside Rick at the altar, he spotted Benae walking toward the church. She was a vision in shades of burgundy. He loved her style and the way her hair blew in the wind behind her. He ran over to her before the wedding planner could stop him.

"Wow," he said aloud holding both of her hands in his.

"Wow, to you," she replied. "You look great."

"Thank you. Come on inside and have a seat on the Groom's side. I have to go up there next to Rick. I'm the best man and I got the rings," he joked. "Don't forget to take some pictures." He kissed her on the forehead and headed down the aisle.

The wedding went by quickly. In less time than he imagined his top dog was a married man. Sincere had to admit, Rick and Kendra looked happy. He thought the picture taking would never end and wondered how Benae was doing alone at the reception hall.

The bridal party entered the small and crowded room, decorated in shades of black, red, and white to lukewarm applause. After two hours of waiting, the guests were aggravated and hungry. The hors d'oeuvres were long gone and they wanted some real food. Obediently they all stood and snapped pictures as the Bride and Groom took to the floor for their first dance. Sincere found Benae and kept his gaze on her until she turned his way. She smiled when she caught him staring at her and he smiled back. He broke their gaze as the bridal party headed to the long, rectangular table set for them at the front of the room. Sincere thought Benae looked lonely sitting by herself and wanted to hurry and be by her side.

He stood up in his place at the table holding his filled champagne glass in front of him. "I want to start off by wishing my man and his girl, I mean his wife..." He laughed and the crowd laughed with him. "I want to wish them all the best. Rick you're more than a friend, you're my brother and that will never change. Kendra, we have had our issues in the past, but I have to give you your props. You're the one that got my man to settle down. Now let's all drink to that."

As the maid of honor began her speech, the magnitude of the step his friend had just taken dawned on him and he felt tears welling in his eyes. He felt Benae watching him and he looked up and returned her gaze not even trying to hide his emotions. He could see her flirty disposition change to one of concern.

He watched as her brows furrowed together and her lips mouthed, "Are you okay?"

It felt good seeing that she cared. He followed the bridal party to the buffet and piled up a plate of food. He walked over to Benae and squeezed in beside her.

"Here babe, they let the bridal table eat first so who knows when you will be able to get something to eat," he said sitting the plate of pork ribs, BBQ chicken, rice and peas, macaroni and cheese, string beans and salad in front of her. He could tell by the look on her face that the food wasn't up to her liking.

"You don't have to give me your plate, I can wait."

"You don't have to wait eat this I can get some more later. He could see that even though she wasn't crazy about the food, she was loving the attention he was giving her.

"Well, let's share," she suggested. "There's way too much food on this plate for me anyway."

"Okay," he said, picking up a forkful of food and feeding it to her. Some of the other women in the room watched jealously. Just as he rose to get them something to drink, Kendra approached. Sincere was surprised that a woman could look so evil while dressed in an all-white Cinderella styled wedding dress.

"Who is this?" she asked rudely pointing at Benae.

"This is, Benae. Benae this is Kendra," he introduced.

"Hello, nice to meet you," Benae said. "Your gown is beautiful."

"Nice to meet you, too," Kendra said phonily. She threw Sincere a look of disgust and shook her head as she walked away.

"What was that all about?" Benae asked.

"Me and Kendra don't get along. I guess, me trying to make it up to her in my speech didn't work."

"Apparently not, but why don't you get along with her. She looked at you like she can't stand you."

"All I know is she's mad because I asked Rick if he really wanted to get married when he told me he was gonna propose. She was putting on mad pressure and I was just telling him not to get pressured into anything. She was ear hustling and heard what I said," Sincere lied. He knew the real reason was that Kendra was expecting to see him here with Bonita.

"Well, I probably wouldn't like you either," Benae said jokingly.

"I think I asked him a valid question."

"I guess, I see your point, but I can also see hers.

53

"That's one of the things I like about you, you're so diplomatic." He rubbed her nose with his.

"And you're so damn cute," she said, giving him a quick kiss on the lips.

Sincere stood up, filled with Benae's compliment, and extended his hand to her. She took it and followed him to the dance floor. The pair danced together in a smooth and sexy unison to *Chris Brown's Come Together.* They garnered lots of stares and attention as they moved effortlessly together on the floor. Much of the energy they exuded came from how much they wanted to act on their desire for one another. He sang along while they danced.

"You and I, it's alright, it's perfect timing. You've been waitin' and I'm anxious for you to dive in. I'm doing for you what I wouldn't do for anybody. So, you might, might get what you want tonight."

She dropped her head back and laughed then picked up where he left off, *"I won't say that I never dreamed of touchin' on you. Ain't that what wild dreams are made of yeah, yeah?"* They laughed together and he couldn't help but pull her close to him.

She smelled so good. Damn, he wanted her. When the song ended, Sincere led Benae over to Rick and Kendra who were getting down on the dance floor themselves.

"Yo', dog we gonna head out in a minute. We have a long drive back to NY and last night is catching up to me."

"No, you can't leave yet, we didn't cut the cake," Kendra said.

"Alright, alright. We'll stay if you're cutting the cake soon. Hey, Rick, take a picture of me and Benae," Sincere said passing Rick his cell phone.

The two stood together and posed for the picture.

"How cute," Kendra said snidely.

BONITA

"Ooohhh listen to that heartbeat!" Shakirra exclaimed so loudly it caused Dr. Brown to flinch involuntarily.

Bonita gave Shakirra the shush finger and frown. She hated going places with Shakirra sometimes, she never knew how to act.

The Dr. pointed at the monitor. "As I was saying, the heartbeat is nice and strong. Things are where they should be at nineteen weeks."

"Thank you, Dr. Brown," Bonita said while lifting herself up from the examination table. "And thank you for seeing me on a Saturday. I don't know how I missed my appointment yesterday."

"It's no problem at all. Just make sure you are drinking enough water and moisturizing, your skin is very dry." The petite doctor gave Shakirra a fake smile and left.

"What's her problem?" Shakirra rolled her eyes.

"You. You are entirely too loud. I know you're excited, but you have to calm down."

"Yeah, yeah, yeah. Anyway, you gonna tell tired ass Sincere he's having a son even though he should have been here with you and not me," Shakirra changed the subject.

"I know but he'll come around. Pretty soon everything will be right back to normal."

"Hmm." Shakirra smirked. "I don't have your patience. I woulda went off on him by now."

"That's you and that's why Joe is never home with your loud ass," Bonita joked, but knew it was the truth.

They left Brooklyn Hospital and walked in silence as they guarded themselves against the chilly, Fall air. "Look the bus is coming." Shakirra took off running leaving Bonita to try to catch up as quickly as she could.

"Hurry up, Nita!" Shakirra yelled from the doorway of the bus.

"Whew, thanks girl. You know I can't run but I didn't want to miss this bus. I'm cold and I have to pee."

"You shoulda went before we left," Shakirra scolded.

"I know, I wasn't even thinking."

"It's okay, you got baby on the brain."

Bonita laughed and thought how lucky she was to have a good friend like Shakirra. She was always there no matter what. She held

55

on to the pole with one hand and took hold of Shakirra's hand with the other and squeezed.

"What's that for?"

"That's for coming with me today and the other two appointments. It would've hurt to come by myself."

"You know you'll never be alone as long as you have me, and I'm not going nowhere," she said loudly.

This time Bonita was not embarrassed by her loud-mouthed friend. "Here's our stop," Bonita said.

"No, I have to stay on to Greene Ave. I have to pick up the kids from Joe's mom."

"Oh, yeah I forgot."

"Go home and relax. I'll probably stay until Joe gets off so he can pick us up."

"Okay then, see you later."

The cool air made its presence known by whipping strong and hard around Bonita's thin windbreaker jacket. She bowed her head and walked as quickly as she could while maintaining control of the two shopping bags that she carried in each hand. She stopped to pick up a few things now so she wouldn't have to come back out. The weather was getting nasty. She managed to keep her footing on the ground that was slick with a montage of colorful fall leaves.

"Whew," she exclaimed when she entered the lobby of her building.

"What's up, Bonita," her neighbor Deidra asked stepping out of the elevator as Bonita entered.

"Hey, Deidra, you better go back upstairs and get a jacket. It's getting cold out there," Bonita cautioned.

"For real?" Deidra asked, stepping back into the elevator. "It was so nice out yesterday."

Immediately, Bonita regretted saying anything. She had unwittingly given her the perfect opportunity to get all up in her business. Deidra was in her late 30's and babysat for the few working moms in the complex. She knew everyone's business and if you told her yours, she wouldn't even pretend that she wasn't going to spread it like germs.

"So, where's your fine ass man? I ain't seen him around here in a minute."

"He's been working a lot but he's been around."

"Oh, that's good. I was beginning to think y'all broke up."

"*Broke up?* No, we're getting ready to have a baby." Bonita could not resist.

"What? When you due?"

"I'm due in February."

"Congratulations girl. Y'all gonna have a pretty baby. Well, this is my floor. I'll see you later."

Bonita went into the warm apartment and began her new Saturday night ritual of making a large cup of hazelnut coffee with whip cream with two hot dogs with lots of sauerkraut and French fries dipped in mayonnaise. Ms. Lucille got a kick out of watching her eat this strange combination. Ms. Lucille loved a good boiled hot dog and enjoyed hers with mustard and her fries with ketchup.

"Oh, Nita, that was good," Ms. Lucille said getting up to put her paper plate in the garbage.

"Thanks Ma. I'm already thinking about what I'll make for breakfast. You want anything in particular?" They both laughed at her non-stop appetite.

"Well, since you asked. I really have a taste for some hash browns and corned beef hash. You can make any type of eggs you want." Her mom smiled at her.

"You got it," Bonita said happily. Nothing made her happier than putting a smile on her mom's face. "Go sit down, I got the dishes, too."

"Okay, I see the little mother in you is coming out. You right on time, that happens at about five months. Uhm hum," she said walking out of the kitchen to return to her favorite chair in the living room.

Little did her mother know that her cooking and cleaning today had more to do with a hopeful visit from Sincere than her maternal instincts kicking in. After cleaning up the kitchen she decided to straighten up the place. Sincere would be making another appearance soon and she didn't want to hear any negative remarks about her housekeeping. She cleaned the bathroom and looked around at her handiwork. The bathroom was the one room that actually looked clean when it was cleaned up and the fresh scent of pine sol enhanced the feeling. She hung a new yellow plastic shower curtain to match the other yellow accessories. The mold on the bottom on the old shower curtain looked gross and she was sure it was making her sick. Her cell phone rang loudly with the basic old school ring and she jogged to her room to answer. It was Sincere.

"Hello."

"Hey, what's up. How you feeling?"

"I'm good. Just cleaning up."

"Alright, I was just checking in. I'll stop by tomorrow after work."

"Why can't you come by tonight? You always used to come by on Saturdays and spend the night with me."

"I can't make it tonight. I'll see you tomorrow, a'ight." He hung up quickly.

I know he didn't just hang up on me. Immediately she dialed him right back. No answer. She was tempted to call again and really go off on him, but she opted for a vent session with Shakirra instead.

"Hello."

"Hey, Kirra," Bonita said getting right to the point. "Sincere, just called me said he's coming over tomorrow and quickly hung up. It seemed very suspicious."

"That's not so bad. It's not like he's really not trying to see you."

"No, this ain't like him. I'm starting to wonder if he got somebody else..."

"I don't know, Nita. He's probably banging some chick but you his main and about to be his baby mama. Where is he going? If you want to talk and find out what's going on, call his ass back."

"I did and he didn't answer."

"Keep calling. Blow his phone up. What's wrong with you? You know all this already."

"I don't know. I just feel like he's not with me."

"Girl, it's your pregnancy emotions. Now stop stressing over what you don't know and call ya man... and call me back after you talk to him.

Once again, Bonita called Sincere's number. The phone rang four times. *I knew he wasn't going to answer,* she thought.

"Hello?" a female voice answered.

"Hello? Can I speak to Sincere?" Bonita asked confused.

"He's not available at the moment. Can I give him a message?" Benae asked.

"Tell him Bonita called. Who are you?"

"This is Benae and I will let him know you called, Bonita." She hung up.

Bonita held the phone in her hand and let the realization of what just happened sink in. *Who the fuck is this bitch answering my man's phone?* she thought. "This shit can't be happening."

She called Shakirra and she picked up on the first ring.

"What'd he say?"

"Girlll..."

CHAPTER 5

99 PROBLEMS

BENAE

After the cake cutting and the bouquet toss Sincere and Benae said their goodnights and hurriedly walked to her car bracing against the wind. The temperature had dropped sharply, and the wind broke through their thin clothing like a burglar. On the drive back they discussed the highlights and lowlights of the wedding. The only things Benae found acceptable about the entire affair was the cake and Kendra's dress.

Everything else she politely said, "Would not have been my choice."

In particular the gaudy venue, buffet style food and DJ instead of a live band. She didn't want to sound as though she was putting down Sincere's friends even if most of it was Kendra's choosing. So, she kept her thoughts on the guest's tacky attire, the flashy black, white, and red theme and twerking led by the bride herself.

Tonight, was the first time Sincere had driven her car. She adored her new Audi A7 but wasn't concerned about his driving because she knew he was a skilled driver. He put on *Kem's When Love Calls Your Name* to set the mood on the ninety-minute drive back to NY. They rode in silence for a while, just feeling the vibe of the music. Keeping his eyes on the road, Sincere reached over and grabbed Benae's hand. Slowly he brought the back of her hand to his lips and kissed it. Benae turned to face him but he kept looking straight ahead without letting go of her hand. She smiled inwardly and relaxed her head against the headrest. She squeezed his hand and closed her eyes as she listened to the message Sincere was subliminally sending her through Kem.

She dozed off and awoke to see that they were in front of Sincere and Tru's apartment. She had been to Sincere' unkempt apartment once and privately decided that she was not going to return to often. The place was filled with too much testosterone to put it nicely. Various pieces of weight equipment, sneakers and clothing were strewn around the place. His bedroom lacked personality. There was only a bed without a headboard, a plain cheap wood dresser with a mirror attached and a 32-inch flat screen TV squeezed on top of it. Surprisingly, his toiletries were lined up neatly beside the TV, but it was his collection of Jordan's arranged with military precision that really stole the show. Towels, socks, and more clothing stayed where they landed. He asked her to excuse the mess and she pretended that it was no big deal, but in the back of her mind she filed it away as a potential problem. Sloppiness was not an attribute she wanted in a man. Fortunately, he preferred spending time at her place as well.

"I'll be right back with Meth. You want to come up or wait in the car? It's too cold for you to walk with us," Sincere said stepping out of the car.

"I'll wait here," Benae said. She checked her phone for messages and thought about finally making love to Sincere tonight. She watched as he walked Meth in his suit with a leather jacket over it. She laughed at Meth's exuberance and energy. He was so excited to be out of the house."

"I feel bad," Benae whined as Sincere got back in the car.

"Feel bad for what?" he asked.

"I feel like Meth misses you and I'm taking you away."

Sincere laughed. "Meth is fine. Tru will be back later to walk him in the morning." He winked at her and flashed that cocky smile.

By the time they got to Brooklyn from the Bronx, the temperature took a bigger dip than it was known to do at night. It was now in the low 40s. The chilly air gave them more reason to cling to one another on the short walk to her apartment. Once inside, Sincere quickly undressed, taking the time to hang his expensive suit on the back of the chair, and slip under the velvet turquoise duvet and turn on the TV. Benae was in the adjoining bathroom, changing and freshening up when she heard the TV.

"Why did he turn the TV on?" she wondered.

She shrugged it off and slid the gold toned chemise over her head. She wiggled around and luxuriated in the feel of the silk fabric against her skin. She tousled her hair and checked her ass in the mirror. She looked good and was ready to present herself to her man. She struck a seductive pose in the doorway and waited for his accolades.

"Nice, very sexy, baby," Sincere said admiringly. "Come get in here with me."

She walked over to the bed and straddled him. "You know you look too cute in my bed with the covers pulled up to your neck." She laughed.

"It's cold in here," he said sheepishly.

"I know. It's better to cuddle when there's a little chill in the air."

"I have to go to the bathroom, but I don't want to leave these covers," he said.

"I'll go turn on the heat. It doesn't feel that cold in here to me," she said walking up the hallway. "You want anything while I'm up here."

"Yeah, a little Henny and some water. Thanks," he said making his way to the bathroom. He was back in the bed and under the covers when Benae returned with a glass of wine, glass of water and pint of Hennessey tucked under her arm. "Now, where were we?" she asked sexily.

"Come here," he said, pulling back the covers so that she could get in bed with him.

He clicked off the TV, leaving the room in darkness with the exception of the blue light from the time on the cable box. Sincere rotated his weight on top of Benae and she relaxed into his weight. He kissed her long and deep, leaving her breathless. His lips found her neck and a low moan escaped her lips as her desire for him surged. Expertly, he lifted himself up and pulled the chemise over her head. She did the same with his undershirt then dipped her hand inside of his boxers and massaged his growing manhood.

He removed them enabling her to gain full access. He guided her back down and took one of her nipples in his mouth. She gasped as the torrid sensation ran through her body. Her hips began to grind against him involuntarily. She licked his neck and ears and could feel his rhythm intensify as his penis rubbed against her outer folds. She watched as he reached under her pillow and pulled out a condom. He opened the package with his teeth and secured the condom in place. He slipped a finger inside of her to make sure she was ready for him. She was. He entered her, squeezing into her moist tightness.

"Mmmm," she moaned loudly and opened her legs wider to receive more of him. Taking her cue, he lifted her legs up and held her thighs up and apart giving himself maximum entry. He pumped slowly at first, but Benae doing a steady grind against him was making him reach his peak. Her speed increased as she got closer to reaching her own. "Oh, God baby, I'm coming!" she yelled as waves of ecstasy overtook her.

She wrapped her legs around his back and moved her hips in a rhythmic rotation. Sincere was pulled along and let go with a force of his own. Spent, they laid beside each other, breathing heavily.

"That took all of fifteen minutes," Benae said laughing.

"I know, that's what happens when you hold back and not let nature take its course."

"Even still it was a good fifteen minutes.

"Hell yeah," he agreed. "That was good but let me show you how it's really done." The second time the lovemaking was just as intense, but a lot slower. Sincere moved in and out of her painstakingly slow, driving Benae crazy. Each time she tried to pick up the pace he would stop and tell her, "I got this baby."

She willed herself to slow it down and let him take control. He plunged himself deep inside her until she could feel him fill her up. The sensation coursed through her body. She was caught up in the sweetest wave after wave of pleasure. She wanted to cry, to call out his name, to say *I love you* but before she could an explosive orgasm took control of her. She felt like warm silk was pouring out of her depths as he slowly continued his conquest.

"Turn around for me, baby," Sincere whispered.

Benae wasn't sure if her legs would hold her up, she was completely undone but she was determined to put it on him, too. She backed her ass up and arched her back like a pro. Sincere rubbed the firm globes of her ass before entering her again. She pushed back onto his long dick and pulled herself forward holding only the tip of him with her muscles. She held him tight within her and backed up taking in all of him. She repeated her seduction until he grabbed her hips and glided in and out of her as he reached his peak and released into her. There was no barrier between them, and she embraced it. For some reason she relished knowing that there was a part of him inside her. Seeming to mirror her sentiments, Sincere wrapped both of his arms around her and kissed the top of her head.

Benae squeezed him back then popped her head up to smile at him in the darkness. "You sleepy?" She grinned.

"I'm tired as hell. I was up all night at the Casinos and bars with Rick. I barely got to sleep."

"Aww poor, baby," she said, leaning over to turn on the light. "Well, I am wide awake. I want to talk and I'm kinda hungry." She took a sip of her wine and handed Sincere his drink. He sat up to take a few sips. "Be right back." Benae came back to the room with Tostitos Touch of Lime chips and a bowl of guacamole. "You know you want some," she said snuggling up beside him and sitting the snacks on top of the covers.

Long after the food and drinks were gone, Benae laid in Sincere's arms with her head resting on his chest. They laid in the darkness and talked for hours, despite the fact that Sincere was tired. The conversation kept him awake. When Sincere confided his previous life as a drug-dealer, Benae sat straight up. She knew he could feel her eyes on him even if he couldn't see them.

"Were you out there selling drugs and killing people?" she asked accusingly.

"Yeah, I was selling drugs, but I never killed nobody. I never even drew my sword."

"Sword," Benae thought, taking note of how his words and tone took on a harsh and menacing inflection. "Wow," was all she could say. For some reason, Benae was intrigued. Then thoughts of her parents invaded her mind. Benae's upper, middle-class lifestyle and super strict parents kept her away from *those kinds of boys,* practically all boys.

"No one is going to knock you up and leave you faster than them fast boys running the streets," Benae could almost hear her mother's voice at the memory.

"You got quiet. Did I say something to upset you?" Sincere asked.

"No, I'm just listening to you," Benae lied.

"Come here," he said, reaching out to pull her back to his chest.

She wanted to push him away but she settled herself in his arms and laid her head on his chest pretending that she was still in a loving mood just like she pretended that his past was okay with her. She laid there wide awake as Sincere's breathing became shallow and she could tell he was asleep. His phone was face down on her nightstand, but she could see it lighting up every few minutes. Finally, she reached over and picked it up. She saw the name Bonita on the screen. She eased out of Sincere' arms and sat on the side of the bed with his phone in her hand. As she expected Bonita called again, this time she took the phone into the bathroom and answered it.

SINCERE

Sincere tried to roll over onto his side but found that he couldn't because Benae was practically asleep on top of him. Her head and right arm held down his chest and her right leg was on top of his. He reached for his cell phone on the nightstand and looked at the time.

"Damn it's one-o'clock already?" he murmured.

"Ummm," Benae stretched. "It's one-o'clock?"

"You kept me up all night girl, and I didn't even get breakfast," Sincere joked.

"Well, we'll just have to have brunch." She smiled.

"Do you have any orange juice? I need O.J."

"Sorry, I don't have any, but I do know a diner we can go to. They make the best omelets, too."

"Cool. Sounds good to me," he said.

After the night he and Benae spent together, he wasn't quite ready to leave her yet. Even if she didn't keep orange juice in the house when she knew he was coming over. He figured he could spend the day chilling and finding out where her head was regarding their growing relationship, especially after the revealing conversation they had last night.

"I'm gonna get in the shower." Truthfully, he sat on the toilet first and looked around at all the girly stuff and girly colors she had placed around the room. The barrage of colors continued into the shower. All he saw was an array of bottles of shower gels from Kiel's, Body Shop, and various fragrances. He chose Caress and had to admit he did feel soft. A blue and white striped towel caught his eye and he chose that one to dry himself off. He stepped back into Benae's bedroom and was surprised to see her showered and already dressed in brown leggings and a beige sweater. She was brushing her hair into a ponytail, but he sensed there was something pensive about her mood.

"What's wrong with you?" he asked

"Sincere," she said looking at him intently, "I think I overstepped my boundaries and I am so sorry."

"What did you do?" he asked, honestly having no clue what she could have done.

"I answered your phone while you were sleeping."

"That's my phone. Why would you do that? Did you want to see who was calling me?"

"I don't know. I told you I'm sorry. It's just that someone kept calling and it was distracting to me even though the phone was facedown. Plus, I want you to myself," she said stepping close to him and wrapping her arms around him.

"You don't have to do all that. You have to trust me." He remained stoic and unfazed by her hug.

"I do trust you. It won't happen again. I promise."

The plan to spend a relaxing day with Benae went out the door with her confession. He really didn't like the fact that she answered his phone. He managed to make it through their meal but in the back of his mind he was worried about Bonita. He knew she was already feeling a way and he didn't want her to know about Benae just yet, especially with the pregnancy.

Little was said on the trip back home from the diner. Sincere turned on the Giants game in the living room and Benae sat at the dining table preparing some documents for work. During a commercial break, Sincere walked over to check on her.

"You alright?"

"No, I can tell that you're still mad at me."

"For real though, I don't like what you did, but I'm not mad. Don't worry about it."

Okay, can I have a hug?" she asked standing up in front of him.

"No doubt." He pulled her into his arms and the ice he felt towards her melted. The tension in the air subsided and the playful banter they enjoyed returned. They ended up on the couch cuddled, watching the game which ended about 9:00 and Sincere decided it was time to go. "Let me get out of here." He stretched.

"You don't have to go."

"I do. I have to go home and get my uniform and Tru is probably tired of taking care of Meth. Let me go check in. I might come back," he said knowing he wouldn't.

"It's up to you. It's already getting late and honestly, I am tired. I know you are, too."

"Hell yeah, I'm tired. You kept me up all night." He chuckled.

"So, that settles it. We'll talk tomorrow?"

"Yeah." They kissed goodnight and he headed out to take the long ride on the train from Brooklyn to the Bronx.

The ride gave him time to think about his situation with the two women in his life. He couldn't really understand what it was about Benae that made him feel the way he did. She was different than any of the women he dealt with in the past. She was pretty, classy, fun to be around, bougie but down to earth and very sexy. Some would say that she was out of his league, but he was doing something right. She was definitely trying to be his leading lady and knock out the competition. Still he didn't like the possessive move she made by answering his phone. More importantly, he couldn't believe he left his phone out like that.

Player's code 101 keep the phone on you at all times. On the other hand, Bonita was going to be the mother of his first child. It's not that he didn't care for her, he just didn't see a future with her. If that was the case, why was he worried about his next conversation with her and spent the day dodging her once again? He realized he had a very real situation on his hands, but he would bide his time and figure out the best way to handle it.

One thing he knew, Bonita was gonna have to deal with it because he wanted to see what could happen between him and Benae. Now that both women knew about each other his whole game plan had to change. The funny thing was Benae never said she spoke to Bonita but he knew Bonita would be the only one calling him that time of night. Benae didn't ask him anything about Bonita but that doesn't mean she still wasn't curious. He hadn't heard Bonita's side of the things yet, but he knew it wouldn't be good.

BONITA

Bonita stayed up more than half the night after her encounter on the phone with Benae. The second cup of coffee didn't help, she was really developing an unhealthy addiction. She gave up alcohol, and the occasional cigarette for her baby, but she wasn't giving up coffee although she felt she needed to cut back. She just hadn't because it helped her cope with the drama surrounding her by way of her relationship with Sincere. The phone call somewhat confirmed what she already knew – Sincere had met someone else.

Still there was a small part of her that just couldn't accept that. There was no way he would be okay with a chick answering his phone. That just wasn't the way he was. *I don't care who the girl is.* Sincere was very private with his phone. One good thing about this chick answering the phone was that she was not going to call again, and she didn't. It's one thing to look like a fool for the man you love, but not for the next female to laugh at. As much as she wanted to talk to Sincere and find out what was going on, she knew she would just have to wait until he contacted her.

By the time she finally drifted off to sleep it was almost 6:00 in the morning. She woke up to the sounds of her mom cooking in the kitchen. *Damn, I wanted to make breakfast for her,* she thought picking up her phone to see the time. It was 10:30. *Well, I guess she waited as long as she could.*

Any other time Ms. Lucille would have had her breakfast no later than 7:00 a.m. She also noticed that there were no missed calls which meant that Sincere hadn't called. She really was in no mood to think about it and rolled over to go back to sleep.

When she awoke again it was almost noon. She still didn't want to get up, but her bladder was about to burst, and she couldn't hold it anymore. Contracting her kegel muscles she slowly got up from the bed and tried her best not to pee on herself. The baby had to be resting directly on her bladder. The pressure was so intense that she feared standing straight and walked to the bathroom bent over like a hunchback. When she was finally able to relieve herself, she thought it was one of the best feelings ever. She shuffled over to the sink and brushed her teeth and washed her face.

"Good morning, Ma," she said passing the living room to go into the kitchen. "Sorry, I didn't get up in time to make breakfast like I said I would."

"It's okay, baby. There's nothing wrong with getting rest when you need it. Pregnancy will do that to you."

"Thanks, ma." Bonita poured herself a cup of coffee and made herself a big bowl of her mother's brown sugar oatmeal, one of her favorites. She crumbled the four crispy strips of bacon and sprinkled them on top. The meal was so comforting and satisfying that she didn't bother going back into her bedroom to get her phone. Shakirra must know by now that she missed their morning breakfast and she didn't care if Sincere called or not. She just wasn't in the mood.

"What you watching?" she asked her mother as she sat on the sofa with her bowl of oatmeal in her lap and a cup of coffee in her hand.

"I don't know some movie on Lifetime it came on about ten minutes ago."

"Okay, I'll watch with you."

Just as she was about to sit her empty bowl on the end table and stretch out on the couch, she heard Sincere' unmistakable knock at the door. *Figures he comes over her when I'm looking busted with my hair a mess and in my pajamas,* she thought. *He gets on my nerves.*

"Oh, that's Sincere. I haven't seen him in a while," Ms. Lucille exclaimed.

Bonita took her time walking to the door. "Who is it?" she asked.

"'Nita you know it's me."

She opened the door but stood in the doorway. "What's up?"

"You not gonna let me in now?" he asked taken aback.

"Come in, Sincere," she said, allowing him entry.

He looked annoyed as he passed her, but she didn't care.

"Hi, Ms. Lucille. How you been?" he asked giving her a big hug.

"I've been fine." She beamed.

"That's good. I'm always happy to hear that you are doing okay. Let me talk to 'Nita real quick and I'll come out here and chop it up with you." He walked into Bonita's bedroom.

She followed and closed the door behind her. "So, who was the girl that answered your phone?"

"It's someone I've been seeing. I wanted to tell you the day that you told me you were pregnant, but I didn't feel that was the right time."

"Oh, I see," Bonita said her voice trembling. "What does this mean for me and our baby?"

"It means that I am with someone, but I will still be here for you and our child."

"Our child, so you know this your baby?" she asked.

"Nita, of course I know. I know you and I know you love me and wouldn't be with anyone but me."

"That's right. So, if you know I love you why are you with someone else? You don't love me no more?"

"It's not that. You know we haven't been getting along or spending too much time together..."

"Yeah, and whose fault is that? To me everything was fine. You just left and came back acting different, but I still believed we were together. I wasn't expecting to hear this shit. Especially, not now while I am carrying your baby. Do you hear me? We are going to have a baby and you are standing here telling me you are not with me? I can't believe what I am hearing."

"'Nita, you're overreacting. I told you I would be here for both of you. What part of that don't you get?"

"Don't you get smart with me. Trust me I get it I just don't know if I believe it. Being here for your family would mean you would choose us over some new bitch."

"She's not a bitch and I am not choosing her over my family."

"Oh, you're defending this bitch? *What!* You caught feelings for her? You in love and shit letting her answer your phone," Bonita mocked.

"You know what, I came over here to respectfully have a conversation with you and let you know that I would be here for you and the baby no matter what, but you on some other shit." He stood up to leave. "Let me know if you need anything, money, clothes, vitamins...whatever. I will make sure you have what you need. I am not abandoning you 'Nita I just can't be your man."

She sat down on the bed, pulled the pillow onto her lap and cried into it as she listened to him chat amicably with her mother about their baby as if he hadn't just beaten her down with his words.

CHAPTER 6

ALL I WANT FOR CHRISTMAS IS YOU

There was no better place to be than New York City at Christmas. The island of Manhattan was transformed from the suit and tie financial center of the world to a quant tinsel town alive with the sights and sounds of the season. The decorative trees, holiday-themed department store windows, vendors roasting chestnuts and the Rockefeller Center tree to top it all off. It was barely noon and the sidewalks along 5th Avenue was already filled with tourists and last-minute shoppers. Since they were already in the vicinity, Benae and Chrissy stopped to admire the tree. The two friends met earlier for lunch at The Sea Grill which overlooked the famous Rockefeller Center ice skating rink. Benae heard that the historic eatery was closing and wanted to make sure she experienced it before it did. After brunch, the twosome walked the ten or so blocks to 57th street and headed to the Spa where Benae had made appointments for them to receive facials and massages. It was her Christmas gift for her best friend.

They took the elevator up to The Spa. Chrissy was overwhelmed by the luxurious surroundings. The magnitude of her friends' gift filled her with warmth and appreciation.

"Benae, thanks so much. This had to cost you a pretty penny and I want you to know I thank you for this from the bottom of my heart."

"You're my girl and you deserve it. Plus, I deserve it too and I need my partner in crime to enjoy it with me," she leaned in and elbowed Chrissy in the ribs.

A petite, dark-haired woman appeared. "Ladies, right this way," she spoke with a strong French accent. She led them into the changing room and continued providing instructions. "The robes and slippers are located in the lockers behind the curtain. Just pick a locker and have a seat in the relaxation room. They changed into plush, white, terry-cloth robes with matching slippers and waited in the circular relaxation room. The room was draped in off white fabrics and there was no sunlight. A round circular sitting area was the focal point of the room. There were pitchers of chilled cucumber water placed on the various tabletops. Within minutes they were called to enjoy their services.

After a couple of hours of blissful pampering, Benae and Chrissy walked out into the crisp air. "Do you want to catch a cab to your place?" Benae asked.

"*A cab?* What's wrong with the train? That's how I got here."

"I don't feel like dealing with the train, right now. I'm too relaxed for that. Getting on the train will just ruin my Zen."

Chrissy had to laugh. Benae was right. After those relaxing massages and facials, the last place they needed to be was on a crowded train. "Okay, but you know how they act about going to the Bronx."

"Yep. The same way they act about going to Brooklyn, but we'll get one." They headed to the corner to flag down a yellow cab. "Or we can use Uber. I don't have the app, though."

"Benae!" She turned to see Max walking toward her.

"Hi Max, what are you doing over here?"

"What do you mean what I'm doing over here? I thought this was a free country."

"It is. I'm just surprised to see you that's all," she explained.

"I have an affair to go to tonight and I needed a new pair of shoes. So, I came to check out Ferragamo. As you can see, I found what I came for." He showed her his shopping bag. "Hey, Chrissy. How you been?"

"I'm good, Max. Thanks," Chrissy answered keeping it short.

"You're looking good, as usual," he said looking at Benae intently.

"Thanks."

"Keep it tight, you know you'll be back."

"Come on Benae, we got one," Chrissy said opening the door for a cab that pulled over for them.

"Bye, Max." Benae turned to enter the cab and Max grabbed her by the arm.

"You still belong to me. Don't forget that."

She snatched her arm away and got in the cab.

"My goodness, what is wrong with him?" Chrissy asked, obviously upset.

"He's just being an ass. He's not taking the break-up seriously."

"Be careful. He made me nervous just now."

"I'm not scared of Max. He just needs to leave me alone."

"Did you tell Sincere about him? If you didn't you should."

"I didn't say anything about Max. Remember when I told you I answered his phone because this girl named Bonita was calling him. Well, I never asked about it because I didn't want him to ask me questions that would lead to me bringing up Max."

"You need to put all that aside and tell him about this nut," Chrissy insisted.

Benae just looked out of the window. Chrissy was probably right, but she didn't feel like agreeing with her right now.

Greg greeted them at the door. He kissed his wife and gave Benae a quick hug, kiss combo and offered up holiday greetings. The Sheffield household was a cornucopia of Christmas delight. A huge spruce tree took center stage in the small living room. Each window was decked out with strings of blinking lights and one even showcased a dancing Black Santa and Mrs. Clause holding candles. Green bows of pine wrapped around the banister leading upstairs and little bowls filled with candy canes were placed around the downstairs rooms.

"Fifth Avenue has nothing on the Sheffield's. My goodness!" Benae exclaimed looking around the room.

Chrissy looked around smiling at her work. "Thanks, the kids and I did it."

As if on cue, both boys came charging down the stairs. "Hi, Auntie Benae! Where's our presents," Marquise the youngest boy asked.

Benae reached down and hugged both of her God sons. "They must be under the tree with all the other gifts. I gave them to your mom weeks ago," she said, grabbing them both and tickling them. She kept going until they cried out for her to stop.

"Are we gonna watch a Christmas Story now?" Kye asked.

"Yep, in a few minutes," Chrissy answered. "Just let me throw the cookies in the oven and spike the eggnog. You get the un-spiked kind." She pointed to her boys.

Benae headed upstairs to the guest room. "I'll be right back. I'm just going to call Sincere real quick. To her surprise and pleasure, he picked up on the first ring.

"Hey, baby. What's up?" she could hear the smile in his voice.

"Not much. Just spending the day with Chrissy and her family. They are like my family too you know. We're about to watch A Christmas Story. The boys love it. We watch it every year. What are you up to?"

"Nothing really, just about to go drop off gifts for my dad. I shipped my mom's already. I'll Probably grab a quick bite then I'm gonna make my way to you."

"Okay sounds good. Why don't you come meet me at Chrissy's since you'll already be in the Bronx? This way you can meet Greg. You can eat here, too. There's a lot of food," she said excitedly.

"Why do women always want their man to meet their girl's man?" he chuckled. "I'll never get it."

"So, you're my man?" she asked coyly.

"I thought you knew that? We've been seeing each other for what five months now. I'm cool with making it official if you are."

"Of course, I am," she gushed.

"I'll call you when I'm on my way."

"Okay. I can't wait to see you."

"I can't wait to see you either."

He's so perfect, she thought as they ended the call. "Thank you," she mouthed clasping her hands together and bowing her head.

SINCERE

Man, I hate Christmas, Sincere thought. *Seems like each year something fucked up happens.* He quickly apologized to God for having such a negative thought. There was no way a baby was a fucked-up thing that happened. It's just that it wasn't in his plan. Instead of staying for dinner at his dad's house, he was going to stop by Bonita's and drop off a gift for her the baby and Ms. Lucille. He hated lying to Benae and knew the time was coming that he would have to tell her about the impending birth of what he now knew would be his son. He decided he would cross that bridge when he came to it. Right now, it was Christmas Eve and it was time to enjoy it.

"Tru, you ready? I'm about to leave man I have a lot of stops to make today."

Tru entered Sincere' room laughing. "I bet you do with your new girlfriend and new baby mama. Damn, she trapped that ass," he teased.

"Yeah, that's what Dad said, too. It is what is now. She's seven months the baby will be here soon."

"I'm just messing with you man. If ole girl really loves you, she'll understand the situation and ride with you."

"I know, but Benae ain't no hood chick. She's a different breed and may not understand the way a girl from the hood would. Know what I mean?"

"Yeah, but love is love. All women love the same. If she ain't down, she ain't real."

Sincere glanced at his brother questioningly. Sometimes Tru seemed to make sense and in those moments Sincere didn't know what to make of it. "Do you know if Glenda cooked today or she's waiting until tomorrow?" Glenda was their dad's wife of ten years.

She was a good addition to the family and kept Leon on the straight and narrow.

"Yeah, I'm sure she did, and I am ready to eat."

"Man, you always ready to eat," Sincere chided.

He waited for Tru's comeback, but he guessed what he said was true since there was no rebuttal.

"I just remembered she said that they have some function to go to tonight," Tru said.

"Even better, so I'll be in and out. I'm leaving now."

"Go head then, man. I'll see them tomorrow. I'll chill at the crib with this new girl since you won't be here. She's bringing some food she made and the liquor."

"Alright, Merry Christmas, man." Sincere hugged his brother and patted him on the back.

"Merry Christmas. Later, "Tru sang and put up the deuces.

Sincere filled his car up with gas and headed across town to see his parents. When he got there, they were already gone so he let himself in with the keys he never returned once he moved out and left their gifts under the modest tree in the corner. The house smelled like Glenda's perfume, so he knew he'd just missed them. He looked under the tree for a gift with his name on it and took it. He hopped back in the car and traveled from the Bronx to Brooklyn to see Bonita.

"Hey, you," she answered the door in a tight black dress, that looked uncomfortable.

"Hey, how you doing?" he said entering the apartment. He was surprised the house was relatively clean. The Christmas tree was nicely decorated, and the house smelled of a good home cooked meal including desserts.

"Looks good in here," he continued. "You cooked?"

"Yeah, me and momma made a little something-something. We even made your favorite sock-it-to-me cake." She smiled up at him. "Did you eat?"

"Actually, I didn't. I'll have a little plate. Thank you."

"Why are you acting all uptight and formal? You used to practically live here."

"Yeah, I remember, but that was a while ago. A lot has changed since then."

Bonita opened the cabinet and Sincere could see a roach scurrying into a less visible place. She rinsed the plate off and began piling food onto it.

"Not too much, I'm not that hungry."

"So, what's the lot that has changed?" She placed the plate in front of him.

"Well, for one, look at your belly. You're really showing now," he joked and reached over to rub her growing belly.

"Yeah." She laughed. "I'm getting big, but the Doctor said I am just where I should be weight wise."

"That's a good thing. How's the baby doing?"

"He is doing fine. He's a good size, too. He's moving right now." She took his hand and placed it on her tummy. "I think he already knows his daddy's voice."

Sincere was amazed by the feeling. He felt an immediate attachment to the mysterious life that he had helped create. This was his baby, his son moving around showing strong signs of life and clearly making his presence known.

"Wow," was all Sincere could muster. He felt tears well in his eyes.

Bonita warmly kissed the top of his head and hugged him to her belly. For a moment he gave into the feeling. He hugged her back and kept his head pressed against her moving belly.

He released the embrace and asked, "Do you need anything. Let me know if you need anything. You look like you can use some clothes," he said knowing he had bought her a few maternity outfits as gifts.

"Yeah, I can use some help with maternity clothes. I was carrying small now all of a sudden, I can barely fit into anything."

"Alright, I got you. I'll get you some things and we'll have to talk about getting everything the baby needs too. Time is flying."

"Yeah, he'll be here in two months."

"Here, I got a little something for you." He handed her a box with the red Macy's logo tied with a big red bow. Inside was a crystal picture frame made for a baby boy. "You can open the rest tomorrow and this one is for your mom."

"Thank you." She hugged him and placed the gifts under the tree. She came back holding a small box for him. "It's not much.

"It's the thought that counts. Thanks. Well, I better get going."

"Where you going?" she asked.

He could tell his quick departure was disappointing her. "I'm going with Glenda and pops to this dinner thing. They bought the tickets and everything. That's why I didn't want to eat too much."

"Oh, okay. Well, have fun, "Bonita said dejected.

"Don't be like that. I'll see you again soon." Before he could stop himself, he reached for her and kissed her lovingly on the lips. She smiled at him and that's what he was going for. "That's my girl," he said. "Now let me get a piece of that sock-it-to-me cake."

He was a little tired from the food and the driving, but he devoured the slice of cake on the way. He left Bonita in Brooklyn to go back to the Bronx to Chrissy's and before the night was over, he would be back in Brooklyn at Benae's. When he pulled up in front of Chrissy's house, he saw Benae standing outside huddled in a powder blue wrap coat and matching scarf and gloves. He felt the tension of the day begin to ease out of him, until she headed for the door and hopped in the passenger seat.

"Hi, baby," she said gracefully sliding into the passenger seat. She gave him a luscious kiss and wrapped him in her arms. "I am so glad to see you."

"I see," Sincere said, a bit taken aback, but he could see all the passion and truth in her eyes. She really was glad to see him. Fortunately, she didn't see the gift from Bonita on the back seat. He tossed it under his seat as soon as she stepped back out.

"Come on inside and meet Greg and the boys."

Sincere had met Chrissy a couple of times when accompanying Benae to Bloomingdale's but had never met her husband. He was looking forward to getting to know another married couple. They spent the rest of the evening eating and drinking with Chrissy and Greg. They even played a couple of hands of Spades before they decided on calling it a night.

"We're not trying to kick y'all out or nothing, but we want some grown up time and our kids will be up at the crack of dawn," Chrissy slurred.

"We are ready to go anyway. We want some grown up time, too, "Benae joked.

"Man, it was nice meeting you. We should do this again sometime, "Greg said to Sincere offering him dap.

"Yeah man, I enjoyed myself. Your two little ones are something else."

"They keep it lively around here," Greg agreed.

"Okay, we're out. Merry Christmas you two." Benae hugged Chrissy and Greg in the doorway. "Call me and let me know if my God sons loved my gifts, as they usually do."

"Whatever! Get home safe. Merry Christmas!" Chrissy yelled too loudly.

"Woman, get in the house." Greg scolded. They all laughed.

Sincere opened the passenger side door for Benae, and watched as she toppled in. This was the first time he'd seen her tipsy and he found it funny

"What are you laughing at?" she asked loudly.

"You," he said. "I think you're drunk."

"I'm not drunk. I'm Merry," she joked and they both laughed.

"So, did you have a good time? I was checking you out and it seemed like you did."

"Yeah, it was cool. They're good people."

"The best, I love them to death."

Sincere put on some music and played *Bryson Tiller's Exchange*. As the music started, he mouthed, "Give me all of you in exchange for me..." He could see her blush and struggle to find something to say. He loved watching a woman react to romantic gestures it told him where her heart was. She acted like a woman falling in love and unable to believe what was happening to her.

After a pause she said somberly, "I love you, too, Sincere." He was caught off guard when she began to discuss her past with Max. She relayed the history of their relationship covering the infidelities, the lies and Max's possessive nature. "The thing that makes me most upset is how he refuses to accept that it's over. I told him it was over before I moved out. I thought moving out would make my position crystal clear but he's not getting it."

Sincere felt his anger starting to rise. What kind of sucker-for-love shit was this? I can't stand dudes like that, but he reigned in his feelings so that his response to her would not betray his raging emotions. "Why is that?"

"I honestly don't know. I did everything I could."

"Did you block him on your phone? Did you maintain a friendship? Like, how did you leave it?"

"I eventually blocked him, but I didn't when I first moved out. I don't want to be friends with him at all."

"Yeah, but did you tell him that?" Sincere glared at her briefly before turning back to focus on the road.

"No," Benae said softly.

"When is the last time you had sex with him?" Sincere asked, once again taking a glance in her direction.

She squirmed in her seat and put her face in her hands. Sincere braced for the worse. "Actually, the last time I had sex with him was the day we met."

"You sure about that?" he asked his voice tinged with anger.

"one-hundred percent sure."

Yeah, and so are those chicks on Maury and the guy turns out not to be the father, he thought, but he said, "You said you broke up months before we met. How you end up having sex the same day we met?"

Benae regained her composure and sat up straight in her seat. "It's true, we did break up, but we lived together until I got my own place." Sincere reflected back on his earlier thought about hating

Christmas. Something bad inevitably happened and this one was no exception.

"Sincere, baby, listen to me." She reached over and placed her hand on this thigh. Sincere continued to drive, keeping his eyes forward and on the road. "I am so sorry for not being clear about my living situation at the time. But I knew I was moving out in a few weeks. I didn't want to take the chance and tell you about it. I didn't want to mess things up with us. The important thing is I am telling you the truth. I promise I will not leave out information like that again. Okay?"

Thoughts of Bonita, the baby that was coming in a couple of months and all the life changing information that he was leaving out were on the tip of his tongue. It was the perfect time to come clean about his situation as well, but for some reason he couldn't bring himself to do it. Once again, he learned something new about Benae. First, she picked up his phone and now she's guilty of lies of omission. He decided to let it ride.

He double parked in front of his house, turned off the car and looked over at her. "Okay."

Benae's disposition brightened and she noticed they were parked in front of his house. "I hope you are not stopping for pajamas, because you will not be needing them with the things that I have planned for you," she said looking at him seductively.

"Oh, word?" he asked brightly.

"Word," Benae responded mischievously.

"I'll be right back. I'm going to get Meth and take him for a walk."

"I want to come I haven't seen Meth in a while."

"I'm bringing him right down," Sincere avoided her invitation."

"Hey, why don't you bring him over to my place? This way he'll spend Christmas morning with us."

"You sure about that?" Sincere asked surprised that she would even consider having his unruly pup in her house.

"Yeah, just bring his cage and he should be fine. I got him some bowls as a Christmas gift, just bring some food and he's all set."

"Cool. I'll go get him and his cage. I'll be right back." Sincere tucked the small gift from Bonita inside his jacket and sat it on his bed. *Tru and his guest must have gone out.* He saw an overnight bag but no signs of anyone.

Parking on Benae's street was non-existent. They drove around and around and just as they were about to park in 24-hour garage, they found a spot five blocks away. A light snow began to fall and Benae released Meth from the cage in the back seat and the two took off running. Sincere walked behind them carrying the puppy cage.

"Okay, boy, time for bed," Sincere said directing Meth into the cage once he'd had a small snack and some water.

Meth whined a little bit but obediently got into the cage and laid down on his pillow. Sincere secured the cage and stood up. Benae was standing behind him with an ice bucket containing a bottle of Dom Perignon and two frosted champagne glasses. She was wearing nothing, but her birthday suit and a red thong adorned with a big bow in the back.

"Whoa," Sincere said clearly pleased with the view. "Damn girl."

Benae turned around and shook the bow on her behind accentuating her ass and toned legs. Seductively, she peered over her shoulder at him asked, "You like?"

"Hell yeah, I like. Come here."

She shook her head no and began walking toward him. "No, Mr. Law, I am in charge and I order you to have a seat on the sofa." Sincere did as he was told and took a seat as Benae sat on the floor beside him pouring the champagne into the glasses. "It's after midnight. It's officially our first Christmas together." She held her glass up. "Merry Christmas, baby."

Sincere clinked her glass against hers. "Merry Christmas."

Looking him directly in the eyes, Benae arched her neck up and they kissed lovingly. The kissed gained momentum and passion as

Benae unfastened his belt and Sincere speedily assisted. She looked up at him for a moment then slipped his hardness into her mouth which was filled with the chilled champagne.

"Oh shit," Sincere mouthed.

The cool, bubbly sensation of the champagne coupled with the warmth of her mouth felt incredible. Sincere leaned back into the sofa and looked down at the woman he had come to love, pleasuring him. He held her head close to him as the feelings of love and the sensations of getting his dick sucked merged. I guess this Christmas wasn't going to be so bad after all.

BONITA

Bonita laid in bed trying to contain her nausea. It wasn't the pregnancy that was making her feel sick it was the stench of chitterlings cooking in the kitchen. Lucille was committed to making them every Christmas and Bonita could not remember a Christmas without them. She never understood how anyone could eat something that smelled so bad. She got up and searched for a can of air freshener.

"Good morning, sleepy head. Merry Christmas," Lucille said cheerfully. She was sitting at the cluttered kitchen table reading the latest copy of Ebony magazine and sipping a cup of coffee. It was good to see her mom in such good spirits.

"Merry Christmas Ma," Bonita said walking over to give her mother a hug. "I see you're making chitlins... as usual." She rolled her eyes behind her mother's back.

"Yes, baby. I hope they don't smell too bad. I closed your door so the smell wouldn't get in there too much."

"It's not too bad but a little Glade or Lysol couldn't hurt," Bonita said spraying the scent of Apples and Cinnamon around the small apartment.

"I made us some breakfast, French toast, eggs and sausage. I made coffee too, I put a little egg nog in mine." Lucille smiled.

"That sounds yummy. I'm gonna put some in mine, too." Bonita danced over to the coffeemaker and fridge.

"Why don't you open your gifts first, they're sitting there under the tree," Lucille said lighting up a Parliament.

"Ma, I thought you were gonna stop smoking?"

"I'll stop. I just don't know when." Lucille laughed at her joke.

Bonita ignored her and walked over to the small but cheerfully decorated tree and picked up the large box wrapped in green and gold paper addressed to her from her mother. She picked up the smaller red box and handed it to her. They both giddily unwrapped their gifts. Bonita was grateful for the two maternity outfits.

"Thanks mom, I needed these." She held up the red corduroy pants and the white top. "I am going to wear this one today. The other one was a black jumpsuit. There were also a couple of outfits for the baby.

"I'm glad you like them 'Nita. I took so much time picking out just the right ones for you and you know I had to get something for my grandson. Oh, and I love my gift. You know White Diamonds is my favorite perfume." Lucille opened a couple of gifts from some of her co-workers.

Bonita opened a gift from Shakirra, a pair of black UGG boots. Shakirra always got her hands on bootlegged items. Last, she opened the gifts from Sincere. There was an array of maternity tops and bottoms and a pair of boots. There were also a few outfits for the baby and $300 in twenties.

"Oh, how nice!" Ms. Lucille exclaimed. "And what thoughtful gifts for you," Lucille said opening the hat, glove and scarf set he'd given her.

"I guess," Bonita said. She was hoping for something more personal.

"Let's go and get ready to visit your daddy's grave. I want to get there early before everyone else starts showing up." She opened the pot of chitterlings and stirred them. "If we get back by 2:00 and finish dinner we can serve dinner no later than 5:00. I told

Shakirra that her and her family are welcome. I expect that Sincere will join us too, right?"

"I don't know ma. He came by yesterday and said he was going to a family dinner so if he comes by it might be later."

"Okay. Now go get dressed."

Bonita looked at her protruding belly in the bathroom mirror. She was days away from her seventh month. She stared at her naked body and lovingly caressed her belly. She could feel the little life moving around inside of her. "Merry Christmas, little one. Mommy loves you so much and so does your daddy. Let's call your daddy and tell him Merry Christmas." Expectantly, she picked up the phone and called him. By the time the call went to voice mail, Bonita was close to tears. The slow and subtle rejection hurt so bad inside. Tears filled her voice as she left a message wishing him a Merry Christmas from her and their son.

As she showered, she let the tears flow even while listening intently for any indication from her phone. There was none. She decided it was Christmas and she was going to be happy regardless. She put on her new outfit, a new wig and bright red lipstick. Her phone rang as she was sliding on her shoes.

"Hello."

"Merry Christmas!" Sincere's loud voice boomed through the phone.

"Merry Christmas to you." Bonita Smiled.

"Did you open your gifts yet?"

"Yes, I did. I love the little outfit for the baby. It's so cute."

"Good, good. What y'all doing today?"

"We're getting ready to go to the cemetery to visit daddy's grave. Later, Shakirra, Joe and the kids are coming over. Of course, you know that I am expecting you to come by."

"Thanks for the invite. I'll let you know if I'm gonna come through."

"Why can't you let me know now? Are you still going out with your dad and Glenda?"

"Yeah, and I'm not sure what I'll feel like doing afterward."

"Oh, okay," she said disappointed.

"It's Christmas, you with your family and friends you know, enjoy that."

"I will, but you're my family, too."

"I know, I know, but I have to go. You make sure you have a good day, okay?"

"I love you."

"I know that, too. Take it easy now. I'll talk to you later."

"Take it easy! Who you fronting for? That bitch that answered your phone. Are you with her?" Bonita let out the attitude that was dying to escape since he dodged her invitation. Shit, she shouldn't have had to invite his ass in the first place.

"Later," Sincere said ending the call.

That lousy piece of shit. He's spending Christmas with this chick and he should be here with me. I can't believe this is happening now. If he didn't want to be with me, he shouldn't have got me pregnant. Tears threatened to fall once again, but she held them in. She didn't want to mess up the make-up she had just painstakingly applied. Besides, Sincere wasn't going nowhere. She was carrying his son and they were going to be a family.

CHAPTER 7

FORMATION

BENAE

Benae closed the door to her office and dialed Chrissy's number. They both went over their holiday week in detail picking up from when they parted on Christmas Eve, covering New Year's Eve to the present.

"Everything is going great with Sincere," Benae said pensively. "But I can tell something is up. Sometimes he just looks so deep in thought. I can tell something is on his mind. The other night I asked him everything under the sun that it could possibly be, from him being on the down low to him being married. He denied everything. I'm just waiting for the shoe to drop."

"Hmm, just trust your instincts. That's all I can tell you. If you feel something is up it probably is," Chrissy advised.

"The feeling is so strong I can barely function here today."

"I'm sorry sweetie, but I have to get back on the floor. People are still coming in for the after Christmas Day sales. I can give you a call later, okay?" Chrissy asked sweetly.

"Okay, I'll talk to you later." The rest of the day was uneventful except for the fact that she had not heard from Sincere all day and he had not returned any of her calls.

She felt lethargic and just wanted to lie down. As soon as she got home from work, she stepped out of her pumps and threw her coat across the sofa. Passing the dining room, an envelope on the table caught her eye. She backtracked and picked up the plain white letter addressed to her. There was only one person that could have left it there. She had left for work before Sincere and he apparently had something to tell her that he couldn't tell her to her face. Benae was not surprised to see that her fingers trembled slightly as she unfolded the note.

My love Benae,

I don't know how to tell you this except to say that it's something I should've told you already. Before I say what I have to say. I want you to know that when I tell you I love you I mean it. I think we have something special and that we can work through anything. I really want to see what we can have together. So, here goes, right before we met, while I was recuperating from my injury I had sex with my girlfriend at the time, Bonita. I was planning to break-up with her by gradually pulling away but that time we were together things happened. The thing is, she's pregnant and...

Benae did not need to read any further. *Pregnant! The one thing I never guessed. I knew this thing was too right and too good to be true,* she thought.

Benae felt the total darkness of the evening engulf her. She squeezed into one of the dining room chairs without pushing it away from the table and just sat there. The house phone rang, and she didn't move to answer it.

Sincere's voice came through on the answering machine, "Babe, it's me, pick up. Alright, give me a call when you get this message."

Over the next half hour Sincere left five more messages, but Benae could not bring herself to answer the phone or her cell. She just sat in the darkness and cried until her head started hurting. By the time she moved from her frozen position at the table it was 8:30 and she had been crying for close to two hours. Drained but somehow strengthened, she knew what she had to do. She began searching her apartment for any signs of Sincere. She gathered his things and put them into a trash bag, his toothbrush, after shave, items from *his drawer* and Meth's bowls, food and toys. Just as she sat the bag in front of her door, her bell rang. Without asking who was there, she buzzed the door to let Sincere in.

"Why is it so dark in here?" he asked walking through the door. Benae didn't answer. "Did you read my letter?" he said tripping over his packed bag. "Mind if I turn on the light?"

She reached over from her spot on the sofa and turned on the lamp. "So, you're gonna be a daddy. Congratulations. When is the baby due?" she said with tear-filled eyes.

Sincere walked over to the sofa and sat next to her. He reached for her hand, but she pulled it away.

"She said in at the end of February."

"What! That's next month. How long have you known?"

"Since the end of September. I didn't say anything because I was trying to deal with the news myself and focus on us," he said kneeling on the floor before her.

"You've known for over three months and didn't say anything to me?"

"I wanted to tell you I just didn't know how."

Benae stood over him. "You open your mouth and tell me! You tell me before I fall for you! You tell me a lot sooner so that you don't hurt me like this. You just man up and do it!" she yelled. Sincere looked down at the floor. "Look at me," she ordered and waited until he did. "You didn't tell me because you are a deceitful coward." She moved to walk away.

"Come sit back down." Sincere tugged gently at her arm. She sat. "Listen, on everything I love, I didn't try to deceive you. I didn't want you to think the worse of me and I definitely didn't want to hurt you. Don't you see I fell for you, too? All this happened at the same time and I thought I was doing the right thing."

"Well, at the end of the day it doesn't matter. I can't deal with this. I just can't." Benae ran her fingers through her hair.

"So, that's it?"

"Guess so. I don't see what else there is to say," she said hopelessly.

"Alright then." Reluctantly he walked to the door and looked inside one of the bags filled with his things. "You packed all my stuff?" The look on his face broke Benae's heart even more but she was not going to let him know that. She wanted him to hurt.

"Yeah, all your things are there." He and Benae locked eyes.

"It seems every time I find happiness it's taken away from me." He sat the bag down and looked at Benae.

Her resolve broke and she walked over to him and threw her arms around him. He looked so sad and so vulnerable. She loved him so much. How could she just let him go? She started to cry in earnest.

"Baby, I'm so sorry." He held her close. "I told you that I love you and if you love me like you say you do we can get through this."

Benae pulled back from his embrace and looked him in the eyes. "You know I love you but this is too much for me, right now. How are you going to feel about her once she gives birth to your child? You can't honestly answer that, right now."

"I can tell you that I want you and want to see what you and I could have. I'm not giving that up."

In spite of herself, Benae was touched by his words. "Let me think about it some more, okay? I'm emotionally overwhelmed, right now."

"I understand. I'll call you when I get home, okay?" Sincere stepped toward her and his towering frame seemed to fill the room. Benae could feel her chest contract as she fought to keep from giving in and forgiving him on the spot.

"Hey, look at me," Sincere gently commanded, placing his hand on her chin.

Benae continued looking down and shook her head no. He wrapped her in his arms and kissed her on her forehead. The sensation was so sweet she couldn't help but smile through her tears.

"I think you should go," she said stepping away once again.

"I'll call you," he said and he was gone.

This time Benae did not follow him with her eyes through the window. In fact, she didn't go to the window at all. She didn't feel like talking to anyone and she definitely didn't want to cry anymore. She walked into the kitchen to pour herself a big glass of wine only to find that she had none.

"Damn! I can't even drink my pain away." Briefly, she considered going to a local bar but didn't feel like getting presentable to go out. So, she put on her favorite floor length satin gown with the matching robe and got in bed with a cup of hot chocolate and a box of blueberry mini donuts. She binged watched the shenanigans and dating disasters of Carrie, Miranda, Samantha, and Charlotte until she fell asleep.

SINCERE

For the first time that he could remember, Sincere was not focusing on Monday Night Football even though his team the New York Giants were playing. Usually, any time football was on it was his time to tune everything out and just chill. But Benae was heavily on his mind. He had been calling her since he left her house a week ago, but she was either still thinking things through or she decided to move on. At half time, he decided to give Rick a quick call and run the situation by him.

Rick exhaled deeply. "Man, that's a tough one. The timing is all fucked up. Benae seemed like a nice girl and if she loves you, she will come around. On the other hand, you and 'Nita been together for a minute and now y'all having a baby. Are you sure you want to let her go, right now? I mean, I know you don't want the next dude around your seed."

"Hell, naw. She won't do that."

"She might if you leave her now."

"True, but if I play my cards right, I can have them both. At least until I see how things go with both of them.

"That's right man. Do that shit, you ain't married." They both laughed

"Talk to you later."

Damn, I forgot to feed Meth. He headed into the kitchen and hoped there was a can or two of food left, the dry food was gone. Meth followed him around playfully nipping at Sincere's bare feet. "You're in luck, Meth." Sincere emptied the last can of food into Meth's bowl and gave him some fresh water. The thought crossed his mind that he paid more attention to his dog than he did to his child. He was surprised when he called Bonita's cell and didn't get an answer, undaunted he tried the house phone.

"Hey, Ms. Lucille. How you been?"

"Hi, Sincere. I'm doing okay. You know I don't get into you and Nita's business. One day y'all together, one day you're not. Y'all speaking, y'all not speaking. I stay out of it, but now you two have a baby coming. You gonna be a daddy and you can't leave her and me to raise it."

"I'm not planning on not being there. I never said that," Sincere protested.

"Well, I am glad to hear you say that. 'Nita never said you weren't going to be here for her and the baby, but I noticed you haven't been around like you used to. I also see her looking sad and I know its cause of you."

All Sincere felt needed to be said was, "I understand."

"Good, you know she loves you and she need you right now. We still need some of everything for the baby."

"Don't worry. I got it. You just take care of yourself and get you some rest."

"Okay, now, I'll call 'Nita to the phone," Ms. Lucille's pleased tone assured Sincere that he was in the clear.

"Hello," Bonita answered the phone.

"Hey, you alright? I didn't get an answer when I called your cell."

"I'm just tired. I am getting so big and the baby is moving around a lot. I'm so excited but I am a little scared too..."

Sincere listened to her ramble on and found himself feeling excited, too. In his mind he saw a small version of himself running around. He smiled as he responded, "Yeah that's my boy, huh? My dad always says us Laws don't make no girls."

"Uh huh, listen to you. The doctor says it' a boy but I trust God the most so boy or girl. I want to name the baby after you."

"I don't know about that. I don't want a Junior." He chuckled.

"Not a Junior but another take on your name. The definition of Sincere is genuine. So, I was thinking Genuine if it's a boy and Sincerely if it happens to be a girl."

"I like that," he said. "That's creative but people are gonna think we named him after the singer."

"No, we'll spell it G-E-N-U-W-E-N," Bonita explained.

Sincere couldn't help feeling excited. "His name will be Genuwen Law. Now that's coldblooded. I like that."

'And I like you," she purred into the phone. Sincere felt his dick jump. Bonita had a way of making the simplest things sound sexy as hell. His line beeped and he could see that it was Benae calling. "Listen, I'll call you right back." He clicked over to the other line.

"Hello."

"I forgot to ask you something," before he could say anything, she continued, "Does she know about us?"

"Who?" Sincere immediately regretted the question as soon as it left his lips.

"Who else, Sincere? You're soon to be baby mama." The attitude Benae exuded took Sincere back, he never heard her sound like this.

"I didn't really talk to her about anything except the baby but yes, I did tell her I met someone. More importantly she knows I don't want to be with her and that we are just going to co-parent. I am going to be there for my child."

"It probably doesn't matter now anyway."

"Yes, it does matter. I love you, Benae."

"I love you, too, but this is bigger than that."

"You're the one making it bigger. Let's just focus on us. The baby is not going to change things between us. I promise you we will be the same."

"I will do my best to believe that, but you have to let her know that we are together. I am not going to be caught up in confusion and drama over this. I am too grown for that."

"That's not a problem. I'll let her know next time I talk to her."

"Okay," he could hear that Benae was back in a happy place. "Guess what I have?" she asked jokingly mysterious. "Don't answer. I have complimentary tickets to see the Nets and OKC tomorrow night at Barclays Center. I can't think of anyone else I'd rather go with."

"Cool. Rick told me Kendra has tickets for them, too. The four of us can hang out if that's alright with you. You and Kendra have more in common."

"More in common than who? Your baby mama? Is that why she was so cold to me at her wedding?"

"That's the past. She'll be fine now that she knows you're my lady and that I wasn't doing something wrong."

"Alright, I guess. I am going to get ready for bed. I have an early start tomorrow."

"I'm going to call it a night myself, after I take Meth out."

"Talk to you tomorrow, love you."

"Love you, too. Later." Sincere leaned back against the sofa. Emotionally, he was drained and ready to get some sleep. One down, one to go. *I have to get Bonita in a good place then I'll be straight.*

Meth started barking at the front door alerting Sincere that his brother was coming in. Tru strode into the apartment with a beautiful lady friend.

He walked over to his brother and gave him some dap. "What's up man, I haven't seen you in a minute." Sincere looked up at his little brother.

"I know. I been out there making that money and spending time with my new lady, Ming. This is my brother I told you about, Sincere."

"Hi," Ming sang. "I am so glad to meet you." She extended her chubby but well-manicured hand toward Sincere. Ming was a big woman, pleasingly plump, half black-half Asian, impeccably dressed in ghetto fabulous garb, nice bling and her God given booty length wavy black hair.

"Nice to meet you, too." Sincere stood up and shook her hand. Tru pulled their hands apart. "Okay, enough of that, enough of that," Tru joked. "But seriously, I been staying with Ming and I'm gonna make it official. I'm moving in with her at the end of the month."

"That's just a couple of weeks from now. You paying for February?"

"Nah, man, I'm out. All I'm taking is my clothes and my flatscreen. That's it."

"Well, thanks for giving me notice." Sincere was pissed. He yanked Meth by the collar and went to the closet to get his coat.

Tru casually strolled over to him and whispered, "I don't know what you're so mad for. You're always at your girl house, too, by the way," he said lowering his voice,

"I suggest you bounce, too. Some goons are looking for me, wouldn't want you to get caught up in the middle." He was smiling, but Sincere knew his brother well enough to know that he was serious.

"Damn, your timing couldn't be worse. I just got into it with Benae but I'll see if I can lay my head there, until I find a place."

"Man, ain't no woman gonna see her man out in the street. If she says no, she ain't for you, man. That's one thing about hood chicks, they stay down. You never have to worry about shit like that with them."

"Benae's not from the hood, but she's down for me. She just proved it."

"Yo, what she do?" Tru asked lowering his voice even more.

"I told her about 'Nita being pregnant and she still down to rock with me. Still told me she loves me and everything."

"So, shorty good. She definitely gon' let you stay. She don't want you running back to 'Nita. It's always good to let 'em know you got options," he said loudly.

"Really Tru?" Ming chimed in from the doorway. "Let me find out, you know I don't play that shit."

Sincere watched as his brother grabbed Ming around her ample waist and whispered some of the famous Law game into her ear. Next thing he knew, Ming was all smiles.

"Alright brother, we're gonna head out."

Ming extended her hand to Sincere. "It was nice to meet you finally."

"Yeah, nice to meet you too."

Once they left, Sincere decided to call Bonita back. She was usually good to talk to when he was in a bad mood or stressed.

"Hello."

"Hey, were you sleep?" he asked not caring if she was.

"No, I was waiting for your call."

"Oh, okay."

"You know you need to get me a new cell phone. When I got you your phone it messed up my credit and now, I can't get another one."

"Damn, sorry about that. I'll come through on my day off and take care of that."

BONITA

Surprisingly, the elevator was there in the lobby. Bonita started unbuttoning her jeans on the ride up. Keys in hand she barged through the door and ran for the toilet.

"Oh, my God, I had to pee so bad," she said as she relieved herself. Just as she was pulling her pants up, the intercom buzzed. "Who is it?" she asked rushing to the intercom.

"Me," Sincere bellowed. She went back in the bathroom to wash her hands and headed to her room to freshen up when the phone rang.

"Hello."

"Hi, this is Benae. I saw your number in my phone. Is this Bonita?"

"Yeah, but why would my number be in your phone? I don't know nobody named Benae."

"Sincere borrowed my phone the other day when he forgot to bring his charger to my house.

"Oh?" Bonita questioned with attitude.

"Well, let me get to the point of my call. He told me that even though you two are no longer together, you are expecting a baby."

"Funny, he never told me a thing about you."

"I may have beat him to the punch, but just so you know, I am Benae Givens his girlfriend."

"Oh, really, well he's at my door right now. Hold on."

"Sincere, I'm on the phone with some bird named Benae saying she's your girlfriend. Who the hell is she?"

Without responding he snatched the phone out of Bonita's hand. 'Hello."

"Hey, it's me."

"Alright, no problem," Sincere stammered. "I'm still coming to get you. I'm on my way right now. I just stopped by to bring her some maternity clothes she needed. I'll be there in about twenty to twenty-five minutes." He disconnected the call and headed for the door.

Bonita followed. "Give me my phone?"

"Oh, here."

"So, you're just gonna leave like that? You just came by to drop off some clothes, Sincere? I thought we were going to spend some time together and talk. She hoped for some dick, too. They hadn't been intimate her entire pregnancy, and she was horny as hell.

"I'll be back. I just have to make this stop real quick." He gave her a peck on the lips.

"You promise?" She kept her face upturned for another kiss.

"Yeah." He kissed her waiting lips again. "I promise."

Now she knew for a fact there was someone else in the picture. She knew it before, now she really knew it. Lazily, she pushed the clothes on her bed onto the floor and laid across it. Her mind was racing over what just happened. Sincere eased out of it for now, but what was really going on? Is he gonna try and have me raise this baby alone? I can't even believe he's trying to be with the next chick while I'm carrying his baby? She was too hurt to cry and didn't even feel like calling Shakirra. She decided that before she took this girl's word, she would have to hear it from Sincere himself. If he did want to be with this girl then he's gonna have to really want her because I'm not gonna make it easy. I'm not gonna make it easy at all.

CHAPTER 8

MR. WRONG

BENAE

Benae stretched the phone cord across her desk so that she could reach and close her office door before her co-workers could hear her hysterical laughter. She and Chrissy were still cracking up from the phone call to Bonita. Chrissy was on the line and had instigated the whole thing.

"Oh, my goodness," Chrissy gushed between breathes. "Did you hear how nervous he sounded? He thought his ass was busted."

"I know, that was too funny," Benae said calming down. "So, what do you think?"

"I honestly think that she's holding on. She's hoping the baby will save their relationship. She basically admitted there is nothing there."

"Same impression I got but I still feel a way. I've fallen in love with him and we are so happy together outside of this issue, but a baby is huge. I feel like I should walk away. But he's told me he will not be with her even if I left so I'd just be giving up the man I love for nothing."

"*Give him up!* No way, didn't you hear what I just said? The baby will keep her in his life, but that's no reason to end your relationship. It's not like she got pregnant while you were together. You didn't even know him yet."

"I get it, but I would have never thought of myself in this situation."

"Yeah, that's understandable," Chrissy said unconvinced. "But he loves you, you love him and he's on his way to you. Why is he picking you up anyway?"

I had an appointment on the Upper East Side, and I didn't want to be bothered looking for parking so I took a car and he said he would pick me up."

"Oh, okay, I bet he thinks you're mad."

Benae giggled. "I am not mad at him, but since he thinks I am, I'll just bust his chops a bit."

"That's the spirit," Chrissy cheered.

"Chrissy, you are so immature and that's why I love you. Anyway, I have to wrap up here and get ready."

"Alright, talk to you later. Bye."

Benae responded to a few emails and clicked off her computer. She sat her make-up case and mirror on her desk, lightly powered her face and re-applied her lip gloss. While she was combing her hair, Sincere texted that he was downstairs. On the way out, she stopped in the ladies' room to check herself out in the full-length mirror. Satisfied that her make-up was perfect, she tied the belt around her camel colored Burberry coat and wrapped the matching scarf around her neck. The brown boots, bag and suede dress looked even better with the coat. All that was missing were her signature Gucci sunglasses. She placed them on and headed downstairs.

Sincere walked toward her as she exited through the revolving doors of her building. *Damn,* she thought as she took in his smooth gait and sexy smile. Just as she was about to smile back at him, she remembered that she was supposed to be mad.

"Hey, baby," Sincere said as he leaned in to kiss her.

"Hi," she responded dryly offering him her cheek. His car was parked in front of a hydrant a few feet away. They walked the short distance in silence.

When he slowly pulled the car into the rush hour traffic, he asked, "What's the matter with you?"

"Just thinking about my conversation with your ex. Or shall I call her your soon to be baby mama?" Benae said rolling her eyes.

"Babe, listen. I don't know what she said to you but ain't nothing going on. I do accept the fact that the baby is mine since she said I was the only one she was with and I believe her. I have to be there for my child, but that's it. Me and Bonita are over with."

"Are you sure? I can't lie, I want you for myself. But if you feel you need to be with her for any reason, I will step aside."

"Trust me when I tell you I want to be with you." He picked up her hand and kissed her palm. His words and romantic overtures convinced her, and she put aside her pretense at anger. She smiled at him. "I want to be with you, too."

After her appointment, they arrived at her apartment and Benae threw on a pair of sweats and her favorite UGG slippers. She was going to order take-out to begin with but thought she should cook dinner since Sincere was over. But after staring in the cabinets and fridge for the third time she still could not find anything to make. So, she returned to plan A. "Babe, I'm just going to order from the Italian place!" she yelled.

"No, you can't keep doing that. I'm tired of take-out that's all I eat at home. When I spend time with my woman, I would think that a home cooked meal is not too much to ask," Sincere spoke to her but kept his eyes peeled on Sports Center.

Benae silently fumed and pulled a package of frozen chicken breasts from the freezer. Trying one more time to get out of cooking, she showed him the frozen package. "It's going to take all night to thaw this out."

"You know you can just thaw them in the microwave. Why you acting like you don't want to cook for me?" he said, his eyes finally on her. The sincerity in his voice touched her and she resigned herself to making him a great dinner. "Of course, I want to cook for you. I just forgot about the microwave," she lied.

He smiled broadly. "Well, get in there and hook me up." He turned his attention back to the TV.

After a dinner of barbequed chicken, baked potatoes, and salad, Benae ran a bath for them. They sat in the warm bubble bath, Benae's back against his chest with a single candle gently lighting the room. "Do you want any more kids?"

Sincere hesitated, "Honestly, I can't really say I want the one on the way but he's on his way. So, I can't say I want any more at least not right now. Why?"

"Just asking," she said softly.

"Talk to me. There's more to it than that."

"I guess I'm wondering how the baby will affect our decision to have a baby in the future."

"We will talk about that when the time comes, okay?" He cupped her breasts in his hands and gently nibbled the side of her neck. Benae abruptly stood up and lifted herself out of the tub. "What's wrong with you?" Sincere asked, grabbing her by the arm.

"Nothing," Benae said, wrapping herself in a towel and leaving Sincere alone in the bathtub.

For the first time today the weight of the conversation she had with Bonita hit her and hit her hard. She realized that the man she had fallen in love with was about to have a child by a woman who was clearly still in love with him. Benae did not want to give Sincere up but she recognized that she may be on the losing end of this developing love triangle. She wasn't silly enough or trifling enough to try to even the playing field with a surprise pregnancy of her own. Yet she worried how her love could be enough when he had love and a child waiting for him elsewhere. She stood gazing out of the window lost in her thoughts and didn't notice Sincere had entered the bedroom until she felt him fit his naked body behind hers. He pulled her close to him and held her tightly in his arms.

She turned to face him reaching her arms up around his neck to kiss him. "I love you," she whispered, her voice cracking with emotion.

"I love you, too." He kissed her back passionately while loosening the towel wrapped around her so it fell to the floor.

He scooped her up in his arms and carried her to the bed. He laid her down and eased downward until his face was in between her legs. She feigned resistance but he only parted her legs further and began licking her depths with short hot strokes. It did not take long at all until she was writhing beneath his skillful tongue and holding his head down into her warmth. When he was done, he got in bed beside her and held her. Though somewhat comforted, she laid awake, her mind racing with negative thoughts of Bonita, the baby and all the drama and pain that they represented.

SINCERE

He could feel the distance between them even though she was laying right beside him. She pulled away from him and turned onto her stomach with both arms wrapped around her pillow. She had never slept that way before, and he knew what was wrong. He sat up and turned toward her in the darkness.

"Benae," he called out and waited for her to turn her attention toward him. "Listen to me girl. I am telling you to stop worrying. I want to be with you. What we have right now is the best thing that has ever happened to me. I'm happy. The thought of my first child coming into this world makes me happy, too. It may be asking too much to have you and my son but that's what I want and that's what I intend to have. The only thing that can stop that is you, but I don't want to see you hurt or unhappy." The subtle moonlight coming in through the window allowed him to watch the emotions playing across her face and he knew his words had the desired effect.

He listened as she apologized for being selfish and professed her love, patience and understanding going forward. When she was done, he reassured her that everything would be fine and once again laid down to get some sleep. This time Benae spooned him and held him from behind. Sincere held her hand and smiled to himself. The vibrations from the cell phone were so strong that it fell out of the pocket of his jeans that were thrown over the chair onto the floor and kept vibrating. Benae sat straight up and Sincere could feel her eyes on him in the darkness.

"Who is that?" she asked loudly.

"How do I know the phone is all the way over there."

"Why don't you go get it?"

Once the vibrating subsided, he took his time walking over to the chair. "Whoever it was, I am not talking to them right now. I need to get some rest." Sincere tried to switch the phone setting from vibrate to silent, but before he could do so it started vibrating again. Benae hopped out of bed and turned on the light.

I guess she forgot all about her promise of love and patience, Sincere thought.

"Hello." He turned the volume down as he spoke.

"Why you ain't call me back?" Bonita screeched. I thought you were coming back over tonight.

"I didn't tell you that."

"Yes, you did. You promised me."

"I don't remember that."

"What is going on with you? Are you with that girl?"

"No. That ain't got nothing to do with it." He glanced at Benae who was staring him down. "I'll hit you up tomorrow." He ended the call and just turned the phone off knowing that would not be the last call from Bonita tonight.

"Who was that?" Benae asked as she slipped a cotton tee shirt over her head.

Pissed that she had put clothes on he answered with a bit of attitude of his own. "Don't worry about it. Let's just go to sleep."

"Just tell me if it was her, I won't be upset."

"No, it wasn't. If you must know it was Tru. I didn't get the chance to tell you but he's moving out. Rather he moved already."

"When did he tell you, he was moving?"

"He told me when he moved out. He was with this new chick and told me he was staying with her.

"That's messed up. You good?" she asked, concern replacing her attitude.

"I'm not sure yet but paying that rent by myself is gonna hurt." He chuckled and sat down on the bed.

Benae sauntered over to him and stood in between his legs. "Well, maybe we can be roommates. I'd love to have you here with me."

Touché, Sincere thought. "I did think about that and said Nah. You just moved here, and you don't want me and Meth in here bringing you down. We live like Vikings." They both laughed.

"True though that may be. You both are welcome here. I can live with a couple of Vikings if you can live with eating out a couple of times a week and a housekeeper." She smiled the smile that he loved but she didn't need to add that to her case.

Sincere was sold since her first offer. "Okay, deal, but don't put me out once we get in here and reality hits.

"Not a chance," she said hugging him tight and kissing him lovingly on the lips. She jogged around to her side of the bed got in and turned off the light. "Now, let's get some sleep," she said sounding wide awake. "Goodnight."

"Goodnight," Sincere responded.

He laid in the darkness with his eyes open thankful that things went better than planned with Benae but wondering what his next steps would be to get into an equally good place with Bonita.

BONITA

"I see your *I'll be back* means, I'll see you whenever," Bonita greeted Sincere with mock attitude.

She opened the door a bit and blocked his entry with her body. She knew she looked cute in the way that turned him on. She had on red denim maternity pants and a stretchy white top that hugged her breasts and belly in a flattering way. The attached ponytail sat high atop her head with a wide bang and hung down her back. She piled on the lip gloss and casually sucked and licked a cherry blow pop. Momentarily Sincere was speechless as he stared at her working the lollipop in and out of her glossed lips.

Once he regained his composure he asked, "You gonna let me in or what?"

Without responding, Bonita just turned and gave him the rearview of her ample ass. Slowly, she switched into her bedroom which was neat and clean. She sat on the bed and patted the space next to her.

Sincere sat. "Nita, you looking good, pregnancy works for you. You really do have a glow."

"Thank you. I feel good, too. There's only one thing that could make me feel better." She looked at him seductively and took a hard suck on the lollipop.

"And what is that?" Sincere asked licking his lips.

"This," she said slipping her candy-coated tongue between his lips and slowly twirling it. She felt Sincere kissing her back but not taking it further as he would usually do. She reached down and stroked him until he was hard. "That's more like it." She smirked.

"Nita, I don't know. You know things are not good with us, right now."

"So what? Who else am I supposed to get it from? I'm carrying your baby, and this is your pussy."

He pulled her beside him on the bed and kissed her like he missed her. The familiarity they had with each other took over and she felt as if they had never been apart. He helped her struggle out of the tight top and took turns licking and sucking her breasts while her arms were trapped in the sleeves. By the time they stood to remove their pants, they were both more than ready. Before he could ask her, Bonita turned and climbed on her bed in the face down ass up position. Sincere caressed her ass and hugged it to him before carefully entering her.

"You okay? I don't want to hurt you or the baby," he whispered.

"I'm good, daddy," she panted. "Put it in." She arched her back to get ready and he did as he was told.

He handled her much more gently than he ever had. His tenderness brought tears to her eyes. She backed into him as their steady rhythm brought her to a leg shaking climax.

"I'm coming too, baby," Sincere moaned as they shared powerful simultaneous orgasms.

Afterward, Bonita laid in Sincere' arms and reveled in his touch as he stroked her belly. Still she needed to know where their relationship stood.

"So, what's going on with you? I feel so disconnected, like I barely know you anymore when I should be feeling closer to you than ever."

"We're just going through it right now. I had to handle business in Chicago. Things were shaky between us even before I left. Now we're having a baby and everything's different," Sincere explained.

"I want us to be a family." Bonita lifted her head to look into his eyes.

"We will be. The baby will see to that."

"What about that other girl? She called me claiming you and shit."

"You don't have to worry about her," Sincere dismissed.

"You sure? She sounded real confident about her place. Like she was your main chick."

"Come on, 'Nita. You should know your position, baby." He reached over and stroked her belly.

"Boy stop it," she cried out knowing she loved every minute of it. "Wait feel this." She took his hand and placed it on the left side of her bulging stomach. She watched with pride as Sincere felt the baby stir within her.

"Wow," he mouthed. The baby put on quite a show, capturing its parents' attention for the next ten minutes.

Bonita got up and threw on an old sweat suit she wore around the house. "After all that I can use something to eat," she said stretching.

Sincere got up and started getting dressed, too. "Yeah, I could eat a little something myself."

"I got some hamburger meat thawed out and some leftover pork chops."

Sincere scowled at her. "Hamburger sounds good."

"Okay, help me make the burgers. While Bonita made the burgers, Sincere mixed a pitcher of Kool-Aid and sliced up some onions, lettuce, and tomato to top them. Bonita popped in a Jay-Z CD and they sang along intermittently while they worked. Bonita glanced at Sincere as she dropped handfuls of the potatoes she'd just cut into French fries into hot oil.

Look at him, she thought, so content and comfortable. *He knows this is where he belongs. There is no way that he is like this with anyone else. I don't care what that Bitch says.* She felt her anger rise but quickly covered it with a cheerful smile. One of the things he always said he liked about her was her cheerful disposition.

"Hey, you wanna play checkers after we eat?" she asked heading to the closet to get the game.

"That's three games in a row. You not tired of getting that ass spanked yet?" Sincere asked standing up from the table and stretching.

"Yes, but you have to give me time to even the score. You can't leave now," she insisted.

"I been here all day, I'm gonna head out," he said, stretching again.

"Head out? You're leaving?" Bonita asked not expecting him to leave after she made it clear she wanted him to stay.

"Yeah, I gotta go home. I forgot to tell you that I had to move. Tru had some beef in the streets and we had to leave asap. I got a place with a new roommate. I don't know him all that well, so I don't want to stay out all night yet. Na mean?"

"Why, what did Tru do now?" she asked, not really caring.

"He just bounced and advised me to do the same. So, I did what I had to do."

"So, where's your place at?" Bonita asked skeptical.

"I'm still uptown, not too far from my old place. Plus, I have to get my stuff for work. I'm working a double tomorrow. I have to get up that dough for you and the baby." He smiled.

"Alright then." She walked toward the door as he put on his coat. "I'm a little tired anyway."

He kissed her on the nose then the lips and they embraced. "Don't let another week go by before I see you again," Bonita threatened softly.

"It won't be. Trust me."

"I love you, Sincere. I never stopped."

"I love you, too." He opened the door and headed down the stairs not bothering to wait for the elevator.

Bonita trotted back to the bedroom and got in bed with the sweat suit on, her mind replaying her evening with her man. She had missed him so much. Now she knew he still loved her and wasn't going to leave her. *I don't even know why I was trippin,* she thought. For the first time in a long time, she fell into a deep comfortable sleep.

CHAPTER 9

FAMILY SONG

BENAE

"You know what? You are too much! Did you really call me in the middle of my busy day to complain about giving orders to your housekeeper?" Chrissy asked incredulously.

"Chrissy, you're making me sound so bad. It's different now that Sincere moved in. He's a slob. Meth is his own story and then there's me and all of my stuff."

"Okay, you knew all that before he moved in. So, what's the real problem?" Chrissy cut to the chase.

"I don't know," Benae whined. "I love having them here but it's not what I was expecting."

"So, what were you expecting?" Chrissy put down the Windex and paper towel she held in her hands and sat down on the side of the tub to listen to her spoiled friend.

"Actually, he's been great." Benae sprawled out on her back and looked up at the celestial scene on her ceiling. "We work out together. We shop together and go out on weekends. The lovemaking is good but not as much as I thought it would be. He complains that I want it all the time and says I must be at my sexual peak. I'm thirty-two nowhere near my sexual peak."

"Everything you've said sounds totally reasonable. So, what you have a higher sex drive than him. Deal with it. Sex isn't everything. Plus, you are both still adjusting to one another."

"Yeah, maybe," Benae half-heartedly agreed. "I wonder if he's reacting to some of my only child ways. For example, I don't share my closet with him even though it's huge. I asked him to use the closet in the guest room."

"That huge walk-in closet and you make him use the guest room? Girl, that's selfish! I wouldn't want to have sex with you either," Chrissy chided.

"You know I love that closet," Benae defended. "It's made for Prada, Gucci and Louis Vuitton, not Timberland and Jordan's."

"Benae, it's horrible to think that way. Where does he keep his underwear and toiletries?"

"There in here. I made room for him."

"Well, that's good. All I can say is you moved in together sort of soon but what's done is done. You both know how he is, and he knows how you are."

"To be honest, I don't think I would have asked him to move in if he didn't have a baby on the way with someone else. I did it to keep him close."

"That's not healthy, but understandable."

"Anyway, enough about me. What's up with you? How are Greg and the boys?"

"Everyone is fine. We're taking them to the movies later and will probably grab dinner at BBQ's. What are you guys doing this weekend?"

"No plans that I know of."

"Well, enjoy lady."

"You too girl. Talk to you later."

Benae crossed the turquoise carpeting and stepped into her closet/dressing room. She looked around at her shoes, bags, clothes, and accessories all organized and in order. She thought about inviting Sincere to share the closet with her but couldn't bring herself to do it. This would be the one place she kept for herself. Her phone rang as she exited the closet and since it was already in her hand, she looked down to see who was calling. It was her parent's landline, so it was either the man she adored most in the world or the woman that caused her the most dread.

"Hey, baby girl," her dad's loud voice boomed.

"Hi, Daddy." If there was someone who could always brighten her day it was her dad.

"I'm checking in on you. Haven't heard from you too much lately. Anything new?"

"I'm sorry, daddy. You know how life in New York can be. Sometimes I just don't have a minute to myself."

"You didn't seem to have a problem calling before. Besides I'm on Capitol Hill all day and I still make time for you and your mother."

"You're right. I will do better with staying in touch."

"Have you had any more run-ins with that nut Max?"

"Nope, I haven't heard from him in a while."

"Good to know. The reason why I was calling is I have to attend a conference at the U.N. at the end of the month. I figured you could put your parents up for a night or two in your new digs? How's that sound?"

Wham! Benae felt like she'd been punched in the gut and paused before responding. She hadn't even mentioned Sincere to her family. For two people that came up the hard way, they chose to forget the past and look down their noses at other blacks who were not high achievers like them. How many times had she heard that they did not spend good money giving her the best of everything for her to take up with a loser? Sadly, the fact that Sincere was living in her place would not go over well.

"Actually, dad I didn't get the chance to get the guest room done yet. I can give you and mom my room and take the ..."

"No, no need to do that," he interrupted her. "We will stay in the city and come by to see your new place before heading back to D.C. Anything else going on?"

There is one thing. I wanted to tell you that I met the greatest guy daddy. I can't wait for you and mom to meet him," she said with genuine enthusiasm.

"Good to know. I look forward to meeting him. I am certain he is a much better prospect than Max?"

"Much better daddy, he makes me very happy."

"Okay, baby girl. Give me a call later this week and tell me more about your new beau."

"Will do. Love you, daddy."

"Love you, too."

"I hope that that, *love you daddy* was to your real daddy and not your pimp," Sincere joked as he entered the bedroom and walked over to hug her.

"Yes, it was my real daddy," she said giving him a kiss on the lips. "He and my mom are coming to New York in a couple weeks. I want them to meet you, but we have to keep our living together between us for now."

"Is that why I had to keep most of my stuff in the spare room?"

"No, that's another issue, we'll get to that later."

"Cool, Get dressed," he ordered.

"Why?"

"Woman just put some clothes on, we're going out."

"Whatever you say," Benae said seductively. "But before I get dressed, I have to get undressed." She opened her satin robe and posed in the gold and turquoise bra and panty set. She took in Sincere's appreciative gaze. "Too bad it's so cold out or else I could have worn this. I can tell how much you like it." She backed up until he she reached the wall and slowly raised her arms over her head. She licked her lips and closed her eyes.

Next thing she knew Sincere was kissing her with torrid passion. He held both her arms with one hand the other pulled at her bra until a ripe nipple emerged. He leaned down and sucked her nipple until Benae's knees threatened to buckle, then he attacked the other nipple just as fiercely. She slid her hands away from his hold and reached down to set his hard dick free. He threw his head back and moaned softly as she massaged his erection.

"Baby, I need you inside me," she whispered into his ear as she dropped to her knees to take him in her mouth.

When he could no longer stand her tonguing his balls and sucking his dick, he slid himself out of her mouth and looked down at her as she protested. He picked her up and leaned her back against the wall. Without hesitation she wrapped her legs around his back.

"Ooohhh, baby, yesss," she moaned as he slid her panties to the side and entered her wet awaiting pussy. In a matter of minutes, they both clung to each other hot, sweaty, and satisfied.

"Damn, baby, that was good," Sincere panted. "But we got to get going."

"Okay, let's take a shower together to save time."

"No, you go head, I don't trust you." Sincere laughed.

"Okay. I can't help it that you make me insatiable." She swatted him on the butt on her way to the bathroom.

SINCERE

Sincere and Benae stepped out of the Brownstone apartment looking like cold weather models. The temperature dove below freezing so it was time to break out the mink coats. Benae's full-length Black Glama mink and Sincere' a short mink jacket, his Christmas gift from Benae. She also bought him a pair of Prada boots, but he chose to wear his black Timbs.

As they neared the destination, Benae recognized the single-lane roads that led to City Island. "We're going to City Island again?" she asked a little disappointed.

"Yep."

"So, why the big hurry? Are we meeting Rick and Kendra or something?"

"Nope."

They drove the rest of the short trip in silence. Benae eyed some of the other seafood restaurants that she wanted to try, but she knew they were headed right to Samuels. That was the only place on City Island Sincere went to, so she didn't even suggest trying someplace new.

"Hey, why you so quiet?" Sincere asked good naturedly.

"No reason."

"There has to be a reason," he pressed. "You always got something to say. Now you're all quiet. Cheer up or else I will be forced to cheer you up." He smiled.

She couldn't help but return a small smile of her own. "I'm fine. Let's go eat."

"You sure you want to eat here? We can go somewhere else," he said as he pulled his car into Samuel's parking lot.

"Sincere, we are here already let's just go."

He smiled to himself. He knew he was getting on her nerves and it was funny. As they walked in one of the owner's son's greeted Sincere. "Yo', my man, how you doing? I just seated your dad. Follow me."

"Of course, lead the way." Sincere glanced to his right to check on Benae who was standing next to him with her mouth open. "You better close your mouth girl, before you start catching flies." He swatted the air in front of her face. Before she could say anything, he took her hand and followed Tony to his dad's table.

"Hey, dad."

"Hey, Sin." He stood up and embraced his son in a strong hug. "So, this pretty lady must be Benae. Did I say it right?" He laughed.

"Yes, you did, sir. It's such a pleasure to meet you."

"All mine, all mine. Please let me take your coat," he said to Benae. "Hey, Tony, can you take these coats and put them in the back? Or else they're going to smell like seafood when we leave."

"Sure thing, Mr. Law. No problem. These are some really nice minks and I know my stuff when it comes to quality," Tony added taking the coats with care. "I'll send Mike over to take your orders."

"Sounds good. Thanks, Tony," Leon Law said turning his attention back to Benae. "Young lady, you can order anything you like. You're my guest and I want you to enjoy dinner. Do you drink?"

"Yes, I do," Benae said with charm.

"Good," Leon bellowed. "This is a special occasion, let's drink up. You know you're the only woman my son ever introduced me to. Now that's not to say that I haven't met other women he dated but you are the only one he called me and formally asked me to meet."

Benae beamed. "Well, that's very nice to know and the timing is perfect. He's going to be formally introduced to my parents in a couple of weeks."

Mike, a waiter Mr. Law knew for years came by to take their orders. Mr. Law took the liberty of ordering huge platters of seafood family style. They dined on a succulent dinner of king crab legs, lobster tails, jumbo sea scallops, mussels and oysters on the half shell all on top of a bed of Spanish rice. Benae and Glenda paired their meal with glasses of white wine, the Law men opted for stronger drinks.

"Oh, my gosh," Benae gushed. "That was one of the most delicious meals I have ever had and like Tony said, I know my stuff when it comes to good seafood."

Sincere gave her the side eye, knowing that they had eaten here many times before.

"Well, I'm glad you enjoyed it. This is one of my favorite places." Leon stretched. "Been coming here since Sincere and Tru were kids. The owner was the first guy to hire me as a distributer when I was just getting my feet wet."

"That's wonderful. I really enjoyed myself tonight."

"Did you save room for dessert?"

"No dessert but I would love a cappuccino."

"Girl after my own heart." Mr. Law nudged Glenda who was looking at Benae like she was sick of her. "I like to have Baileys and coffee after dinner," Leon said.

Sincere sat back and watched the easy and comfortable banter between his lady and his pops. She was everything he'd ever wanted – beautiful, respectful, classy, successful, loved sex and she genuinely loved him. Tonight, was just the cherry on top.

After sitting and chatting until the restaurant was almost empty, the foursome headed to the parking lot to say their goodnights. It was even colder now as a fierce wind blew over the waters surrounding the tiny island. Benae shoved her hands into the warm folds of her fur coat and pulled her shoulders up to shield her face.

Mr. Law leaned in and grabbed her in a one-shoulder hug and kissed her cheek. "My darling, it was such a pleasure meeting you. Son!" He and Sincere embraced and patted each other once on the back. "Let's do this again soon you hear. Now get home safe, take your time out there. The roads up here are frozen, watch out for black ice."

"Okay, Dad, you, too. Goodnight Glenda."

"Bye Glenda, bye Mr. Law!" Benae shouted, walking toward the car.

"No more of that. I am going to call you daughter. You can call me dad. I got two boys and never had a chance to spoil a girl."

"Alright, dad." She smiled as she took Sincere's hand and walked towards the car.

"Wow, your dad is so nice. That was such a sweet surprise babe. Thank you. I can't believe I'm the only woman you ever introduced to your dad." She reached over and put her hand on his thigh as he maneuvered the Lexus out of the parking lot. "Hey, look at me," she said softly.

He stopped at a stop sign and turned to face her.

"I love you Sincere, I really do."

"I love you, too." He really felt that he did.

He could tell by the way she reached over and kissed him that she was feeling it, too. The love that was growing between them was deep and profound and he was ready for it.

BONITA

Surprise!

Bonita jumped back from the shock of hearing a room full of people basically screaming at her but as it subsided, she quickly realized that little Jo-Jo's birthday party was really just a cover for her baby shower.

"Got you!" Shakirra screamed over all the other voices.

"Oh, my God! I'm so surprised. I got a gift for Jo-Jo and everything."

"Since it is Jo-Jo's birthday tomorrow it won't go to waste," Shakirra said, taking the gift from her.

"Come here, baby." Lucille emerged from the group of girls gathered in the middle of the community center. "Come here and sit in the pretty chair we bought for you."

"Okay." Bonita waddled over to the white wicker chair decorated with coordinated dark and light blue bows. She sat carefully, making sure the chair could support her weight.

She was nearing the end of her ninth month and felt she was as big as a house. Now she had a chance to look around and take it all in. Everyone knew she was having a boy and mostly everything was blue – blue decals of ducks, pacifiers, booties, blocks, and rattles. A table off to the side was loaded with gifts and Bonita could not wait to open them and see what was inside. The baby needed everything. On the other side of the small room tables held a variety of food heated by sternos – fried chicken, barbeque chicken, baked beans, corn on the cobs, mac and cheese and tossed salad. The cake in the middle of the table clearly came from Little Shop of Sandra's.

The signature organza wrap was baby blue and adorned with little brown baby boys throughout. It was beautiful and Bonita wanted to cry, she was so grateful. The only thing missing was Sincere. She wished he was there to share this day with her. Her eyes scanned the room looking for his unmistakably tall, muscular physique but it was obvious he wasn't there.

As if on cue Shakirra stepped over to her. "Before you ask, your mom told him the shower was today he said he would come through."Shakirra made air quotes with her fingers and made a snide face.

Bonita ignored Shakirra's sarcasm and got up to help herself to a big plate of food. "Alright everybody, let's get this party started."

Shakirra organized an intimate shower that was fun and memorable. They played some of the traditional shower games and a few games Shakirra created including a version of truth or dare that was strictly related to sex. By the time, the games were over everyone was giving Shakirra props for throwing a banging shower.

"Okay, everyone." Shakirra summoned while taking her place in the center of the room. She was a vision in blue – blue patent leather pumps, blue tights, blue dress and blue ponytail holder. "We're gonna cut the cake now, so that you can eat it while 'Nita opens her lovely gifts."

Lucille and Bonita shared a glance. "I didn't know she had it in her," Lucille whispered to her daughter.

"Neither did I, ma. 'Kirra is full of surprises." They both laughed softly.

As Bonita opened the tiny items to a room full of *"oohs"* and *"aahhs"* she felt truly loved by her friends and knew that her baby boy would be, too. There were plenty of onesies, bottles, blankets, outfits and of course tons of diapers. There were two gifts remaining, one from her mom and the other from Shakirra. Throughout the gift unwrapping, her eyes kept going to the door hoping to see Sincere walk through. She opened the gift from her mom. It was a baby's book of memories and her mom had taken the time to neatly fill in the family tree information for herself and Bonita's dad.

"Oh, mom, this is precious. Thank you so much."

"Make sure Sincere gets his people to fill in his side so the baby knows his history."

"Well, you can tell him yourself. He said he was coming right?" Lucille looked away and sat back down in her seat.

"Last but not least, this is from me." Shakirra rolled it over to Bonita.

It was completely wrapped, but it was easy to tell that it was a stroller. As she peeled open the blue and white checked wrapping paper Bonita was overjoyed to see that it was filled to the brim with everything the baby would need. "Oh, Shakirra, thank you! You are too much. Everything is in here. Wow," Bonita exclaimed.

Shakirra was ready to take the spotlight and go through the items inside the stroller when she was preempted by Sincere' loud voice coming from the doorway.

"The Champ is here," he exclaimed loudly while strolling over to Bonita and planting a kiss on her cheek.

"Well, well, well look what the cat dragged in." Shakirra smirked and looked him up and down.

"You look like someone should drag you out," he retorted. "You're killing me with all that blue." He shook his head and glared at her with distaste. Rick who had accompanied him to the shower was cracking up laughing.

"Whatever." Shakirra waved her hand and walked away.

Sincere turned his attention back to Bonita. "Look at all this stuff. My little man getting a good start."

"I know." Bonita smiled. "I am so happy we have so much stuff for the baby. We needed everything. All we need now is the crib."

"I told you I got that covered."

"Well, I'm due in three weeks when do you plan on getting it?"

"Slow your roll, it's outside in the car. I didn't want to bring it in because it looks like I'm getting a gift for my son. It's not a gift, it's what I'm supposed to do as his father."

"Oh, you got it!" She wrapped her arms around him and tilted her face upward for a kiss that never came. Slightly embarrassed she released her hold on him as he explained the features of the crib.

Rick chimed in, "The layette Kendra got is gonna look good with it and she got the mobile."

"Thanks for the gift. I opened it earlier and Kendra said it was from both of you."

"That's because it was," Kendra stated as she walked up to them and gave Rick a hug and a kiss.

"Yo', Rick, Man you ready to help me take all this stuff upstairs?"

"Yeah, let's get to it."

While the guys started packing up the gifts, Shakirra, Bonita and Kendra put away the food and chatted.

"So, how you like married life Kendra?" Shakirra asked.

"It's really not much of a difference since we were already living together, but it does give me more rights."

"More rights?" Bonita asked stopping what she was doing to hear the answer to her question.

"That's right more rights to check his phone, pockets, time and right to be more demanding."

Shakirra raised her hand for a high-five. "I know that's right."

Kendra gave her a hearty five and they both broke out laughing. "So, Nita, what's up with you and dog-ass Sincere?" Kendra asked with attitude all over her face.

"What you mean what's up?" Bonita asked feigning naiveté.

"I meant to give you a call right after the wedding, but I was preoccupied with other things and forgot. But he came to the wedding with this chick I never met. Rick didn't know her either or at least he said he didn't."

Bonita couldn't hide the shock she felt inside from showing on her face. "*What?* He told me that he didn't bring me because he would be too busy being the Best Man that he wouldn't have time for me. He never said he took someone else."

"Don't stress it. I just thought you should know because if you have any competition you need to check that bitch. Let her know you're the baby mama and she better step the fuck off."

"I don't know. I'm not really like that..."

"Do you know how many bitches I had to check? You see how fine Rick is right? And although I can't stand his ass, Sincere is fine. All types of chicks be coming at them. So, you have to protect your territory," Kendra said fiercely.

"Dang, Kendra, you ain't no joke," Shakirra chimed in. "I thought I was bad."

"No, these bitches out here ain't no joke. Men are weak you have to be strong for they trifling asses. Let that chick know you ain't going nowhere. If she still wants to stick around just become the baby mama from hell. Need everything all the time. Just make sure you keep your man."

"Kendra, we need to hang out more often. I need you in my life," Bonita joked.

"Shit, me too. Don't leave my ass out." They cracked up laughing at Shakirra and finished packing up the food.

CHAPTER 10

JUST BE A MAN ABOUT IT

BENAE

Benae made a quick dinner of fried fish, mashed potatoes, and spinach. She paired dinner with a bottle of Riesling. Since she and Sincere always ate dinner on the sofa she picked up a set of trays to for them to eat on. For some reason she was proud of the little meal she prepared and took her time nicely plating the food. She folded the napkins in half and sat the fork and knife on top of them. Last, she poured them each a glass of wine and carried the trays one at a time into the living room. Sincere sat up from his slouching position on the couch.

"I'm starved babe, thanks. What's up with the tray and the wine?"

"Just felt like doing something new."

"Nothing wrong with that. Cheers!" He lifted his glass. He clinked his glass with hers and took a sip. She saw him turn to look at her, but she kept her eyes on the TV.

"Babe, what's wrong now?" he asked.

"Nothing, really. I'm just thinking about you meeting my dad. He's not as cool as your dad."

"Be honest, what you trying to say?"

"I don't know. I just want you to be prepared for questions my dad may ask regarding your future goals and career plans."

"So, what you're really saying is you're worried about him thinking that I'm not good enough for you. Well, I'm just gonna be myself. An EMS worker is a respectable job and I have no plans to go to college and play the Corporate America game. It's not for me."

"You know it's not my issue, but I know my father. I just want him to like you."

"If he loves you like you say he does, he'll respect your choice, right?" He set his fork down on his empty plate and finished off his glass of wine.

Benae took his empty plate, sat it beneath hers and stacked his tray under hers. "Babe, I have a question. What about the baby? Should we tell my parents now or wait?"

"You know, I thought we could save it for later, but I'd rather be upfront with it. My son is gonna be a part of my life. So, we should just..."

"Your son!" Benae cut him off.

"Yeah, 'Nita said the baby is a boy."

"Oh, so now she's 'Nita. I can't with this shit," Benae said standing up and carrying the trays to the kitchen.

"Look, don't start tripping now. We got this far together. We can do this. We have a good thing. There's no reason we can't make it eventually as husband and wife."

Benae turned to face him, one hand on her hip. "Are you telling me what you think I want to hear?" She could see frustration cross his face.

"Nah, I'm serious. I'm gonna marry someone eventually and right now I see no reason why it shouldn't be you."

Benae felt her anger subside. "You know I love you, right?"

"Yes, I know it. Question is do you know I love you? Cause if you did a nickname wouldn't get you shook," Sincere said emphatically.

"Alright babe, you're right. I apologize for acting so insecure."

"Cool. Now I believe we were talking about your parents' visit. I was thinking of taking them to Spain's my favorite spot in Jersey. That way I can cover dinner and I know it's someplace they never been."

Benae was taken aback but in a good way. It never occurred to her that Sincere had thought about her parents again after the first time she had mentioned it.

"Babe that's perfect. My parents love Spanish food and Spain's is a classy spot. They will love it." She walked over to him while he was loading the dishwasher and gave him a peck on the cheek. "I must say I am impressed with your thoughtfulness and desire to show my parents a good time. You know they are not suckers' for a pretty face like I am."

"Lucky for you, I'm a sucker for a pretty face, too." He winked at her and closed the dishwasher.

"You're so silly," she sing-songed.

"And you're so pretty," he mimicked. "Come on let's finish watching this movie."

As she rested her head on Sincere's chest, she smiled and thought of how happy she was. Things just seemed to keep getting better and better with him. She was going to be his wife and that baby on the way did not matter to her at all.

SINCERE

"Yo man, I'm following you. Stop driving like a fuckin' asshole. I'm not trying to get pulled over!" Sincere yelled into his Bluetooth.

"Can't help it if you drive like an old lady" Tru joked back and increased the speed on his Escalade.

"I ain't joking. Slow down or I'm turning around. This was your invitation."

"Alright." Tru laughed. "We here anyway. Start looking for a park."

Sincere slid his new Silver BMW X6 into a spot beside Tru's Escalade. He had used the last of the $50,000 he'd made from selling guns to buy the car. Some of it went to Bonita and the baby but the most of it went to him freshening up his wardrobe to match Benae's and just the spending that came along with being with a woman of her caliber. Now that he lived with her, he was able to save more money since she paid most of the bills.

The two brothers stepped out of their vehicles and walked toward each other with silly grins on their faces. "Why you always gotta be an asshole man?" Sincere asked grabbing his little brother in a mock headlock.

Benae sauntered up to them looking like the boss lady she was – black leather trench coat belted at the waist, Saint Laurent booties and oversized Gucci tote. Sincere watched as Tru stopped wrestling with him to give his attention to Benae.

"That's you?" he whispered.

"Yes, this is my lady Benae. This is my brother, Tru."

"Hi, Tru." She smiled and extended her hand. "It's nice to finally meet you. I've heard so much about you."

"Yeah same here." He shook her hand and turned his attention to a beautiful, heavyset woman emerging from his SUV. "This is Ming, my girlfriend."

"Hey, girl," Ming said like she'd known Benae for years. "Look we have on the same boots just different colors. I like you already," Ming said as she grabbed Benae by the arm and headed inside East, an upscale buffet.

They were seated at a large booth toward the back of the restaurant at Tru's request. As soon as the waiter took their drink orders Ming and Tru made a b-line to the buffet tables. "Y'all better come on if you want to get the best crab legs. They just put out a fresh pan!" Ming yelled.

"We're coming!" Benae yelled back and started laughing.

Sincere raised his eyebrow and looked at his usually classy lady. "Don't ever call me ghetto again," Sincere teased. She linked her arm with his and they walked to get some food. "You're rubbing off on me."

The two couples indulged in everything from seafood and sushi to Chinese food and simple desserts. Sincere noticed the ladies talking in that soft conspiratorial tone women used when they were talking about their men. He figured this would be a good time to talk to his brother about some business moves he wanted to make, but Tru was on his fourth trip to the buffet. He came back with another plate piled high with all his favorites.

"Damn, you gonna eat all that?" Sincere asked loudly. "How much you weigh now?"

"I ain't got no scale. How da fuck I know?"

"Never mind, forget that. I need to holla at you a minute," Sincere lowered his voice and leaned in closer towards his brother. "How's business?"

Tru nodded affirmatively and took a bite of the warm buttered rolls he couldn't seem to get enough of. "Good. I may need to help you unload some merch."

"Just say the word. What's up?"

"A lot going on. I spent the money from the Chi-Town job on the whip and the insurance is no joke. So, she pays the mortgage on her condo and I pay the utilities. It sounded all well and good until winter hit. The gas bill is a bitch. Now with the baby coming I have to take out a family plan for medical. I don't want my son getting welfare if you know what I mean. But the main thing is her mom's be pressing me to get them an apartment outside of the PJs. She don't want the baby raised there and honestly, I don't either."

"Damn, that is a lot."

"Even if she wasn't on me, I don't want my seed raised in the PJs. I would get a place for 'Nita and the baby if she would at least do her part by getting a job or something. All she wants to do is sit on her ass all day and bullshit with Shakirra. She never had a job since I knew her."

"You sure you want to do that? If you get her a place, she gonna expect you to be there...every night," Tru said emphatically.

"Nah, I'm not worried about that. I'm gonna tell her I'm with Benae. I just want to wait until after the baby gets here. I don't want to stress her right now."

"You definitely got a lot of shit going on. I'll put you on. We can talk about that later."

"Talk about what later? If y'all talking business, you know I know."

"Ming how many times I gotta tell you about that shit? When men are talking play your position," Tru said staring at her intensely.

"I'm sorry. It's just that I have some ideas and I know you trust your brother."

Tru relaxed and stretched his arm out behind Ming's chair. "See this here is my ride or die. She's down for me." Once again Tru's demeanor changed from jovial to dead ass serious in a matter of seconds. He placed both elbows on the table and leaned across the table facing Benae and asked, "You down for yours?"

Sincere watched as Benae's eyes nervously found his. He remained stoic and waited for her response. "If down for mine means that I love him and got his back then the answer is yes."

Tru nodded and laughed out loud. "That was the whitest motherfuckin' answer but at least you got it right." They all joined in laughing, including Benae.

"You know us Law men only mess with the best. Benae is a diamond girl, that's my baby." Sincere pulled her close and kissed her lips.

"Aww," Ming said. "Now raise your glasses. A toast to love, happiness and getting this money."

BONITA

Bonita stood in the doorway of her bedroom surveying the clutter. She had done her best to make room for the baby and when Sincere puts the crib up she'd have just enough room to scoot between her bed and the crib. The big bureau at the foot of her bed was taking up a lot of the space but she needed it to keep her clothes in and plus her TV was on top of it. Rubbing her lower back she walked over to the junk room. There was no way she could tackle that room no matter how much nesting she was in the midst of doing but it would be nice to have the baby in his own room.

Lucille started down the hall and peeked into the junk room when she saw that the door was open. "I know what you're thinking

'Nita. We need to clean out this room. I don't know how we let it get so bad."

"Ma, my back is killing me. I think I did too much already."

"Go sit yourself down. I'll get this together."

"You can barely move around. Your knees hurt you all the time.

"I'm not doing all of it. When is the last time you spoke to Sincere?"

"Earlier. We speak every day."

"Umm hmm. Speaking ain't doing you no good. He planning on getting you a place?"

"He spoke about it, but I'm not sure I want to move out. At least not right away. I would rather stay here with you until I'm sure I know what I'm doing with my baby."

"Listen to me. I don't want to see you raise a baby here in these projects. Let Sincere get you out of here. You know I'll follow you."

Bonita wasn't too thrilled with that idea either. "For now, I want to stay here and get this room together. I can't deal with a newborn and a new move at the same time."

Before Lucille could protest further, she was interrupted by Sincere' signature knock on the door. "You knew he was coming by?"

"Yeah, he said he's gonna put the crib together and help me get organized." She went to open the door and realized she wasn't excited to see him like she usually was. In fact, she would be more excited if she could sit down with a Big Mac, large order of fries, a coke and watch Judge Mathis.

"Hey, Ms. Lucille, how you doing today?" Sincere gave her a hug.

"I'm good. Good to see you. You know we need help getting this place straightened up. I feel so bad that we let it get this way."

"That's why I'm here. I took the day so I could knock it out in one shot."

Bonita brushed past Sincere and over to the junk room door. She opened the door wide and stood aside. "I don't know about one shot. This room is packed with all kinds of crap."

Sincere surveyed the years of tossed aside, broken and no longer used items. There were boxes stacked everywhere, box springs, broken lamps, stuffed animals, an old floor model TV a couple of full bins and stacks of blankets. Sincere peered inside and frowned his nose. "It smells sort of rank in here. Can't we just throw it all out?"

Maybe so, but maybe someone might be able to use some of that stuff. I'd sure hate to waste it."

"Ma, that's how this mess got started in the first place. Always saving something for somebody and never give nothing away."

"Alright, here's what we're gonna do," Sincere interjected. "I'll give Rick a call and see if he can come by when he gets off. What's Shakirra and Joe doing?"

"Nothing. Neither of them working now."

"Call 'em. Tell Joe we need his help. I got a few bucks for him if he needs it," Sincere said heading towards the door.

"Wait where you going? You just got here," Bonita exclaimed. She couldn't believe he was going somewhere already.

Sincere laughed. "Damn, girl calm down. I'm just going to get something to eat before I get started. What you want?"

"Can you get me some McDonald's? I been craving it all day."

"Big Mac, large fries and a coke. Ms. Lucille can I get you something?" he asked holding the front door open.

"You know what. I'll take the fish sandwich and iced tea."

"Alright, I'll be right back." He zipped up his North face vest and headed for the stairway.

Bonita yanked open the door and yelled down the hallway. "Sincere don't play, you better come right back." He looked over his shoulder and presented her with a sexy smile and wink that made her moist. *Damn, that mofo is fine,* she thought, forcing herself to get back to the issue at hand.

After another fast food run and a trip to Home Depot, Joe and Sincere had emptied out the entire room. Joe and Rick applied a fresh coat of light blue paint over the primer.

It was going on 9:00PM and Ms. Lucille was ready to call it a night. "Fellas you did a really good job in here. I almost thought I'd never see this room look like a room again," she said looking around appreciatively. "I'm going to lay me down to sleep. Y'all have a good night."

Bonita stood near the window and imagined how she wanted the baby's things arranged in the small room. The sound of Sincere's phone vibrating snapped her out of her daydream. She watched as he pulled the phone from his pocket and glanced to see who was calling and put it back in his pocket.

That's right, Bonita thought. *Whatever chick is calling my man has to wait. This is my time.* She walked up to Sincere, put her arms around his waist and barely rested her head against his back due to her outstretched belly. "I'm so excited," she said. "We're gonna have this room looking so cute."

The baby started kicking and moving around frantically, causing a ruckus on Sincere's back. "You're not the only one excited. He's ready to come see his room," Sincere said proudly.

"That's how LJ was," Joe chimed in. "No patience." He shook his head.

"Well, that's fine with me. I'm ready when he is." Bonita sat in the kitchen chair she pulled into the hallway to interact with the guys while they worked.

Sincere' phone vibrated again. This time he hurried into the bathroom and closed the door. Bonita eased over to the bathroom door to listen.

"Nah, we're not finished. We're almost done. You know how Kendra is. She wants everything to be perfect...I'm not sure why she picked today. I been here since I got off. I'm tired as hell. I should be home no later than between eleven-thirty and twelve. Okay. Yeah. Me too."

Bonita moved away from the door faster than she had moved in months. She listened to Sincere use the bathroom and wash his hands.

He came out drying them on his sweatpants. "Yo', Rick man, Tru is nosey as hell. He trying to be up in my business."

Rick rested the paintbrush on the side of the paint tray. "Should've told him to come over here and help."

"You know this is not his type of gig. Plus, he and Bonita can't stand each other."

He's not the only one I can't stand at the moment, she thought at the same time giving Sincere a warm, fake smile.

By the time the room was completely painted, and the crib was put together it was going on 11:30. Joe had left them about an hour earlier. Rick was ready to make his exit as well.

"Yo man, I'm out. Kendra's been cool the whole time I was here, and I want her to stay that way. Only one thing a man need after putting in work like this.

They slapped five. "Hell yeah," Sincere agreed.

"I know what he means, too." Bonita rubbed Sincere's chest.

Rick headed to the door. "That's my cue. Night y'all."

Bonita continued her seduction. "You know what they say, good sex can make the baby come faster."

"Come on 'Nita, I'm dead ass tired," he said looking down at her 5'3 height.

"*Tired?* Well this will put you right to sleep." This time her hand headed north and rubbed his dick through his jeans. She thrust her hand between his legs until she was sure she was getting the balls and the dick. Getting up on her toes she used her other hand to grab him behind the neck for a kiss. "Just as easy as I knew it would be," she said to herself as she led him to the bedroom.

He sat down on the bed as she closed the door and crossed the room to turn on the radio. Alicia Keys sang, *"If I was your woman, I'd never, never, never stop loving you."* Sincere seemed to take Alicia's words as his own. He pulled Bonita close and kissed her deeply. Slowly and rhythmically their tongues swirled in each other's mouths stopping only to allow her to suck his bottom lip. She knew he loved that shit. He laid her down gently on the bed and removed her pants, panties and buried his head into her pussy. Bonita spread her legs wide to give him all the room he needed to do the job right. She grabbed her pillow to muffle the sounds as she came and came. It had been so long since she'd had her pussy eaten and this shit was so fucking good.

Sincere patted her on the thigh and whispered, "Turn around for me baby."

Without a moment's hesitation she was on all fours. Sincere stood on the floor and entered her from behind. He went in deep and slow holding onto her DDs while he worked his way in and out of her throbbing pussy. She could tell by his jagged breathing and quickened pace that he was nearing his peak, so she pulled forward to try to take control of the motion. She slowly slid her pussy up and down his dick until he matched her easy rhythm. She wasn't ready for the sex to end but she could no longer hold back the orgasm that was building inside her.

"Don't stop, don't you fucking stop! Oh Gaaawwd!" she screamed not caring if her mother heard her. She needed that nut and momma would just have to understand. They laid on the bed, Sincere on his back, Bonita curled towards him.

"Sincere I love you so much." She noticed he didn't look her way when he returned the sentiment. Still she was determined to remind him of what they had. "Do you want to take a shower and come back to bed? You look hot."

"That sounds good, but I need to get home." He looked at the time on his phone.

"So, you're just gonna leave like that? After what we just did?" Bonita was pissed.

"Come on don't start that right now."

"I'm sick of this bullshit, Sincere. You need to tell me what is going on."

Before he could answer his phone started to vibrate and the bright light flashed in his hand. "You gonna answer it?" she asked standing in front of him her naked belly in his face.

Sincere ignored Bonita and the phone. He pulled on is pants and slipped his sweater over his head.

Bonita glared at him. "You're going to see that bitch, right? The one who said she's your girl. You really got someone else. I can't believe you would do that to me." She sat on the bed and covered herself with her bathrobe.

"Nita," he reached for her.

"No, don't touch me. I heard you on the phone lying earlier. Talking about you were helping Kendra." Sincere bent down to tie his boots.

"Get out, get out of my house!" she screamed.

"What?" Sincere asked incredulously. "Yo', your hormones must be off the chain right now cause you buggin."

She walked past him and into the dark kitchen. "Here I am pregnant with your first-born son and you do me like this? This ain't right."

"Go take a shower and calm down." The phone vibrated again. "I got to go."

"Go then you bastard." Bonita picked up a knife from the butcher block and charged at him with it.

Immediately Sincere put his hands up to defend himself. Bonita sliced the air wildly and caught him across the palm.

Sincere hustled over to the door and held the knob. "Are you fucking crazy? What's wrong with you?"

Using the knife as a pointer, she emphatically let him know that she was not playing. "I am giving you to the count of three to get the hell out. One..."

"Alright, I'm gone," he said and slammed the door as he left.

Bonita leaned over the sink, dropped the knife, and cried. Her mom crept out from her bedroom. "What's going on? Where did this blood come from?" she asked looking at the trail of blood on the floor.

"Oh, mama," Bonita cried and headed toward her mother's waiting arms. She stopped in her tracks as the warm fluid surrounding her baby came trickling out of her.

CHAPTER 11

LOVE, I THOUGHT YOU HAD MY BACK

BENAE

Benae turned over onto her stomach and snuggled deeper under the down comforter, but not before stealing a glance at the digital clock that glowed 12:48 A.M. She told herself she wasn't going to call him again. Her mind battled with her heart. *I love Sincere and I know he loves me, but he is having a child with someone else. There has to be more going on than he's telling me. Look how long it took for him to tell me about the pregnancy. He says he wants to be with me, even says he wants to marry me but right now we are not married, and I have no ties to him...* She paused her thoughts to listen and verified that she heard the sound of his keys in the door. She lay extremely still, relaxed her eyelids and pretended to be asleep. She listened as he stopped in the bathroom, ran some water, and emerged.

"Bae," he called softly. She stirred slightly. "Wake up," he said sort of gruff.

Benae stretched and turned around to face him, her eyes squinting from the brightness of the lamp Sincere just turned on. "Hey, you're just getting in? What time is it?"

Sincere brushed off both of her questions. "It doesn't matter. Look at my hand." He stuck his hand out so she could see the deep gash he had across the palm. "Oh, my God, what happened?" she asked

"I cut it messing around with a knife at Rick's. Shit won't stop bleeding," he said applying more tissue around it.

Benae hopped out of the bed and threw on the jeans and sweater she had on earlier. "We have to go to the emergency room. I think you need stitches."

"Probably so," Sincere said, reaching down to pet Meth with his good hand.

"See, you laying here thinking foul thoughts and your man was working hard and injured himself," she admonished under her breath.

The Long Island College Hospital waiting room wasn't too busy. Two sick kids were sprawled out across a couple of chairs each, one man with his arm in a makeshift cast and a few other folks whose ailments were not obvious. Sincere signed in and took a seat beside Benae. She took his injured hand and held it gently between both of hers. The unmistakable sensation of a vibrating cell phone intruded upon what Benae felt was a private moment. She released Sincere's hand although she knew he would retrieve the phone with his other hand.

He took a quick glance to see who was calling. "It's Tru. No one else would call this time of night. I can't be bothered, right now," he said as he turned the phone off and dropped it into his vest pocket.

Benae didn't believe him. She had a strong feeling he was lying to her. Aggravated she stood up and announced that she was going to the vending machine to get a bottled water. "I'll be right back." She leaned down to give him a kiss and inhaled traces of what could only be identified as pussy. She stood straight up and eyed him suspiciously. "Let me make sure," she said to herself. She smiled sweetly and pretended to reach down for a hug.

Sincere twisted in his seat and held his hand out in agony forcing her to step back and acknowledge his pain. "I wish these doctors would come on. This thing is really starting to hurt."

Benae looked at him like he was full of shit and walked off to find the vending machine.

SINCERE

Damn, that was close. He remembered that he didn't get the chance to wash or rinse his mouth out after going down on Nita. *All that damn drama. I forgot the most important thing.* As soon as he saw Benae exit through the automatic doors, he slipped into the restroom nearby. He rinsed his mouth with hot water and dampened a paper towel with his good hand to wipe his face off. He didn't use soap. He didn't want to arouse suspicion if he hadn't already. When he opened the door, he heard a petite Hispanic woman in scrubs calling his name. "That's me," he said heading over to her.

They got back home at 3:30 in the morning, but Sincere was up three hours later getting ready for work. He was careful not to disturb Benae who was unusually quiet last night. She didn't say anything, but he could tell something was wrong with her. He was sure he would hear about it. However, when they got home, they were both too tired. She called off work and was still asleep. He brushed her cheek with his lips and quietly signaled to Meth before heading out the door. He could tell it was going to be one of those NY days, sunny yet freezing. Meth ambled along ahead of him looking for the perfect spot to do his business. Sincere turned his phone back on and checked his messages.

"Damn, twenty-one missed calls. She knows she's wrong for that. I bet her ass ain't apologize either." The phone vibrated in his hand as he attempted to press the button for voice mail. He picked up even though he wasn't in the mood to start his day hearing from Bonita.

"Yeah, what's up," he said dryly.

"I been calling you all night."

"Ms. Lucille?" He was taken aback. "Everything alright?" She was calling from Bonita's phone.

"Yeah, 'Nita's water broke this morning. She's not in labor yet but we're here at the hospital."

"Alright, keep me posted." He hung up before she could protest.

Of all days, she going to have the baby the day after she stabbed me, he thought. He needed to talk to someone. He thought about his dad but decided that this one was for Rick since he was an early bird, too. "Yo', Rick, you had breakfast already? I need to talk man."

"I was about to stop by the diner on twenty-third street. Where you at?"

"I'm home. I have to take Meth back home and I'll be there in fifteen minutes."

"Cool, see you then."

Sincere quietly let Meth back into the house and headed to his car which on this rare occasion was parked in front of the house. In no time he passed over the Brooklyn Bridge and was on the FDR heading for the 23rd Street Exit. It was early so parking wasn't a problem. He usually enjoyed the pre-bustle of the City but today neither his mind nor his spirit was with it. He saw Rick through the glass pane with a cup of coffee scrolling through his phone.

"Look at you sitting in here looking all sophisticated and shit. Marriage changed you man." They clasped hands and laughed.

The waitress came by for their orders and walked away with more switch in her walk than was necessary. Sincere and Rick were used to it, but they looked anyway.

"So, what's on your mind?" Rick asked.

"Man, I don't even know where to start. Last night after you left Nita's..."

"You hit it?" Rick cut in with sly smile."

"Damn, man, yeah," Sincere admitted. "She was coming at me and saying she was backed up and needed it. What was I supposed to do? Know what I mean..." He paused while the waitress brought their food.

"Anything else fellas?" she asked flirtatiously.

"Nah, we're good." They both said.

"So, after you hit it..." Rick joked.

"After I hit it her crazy ass tried to stab me." Rick looked at him confused. "Yeah, I know," Sincere continued. "She got pissed when my phone rang a few times and I didn't answer it. It was Benae and she figured it out and went bat shit crazy. You see my hand, right?" He showed Rick his stitched-up hand. "Eleven stitches."

"Damn, she fucked you up."

"It gets better," he continued. "So, I get home real late, like one in the morning. Benae had been calling and I didn't answer. So, I knew she was gonna have an attitude, but I countered it by showing her my hand. I told her I did it by mistake at your house. So, it's all good, she's showing concern, hops up to go the ER and everything. When we get there, she comes in for a kiss and shoots straight up like she smelled something. That's when I remembered that I never cleaned up after fucking with Nita."

"Damn, yo'!" Rick exclaimed. "How you forget?"

"She started with the stabbing shit, so I had to break out. When I got home, I went into my injured spiel I was just thinking about keeping Benae from going off on me. Plus, Nita called while we were in the emergency room. I told her it was Tru, but I don't think she believed me." Rick just shook his head and ate some more of his pancakes. "So, I just turned my phone off so I wouldn't have to worry about no more issues with my damn phone. I turn it on this morning. I got twenty-one missed calls and three voice messages all from Nita and her mom."

"Her mom?" Rick asked, confused once again.

"Yep. You know why? 'Nita's water broke this morning."

"Word?"

"Yeah, but she's not in labor yet."

"Man, she can get in labor anytime. Babies come when they want to. Call and see what's going on?"

"Yeah, I should do that right?" He called and this time Bonita informed him that her water broke but nothing really happened since. Still she wanted him there with her. "She good," Sincere reported. I better get going. I'm still feeling pissed about last night, but I have to be there to see my son born."

"Yeah, my dude you don't want to miss that," Rick said. Sincere reached for his wallet. "Nah, breakfast is on me."

"Thanks man. Appreciate it. Damn, I have to call my job and let them know I'll be off today, too and I have to tell Benae today is the day."

"How you think that's gonna go?" Rick asked on the way to his car.

"I'm about to find out. I'll hit you up later."

Sincere headed back to Brooklyn as quickly as possible with rush hour traffic quickly approaching. He decided he would tell Benae in person and make the ten-minute trip to Brooklyn Hospital. He replayed over and over in his mind exactly what he would say to appeal to her understanding and loving side but when he got home, she wasn't there.

CHAPTER 12

HALF ON A BABY

BENAE

The Brooklyn Promenade bustled with activity as pedestrians hurried, jogged, walked pets, and took in the view of the Manhattan Skyline across the water, even in the cold February air. Benae jogged along the waterfront at an easy pace. She held Meth's leash tightly as he walked briskly beside her. She decided to start jogging again, so many late-night meals and time spent lounging around the house with Sincere was starting to add pounds. Since their conversation about his child, things between them had settled into a comfortable routine. Sincere did his share of the cooking but his housekeeping habits were non-existent.

Instead of nagging him to change his self-proclaimed Viking ways, Benae hired a housekeeper, as per their agreement. She came by once a week and both were happy with her help. Initially, Sincere tried to encourage her not to, he felt a real woman should take care of her house herself, but he came around. She decided to head out and stay out of Honey's way while she cleaned. As she jogged, she thought about her parents' upcoming visit and how much she was looking forward to introducing them to Sincere.

Although she was starting to wonder if he was still seeing his soon to be baby's momma. She was sure that she smelled pussy on him last night but then again, she wasn't sure. Even if he was cheating, surely, he wouldn't be that sloppy or stupid. She thought about calling Kendra but realized they had never exchanged numbers. She was very happy with the way things were going in the seven months since they had been together, and she didn't want to bring negativity to the situation if she wasn't 100% sure. She stopped to take a breath when her phone rang loudly in the phone holder attached to her arm. Breathing heavily, she stopped and answered the phone.

"Hey, babe," Sincere sounded upset.

"What's the matter?" Benae reacted.

"It's time."

"It's time?" Benae asked confused. "Time for what?"

"'Nita called, she's about to have the baby."

Benae was stupefied. Somehow this moment never registered in her mind. It was like she knew the girl was pregnant, but never truly anticipated the birth. Sub-consciously she stumbled over to a bench and sat down ignoring the cold permeating her clothes and freezing her butt and thighs.

"Hello?"

"I'm here," she said softly. "I'm just a little surprised."

"Where are you?"

"I'm on the Promenade."

"Why don't you come home? I'm already back at the house, okay?"

"Okay," she said disconnecting the call. "Come on let's go, Meth." Meth was more than ready and broke into a light jog beside her as she ran back home. For some reason she needed to see Sincere, to be near him.

When she reached her apartment, she realized she had run the whole way and stopped to hold onto the cold stone stairway. Breathing heavily, she glanced up at her window to see Sincere looking down at her. Meth was already at the top of the stairs waiting for her, his tail wagging excitedly. Benae walked into the house, past Sincere and into the kitchen to grab a bottled water from the fridge. Honey was in there cleaning out the microwave.

"Hello, Ms. Benae," she said in her cheerful Indian accent.

"Hi Honey, you know what. I'll pay you for today, but you can take the day off. Sincere and I need the house to ourselves."

"No need, I can leave and come back. No problem."

"No really, take the day," she insisted.

"Okay, if you say so." She grabbed her coat and left them alone.

"What's all that about?" he asked concern written all over his face.

Benae fought the urge to roll her eyes. Instead she walked into the living room with Sincere following behind. "I don't know,' she whined. "Sincere, I know it sounds crazy, but I wasn't expecting this. I don't know what to do, how to feel, what to say..." She sat the bottled water on the table and stared at him helplessly.

"Come here," he said pulling at her arm gently. When she didn't budge, he pulled a little harder. "Come here." He grabbed her into his embrace.

Her knees buckled and he held her up, keeping her from dropping to the floor. She tried to hide her tears but knew the slight jerking of her body gave her away.

"I don't want you to go," she cried out.

"Baby, I have to go. I have to be there for the birth of my son. We talked about this and I told you I was gonna be there." Somewhere in the recesses of her mind she remembered that he had. He sat them down on the sofa pulling Benae onto his lap. "Benae, look at me." He lifted her face up to his. "Listen to me. I know this is hard. I understand how you're feeling, right now, I do. I promise you nothing will change between us and I mean that. I love you girl." He kissed her lips then her nose. "Everything is gonna be fine, but I have to go. I have to go to the hospital alright?"

Benae gathered her composure and stood up. She reached both of her hands out to him. He took them in his hands and stood up facing her. "Sincere, I understand that you have to go. I also hope that you can understand that I won't be home when you get back."

"Don't be like that. I have to go, but I came home to make sure you were alright. She's already in the hospital. I don't want to leave if you are not okay, but I will," he threatened.

Benae's face was stricken with horror as the full effect of what was happening took hold of her. "I guess you have to do what you have to do," she said sadly.

"Yes, I do," he pleaded as he leaned down to kiss unresponsive lips and searched for eyes that would not meet his. "I have to go. Don't worry everything will be okay." Benae heard the door close behind him.

She knew she was going to break-down and was happy that she sent Honey home. She walked to her bedbroom and sat on the bed. She felt mocked by the bright sunshine beaming through the windows. She needed her best friend.

"Chrissy," she cried into the phone.

"Benae what's the matter?"

Benae was crying so hard she could barely get her words out. "She's, she's, she's having the baby."

"What?"

"Sincere's baby mother is in labor."

"Is he with her?"

"He just left to go to the hospital."

"Well, that's good. He should be there. That's his baby too, Benae," Chrissy said carefully.

"I know. In my heart I know, but I just can't deal with it right now. My emotions are all over the place. I need to get out of here. I'm packing a bag and I'm coming over."

"That's a good idea. You don't need to be alone, right now..." she paused and could hear her friend crying hard but softly. "Get an Uber and come over. I'll have all your favorite things by the time you get here."

Benae couldn't help but feel a little better. Chrissy was just too good of a friend not to. "Okay," she said brightening up a bit. "For once in my life I am going to do exactly as I'm told."

"Great, a couple of bottles of wine, an order of chicken Chow Mein and pralines and cream ice cream coming right up. I can also throw in a snuggie and one of your favorite movies if we need to go there," Chrissy warned lovingly.

"I love you, Chrissy. I'm so glad to have you as my bestie," Benae said softly. "But this hurts so bad," she whined. "I know this is it for us. Why would he stay with me when he has a whole family? I should have left the day that he left that stupid letter. I am so stupid. Just like my mom says, I am so smart but so stupid."

"Don't say that. I don't know how I would handle this situation if I were in your shoes. I honestly don't."

"I know. I can't believe this is happening to me. I meet this great guy now this. It's almost surreal."

"It is. But we can talk when you get here. Just get yourself together and come on over. I'll be home when you get there. I'll tell my boss I have a family emergency and get the hell out of here."

"Chrissy, I forgot you were at work. You don't have to do that," Benae said firmly.

"Don't worry about. I want to do it and it is a family emergency," she emphasized.

"I know it's no point in arguing with you. I'll be on my way soon."

BONITA

"Oh, My God! Ma it feels like something is ripping me apart. Please I just need a minute to rest," Bonita panted.

"Ms. the contractions are ten minutes apart and the baby's head is crowning. You have to keep pushing." Doctor Patel said.

"I can't, I can't," she cried.

Ms. Lucille wiped Bonita's sweat soaked face with a cool cloth. "Take a deep breath and push baby."

"Let me talk to her." Ms. Lucille moved away from the side of the bed and let Sincere take his rightful place.

Bonita knew that voice anywhere, even in the midst of unbearable pain. She opened her eyes to see Sincere dressed up in the required blue scrubs.

He took her hand and looked down at her. "How you doing?"

She looked up at him displaying more love than she realized, then looked away and rolled her eyes.

"Keep pushing baby, I can see the head." He said.

Bonita pushed as hard as she could. She had been in labor for eight hours and her energy was just about gone. She squeezed Sincere's hand and pushed again until the need to do so subsided.

"Here he comes," Dr. Patel exclaimed as she pulled the tiny newborn from Bonita's womb. "Congratulations mom, dad and grandma," she said as she lay the baby on top of Bonita's heaving belly and picked up a pair of surgical scissors. "Would you like to do the honors," she asked, handing the scissors to Sincere.

Bonita watched as Sincere cautiously took the scissors and carefully severed the lifeline between her and their son. Before she knew it, the baby was whisked away by the delivery room nurses for newborn observation and care.

"That don't hurt?" Sincere asked as Dr. Patel stitched up the incision from the episiotomy.

"No, I don't feel a thing," she replied dreamily. "We have a son." She smiled.

"Here he is." A bubbly nurse carefully handed the tiny bundle to Sincere only now he was cleaned up and wrapped in an official hospital issued blanket.

Sincere tilted the baby in his arms downward so that they both could get a better look. Neither had the words to describe how they felt at the moment, so they didn't try to find any. When Sincere kissed the baby's forehead, Ms. Lucille was ready with her cell phone to snap the first pics of father and son. Bonita reached for the baby and Sincere pulled out his phone to capture more photos of the precious moment.

"He's perfect," Bonita cooed.

"Of course, he is," Sincere said proudly.

"I wish I could hold him forever, but I am so tired. I think I'm gonna fall asleep. I just want to know that you are gonna be here."

"I'm not going nowhere. I'm about to go out there with your mom and make some calls. We about to set it off in here," he exclaimed.

Bonita shared his enthusiasm, but she couldn't show it. She was so tired. "You're gonna have all these people come up here and I must look horrible."

"Actually, you never looked more beautiful." He leaned down and kissed her on the lips. I want you to know, I'm sorry for the way I acted in the beginning and I'm glad you didn't listen to me. Thank you for my son."

The bubbly nurse re-appeared at the door. "We need to take the baby for a minute."

"Oh, okay," Bonita sighed. "I can barely keep my eyes open," she said handing over the little bundle. \

As the nurse scurried away, Sincere headed toward the door behind her. "Nita, I love you. I hope you know that."

She closed her eyes. "Thank you, God for giving him the change of heart I prayed for. Thank you, thank you, thank you," she said aloud before drifting off to sleep.

CHAPTER 13

WHY ME BABY?

BENAE

Benae woke up in the same spot on Chrissy's couch she'd curled up in after polishing off an entire bottle of wine while overeating Chinese food and ice-cream. It was 10:30 a.m. and she felt like she'd slept the day away. She sat up in the semi-darkness encouraged by the heavy drapes and replayed her last conversation with Sincere in her mind. The sadness was so severe it actually ached within. Wrapping her arms around herself, she gave herself a hug then stretched her arms upwards and stood up. She could hear Chrissy upstairs laughing at something on TV. The boys must have been very quiet this morning to not disturb her sleep. She heard the soft sound of her phone vibrating on the end table beside the sofa.

"Hi ma," she said dryly.

"Hi baby, are you busy? I called you twice already and didn't get an answer."

"I was sleeping. Sincere cut his hand and we were at the emergency room all night," she lied.

"Well, how is he?"

"He's fine, just needed a couple of stitches."

"That's good. Now about your dad's and my visit, I can email you our itinerary. We left Saturday night open for dinner with you and Sincere."

"Mom I don't know. Things are not that great with us right now. We have a situation we need to work through."

"I'm sure you two will be fine. Just talk to him. Remember communication is the key."

"I remember." *Why is it that she never bothers to find out what the problem is before she starts with her tired advice?* Benae wondered.

"Be on the lookout for my email and I'm looking forward to seeing you this weekend. Smooches."

"Smooches," Benae replied rolling her eyes. *My God she gets on my nerves. Now I have to worry about keeping her happy while my life is falling apart.* Tears brimmed her eyes, but she wiped them away when she heard Chrissy coming down the stairs.

"Good morning," she sang cheerily. "You feeling okay?" She looked Benae up and down. "There's coffee in the kitchen."

"Thanks. Coffee sounds good. I'm going to hop in the shower and try to do something with my face. I know I look like death warmed over."

"Your eyes look a little puffy that's all," Chrissy corrected. "Are you going to the office today?"

"No, I'm taking another sick day. What time do you have to go in?"

"I'm about to leave now. I'm working eleven to seven today," Chrissy said grabbing her keys and coat. "Get some coffee, take a shower and just put the slam lock on when you leave. No rush, though. I got to go but make sure you call me later."

Benae poured herself a cup of coffee and sat down and looked at her phone. There were five missed calls from Sincere. She briefly thought about calling him, but she really didn't want to hear anything he had to say. Not now anyway. Before she could sit the phone down, it vibrated in her hand. It was Ming.

"Hey, girl, Tru told me the news about the baby. I figured you could use a friend. I know I would."

"I'm at my friend Chrissy's house. I came here to spend the night but I'm still a mess. I'm trying to get myself together now."

"If y'all ain't doing nothing why don't y'all come by here for lunch. I got some veal cutlets and I was going to make veal parm and throw together a Caesar salad."

"Okay, that sounds good. I can pick up a bottle of wine. Chrissy had to go to work."

"You could if you want to, but I have a full bar. You know me and Tru like to get out drink on. What I need is some cheesecake."

They both laughed. "Too bad I'm not home I could have stopped by Junior's."

"I don't need it. Just come on over."

"Okay, send your address. I'll GPS it and be on my way." Benae was happy for the added distraction and it would be good to get Ming's take on things since she gets an inside scoop from Tru.

Of all the highways in New York, Benae loved the FDR Drive. Riding alongside the East River was so soothing. Even through her pain, she still felt the calming effect of the glistening water and bright sunshine. It wasn't enough to comfort her heart, though. She pictured Sincere holding his newborn son while his affection grew for the woman that gave him to him. She blinked away tears as she exited the highway and headed to 5th Avenue and 138th Street in Harlem.

The vestibule of the four-story walk-up looked pretty basic but it was nice and clean and Benae appreciated that. She didn't have high expectations for Tru and Ming's living space. By the time she reached the top floor she was slightly out of breath. She knew it was due to the lethargy she felt because of Sincere. Any other time she would have taken those stairs like nothing.

Ming stood in the doorway looking like a page out of a high-fashion magazine. "Hey girl," she exclaimed, "Come in. Have a seat. Put your feet up." They embraced deeply.

Benae stepped into the lavish living room and was astonished by the glamorous surroundings. Ming's exquisite taste did not end with her wardrobe. They had taken two apartments and converted them into one. Benae took a seat at the black and white solid marble dining table with high back matching leather chairs. Underneath the table was a beautiful alpaca rug and above hung an intricate crystal chandelier.

From her vantage point she had an overview of the large sunken living room which was decorated in various tones of tans and browns. The leather sectional looked inviting and Benae was ready to sink into it. Other than that, most of the furnishings were a bit too gaudy for her taste, but still she was impressed. She knew good quality when she saw it and nothing in here was cheap.

"Hustling is apparently good to you and Tru. This place is beautiful."

"Why thank you darling," Ming said beaming. "It means a lot coming from a classy lady like yourself. Plus, Tru is gone so much, I spend most of my time decorating. It's a hobby."

"What about your friends? Don't you hang out with them?"

"What friends? I don't trust women like that. Most of my friends are dudes and Tru's not having that."

"What about family?"

"Same thing basically. Mom died when I was a kid. I see my dad now and then. He's an addict so he finds me when he wants to. I don't get along with my sister. She accused me of sleeping with her man and she came at me. I kicked her ass and we never spoke again. That was three years ago."

"That's crazy!" Benae said loudly. "I always thought that if I had a sister, we'd be the best of friends."

"We're sisters now. We had this connection. I liked you from the jump and that's not me."

"I know, we clicked for some reason. I feel I can trust you."

"Yeah, yeah, yeah, me too," Ming said killing the emotional turn the conversation was taking. "Now let's get some drinks flowing, get you comfy and sit down and talk," Ming said heading into the red and white kitchen.

"Can I ask you a question?" Benae asked with a smile on her face. "Did you sleep with your sister's man?"

"Yeah, I fucked him, but she can't prove it." They both cracked up laughing.

Having feasted on veal parmesan, Caesar salad, garlic bread and two glasses of red wine they curled up on opposite ends of the sectional where Benae relayed the story of how she and Sincere met, fell in love and how she learned about the baby.

"I can't believe he's a father now. I won't be his first priority anymore, but he'll still be mine. I'm not sure how I feel about that. I've never dated anyone with a child before and that's the primary reason why."

"What! You worried about not being his first priority?" Ming wanted to know. "That's the least of your worries. What about his baby momma?"

Baby momma. The term sounded like some foreign disease. Benae cringed a little and Ming didn't miss it.

"That's right baby momma," Ming restated. "And trust and believe that bitch ain't trying to go nowhere now."

"If that's where he wants to be, he can go. I am not fighting over him. The fact that I'm willing to still deal with him and this whole messy situation is as much as I'm willing to take," Benae said displaying attitude.

Her façade did not fool Ming, she saw the sadness in her eyes and heard the heartbreak in her voice. She walked over to Benae's end of the sofa. "Look at me. You don't have to be strong and put on a front for me. You cried your eyes out earlier. I know you love that man and he loves you. Tru and dad talk about how much Sincere loves you. They don't talk about her except to say she tried to put the trap down but Sincere ain't no sucker. He's not going out like that so why should you? Don't let your pride write a check your ass can't cash. You have to be united with your man and let that trick know, she better be happy with her son because that's the only Law man she gonna get."

"You're right," Benae said softly. "In my heart I know you're right but I'm just so, so...everything...sad, mad, scared..."

"That's okay, all this is new. Once it all settles down. You will be alright, and you and Sin will be fine."

"What time is it?"

"It's going on six why?"

155

"Oh, God, I have to go to work tomorrow but I don't want to go home. I don't want to hear about the birth, the baby, none of it. It hurts." Benae managed to get out before dropping her head to her hands and crying.

Ming put her arms around her shoulders. "It's okay. You know what, you can stay here tonight. You can sleep in the spare room. I have more wine if you want or you can get some rest it's up to you. Plus, I don't see why Miss High Powered Executive can't take another day off. Can't that place run a day or two without you? You can't be that damn important. Stay home with me, you know I ain't got shit to do."

In spite of herself, Benae felt her tears turn to laughter. "Ming you are so crazy," she said through the tears. "I'll stay, I'm sure your guest room looks like a room out of Caesar's Palace."

"As a matter of fact, it does. It has a Roman theme." They laughed again.

"Well I can't turn that down," Benae joked. "And yes, I'll take another glass of wine and some more parm for that matter." Benae got up to head to the kitchen.

"Sit your ass down. I'll get it," Ming ordered.

Benae did as she was told. She pulled her silenced phone from out of her bag to see eleven missed calls from Sincere. She turned it off, plugged it into the charger and yelled out to Ming, "You may as well break open another bottle! It's going to be a long night."

It definitely was, Benae cried and Ming comforted her into the wee hours of the morning. As the night wore on, both realized that they were developing a true friendship.

SINCERE

Once again Sincere called Benae and once again his call went unanswered, in fact the call went straight to voice mail. He was more confused than he was when he left.

He kept saying to himself, "I didn't do anything wrong, why is she so mad?"

Their last conversation played over in his mind here and there. He just couldn't find a reason that would give him this response or lack of one from her. She was really fucking up a blessed occasion. He was a father and even though Benae was not the mother of his child he wanted to share this with her, too. He headed back to the nursery to check on his son and decided to he would wait for Benae to call him or just see her at home. Overall, today was a great day and he wasn't gonna let her ruin it for him. His Dad, Tru, Rick and Kendra, some co-workers and even his mom came up from Florida to meet little Genuwen. Everyone that mattered to him showed him love except one.

"Son, I'm gonna head on home now," his dad said. Sincere didn't see him there until he spoke. "If you want to stop and grab something to eat, we can do that first."

"Damn, I didn't eat all day. I didn't realize it until you said it but man, I'm starving."

"Well, let's eat. Where you wanna go? It's on me," his dad sad slapping his arm around his son's shoulder as they both gazed down upon the newest member of the family through the looking glass."

Sincere could feel Dad's pride beaming without looking at him and it felt great. "Sorry dad, but I'm gonna go home. Benae probably made something for us at home. Plus, I want to get some rest, I been up all day."

"I hear you son. Go on home and get some rest. Tell Benae I said hello." He turned to walk away and said loudly, "Congratulations Sincere, the first member of the next generation of Laws." He tipped his hat and turned his attention to one of the pretty nurses passing by.

Sincere shook his head and smiled. *Dad's gonna be dad,* he thought as he followed him out of the hospital to the parking lot.

"Hey, dad, when did Tru leave? I left to go to the bathroom and when I got back, he was gone?"

"He left to take your mother to the airport and said he had some business to tend to. You know with your brother that can be anything got damn thing."

The weight of the day was bearing down on him and he was in no mood to entertain one of Dad's drawn out conversations about the state of his youngest son's life. "Alright, dad, get home safe," Sincere interrupted.

"When you bring that baby home you make sure you come see me. I ain't got nothing against that girl. I just don't like her ways, but we family now so that's that."

On the short drive home, Sincere felt anxious. He didn't know what to expect when he walked through the door. When she didn't come home last night, he wasn't too surprised since she had told him as much. Still he hoped that whatever issues she was dealing with, she had worked them out within herself and was sitting at home waiting for him with the love he had grown so accustomed to. There were no parking spaces on the block. He drove around until her found a spot three blocks away. He walked home with thoughts of his son and Bonita.

He couldn't deny the love he felt for her after watching her squeeze his son into the world and sharing that moment together and of course hearing her affirmations of never-ending love for him. For the first time he felt as though his heart was in two places. Benae had qualities that deeply appealed to him – beauty, honesty, intellect, drive, style, class and the lifestyle he saw for himself. While Bonita was sexy, submissive, caring, simple, domestic, and easy to please, life with her would be uncomplicated and he would be in complete control. Sometimes that's what he wanted at other times he wanted a female version of him and that was Benae. Now he had to add mother of my son to Bonita's list.

He knew what he liked in each woman but there were things that he didn't like. On the negative side Benae was financially in control, more than a little bougie, superficial, not domestic and from what he experienced recently unsupportive. The flip side of Bonita is that she was childish, uneducated, boring, lacked ambition and was unpolished.

Sincere chuckled to himself. "Now I remember why I started looking elsewhere in the first place. I got tired of feeling stagnant. I wanted a lot more than Bonita could give or even think of. I chose Benae, she lives the life I want. She's the kind of woman any successful man would want beside him." Satisfied that he had resolved the conflict within, he put the key in the door and walked into a blackened apartment. He switched on the hallway light and walked towards the bedroom. *She must be in the bed,* he thought as he turned on the light. All that greeted him was an unmade bed, and clothes strewn about. "Where the fuck is, she?" he said aloud.

Now he was furious. The anger and disappointment he held in all day unfurled. She didn't answer the phone all fucking day, acted like she didn't know the baby was due, now this disappearing act bullshit. He grabbed the drapes and pulled them from the wall then snatched the pillows from the bed and threw them around the room. Not fully spent from the hurt he felt inside, he sat on the edge of the bed and willed himself to calm down. *Losing control and destroying things is not the way to go.* He thought about working out or going to get something to eat. He pulled up Grub Hub to see what was still open for delivery and settled on Soul food even though he really didn't want it. While he waited for the food to arrive, he contemplated trying Benae one more time.

"Fuck that," he said and dialed Bonita. She didn't answer either, but he knew she would have if she wasn't in the hospital recuperating from delivering his baby.

BONITA

"That's right look at me, look at me," Shakirra cooed to little Genuwen who was bundled up in her arms. "Yes, get to know your auntie-God-ma."

"You can't be both silly," Bonita chided and laughed at her crazy friend.

"Yes, I can, watch me. Plus, I have to be both. You don't have no sisters or other best friends!"

"Whatever Shakirra," Bonita said standing up cautiously. The stitches from the episiotomy were tight and she didn't want to pop them. "Why did my mother give you these jeans. I told her to give you a jogging suit."

"She said she couldn't find it."

"I don't want to come home looking all busted."

"You won't' look busted. Put on the cute top. It'll show off your hourglass boobs." She laughed. "I bought two wigs, see which one you want."

"Thanks girl," Bonita exclaimed and gave her bestie a big hug. "I'm going in the bathroom to take a wash up and get dressed. You got my little man, right?"

"Of course." She smiled down at the baby.

"Where my little man at?" Sincere' voice boomed across the room.

"Shhh, you gonna wake him up," Shakirra whispered. "I'm surprised to see you are here."

"I know you are," he said annoyed. "Where's Nita?"

"In the bathroom." Shakirra rolled her eyes at him.

"You can save the attitude and learn to mind your business. Take your ass home and take care of your...what...four five kids?"

"Three and with my *husband*. No baby mama, baby daddy bullshit in the Jones household."

"Okay, y'all cut it out!" Bonita opened the bathroom door and yelled. "This is a happy occasion, don't ruin it."

"You're right," Sincere said walking over to her and giving her a hug. "How you feeling? You look good."

"Thank you." Bonita beamed and glanced slyly at Shakirra who in return gave her the side eye.

The trio headed down to Sincere's car with him holding the baby in the car seat, Bonita holding her flowers and balloons and Shakirra carrying Bonita's bag. They pulled up to Monument Walk and headed into Bonita's and Shakirra's building. People who knew them, and some they casually knew from the neighborhood, stopped, and tried to get a peek at the baby. Shakirra visited for a short while until she sensed the two newly minted love birds wanted to be alone.

"Alright, y'all I'm leaving," she said grabbing her coat from the back of the kitchen chair. "Y'all know you can't do nothing for six weeks. Don't let him try to get some before then," Shakirra cautioned.

"Bye, Shakirra," Bonita said walking her friend towards the door. "Don't worry I'm fine. I got him back," she whispered in Shakirra's ear as she walked out. Bonita felt slightly offended when her friend did not give her any encouragement or even a smile.

She walked into her bedroom where Sincere had taken Gen and saw Sincere looking at his phone. It got on her nerves when he checked his phone, but she forced herself to ignore it and smiled. "So, baby-daddy how you feeling? It's our first time at home with our son."

"I'm on top of the world, right now. Never knew I could love someone so much."

"I know right." She slid on the bed beside him and caressed his back.

He glanced her way and his eyes were filled with emotion, emotion she interpreted as his love for his son, for her, for their family. She was about to kiss him when she heard her mother's voice.

"Hey, 'Nita, I didn't hear you come in. Hello Sincere."

"Yeah, we got in a little while ago. I saw that you were sleeping so I didn't bother you."

"How's the baby doing?"

"He's good. Sleeps a lot." She giggled.

"That's good," Ms. Lucille said coming over to hold her grandson.

Sincere stood up and walked out of the room. 'Nita could hear him talking softly on the phone. She knew from the timbre of his voice that he was talking to a woman and that he was a little upset. She could also tell that whatever was being said was soothing him. Bonita felt tears sting her eyes a little bit. What was it going to take to get her man back? She was here first and now they were a family.

Sincere came back and made sure Bonita and the baby had everything they needed. He even asked if she wanted him to bring her something to eat but Ms. Lucille had already made dinner and announced it before Bonita could take him up on his offer.

"I'm about to head out. You get some rest and if you need anything just call." He gave her a peck on the cheek and headed for the door. "I'll be by every day, okay?"

"Sincere."

"Yeah." He stopped and turned around.

"Remember, I love you."

"I know. I love you, too," he said and left, but for some reason it seemed like he didn't want to go.

CHAPTER 14

HIS STORY

BENAE

"Good morning, Ms. G," her ever cheerful assistant Candice greeted.

"Good morning," Benae replied barely audible.

"You okay?" Candice asked standing up from her desk, preparing to follow Benae into her office.

"I'm fine just a little tired. I didn't sleep well. Give me an hour. If anyone stops by tell them I'm on a conference call.

"Sure, no problem. Do you need coffee or anything?"

"Actually, coffee sounds good. Grab a bagel with butter too and get something for yourself."

"Okay, I'll be right back."

"Thank you." Benae slid into her office and closed the door.

She wished that she had total privacy, but the big glass pane next to her office door prevented that. She was slightly hung-over and very sleepy, but as Ming told her before she left, neither showed on her face. She took a look in the mirror she had posted beside her monitor. She had to admit she looked fine. No one could tell the two rough nights she had by looking at her. It took her a few minutes to remember her password to log on to her computer. Once she got in, she sat and watched new email messages quickly fill up her mailbox. Before opening any messages, she checked her office voicemail, fortunately there was nothing urgent. As she started tackling the email messages which lead to lengthy responses, phone calls, or quick meetings the day passed by before she realized it. The monthly forecasts were almost done. She just needed information from a few of her colleagues before wrapping up that week-long task. She pushed back from the computer screen and stretched her arms above her head.

Candace knocked and opened her office door simultaneously. "Looks like someone needs to go home," she joked catching Benae in mid-stretch.

Benae chuckled. "I know right. What time is it?"

"It's five-thirty. I came in to say goodnight."

"Okay, well you have a good evening. I am going to get out of here myself."

Even in NYC traffic the trip from downtown Manhattan to downtown Brooklyn took about thirty minutes. The fish market was not far once she crossed the Brooklyn Bridge, so she double parked and hopped out to pick up some jumbo shrimp. As she headed home, she figured making Sincere a nice dinner of shrimp scampi would be step one of her apology. Throughout the day she pondered the situation and the net takeaway was that she loved him and wanted to work things out. The fact that he was there for his child's birth was a testament to his good character. She should be upset if he chose not to be there. It was just fear that caused her to act so selfishly. The fear of losing the man she loved to the woman who bore him a child. Any woman in her shoes would feel like she did. In the end, she resolved to salvage her relationship and let go of the fear and insecurity. She was ready to make amends.

She expected Sincere not to be home, but what she hadn't expected was to see the place in such a mess. Clearly, he had slept on the couch and had some sort of tantrum. The curtains were pulled from the rods and lying on the floor. The clothes he wore the day before were thrown across various pieces of furniture, empty food cartons were left behind and the bedding from the bedroom was piled up on the sofa. The sight touched Benae's heart and she felt even worse about the way she acted. She looked at the time on the cable box and saw that it was a quarter after six. If she wanted to surprise Sincere with a celebration for his new son, she needed to get started. But first, she needed to do something she hadn't done in two days.

"Hey baby," he said when he picked up the phone.

The sound of his voice and the fact that he was not mad touched her. "Hi," she croaked.

"Are you home? I need you home with me."

"Sincere," she cried. "I am so happy you still want me. I thought you were going to leave me. So, I guess I left first."

"No, baby never that. Yes, I have a son now and I love him. That changes nothing between us. I love what we have, too. I need you understand that."

"I do now," she whispered. "And yes, I'm home."

"Sorry about the house." He chuckled. "But I was pissed off when I came home, and you weren't there."

"No, babe, I'm the one that's sorry. Don't worry about the house. I got it. When are you coming home?"

"I'll be home around eight...eight-thirty, I'm off now. I am going to stop by to see my son and I'll be home right after that."

"What's his name?"

"Genuwen Jamison Law. It's another way of saying Sincere except we spell it G-e-n-u-w-e-n."

Benae winced when he said, "we", but she continued with the conversation like nothing happened. "Genuwen," Benae repeated. "That's clever," was all that she could come up with.

"Thanks, I think it's fly as hell," he said proudly.

"Oh Lord, here you go," Benae rolled her eyes. "Well go do what you have to do. I miss you and will be here ready and waiting for you," she said affectionately.

"Sounds good to me. I'll see you in a little while. I love you."

"I love you, too." For some reason she felt like crying.

Instead she dropped to her knees, placed her folded hands on the sofa and prayed. She asked for guidance, patience and discernment. After praying she felt better. She plugged her phone up to the Bose speaker and listened to her chill playlist while she cleaned up. When she was done cleaning the living room and bedroom, she gathered the ingredients for the scampi, and added fresh broccoli and garlic bread to round out the menu. In no time at all, the house was filled with the aroma of fresh garlic, shrimp, and butter. She put the food on warm and headed to the bathroom to run a hot bath. She looked around for the package of votive candles she'd purchased awhile back and found them in the cabinet under the sink. There were five left and she lit them and sat them around the bathroom.

The look was very sexy, and the fragrant Jo Malone London Pomegranate Noir Deluxe candle scent was romantic. Pleased with her work she striped down and lifted her leg to step into the tub that was overflowing with bubbles. Before she put her foot into the water, she remembered the *Congratulations* and *It's a Boy* banners she'd picked up. Quickly she pulled the banners from their bags and clumsily hung them in the living room. Giddy, she ran back down the hallway and carefully stepped into the steaming hot bath and waited to for her man to come home.

SINCERE

He didn't mention it to Benae but he had spent the entire day with Bonita and his son. He completely enjoyed himself, too. Little Gen captivated him even though all he did was eat and sleep. Sincere found everything he did worth seeing and didn't want to miss a thing. It was hard to believe that only two short days ago this tiny human did not exist at all. Walking to his car, he felt a moment of absolute perfection. He had a beautiful son that he loved more than he knew he was capable of and the woman that he loved still loved him. He felt undeserving of such goodness and teared up a little as he said a silent thank you to God. He called Benae as he neared home.

"Hey, baby," Benae sang into the phone.

"Hey, I'm checking to see if you need anything from the store before I come in?"

"No, I have everything I need except for you," she said and hung up.

Sincere looked at the phone. "This chick got me confused as a mafucka." He smiled, slid his phone into his pocket and jogged up the stairs.

"Surprise!" Benae yelled spreading her arms wide. "Welcome home, Dad."

Sincere couldn't help but smile even wider. He read the banners and felt a little bashful at her unadulterated attempt to please him. "Thanks babe. I wasn't expecting nothing like this," he said looking around sheepishly.

He watched as she slowly walked toward him, and he got a good look at her in the floor-length sheer gown she was wearing. She stopped right in front of him and looked into his eyes. He loved the love he saw there and softly placed a kiss on her forehead. His body reacted as she held him by the face, stood on her toes and slid her tongue into his mouth. He wrapped his arms around her waist and pulled her into him. They kissed passionately until it built into a lustful crescendo.

Benae pulled away and planted tiny kisses all over his face, "Baby, I am so so sorry for acting the way I did. If we could do it over, I would be your support and give you the love you needed."

"It's okay, I understand. You thought you were losing me. The important thing is we're good now."

"Yes, I just don't want to ever lose you."

"Never, don't ever worry about that. You got me." He flashed her the smile that melted the hearts of many women and slid his hands down to her butt. She removed his hands, "No, no we have plenty of time for that. Let's have dinner before it gets cold. I made your favorite."

"You threw down on some scampi?" he asked sniffing the strong aroma of butter and garlic in the air.

"I sure did." She led him into the dimly lit dining room.

The lights on the chandelier were dimmed to the lowest setting. Two 12-inch tapers burned brightly in the middle of the table casting a soft glow around the room.

Sincere was more than impressed. "Babe, this is real nice. I never had a candlelight dinner before."

"Well, I'm happy to be your first at something." She grinned, pulling a bottle of Dom Perignon from the wine fridge. "Here open this."

"Dom, too! This is another first," he said popping the cork.

"Good it's my favorite. Now tell me all about your baby boy and show me some pics."

Damn, I love this girl, he thought as he pulled out his phone and scrolled through pictures of his son taking care not to show any with Bonita.

After dinner Benae picked up the half-burned candles and carried them to the bedroom. Sincere was right on her heels ready for whatever else she had in store for him. He saw the massage oils on the nightstand and knew she was preparing to please him, but he decided that she had done enough, and it was time for him to return the favor.

"Come here," he said sitting on the bed. She came and sat beside him as he expected. "Now lay down."

"No, I want you to lay down. I'm not done with you yet," she said smiling at him seductively.

Benae untied the sheer gown and let it fall to the floor before straddling Sincere and kissing him deeply. He reached down to squeeze her ass and she began a slow sensual grind. In no time, he felt his dick pushing up against her soft skin. She lifted her breasts to his lips and he licked around the breasts and took his time getting to the nipple.

"Yes," she cried when he finally closed his lips around her areole and gently teased it with the tip of his tongue.

He switched to the other breast knowing it would drive her crazy. Quickly, she climbed up to his face and spread her pussy lips while hovering over his awaiting mouth. He stuck his tongue out and lightly flicked it over her clit. He knew she would not be able to stand it for long and she began grinding his face the way he loved. He sucked and licked her until he tasted her creamy goodness. She didn't cry out, but he could hear her breathing deeply and whimpering, which sounded so good to his ears. She climbed down off his face breathless.

"I didn't mean for that to happen. I just wanted to tease you a little, but it felt too good," she breathed. "Now you lay down like I told you to."

Sincere laid on his back with his dick sticking straight up. They both glanced at it and smiled. Benae kneeled on the floor before him. He'd closed his eyes in preparation of getting some head but nearly kicked her in the face when she wrapped her warm lips around his big toe.

"Oh shit," he whispered lifting his head to see her sucking his toe like it was his dick. He had to reach down and grip his balls to try to gain control over the sensation and the view.

"Relax baby," she said switching to his other foot.

He released a soft, "Damn." His rock-hard dick begged for attention.

Still she made him wait and thoroughly licked his inner thighs before licking and sucking his balls while stroking his dick from balls to tip. When he could barely take any more, she took him into her mouth and gave her man the release he was waiting for. He bucked on the bed and called out her name as he came. He'd never done that before, but that shit was good, especially when she swallowed every drop and cleaned the tip. She smiled up at him obviously very pleased with herself.

"Come here," he said, pulling back the covers and sliding under them. "Where you going?"

"I'm going to blow out the candles."

"Put on the lovemaking playlist and get back in here. We ain't done." He laid back on the bed satisfied.

Satisfied that things were going to work out just the way he wanted them to with both of the women in his life. He knew Bonita was never going anywhere, especially now that they had a child together. Now that Benae has come around to fully accepting the situation he couldn't help but feel like he had everything he wanted.

BONITA

Bonita wrestled into a pair of denim cut-offs and a blue t-shirt. She piled her hair into a bun on top of her head. *That feels better,* she thought.

The honey-blonde weave hanging down her back looked good, but it was hot as hell. That's one thing about the projects, they had good heat. She crept into Gen's room and turned on the baby monitor so she could hear him when he woke up. The baby monitor was one of her favorite gifts. She sat on her bed sipping iced coffee and nibbling on strawberry pop-tarts. The TV was on, but her mind had drifted away from Maury to Sincere. Since she had the baby things had been great. He had returned to his pattern of calling 2-3 times a day. Mostly to check on his son, but once she got him on the phone, she kept the conversation flowing. She also loved that he stopped by almost every day after work.

Apparently, he stopped seeing that bitch, she thought. *Because he's not running to pick her up or sneaking to answer her calls.*

He was still a little distant and didn't try having sex, but she chalked it up to the fact that he was uncomfortable since the birth. She had heard that men are weird about the baby coming out of their pleasure spot. She thought giving him a key would once again solidify their bond, but Ms. Lucille wasn't having it.

Gen, as everyone called her son, whimpered softly. Bonita sat and listened to his sweet sounds for a second before going to retrieve her baby. "Hey there mama's little boy," she cooed. "Let's get you some milk." She loved being a mom.

The late night and early morning feedings, changing diapers, doing laundry, endless crying none of it fazed her. Her cell rang as she sat on the bed to feed her baby. Propping the bottle up against her chest so she didn't disturb him, she quickly pressed the speaker button on the phone.

"Hello."

"Yeah, it's me," Sincere said, "I'll be on my way there in about an hour. You need anything?"

"He's a little low on diapers but he can make it another day or two."

"Alright, I got it."

"Okay, see you soon."

"Oh, and Nita..." he paused, and she thought he was going to say, *I love you.* "I have to talk to you."

"About what?" she asked anxiously.

"I'll tell you when I get there. Aight?"

"Alright," she said reluctantly.

Bonita finished feeding Gen, wiped him down, changed him into a fresh onesie and laid him down on his blanket in the center of her bed. She wanted to be optimistic about what he had to say but she had an overwhelming feeling that it wasn't good. When she heard him at the door, she took her time answering. He came in with his usual noisiness.

"Damn it's hot in here," he said with his face scrunched up in discomfort. He headed straight to his son and picked him up. "Hey, what's up man?" The baby wiggled and smiled up at his daddy. "Look, Nita, he's smiling at me."

Bonita peeked over just in time to see the smile before it disappeared. She had seen a few already but she didn't want to spoil his moment. He played with his son until he started yawning and dozing off. "You can lay him back down on the bed," Bonita said sitting next to him. "What do you have to talk to me about?"

He turned to look at her. "First I want you to know that I love you and I am grateful for our son. I'm gonna always be here for you nothing will change that. You feel me?" She nodded but did not meet his eyes. "Good," he continued. "We have a son now, so we got to be real with other and be honest. There are some things in my life you need to know about."

"You can trust me and tell me anything." She saw frustration flash across his face.

"Nita, just listen. You are making this harder. Now, I know you got love for me. You got a lot of love for me, but there is someone else who has a lot of love for me and I got love for her."

"What!" Bonita stood up. "Who? That bird bitch, Benae or whatever her name is?"

"Yeah, her name is Benae, and don't call her a bitch. She never called you out your name."

"I thought that was over. Why now?" she shouted.

"I didn't want to stress you while you were pregnant. But now everything is going smooth and we cool with each other. I want to do the right thing and be honest with you."

"This is what you call doing the right thing? I still don't understand why you are doing this to me?" She let the tears flow and didn't bother wiping them away.

"Nita, I don't want to hurt you. This why I said we have to be honest. You know why I am doing this. We argued all the time. You never wanted to go nowhere or do anything. You have no ambition. You're scared to move out of the projects. You don't want to get a job. There's a whole bunch of reasons why. We were deaded when I left last year. The only reason I came back is because you were pregnant."

"You never told me you felt like that. You complained here and there but if I knew it was that serious, I woulda done something about it," she pleaded.

"Maybe so, but I was moving on. I knew you cared for me and I didn't want to hurt you. I don't want to hurt you now."

"I can't believe you're saying this to me." She stared at him, not finding the sympathy she wanted. "I thought, I thought..." she struggled to get the words out.

"I know what you thought. You thought having a baby was going to change my feelings toward you. They did change. I love you for giving me my son but that's it." He left the room and came back with a wad of toilet paper.

"Thank you," she said taking the paper. "I didn't get pregnant on purpose but when I found out I was. I thought it was a sign that we belonged together," she lied.

"I'm grateful for Gen and that's who we need to focus on. We need to be here for him even if we are not together."

She nodded and blew her nose. "So, that's it? We just gonna co-parent?"

"I'm not saying it like that. We'll always have love." He stood up and reached for her.

She just looked up at him. *Why does he have to be so damn fine? Standing here looking good with his golden-brown skin, crisp hair-cut, 7 jeans and fresh white uptowns.* She didn't miss the two carat studs in his ears, or the watch flooded with pave diamonds. He was probably choosing that bitch for her money. She stepped away from him. "There are some things in life that money can't buy. Things like real love. My love. Remember all that glitters ain't gold."

He looked confused. "What you talking about?"

"You'll figure it out," she said glancing at his watch.

"Yeah, alright, I'm gonna head out."

"Okay, so when you gonna see your son?"

"I'm gonna see him every day like I been doing."

"Humph. You got everything all planned out. You never think about me with the next man and him being around your son?" She watched his face briefly cloud over at the impact of her words.

"We'll cross that bridge when the time comes. I really don't want my seed around no other dude."

She stood close to him and stroked his dick through his shorts. "There doesn't have to be anyone around your son but you," she said reaching up to kiss him.

"'Nita don't do this."

Was that pity in his eyes? My God, he is really serious. She backed away from him and copped that immediately available Brooklyn attitude. "That's alright, I'm good. Your loss, cause trust me you will miss this," she said indicating her body. "Now get out."

"Oh, it's like that?" Sincere asked.

"Yeah, it's like that," she said walking to the door and opening it. She slammed the door hard behind him and made sure he heard the locks click.

CHAPTER 15

LOVE AND WAR

BENAE

"My hair won't fall right," Benae muttered to herself. She was standing in front of the mirror in the master bathroom. Sincere was in the guest bathroom getting ready. She dug her hand in the ceramic bowl that her parents bought her from China and searched for a bobby pin with bling. She secured the pin to a swooped section of her hair and smiled. "Much better."

Wearing a Victoria's Secret half bra and matching panty set, she pranced into the bedroom and sat on the bed to fasten the thin straps of her designer shoes around her ankle. She got up to get her dress from the closet. Sincere sauntered into the room dressed and ready to go. He looked amazing in his black suit and grey, crew neck silk shirt beneath it.

Before she could say anything, he walked up behind her and pressed his manhood against her semi-bare ass. "What you trying to do girl? You know we have to go get your parents."

"I know." She giggled. "I was just trying to put on my dress."

"You could have put on that dress before you put on those shoes." They both laughed.

She pulled the navy-blue body-con ribbed dress over her head. "Look at you," she said eyeing Sincere. "What you tryna do?' she imitated. "No, really, you look great." Sincere posed and tugged at the sleeve of his jacket. "We need to find more occasions for you to wear a suit. I haven't seen you in a suit since Rick and Kendra's wedding."

"Duly noted. Now let's get this show on the road."

They headed to the Millennium Hotel near the United Nations Headquarters. Benae's dad liked to stay there because there was less traffic and it was easier for him to get to meetings that he had at the U.N. Sincere thought it was a good location too, it was a quick trip to the Holland Tunnel which would get them to Jersey in time for dinner at Spain's restaurant. Benae called her dad's cell to let them know that they were nearby.

They pulled up in front of the hotel and Benae's parents walked out and approached the car. Sincere and Benae stepped out to greet them.

"Daddy!" Sincere watched as Benae embraced her dad and placed a kiss on her mom's cheek.

"Is this the man of the hour?" Mr. Givens inquired.

"Daddy!" Benae admonished.

"I'm just kidding with you," he said to Sincere. "Watch out I love a good- natured joke."

"Yes, he does," Benae added. "Mom, Dad this is Sincere. Sincere these are my parents Rhonda and Reed.

Sincere extended his hand. "It's a pleasure to meet you both."

"You as well," Rhonda said giving her daughter a look of approval. Sincere's good looks were not missed on her. "You're a good-looking man, I hope your name suits you."

"Thank you. I believe it does." He smiled.

"Do you go by any other name? Do your friends and associates call you, Sincere?" Mr. Givens smiled mischievously.

"No Sir, most people call me, Your Majesty," Sincere joked. They all laughed. "But you my good man, can call me Sincere or Mr. Law."

"Alright then, we'll see what comes out," Reed joked.

Benae enjoyed the banter and was glad her dad was in more of a jovial mood than usual.

Sincere opened the back door of the BMW. "Isn't this Benae's car?" Rhonda inquired. "Don't you have your own car?" She looked at Sincere.

"Mom," Benae interjected. "This is Sincere's car, I have an Audi. I got rid of the beamer a while ago."

"We could have taken Benae's car. But we thought you would prefer the space of my SUV over the sedan," Sincere explained.

"Oh, how thoughtful," Rhonda said sliding into the back seat.

On the ride to the restaurant Benae admired the easy way Sincere joked with her father and smoothed over her mother's disdain for China Town. The unpleasant smell near the Bayonne Bridge, New Jersey overall and finally the area surrounding the restaurant.

"This can't be where we are having dinner," Rhonda exclaimed as they pulled into the dark, unattended parking lot.

"No, we are eating across the street. They just provide parking over here. Don't worry Mrs. G, you're in good hands."

Benae couldn't believe that actually shut her mother up. It would not have worked if she said it. When they entered the beautifully appointed restaurant, Benae read the looks of approval on her parents' faces. The overly attentive wait staff showed them to their table, poured sparkling water and simultaneously took their drink orders. Another waiter came by and presented the specials.

"May I suggest the mussels marinara or the stuffed clams to start," Sincere said. Benae was astonished but managed to give Sincere a supportive glance as if he spoke this way all the time. "The mussels sound good," Rhonda said. "I'll have that."

"I'll try the clams then," Mr. G said.

"Good choices, you won't be disappointed," Sincere added. "I also recommend the Sangria. They have their own homemade recipe. I'll order a couple of pitchers for the table if everyone is fine with that."

The Givens clan answered yes in unison and Benae marveled at how Sincere seemingly held her family in the palm of his hand. To top things off, his recommendations did not disappoint. They went on to dine on authentic Paella, lobster stuffed with shrimp and scallops stuffed with crabmeat all served with delicious yellow rice. For dessert Sincere ordered each of the six desserts offered. The caramel flan and amaretto cake were the favorites. They ended the meal with Spanish coffee.

"I must say, that was a fabulous meal and very different than anything I remember ever having," Rhonda gushed.

Once again, Benae was shocked. Her mother who found a way to complain about everything, was completely happy.

"I second that," Reed chimed in. "Good choice." He turned to Sincere. "Talk to me. So, how did you two meet? How are things going? And what are your plans together?"

"Well Sir, we met at a nightclub in the city. I had just got back from Chicago and wanted to have a drink and listen to some music. But that night my life changed. I met your beautiful daughter and fell in love with her."

"Love at first sight?" Reed asked.

"I wouldn't say that, but I did know that she was special," he said smiling at Benae.

Most of the night, the Reeds regaled Sincere with stories about Benae as a sweet little girl who transformed into a prissy teen, and ambitious young adult. Sincere told half truths about his parents and upbringing in the Bronx. Benae was surprised it took this long for these questions to come up. They both entertained her parents with tales of how they met at The Lounge night club, Rick and Kendra's wedding, and dinner with Mr. Law. Then the conversation took one of the turns Benae dreaded but knew was inevitable.

"So, Sincere what part of the city do you reside in?" Rhonda asked.

He glanced at Benae before answering. "Brooklyn."

"What part?" Reed asked. Again, Sincere glanced her way.

"Uh, Daddy, Sincere and I live together. He and his brother had a place together in the Bronx. When his brother moved out, I asked him to come move in with me."

"I see." Mrs. Givens pursed her lips. "That was a mistake. A man is not going to buy the cow if he is getting the milk for free. And besides it's tacky. I see you still haven't learned."

Benae hated her mother's ability to make her feel stupid. She was sitting there thinking of a response when once again Sincere took over.

"Mr. and Mrs. Givens, I want you to know that I love your daughter. I've never met anyone like her. She's good to me and she loves me. I have nothing but the best intentions towards her."

"Well, that's reassuring," Rhonda said.

"Intentions are good, my man, but actions speak louder," Reed stated.

"You're right. I just have some things I want to handle to make sure I take care of her the right way. Me and my brother, uh...my brother and I are looking into starting a couple of businesses. The ones I told you about earlier."

"Looks like you picked a good one, baby girl. He has a good head on his shoulders. Old-fashioned values and no kids," Reed stated boldly. "I'm not trying to rush you into anything, but this gal is walking around with thirty-three-year old eggs." He laughed heartedly.

Benae laughed tightly. This was the second subject she was dreading. "Dad, actually Sincere has..."

"Look, Reed, you've hurt her feelings," Rhonda interrupted. "Sweetheart never mind your father. Women these days are having babies well into their forties. So, there is no need to rush."

"Rhonda her feelings are fine. She knows her dad loves to pick on her. Right baby?" Benae nodded. "When you do marry and get pregnant, you will have some gorgeous grandkids for us. You both were fortunate to have swam on the good side of the gene pool." They all laughed.

The rest of the evening continued with light-hearted conversation and good-natured jokes. At the end of the night everyone was tipsy except Sincere. Though he kept playing nice with her parents, Benae knew he had something on his mind and she knew exactly what it was.

SINCERE

As soon as they said their goodnights to Benae's parents, Sincere turned off the music and said what he had been holding back since dinner. "Yo, you made me feel like I was denying who I am and definitely my son." He could see the shock on Benae's face, but she was just gonna have to deal with it because he wasn't about to hold back his anger.

"I tried to tell them...my mom cut me off and it just didn't seem like a good time to bring it up again," Benae stammered.

"That's not even the point. I thought you told them already. You didn't tell them shit. Not even that we lived together. What kind of games you playin'?" He stared at her. "You ashamed of me or something? You think I'm not good enough for you?"

"Of course not, everything just happened so fast." Benae tried to hold his hand but he kept it tightly wrapped around the steering wheel.

"Nah, that's bullshit!" he yelled. "I've been living here for months. My son was on the way for months. Ain't shit happen fast, you handling business slow." They crossed the Brooklyn Bridge and drove home in silence. He pulled into a parking spot across the street from the house. Benae quickly grabbed the handle to get out. "Uh-uh, I'm not finished," he said grabbing her by the arm. "You cried your eyes out the day my son was born, ignored me all day, and left me with no one to come home to for two nights. You said your reason for this was because you were afraid you were gonna lose me. I told you I wasn't going nowhere. I set everything up the way it's supposed to be. I told Bonita that she had to let go and realize that we have to be here for our son and that's it. I let her know I'm here with you and how I feel about you." He watched her swipe tears away. He was so mad that he didn't feel like consoling her and he didn't. "You don't trust me, Benae. You doubted every single word I said to you and that's fucked up."

"No, that's not true." Her teary-eyed, runny-nosed face looked beautiful to him, but he didn't show it. "Sincere that's not true. It had nothing to do with that and everything to do with my parents. I know how they are and what they expect from me. I knew they wouldn't like they fact that we were living together so soon. It would seem like I am repeating mistakes I made in the past."

"You're such a hypocrite." He chuckled, not believing how she was turning things around.

"I am not a hypocrite. I was going to tell them, okay. I thought they would come over and it would naturally come up."

"Yeah? So, when was my son gonna naturally come up? When we drove past Brooklyn Hospital?" he asked sarcastically.

Benae yanked the car door open and stepped out. "You are being an unfair ass," she said and slammed the door.

He watched her strut across the street and march up the brownstone steps just to stand in the doorway holding the door open for him. He took his time exiting the car and making the short trip to their building. He brushed past her and headed up the stairs.

"Sincere," she was on his heels. "I am sorry I didn't tell my parents everything when I was supposed to. The good thing is they know now, and we will tell them about the baby as soon as possible."

He felt himself relaxing as she held him tightly from behind. He opened the door to the apartment and stepped in. Before he could turn on the light, she stepped in front of him in the darkness. "Look at me," she prodded him to face her. "I haven't even met your son. How am I supposed to talk about him, and I don't even know him? When I do bring him up to my parents, I want it to be with love and care from my heart not like secondhand gossip. Can you understand that?"

"I do," he said flipping on the light and heading to the bathroom. "It's a different type of situation!" he yelled over the sound of his pee forcefully hitting the water. "I respect that or else I could have just told them tonight myself. I wanted to see where your head was at." He closed the door and prepared to take a seat realizing he had more bathroom business to tend to.

He hung his suit jacket on the hook behind the door, took off his shoes and made himself comfortable. When he was done he took a quick shower and walked into the bedroom butt naked fully expecting Benae to be waiting in something sexy to show him how sorry she was, but when he got there she was under the covers asleep.

BONITA

"I don't believe he pulled this shit again," Shakirra shrieked. They were drinking coffee and eating the scrambled eggs, grits, and sausage, she prepared.

"I can't believe it either. I wasn't expecting it. Things were going so good," Bonita said solemnly.

"What do you think the real reason is?"

"I'm gonna take his word for it. He said he loves her, she loves him, and they live together and shit."

"Damn girl." Bonita could see that Shakirra felt bad for her. "You just gonna let him play you like that? I mean just let him go to some new bitch while you been here for him?"

"I don't like that he's trying to act like he's coming correct for this bitch. If anything I'm used to him at least lying about bitches and keeping them in they place but this is new to me. Still no matter what, I got his son, his only child and I know he loves his son. I ain't gon' lie though, I thought having my baby was going to get him to come back to me," her voice cracked. "I really did."

"Don't cry girl. Like you said you baby mama now and he ain't going nowhere." Shakirra walked over to her friend and wrapped her arms around her from behind. "You worked too hard and y'all been through too much. He's not going nowhere. He's just setting up that game bullshit. So, he can go back and tell her he told you what's up so she'd put down her guard and trust that ain't nothing going on with you. But on the low he gone be right here like he always been," Shakirra said walking back to her chair and taking a sip of her coffee.

"I know but I don't want to be his side chick. Why should I settle for that?" Bonita said angrily.

"You're not settling, you just waiting him out," Shakirra explained. "If he come over and want some pussy you gonna tell him no?"

"No," Bonita said with a slight smile.

"I know you're not and you're not gonna say no to getting some money, making him something to eat or spending time with his son. So, he's basically still your man. When he gets tired of the next chick, he'll be right back home with you. Let that motherfucker know just how much you love him."

"I know you're right but I'm sicka this shit. I just had a baby for him, and this is what he do? What's up with that? I don't understand why now?"

"That is something you have to ask him because I honestly don't understand that shit either. Ask him if he plans on bringing Gen around her and ask how would he feel if you have him around the next man," Shakirra suggested. "I know he don't want no dude around Genuwen."

"He made that perfectly clear."

"Uh huh, thought so." Shakirra gave Bonita a knowing look. "Now all you have to do is set it up. Get one of your pocket dudes and chill with him outside or something when Sincere is coming around."

Bonita started laughing. "That's a good idea." She put up her hand for a high-five and Shakirra slapped it with relish.

"Okay, now here's the other part. You can't forget about what's her name...Bean? Beano?" They fell out laughing. "You can't leave her out. Make sure you are the baby mama from hell." They laughed some more. "Yes, call his ass for every little thing, all times of the night. Be super needy like Kendra said."

Bonita looked impressed. "When did you get so smart?"

"Bitch I always been smart. What I need to do is get my ass back in school and parlay these skills into a career."

"That or find a way to make some money advising women how to deal with these negroes from the hood. They are definitely a different breed." They fell out laughing again.

"Girl let me go pick up J.J."

"Okay," Bonita said reluctantly.

"Everything is gonna work out fine. Sincere does not deserve you but if you want him, you will have him. Trust me." Bonita did.

CHAPTER 16

ANNIVERSARY

BENAE

The gentle prodding and thumping on her back released the pressure held within her tense muscles. Benae often treated herself to the benefits of Magda's deep tissue massages, but today was special. Sincere had accompanied her. She briefly lifted her head and glanced over at him as he received the same treatment from Magda's colleague, Irina. Content that he was relaxed she placed her face back in the oval opening on the table. The day had been peaceful, fun, and relaxing. Pretty much the way things have progressed between them since the blowout after her parents visit. They started the day with a shower together and a quickie, followed by a run along the promenade. Their spa appointments were at 2:00 so they had time to drive into the city for a bite to eat and take their time walking the few blocks to the Spa.

"How you feeling, baby?" Benae asked after the massages were done and they were alone.

Sincere stretched. "Great. I have to get these more often."

"Good," she said sliding off her massage table, walking over to his. She stood in between his legs and wrapped her arms around him. "Now let's get dressed and continue with the rest of our special day." She kissed him on nose, then released him and took a step backward.

Sincere held her where she was. "Thank you, baby. Today has been great. You don't have to do anything else. I appreciate everything so far and I love that you took the time to plan this day for us. I love you, Happy Anniversary."

"Happy Anniversary! I love you too, babe, that's why I did it. I want you to know how much I love and appreciate you. I feel guilty at times that you are with me instead of with your son, but after talking to Chrissy and Ming they made me realize that it was your choice and I should be happy. I want you to know that I am so happy that you didn't leave me. I am so in love with you Sincere Law."

"Well, damn, I wasn't expecting all that, but Chrissy and Ming are right. It was my choice to choose you. It doesn't mean I'm not choosing my son. I love my son, I love you, and I love what we have built together. We've been through a lot for this to be year one." He leaned forward and kissed her gently on the lips, pulled away to look into her eyes then leaned in and kissed her again, this time his tongue found hers and he gripped her ass tightly.

"Babe, we need to stop and get dressed," Benae moaned. "We're going to get kicked out of here.

"Now you saying no?" He stood up and patted her on the butt.

They retreated to their separate locker rooms and Benae planned the rest of their Saturday. *Maybe we can go to Benihana. I've never been, and I've always wanted to go,* she thought. Playfully, she pulled out her cell phone and called Sincere.

"Hello, I'd like to speak to Mr. Law please?"

He played along, "Speaking."

"Well, Mr. Law Ms. Givens has decided to invite you to stay the night with her at the Renaissance Times Square. The remainder of the evening will include dinner at the world-renowned Benihana restaurant, followed by two desserts. The first provided by Serendipity, the second provided by Ms. Givens."

"Sounds good, sounds real good," she could hear the smile in his voice. "You're too much, girl."

"She thought you would be pleased. She'll meet you in the lobby in ten minutes," she said ending the call. She re-applied her make-up and pulled the white strapless sundress up over her hips. She slipped on her favorite turquoise sling backs and swung her white Tory Burch tote bag over her shoulder.

Sincere reached for her hand as they walked back to her car. Benae loved when he held her hand it made her feel like she was in her rightful place in the world. "I figured we can check into the hotel and park the car there and put our bags down."

The ambiance of the Renaissance Hotel suited Benae's tastes. She always stayed at the Renaissance when she traveled on business. Once they stepped into the tastefully appointed room, Benae flung herself onto the King-sized bed. She noticed Sincere glance at his phone again. It was the second time he checked it but didn't answer it. She sat up and patted the space beside her on the bed. She watched him inhale and exhale deeply before making his way over to the bed.

"What's the matter? she asked.

"Nothing."

"Are you sure? You seem like you have something on..." He cut her off.

"I have to get this. It's Bonita and she texted 911."

Benae's face and heart filled with concern as she intently listened to the one-sided conversation.

"Yeah, what's going on? He what? How the fuck that happen? Damn, I'm in the city. I'm on my way now. No just meet me there." Before Benae could ask he started, "She said he fell off the bed and busted his head."

"Oh, my God," Benae said horrified.

"Come on we have to go to the hospital." He picked up his unpacked bag signaling to Benae that she should do the same. She quickly threw the items she'd unpacked back into her bag and rushed out to catch up to Sincere who was already at the elevator doors.

SINCERE

Sincere knew he was driving recklessly, but he didn't care. Fortunately, the traffic was pretty light for a Saturday afternoon in the summer. Focusing on bobbing and weaving through the parade of cars was better than seeing visions of his son hurting. Just the thought of it hurt and it pissed him off. He could tell his driving was making Benae nervous by the way she stared ahead with her hands gripped tightly together in her lap. He also knew that she wasn't going to say nothing about his driving, even though it was her car. He liked that about her. She was the type of woman that knew when to shut the fuck up. He found a spot near the hospital entrance and the desire to get to his son consumed him. He didn't realize that he had turned off the ignition but left the keys inside. He strode purposefully through the sliding doors. Benae grabbed the keys and ran behind him until she caught up to him.

Timidly, she tugged at his arm. "Babe, listen to me for a minute." Coldly, he glanced down at her and her grip on his arm. Surprisingly, she didn't back off as he expected. "You need to calm down. You're no good for anyone like this. Your son needs to feel your love, not your anger." Her last sentence provided the words that got through.

Within himself, he took a step back and redirected his emotions. She trailed behind him as the headed into the emergency room. Sincere scanned the crowded room until he spotted Bonita gently rocking the baby back and forth.

"How's he doing?" Sincere asked reaching out to touch his son.

"He has a gash on the side of his head." Bonita pulled back the gauze she was holding against the baby's head to reveal a nasty cut that was about two inches long but deep. "The Triage Nurse said that he will probably need staples."

"What they waiting on?" Sincere said loudly looking around to face the Triage windows.

"We have to wait for the Pediatrician. There's only one on call today."

"Figures," Sincere said. "Let me get him." He reached for his son who smiled up at his dad as soon as he saw his face. "Hey, son, daddy's here. Daddy's here now. It's okay." He looked around the room and saw Benae sitting across the room. "Be right back." He walked away before Bonita could protest.

"Hey." He walked up to Benae. "See my son. He's a little banged up but he's a trooper. Not even crying or nothing," he said proudly.

Benae stood up and glanced down at Genuwen who just looked back at her uninterested. "Aww he's adorable. He looks more like you in person." Sincere brought Benae up to speed on the baby's prognosis. "It shouldn't be too much longer before he sees the doctor. So, let me get back over there and see what's up." He could tell Benae was going to give him a kiss, but he shifted Genuwen to his left arm effectively thwarting her attempt. For some reason he didn't want 'Nita to see them kiss. He knew he had hurt her enough, and he must say she was handling it better than he thought she would.

Uh-oh, I spoke to soon, he thought. By the look on her face Bonita was pissed. Before he could sit down beside her, she exploded. "What the hell you bring her for? This is about our baby. There's no reason for her to be here."

"We were together when you called. What was I supposed to do, drop her off first?" he said keeping his voice low.

"You could have just left her ass home."

"Who said, we was home? You know what, now is not the time for this, man," he said aggravated. "Now tell me how this happened to him?"

Bonita rolled her eyes and began relaying the events that led to Gen's slip from her arms onto the side of the tub. As she was wrapping up the story the baby's name was called. This time Bonita was spared because Sincere was about to rip into her for not being more careful when bathing the baby. He grew angrier still when he had to hold down his son so that the doctor could apply staples to close the gash on his head. By the time Genuwen calmed down and had undergone his final round of observation, the sun had set, and it was getting dark. The parents walked down the long corridor drained from the day's events.

"So, what you just gonna leave us now and go home?" Bonita asked with slight attitude.

"No, I just want to let Benae know everything's good. I'm gonna carry him and walk you home." He decided this was best since the hospital was just a few blocks away. He was happy when his words had the desired effect and the scowl on her face was replaced with relief.

"Okay, hurry up."

Sincere jetted through the heavy swinging doors and headed toward the waiting room. "Mr. Law," someone called out to him.

"Yeah." He turned around and saw that it was the pretty Pediatrics receptionist.

"This lady kept asking how long you were going to be then finally she just said to tell you that she was going home. So, I'm letting you know." She smiled sexily.

Sincere couldn't help but notice her hazel eyes and full lips colored in a coral tone that complimented her brown complexion.

"How long ago was that?" he asked taking a step towards her.

"About half an hour. She was upset when she left. She barely said thank you when I complimented her outfit."

"Damn," Sincere said more to himself than to this girl who really seemed to enjoy her role as messenger.

"But as they say," the pretty stranger said stepping from behind the counter that separated them. "When one door closes another one opens. Now a girl like me wouldn't have left," she said smiling up at him knowingly.

"It's all good."

"Why don't you take my number so you can call me tonight? Your girlfriend is gone, your baby mama is gonna be tending to the baby. You need someone to tend to you."

That shit sounds good, Sincere thought. He pondered the situation. On one hand the last thing he needed was to add another female to the mix but on the other hand she may be just what he needed to release the tension of the tug-o-war he was obviously in with Bonita and Benae. Plus, with the stunt Benae pulled by leaving with the car and Bonita getting an attitude because Benae came with him, he didn't really feel like being bothered with either one of them. *Fuck it,* he thought. He pulled his phone from his pocket. "What's your name?"

"Angela."

He'd taken her number and put his phone back in his pocket as Bonita came through the doors. "Come on, let's get him home," he said putting his arm around Bonita and winking at Angela.

BONITA

Bonita made sure Gen was fed and sleeping peacefully before she pulled out her phone and texted Shakirra, *call me.* She stood in the doorway of her bedroom watching Sincere propped up on her bed like he lived here. "Boy, get off my bed like that."

He didn't move. "You got something to eat, I'm starving. I didn't eat since breakfast."

"Don't you think you need to go home and eat?"

"What I can't get a meal here no more?"

She pointed at him. "Hold that thought,' she said stepping into the hallway but lingering near her bedroom door.

"Hello," she purred into the phone. She laughed giddily. "I have to call you back. No for real I'm gonna call you back in a few minutes. I had a long day and I just got home. I need to take a quick soak in the tub. I'll call you when I get in bed. Stop it. Get your mind out the gutter." She laughed again. "Okay, I'll call you back in a little while. Bye." She ended the call and walked back into the room nonchalantly.

Sincere stood up. She could tell he was emotionally affected by her phone call. He put a puzzled smile on his face and asked, "Yo, who was that?"

"No one you know," she said flouncing down on the bed.

He put on the sexy grin that she was all too familiar with, but she was not going to give into it, so she turned her attention to the TV. "Listen, I don't know what you trying to do. I know you still love me. Whoever, you trying to talk to can't replace Sin, baby. Don't play yourself by running to the first man that throws you some attention," he said his cockiness on 100.

Two can play that game, she thought. She leaned back on the bed propping her breasts up and giving Sincere a sultry look. "Now you listen to me. You see all this woman, right here. I ain't gonna be lonely whether I still love you or not."

Sincere smirked. "'Nita I know you better than that. Why don't you just chill."

"That's what I am about to do. I think it's time for you to go home."

"A'ight, no problem. I see you got a call to make."

"Yes, I do," she said walking to the door. "Goodnight, Sincere."

"Goodnight, Bonita," he said brushing past her.

She closed the door and suppressed laughter. Sincere was making this easier than she thought. She walked into the bathroom, turned on the faucet and began to fill the tub. She decided to take a hot bath after all then she would call Shakirra back and let her know the plan was working.

CHAPTER 17

MAKIN' PLANS

BENAE

"It's just a lot harder than I thought it would be," Benae complained to Chrissy and Ming. They were sitting outside on the boardwalk having lunch on the Jersey Shore. Ming suggested they drive out there and relax by the beach.

"Not to cut you off," Chrissy interrupted. "But this steak is the bomb, nice and rare the way I like it. And this steak sauce...girl, I like this place."

"I'm glad you like it," Ming responded. "It's a little place I found when I was out here doing business."

"I've been meaning to ask, what is it exactly you do?" Chrissy asked between chews.

"I'm a Jill of all trades, suffice it to say I'm never broke and will never be broke."

"I hear that," Chrissy said.

Benae decided it was time to bring the conversation back to her. "Ahem, as I was saying. I need help deciding what to do. I know some women would have left the moment they heard about the baby and some would say the pregnancy happened before they were in the picture and stick by their man regardless. I feel like I'm somewhere in the middle."

"Listen you and I are sisters and we are going to be sister-in-laws. The sooner you realize that the better. Like Tru says once you're in it, you're in it. You can't just run away on love."

"Well, too late now. We should have told her that before she stranded him at the hospital. You have to admit that was funny," Chrissy said laying down her fork for a few seconds.

Benae joined the laughter in spite of herself. "Seriously, I wasn't trying to be funny. It just felt stupid sitting there. I didn't like that he was sitting with her, but I also felt like he shouldn't have sat with me. After they were gone so long, I realized I had no purpose there."

"Bingo!" Ming exclaimed. "That's it right there. You have to play your position. You're Wifey. He comes home to you every day and lays with you every night. If he has to play family man with his baby moms at times so what. Let them do that and you be sure to be there for him at home. Let no awkwardness, no confusion, or no petty bullshit come between you and your man."

"Damn, Ming," Benae scowled. "You are so blunt."

"Benae, she may be harsh but she's right. Getting overly involved will only aggravate you and you know how you get when you're upset."

"So, I have to apologize again?"

"No, what happened when he came home that night anyway?"

Benae shrugged. "Nothing, he got in the bed with me and said I was wrong for leaving. I skipped over that and asked about Gen. He told me he had to get some staples and how traumatic it was to watch. I told him I was sorry that he had to go through that but I'm glad that the baby's okay. After that I told him we need to re-celebrate our Anniversary. He said we would, and we went to sleep."

"Well, it sounds like that issue is over, don't bring it back up again." Chrissy ate the last of her rib eye. "That steak was so good. If I wouldn't look greedy, I would order another one." She burped. "Ooh, excuse me."

"Chris, are you pregnant?" Benae asked giving her the side eye.

"Yes, six weeks," Chrissy beamed.

"Me too," Ming sing-songed.

"No way, you heifers must be kidding me!"

"I'm due April second," Chrissy said.

"My due date is March fourteenth."

Benae watched as the two grinned at each other and squeezed each other's hands. "When were you planning on saying something?" Benae looked side to side at her friends.

"Today," they both said in unison.

"We've been together all day and neither of you said anything. What were you waiting for? For me to figure it out, like I just did?" Benae was feeling a way.

Chrissy leaned toward Benae. "Benae Givens, you know you're my girl but it's always about you. All this time we've been listening to you. After that we have to find a solution for you and finally, we have to make sure you're okay. Then, we can talk about what's happening in our lives..." She paused and looked at Ming. "You're kind of new, but I know you know what I'm talking about."

"I was just waiting for you to ask me about my day...my life but I was going to get to it even if you didn't."

Benae refused to accept the picture they painted of her. "I'm not like that all the time. Only when I'm going through something. Tell the truth, Chrissy."

"I told the truth and I'm sticking to it."

"Okay, well, then...I have one question for each of you. Chrissy, is Greg happy about baby number three after telling you he was fine with two? Ming, is Tru happy and does he want to get married?"

"That was two questions," Ming said.

"Whatever, answer them."

"Tru is okay. Not that you asked, but I'm very happy to have our first child. He hopes it a boy and so do I. As for marriage, I think he'll marry me, but we haven't spoken about it."

"Congratulations, sweetie," Benae said, standing up and hugging Ming. "Congratulations to you as well, Chrissy." She squeezed her friend and kissed the top of her head.

"Well, Greg's not happy. He keeps telling me we don't need another one," Chrissy said flagging down their waiter.

"It's alright. He will come around," Benae said.

Ming added, "Yeah, you know how men are."

"Yeah, let me get another grilled steak no sides and another lemonade with extra lemons." Chrissy placed her second order. "Anyway, I'm happy and I'm hoping for my little girl."

"We're hoping for her, too." Benae smiled at her friend.

"Can I get you ladies anything else?" the waiter interrupted.

"I'll have the chocolate brownie with vanilla ice cream," Ming ordered.

"I'm good," Benae said.

They sat in silence for a moment looking out at the beach and enjoying the breeze. Benae took a sip of her Chardonnay and sighed. "Okay, I guess you two are right about me," Benae said feigning sadness. "I have an issue and I need a solution."

"I already know what it is. You want to get pregnant now and you know Sincere ain't ready because he just had one. So, you want to know how to get around that little problem," Ming said knowingly.

Benae nodded slowly. "That shit you do doesn't even surprise me anymore."

"And it shouldn't surprise me how needy you are, but it does. We shouldn't have to tell you how to seduce your man and get him to cum inside you. You got dick in your bed every night and you can't get knocked up. Come on Benae think," Chrissy added.

Benae was quiet for a second. "Okay, enough of the insults tonight alright. Has pregnancy made both of you mean? Anyway," she continued. "It's not that simple. Since Genuwen was born Sincere has made it very clear he doesn't want another baby anytime soon. He warned me that it didn't work for Bonita and for me not to get any ideas. I use my diaphragm and sometimes he asks if I put it in. I don't want to lie."

Ming shook her head at Benae pitifully. "I see you do need help. This man kept a whole pregnancy from you for months and you worried about lying to him. Miss me with the bullshit."

Benae was getting a little put off by Ming's slick mouth. She picked up her glass and took a long sip.

"Or you can do one of my moves," Chrissy chimed in. "And wake him up in the middle of the night. Give him some head and get on top. He'll think he's dreaming and fill you up."

"You know when you're ovulating right?" Ming asked. Benae gave her the *really* face. "Good, hold out on giving him some until you're ovulating. He'll be backed up and not thinking about no protection."

"So, you really think I should do this? I'm afraid because I could end up a single mom."

"No, you won't. You will end up married," Ming said emphatically.

"How can you be so sure?"

"All I can say is this, brothers talk, and men talk to their women. Tru told me some things about Sincere and he wants to get married to someone like you. He wants what Rick has with Kendra."

"No way," Benae said, shaking her head. "Sincere hates Kendra."

"He does but he loves her ambition and style. She's from the hood but she ain't no hood chick. And you better not say a word, but he told Tru he wants to marry you. They are supposed to pull one last lick so that he can get you this ring you showed him in Tiffany's."

"*A lick?* What's that? It sounds illegal."

Ming glanced at Chrissy. "Is she for real?"

Chrissy nodded and gave Ming a look that told her she said too much. "Perfect timing," she said removing her napkin from the table and placing it back in her lap so that the waiter could sit her plate down. "Yes," Chrissy exclaimed rubbing her hands together greedily.

"Nice try, Chrissy. You didn't distract me," Benae said dryly.

"Don't worry about the boys. Just focus on locking down your relationship so you can stop going back and forth with this," Ming said. "I'm telling you the ring is for the taking. It's up to you to seal the deal."

SINCERE

Sincere walked through the door and immediately detected the fresh smell of lemons and pine. He looked down and sure enough the wood floors were glistening. All around were the signs of a freshly cleaned house indicating that Honey had been there. He came to love Honey coming through every two weeks, especially after too many times of running out of clean clothes and listening to Benae complaining. He kicked off his work boots to allow his feet to breathe after 12 hours of suffocation. The uniform was next. He stripped down to his underwear and laid across the bed on his back. The stars in the celestial scenery on the ceiling seemed to twinkle at him.

He chuckled and thought about the crazy woman he was in love with which in turn led him to think about making more money. It's not that he cared about her making more money, he just wanted to bring more to the table. He agreed with one of his favorite rap lyrics, *If you can't get paid on an earth this big, you're worthless kid, don't even deserve to live.* The fifty thousand that he made last summer was gone. Getting that money was fast and easy, but risky. Almost every day Tru and his Chicago connect presented him with compelling reasons to get into business with them. He would have more money for his son, his woman, and his overall lifestyle.

Tru made it very tempting with his tales of easy money and showboating. Sincere trusted his brother but he was too well-known in Brooklyn, The Bronx and Chicago's Southside. In the streets, he was practically guilty by association because everyone knew Tru was his brother. Still that was not the main reason he refrained from getting back in business with his brother. Other than the risk of getting locked up and not being around for his son, he didn't like or trust Ming. She was too involved in Tru's dealings for Sincere's comfort. Something about her just didn't sit right with him. More important than all of it, he simply wanted to do his own thing – no partners, no negotiating just him running the show. So, although he approached Tru for a cut of his business he decided against making that move. The more he thought about it, he knew exactly what he was going to do. He was shaken out of his thoughts by the vibration of his phone. He reached over the bed to pull the phone out of his pants pocket. It was after 7:00 and Benae was calling from her office.

"Hey, baby, calling to let you know I'm on my way home now."

"They got you there late again, huh? I thought you were about to walk through the door?"

"Yeah, the International Board meetings are scheduled next week, and we have a lot of preparing to do."

"I hope you didn't use up all your energy. I got something for ya."

He could hear the smile in her voice. "That sounds good. I can use some loving."

"Then stop wasting time and bring that ass home."

"Alright, I'm leaving now. Want me to pick up dinner? I was thinking the Dominican spot."

"Cool, I'll call it in, so it'll be ready when you cross the bridge. You want your usual right?"

"Yes, babe, oxtails, white rice and cabbage."

"I got you. Now, come on home. I miss you." He stood up and adjusted his dick. *Let me get back to Tru real quick and then check on my son before I order this food.* Tru didn't pick up so he just left a message and called Bonita. "Hey, what's up? How's Gen doing today?"

"He's okay. His nose is a little stuffy and he's been very cranky. He doesn't want me to put him down."

"I told you that was gonna happen when you kept holding him all the time."

"I don't hold him all the time," she barked. "You not here to see what I do so don't tell me what I do."

"Dang, what's wrong with you?"

"I'm sorry," she said sounding like she was on the verge of tears. "I feel so overwhelmed at times. I'm so tired. He wore me out today."

Sincere felt bad. He knew things would be easier for her if he was in the picture more often. He saw his son almost every day, but it wasn't enough. "You know what, let me come get him sometime and give you a break. He's almost six months and you know he loves being with me."

"Wow, I wasn't expecting that," Bonita said. "And he gets so happy when you come by. The question I have is, are you going to have him around that chick you live with?"

"'Nita, she lives here so he'll have to be around her."

"Where's he gonna sleep at? I don't want him on y'all bed even on his blanket."

Sincere thought about how clean his and Benae's house was compared to Nita's but left it as a thought and proceeded with positivity. "We can get him a crib over here matter of fact he can have his own room." When Bonita didn't say anything, he continued, "I'm off tomorrow so what I'll do is get him all set up here then come pick him up. I'll bring him back Saturday or Sunday. Alright?"

"Alright, Sin, we'll see how this goes but you betta answer every time I call."

"I will as long as you ain't ODing. There's no need to be doing extra calling. He'll be with me and he'll be fine." He thought that would be it and he could get on with his night since tomorrow he was going to be on daddy duty, but Bonita kept droning on and on. She was usually long winded, but she was killing him tonight. "'Nita, Nita," he interrupted. "Listen, I got to go. I'll see you tomorrow afternoon. Give him a kiss for me." He ended the call. "Damn, that girl can talk," he said aloud. He was about to make the call to the Dominican restaurant when Benae called him.

"Babe, what happened? They don't have the order," she sounded confused.

"Damn, I got sidetracked and forgot. You mind stopping by the Jamaican spot instead. I want some Jerk chicken."

"Actually, that sounds better. I can go for a beef patty and coco bread."

He started the shower in the master bathroom. As he worked the soap into a creamy lather and sloshed it between his legs, the heat he felt earlier returned. He couldn't wait to get inside Benae, she had put him off the last few days complaining of headaches and cramps. Today it sounded like she was good to go and he was more than ready. If all went as planned, he would have Benae as an appetizer, the food she was bringing for dinner and a good night's sleep for dessert. He would be 100% ready for the changes that were sure to come.

BONITA

What a difference a day makes, Bonita thought to herself. The breeze coming in through the slightly opened window chilled Bonita's arms, subconsciously she sat rubbing them before leaving her seat at the kitchen table and closing the window, pausing to look out into the gloomy skies that threatened to let loose a barrage of rain at any moment. She tossed her breakfast dishes in the sink and retreated to her bedroom. Gen was down for his first nap of the day and Bonita debated between grabbing a shower or grabbing a nap. Without really thinking about it she pulled back the covers and got in. Lying there she picked up the photo of her and Sincere that sat on her nightstand. In it he stood behind her with his arms wrapped around her as they both smiled for the camera.

"We were so in love, what happened to us?" she wondered. Now that he was picking the baby up for visits at his house the distance between them grew. She knew he still cared but he was definitely focused on co-parenting right now. No matter how often she called or complained he never said anything negative about her antics. God, she loved him and wanted him so bad. She needed to talk to him.

"What up, shawty," he answered playfully.

"I miss you," Bonita said knowing that she sounded sexy and vulnerable.

"How you miss me when I come through or call every day?"

"It's not the same," she whined. "Don't you miss me? Don't you miss what we had?"

"What's going on here? Somebody die on TV?"

"Stop playing, I'm serious. We should spend some time together and have fun like we used to. Remember that time we went to Great Adventure? That was the first time we told each other I love you."

"Yeah, I remember," Sincere said softly.

"Sin, I know you live with this girl and you think y'all all in love but what we had was real. I gave you my all. I was good to you and I was always faithful. I still can't believe you left me to raise our son alone."

"First of all, nobody left you to raise him alone don't say that shit no more. Second, sometimes I do miss what we had then I remember all the jealousy, arguing and us just not getting along."

"You're only focusing on the bad times it wasn't always like that. And if I recall correctly, you gave me plenty of reasons to argue and feel jealous," she retorted.

"Probably so, but that's why all that is in the past."

"*Probably so,*" she mocked. "But you still love me. You know you do."

"'Nita, we've been through all this before. It is what it is now," he huffed.

"Don't get frustrated. I just have some things I want to remind you of because I really think that you forgot." For the next thirty minutes she regaled him with a trip through memory lane, from the day they met, highlights of their sexcapades, struggling through hard times and of course the birth of their son. She ended by telling him, "If you think some new chick is going to come in between all of that. You are wrong. I don't give two shits about her. So, what we had we can still have. Eventually, you will realize what you have and come home because at the end of the day Gen did not ask to be here. He deserves a home with two parents."

"I hear what you're saying, and I see how much you love me. Let me get some things together and I will make some changes."

Bonita couldn't believe what she was hearing. "Thank you, because I can't stop loving you."

"Love you, too. Talk to you later."

Still in bed and feeling good about herself for not listening to Shakirra and doing things her way, she fantasized about making love to Sincere. Hopefully, next time he came by he would *bless her* as he called it with some dick. Spreading her legs, she reached down and gently stroked her clitoris. The small circular motions quickly got her juices flowing. Keeping her eyes closed, she focused on the mental picture she had of Sincere's head buried between her legs. She slid her left hand up to fondle both her breasts while she continued pleasuring herself with her right. She slid a couple of fingers inside and rubbed her clit against her fingers as she stroked herself.

"Ooohhh," she moaned as the pleasure she was giving herself increased.

She began to swivel her hips feeling more excited by the sexy movement. Remembering that her mother was in the living room she got up and closed the door. This time she took off her clothes, got under the covers and spread her legs wide and continued fingering herself. She propped herself up on her pillows and caressed both of her large breasts.

"Mmmm," she moaned as she pulled them both towards her mouth and licked her nipples.

She continued to lick and suck one of them and stroked her pussy with her other hand until she lifted her ass up off the bed and gave into a luscious cum. When she was done, she hugged her pillow and thought about the vibrator she hid in her closet. Still feeling frisky she turned up the volume on the TV and set the vibrator on high until she was undone again.

CHAPTER 18

FEELING GOOD

BENAE

Benae enjoyed the feeling of Sincere's arm around her shoulders as they walked down 19th Street. Usually, he held her hand but tonight he held her close and allowed her to slip her arm around his waist. In fact, she realized he had been extra nice all day. Who was she to complain? They had seen the movie she wanted to see and were now on the way to her favorite soul food spot. She knew this was his way of showing her love before she left to spend Labor Day weekend with her family at Martha's Vineyard. She wanted him to come with her, but he couldn't get the time off. To EMS, Labor Day was just another day and they were usually understaffed on holidays. They had called ahead, and their orders were ready for pick-up when they arrived. The smothered chicken, mac and cheese and potato salad was for her and baked chicken, mac and cheese and collard greens was his, along with a slice of red velvet cake. On the drive home he played soft music and held her hand with one hand and drove with the other. She loved when he was in a romantic mood. He was so vulnerable and open with a hint of sensuality that only awakened the sensuality within her.

They walked into the stifling apartment. "It's hot in here," Benae said.

"Yeah, it feels hotter in here than it is outside," Sincere responded while adjusting the Nest thermostat. "No wonder," he said. "The thermostat was off."

"Sorry, my bad," Benae said. "I was freezing this morning and I turned it off. Anyway, leave it off. Let's open the window for a change!" she yelled from the bedroom. "What are we watching while we eat?"

"Let's watch Luke Cage. We're up to the fifth episode, right?" Sincere asked, reaching for the remote and turning on the Smart TV. He sat the food on the coffee table and began pulling out containers of food. "Babe, can you bring me something to drink?" he yelled out to her.

"Okay, just give me a second!" Benae yelled back while changing into one of his t-shirts.

She didn't want to put on more clothes since she was definitely having some goodbye sex before she left. This was the first time she and Sincere would be apart from one another in the year they had been together. She trusted him but thought making sure he got some before she left couldn't hurt. She hurried down the hallway into the kitchen and poured them both some Minute Maid Berry Punch. She carried the drinks into the living and scurried over to the sofa to catch the beginning of the episode. She noticed Sincere had removed his pants and was digging into his food like he didn't know where his next meal was coming from.

After they ate, instead of getting on top of her as she expected, he laid beside her and pulled her on top. "Ohhh, you gonna let me take control tonight, huh?"

"I didn't say that. I just want to see you. I get a better view this way."

"Yeah, but now I'm going to get rug burns," she whined.

He ignored her, pulled her down to him and began tantalizing her breasts with his tongue. She moaned and grinded herself against his hardness as he pleasured both breasts simultaneously. Without removing her breasts from his mouth, she lifted her hips and tugged his underwear down until he was able to kick them off the rest of the way. She pulled away from his mouth and held his erect dick straight up so that she could easily slide down its length. She closed her eyes and felt him pulsing inside her. Her wetness oozed out of her completely coating him from head to balls. Initially, she rode him slowly up and down. She closed her eyes and was basically in her own world until she opened her eyes a bit and saw Sincere staring at her. He looked so fucking sexy. She leaned down and kissed him hard, sloppily dipping her tongue in and out of his mouth while quickening her pace riding him. She rode him furiously unable to contain any semblance of control. He sat up with his back against the couch and once more attacked her breasts. She was done. She gripped the pillows on the sofa as the waves of her orgasm built within her.

"Come with me baby," she panted.

"Oh, shit, yeah." Sincere moaned, while taking control of her hips and busting his load. "Damn, girl, woo that was needed."

"You drive me crazy. I love having sex with you," she panted

"I know you do." He smirked.

"You're so conceited."

"Yeah, and you love it," he said slapping her naked ass.

"Let me get up and finish packing," Benae said heading to the bedroom.

"Babe, when we going shopping for new living furniture? I'm tired of this light ass couch. All this is you we need some me in here."

"I know, bae, we can start looking when I get back. I'd like to have the place redecorated by the holidays!" she yelled from the bedroom.

She packed while Sincere laid in bed half watching her, and half watching TV. She got in bed with the intention of giving him some head, but they just talked into the wee hours of the morning and eventually fell asleep. Later that morning, Sincere drove Benae to JFK International Airport. He stayed with her while she checked-in. When the time came for her to head to the gate, she felt an overwhelming sense of sadness.

"Babe, are you crying?" Sincere asked concern etched onto his fine features.

"I feel sad leaving you. We haven't been apart since we met."

He chuckled. "Benae, you're only going to be away four days. I'll be right here to get you on Tuesday, and you know I'll call you every day."

"I know." The emotions just came rushing through. "It amazes me how much I love you." She smiled.

He took his thumbs and wiped the tears from her eyes. "That's better," he said pulling her close to him.

Benae felt that their love couldn't get any better. She hugged him back and they kissed warmly. "Okay, I'll call you when I arrive." She stepped away and headed towards the gate. "Love you."

"Love you, too," he said watching her.

She turned her head slightly to see if he was still standing there watching her walk away and he was. She smiled and chided herself for allowing herself to feel so insecure about leaving him alone for a long weekend. "That man loves my dirty drawers. I have absolutely nothing to worry about." She boarded the plane, plugged in her earphones, positioned her neck pillow, and went to sleep.

SINCERE

Sincere hurried home to pack and get ready. He had a getaway of his own planned. He had done everything he could to keep Benae happy and focused. He didn't want her to think anything was up with him and he knew how suspicious she could be. He and Tru were flying to Chicago to take part in a big gun deal that he put together. He threw a couple pair of jeans, shirts, sneakers, and caps into a duffle bag. He packed some toiletries into a smaller bag and threw that in too.

"Hey, Meth, come here boy." The almost full-grown dog came bounding toward Sincere. "Hey, boy," Sincere said fluffing Meth's ears. He let him lick him to his heart's content. "I have to go away for a minute. You gonna go stay with grandpa for a couple of days."

Meth stubbornly tugged against the leash and planted himself firmly on the ground in front of Dad's apartment building. Sincere, fed-up with coaxing the pup, yanked hard on the leash harshly bringing him to his feet. Leon walked outside of his building just in time to witness Meth's reluctance to visit him.

"Hey, dad."

"Hey what's going on? What's up with the dog?" Leon asked.

"I don't' know, but ever since Benae got him spoiled with his bed and toys and a water dish that releases cold water, he never wants to leave."

Henry laughed out loud. "Well, I wouldn't want to leave either, especially not to come over here." Henry kneeled and petted Meth on the head. "Pass me the leash. I'll take him to the park and tire him out a little. I don't want him howling in my house."

"Okay, I'll take his stuff upstairs and wait for Tru to pick me up."

"I hope you're not getting into no trouble. You got your life on track, Sin. Don't let your brother and his bullshit bring you down."

"It's nothing like that. It's a legit opportunity to invest and make some money. I ain't gonna be with EMT all my life. Man, I got a son to get out of the projects and when I do ask Benae to marry me, I want her to feel comfortable that things are taken care of on my end. I don't want to worry about money."

"Okay, son, I understand. Just don't do nothing stupid. Don't let money rule you."

As Sincere headed down the stairs of the second-floor walk-up, he could hear the sounds of Tru's souped up music system beating hard. He quickly hopped into the Escalade that still looked like it came straight from the showroom.

"Yo' man, you hungry? I'm not eating no airport food," Tru lamented.

"We only have two and a half hours before our flight. I need to make a stop, too."

"For what?" Tru said irritated. He turned to frown at his brother before turning his attention back to the road.

"I need to leave the just in case money with 'Nita."

"Why you ain't do that before? You know we on the clock."

"I didn't have time. I had to take Benae to the airport, pack and drop off Meth. I been busy all day."

"Why you ain't leave the stash with your girl? You gon' trust that broad like that? You know she sheisty.

"Man, I'm not getting into that with you, right now. Just drop me off. She's waiting for me. Plus, I want to give my son some love before I go."

"Alright, I'll stop over there. While you're doing that, I'll hit up that KFC on the Ave. From there I'll hop on the BQE to the Van Wyck and we'll be at the airport in no time."

BONITA

I don't know who Sincere thinks he's fooling. He knows he still loves me and that I'm always going to be down for him. She admired her reflection in the mirror as she replayed the conversation with Sincere in her mind. He asked her to hold $5,000 for him just in case something went wrong with the deal. "The funny thing is he can't trust *his woman* because she don't understand the game," she spoke out loud as she styled her hair. "That's why he don't need that uppity bitch anyway. He could have his fun with her, but he is still mine." Just as she finished sweeping her hair up into a ponytail, she heard him banging on the door.

Instead of rushing to answer, she took her time. She powdered her nose and applied two layers of lip gloss. She checked her appearance once more before sauntering to the door.

"What took you so long to open the door," he barked while barging into the apartment.

"I was in the bathroom, if you must know," she lied. "And you're banging on the door like a nut."

"Oh, my bad. Listen I got to go. My flight is at 7:15." He walked into Gen's room and leaned down to kiss his son on his head. "I'm doing this for you, man," Bonita heard him whisper. It touched her to see how much Sincere loved his son. He looked up and saw her standing in the doorway. He pulled an envelope from a pocket inside of is jacket. "Put this somewhere safe," he said handing her the envelope. "Nothing should happen, but you never know. Thanks for looking out."

"Always," she said and tipped her face up for a kiss. She wasn't surprised when Sincere held her in his arms and kissed her passionately. "Make sure you call me when you get there," she said as he broke free of their embrace and walked towards the door. "Be careful, I love you." She moved closer for another kiss.

"Love you, too," he quickly gave her a peck on the lips and left.

Bonita waited by the window and watched as he jogged toward Tru's shiny black Escalade. Still standing by the window, she placed her hands together, bowed her head. She silently prayed for Sincere's safe return. Sure, that he was now in God's capable hands, she peeled $200 from the stack of cash he'd given her. Thanks to Sincere their son had everything he needed. She could use the money to get something for herself. Or better yet, she would get something special for him to show her appreciation for all he does for her and their son. Yep, it was only a matter of time.

CHAPTER 19

CRAZY, SEXY, COOL

BENAE

Benae sat at the mahogany dressing table and stared at her reflection. She was in a quaint room in one of the cottages by Menemsha Village on Martha's Vineyard. It was reminiscent of many of the rooms she'd slept in during memorable summers at the vineyard. Not too much had changed since the last time she'd been here four or five years ago. Usually, being here made her feel happy and like a kid again, but the sad face staring back told the story of the current state of her heart. She knew something was wrong. The three days that she had been away she hadn't heard from Sincere except for very brief calls when he was, *"just checking in"* or *"tired and about to hit the sack."*

At times the heart battled with the mind, emotion squared up against reason but this time both were in sync. Sincere was being evasive and distant which translated into him hiding something from her, which in turn tampered with her trust and that made her sad. If this wasn't her twentieth time calling him today, she hadn't called him at all.

"What is going on?" Benae cried out in despair when once again he failed to pick up.

"Hi sweetheart, are you on the telephone? I thought I heard you talking." Her mom breezed into the room in a beautifully tailored St. John dress.

"No mom, I was just talking to myself," Benae said and busied herself with her phone to keep her mother from seeing her face.

"*Talking to yourself?* That's not good," she said as she walked over to the two large windows and tied back the drapes. "It's so gloomy in here. I thought you wanted to go shopping before the festivities later. You need to get dressed."

"Okay, give me a half hour," Benae said with fake cheer. Of course, Rhonda didn't notice.

"You don't look like you're ready to go anywhere. Why are you so tired? Did you and dad stay up too late?"

"No, mother." Benae was starting to feel even more aggravated.

"Is something wrong?" Rhonda asked finally detected that something was bothering her daughter and walked over to her.

The last thing Benae wanted was to discuss the situation with her mother, but she needed to talk to someone, and she wasn't about to bother her two pregnant friends who had already called her out. She turned around, allowing her mother to see swollen eyes, tangled hair and disheveled pajamas. Rhonda didn't say anything but her slightly raised eyebrow and puckered lips told Benae exactly what was on her mind. She would have liked for her mom to sit beside her and hold her hand or give her a hug but Rhonda stood in place near the dressing table and waited patiently to hear what her daughter had to say.

"I'm not sure if something is wrong or not but I really haven't heard from Sincere since I got here. It's not like him and I'm worried that something is wrong."

"Something like what?" Rhonda asked sitting down on the bed.

Oh, now she wants to come closer. Now that she's ready to hear some dirt, Benae thought.

"I don't know. Forget it." She jumped up from the vanity and opened the closet in search of something to wear. "I'll be down in a half hour. I'm just going to shower and throw my hair in a ponytail."

"Okay," Rhonda said heading toward the door. "But take an hour. Put on something nice and make sure to do your make-up. Lots of people are going to be out today and you never know who you may run into."

Benae rolled her eyes and selected a bright yellow sundress with metallic gold sandals. It was chic yet comfy. She was not going shopping in heels. She didn't know how her mother did it. Determined to get on with her day, Benae stepped into the shower and let the scent of the Bvlgari au the vert soap refresh her. After washing her face and brushing her hair she felt better. She brushed her hair up into a high ponytail, applied gel to the edges and tied a scarf around her head to set while she dressed.

She barged into her parent's bedroom and sprayed herself with the matching Bvlgari perfume. Her phone rang and she and ran back to her room to answer it, but she missed the call. Damn, the call was from Sincere. She played the voicemail which said that he would be working all day and he would be hanging out later and he'd call her tomorrow.

"Tomorrow? Is he crazy? It's only eleven thirty in the morning and he's talking about tomorrow," she said aloud. "Oh, hell no." She called their house, Rick and his dad. She didn't get an answer anywhere. Upset again, she decided to call his job. "Hello this is, Benae Givens, I'm trying to reach Sincere Law. Is he available?"

"No, I'm sorry Sincere is out on vacation. Can I take a message?"

"Are you sure?"

"Ms. that is the information I have."

"Okay. Thank you."

Benae felt sick to her stomach. She couldn't believe Sincere lied to her. She had proof that he did. Now the question was why.

SINCERE

So far, the flight from Chicago to NY was anything but relaxing. Not only had the deal he'd put together not bring in the money he thought it would, they almost got popped by the cops. Tru decided to stay and try to broker another deal to make up the rest of the money. On top of that he knew he would have to deal with Benae. Her messages were getting more and more intense.

"What can I get you, Sir?" Sincere looked up to see a petite, light complexioned pretty girl with a pixie hair cut smiling at him. He flashed her an appreciative grin before replying, "I'll take a Coke and I want the whole can."

"Sure, no problem," she replied putting ice in a cup and handing him the can.

"Thanks, what's your name?"

"Melissa." She smiled and moved on to assist the next row of passengers.

He kept his eyes on her while she worked. He could tell she knew he was watching her. She came back with a freshly wrapped pillow and blanket. She said she would move him to First Class but there were no seats available. Sincere assured her that getting her number would make him happier than being in First Class anyway. Melissa discreetly handed him her number on a napkin. When it was time for him to deplane, she whispered for him to call her tonight so they could have fun while she was in NY overnight.

When Sincere walked into the house the time on the microwave read 11:37 am. He booked an early Saturday flight home just to make sure he got back before Honey came through to clean and do laundry. He unpacked and put his dirty clothes in the hamper and left some on the floor for effect. He placed clean plates and cups in the sink and ran water over them, messed up the bed and sat his toiletries around the bathroom. He even lifted the toilet seats in both bathrooms for good measure.

Honey showed up while he was watching the recorded Summer League Basketball games and making something to eat.

"Hey, what's good?"

"Hello, Sincere. It feels good in here. It's so hot outside today," Honey said.

"Not too bad to me. I like the heat."

"Yes, I do too, but it's the humidity that gets to me. By the way, I wanted to tell you that I will be going home to India for four weeks. I will not be able to clean for you, but I have someone that can help while I am gone."

"You have to talk to Benae about that. When you leaving?"

"Next week."

"Oh, okay. I was thinking of taking Benae to Jamaica for vacation."

"Jamaica," she repeated. "I heard good things. Where's Meth? He's usually all over me by now."

"He's at the vet," he lied. "I'm going to pick him up in a little while."

"Aww, poor Meth. He hates the vet."

"He'll be alright," Sincere said taking his stacked sandwich and chips to the couch.

"Where do you want me to start?" Honey asked. "Benae usually leaves instructions but I don't see them."

"Just do the basics. It's not too much mess in here this week."

"Okay, don't worry. I'll see what needs to be done and I'll do it."

Damn, Honey was sexy in her own little way. Her apparent willingness to please and submissive ways were a turn-on. It wasn't the first time Sincere wondered if she treated her man like that. But Honey never flirted or crossed the line and he wasn't about to either.

Sincere got in the car and let the windows down. He preferred the natural breeze over A/C. His plan was to pick-up Meth and then hit Melissa up to see what she was up to. He often took phone numbers from women because he knew he could, but since meeting Benae he hadn't called any of them. That was about to change, He was definitely gonna hit Melissa up. He remembered he hadn't turned his phone back on since the flight. He had five messages waiting to be retrieved. First message, *"Sincere I know something is going on. I'm hurt and upset, you need to call me before I get home tomorrow.* Delete. Next message, *"Boy where you at? Are you back?"* Delete. Next message, *"Yo, what up playa. Hit me up. Let me know what's good for tonight"* Next message. He didn't delete Rick's message. A message from the homie on the night he was planning to meet up with a chick might come in handy. Next message, *"Hi Sincere, it's Melissa. You're probably settling in, but I hope to hear from you before I head out tomorrow. Ciao."* Delete. Next message, *"Sin, when you coming to get this dog?"*

All he wanted to do was pick up Meth and get some rest, but he slipped in his earpiece and returned calls starting with Benae. Surprisingly, he got her voice mail. He left a message promising to call again and ending it with I love you and miss you. He called Bonita and let her know he would be stopping by but couldn't stay long because he had to pick up Meth. He called Rick and told him about Melissa. Rick also had a chick that he wanted to hook up with later. So, they agreed to make it a foursome. He called Melissa and let her know what was up.

BONITA

Bonita struggled to close her skinny jeans. When she couldn't button them, she turned around and admired her ass instead. "You got to focus on the positive," she said. At least now she was in them, last month she couldn't get them past her thighs. The baby weight was coming off little by little. While she tugged the jeans off, her cell phone rang. She was surprised to see Kendra's name on the screen. They'd only spoken once or twice since her baby shower.

"Hey, Kendra. What's up girl?" she asked.

"I'm good. What you been up to? How's the baby. He's getting so big. I saw pictures when Sincere came by the house."

"He's doing so good. I can't believe he's almost seven months already."

"I know, they grow so fast. It seems like I just had Deja and she'll be four this year."

"So, tell me how you been. How's married life? I heard that first year is tough," she joked.

"It's work, but it's worth it. You know I love Rick to death. That's my heart. But I'm not gonna lie, he does get on my nerves sometimes especially when he out with ya boy. Since he got with that new chick, he and Rick don't hang out as much or maybe it's since we got married since she came around at the same time. Whatever the reason, I ain't mad. Anyway, I'm calling because they're going out tonight."

"Humph, yeah I bet cause she out of town."

"Ohhh," Kendra said. "How you know?"

"You know me and Sincere talk. Ain't nothing changed. I'm still his confidante. She's just a phase. Eventually he will realize that real love and his family is what he needs. Rick goes home to his kid every night and Sincere is gonna want that too and the only one he can have that with is me."

"Not if he has a baby with her, then what?"

"He wouldn't do that to me."

"Okay, if you say so." Clearly conveying to Bonita that she did not co-sign her naiveté.

"I know so," Bonita insisted. "He went out of town to handle some business with Tru and he left me with the just in case money. He probably didn't tell her about none of it."

"That's good," Kendra said unfazed. "What he needs to do is marry you, but Rick tells me he wants you to get a job with a career. He basically left because he thinks you're lazy and don't want to work. If you get that together you can definitely get him back and for the right reasons, not just because you have his son."

"Do you think you can help me get a job at your company?"

"Maybe. First get your resume together so I can see what you're working with."

"I can do that, but I don't have a lot of experience. I really didn't work since I was like twenty. That was about six years ago."

"We can talk about that later," Kendra said, purposely changing the subject. "I was calling to see if you wanted to hang out. My cousins are here for the weekend and they want to party in NYC before heading back to Buffalo."

"Hell yeah," Bonita squealed. "I need to get out myself. Where y'all going?"

"Probably to BBQ's then to a club somewhere."

"Can Shakirra come? She'll be mad if I go without her."

"She so damn skinny, we can squeeze her in the car."

"True." Bonita laughed. "I'm gonna go get me something to wear with the money Sincere left and I'll be ready when y'all get here."

"Alright. I'll call you when I'm on my way."

"Okay, see you later." Without putting the phone down Bonita dialed Shakirra to fill her in on the unexpected call from Kendra and the fun they were gonna get into.

CHAPTER 20

ONE OF THEM NIGHTS

BENAE

Benae felt better after talking to Sincere. She was surprised at how quickly she was able to distrust him and suspect that he was up to something with Bonita. *He keeps warning me about that,* she thought. I really don't want to be that woman who lacks trust in her man and her relationship. Earlier she had taken a moment to slip away from lunch with her mom and her friends to make a quick three-way call with Chrissy and Ming. They both assured her that she was stressing herself out for nothing. Benae was not convinced until Ming told her about the deal in Chicago. She wasn't supposed to tell her about it but Ming decided that Sincere fucked up, so she had to save his ass. If he was mad about that fuck him. Benae wasn't happy that Sincere was still dabbling in illegal activities but she was much happier to hear that than to hear that he was cheating on her.

She concluded her friends were right. She just missed him and loved him so much that she knew that something was going on with him. She pulled out her phone and gazed at the picture of them. Just as she was about to sit the phone down and start organizing all the shopping bags surrounding her, it rang. She smiled and answered Sincere's call.

"Hey, babe," she cooed.

"What's up?"

"Not much, I overspent and now I have too much stuff to bring back on the plane."

"Sounds like typical you."

"It's mostly stuff for the house and now I have an extra little boy to shop for," she teased.

"Aww, that's what's up."

"Babe, I know that you're on vacation..." she paused. "I also know that you did business out of town with Tru." Sincere didn't say anything. "I was upset because I found out you were not at work before I knew why, and it hurt me that you lied to me. I don't like that you're still doing things like that with your brother, but what I really want you to understand is that you can't lie to me."

"I didn't lie, I just didn't tell you," he defended.

"A lie of omission is still a lie. Just like you want me to trust you, you have to trust me. I'd rather know the truth and discuss it or even argue about the truth than have to deal with a lie. You feel me?" she asked using his line.

"I feel you. You're right. I have to trust you, too," he agreed.

"On another note, I miss you,"

"I miss you, too. That's why I'm standing outside talking to you when I should be inside with my boys."

"You are? Where are you?" she asked sitting down on the bed.

"Some bar uptown with Rick. We just had something to eat. We might head to a club or something. Kendra and her family are hanging out. You're out of town so me and Rick keeping each other company."

"We'll have fun, tell Rick I said hello."

"Alright, now you have fun tonight, too. I'll be there to pick you up tomorrow. You're flight gets in at two, right?"

"Yep, I'll text you the info again if you need it."

"Nah, I got it."

"Okay."

"Love you, girl."

"Love you, too."

Chrissy and Ming were right. He's out with the boys thinking about me. Feeling festive for the first time in days, Benae changed into a flowing electric blue maxi dress and matching sandals. She pulled her hair up into a high bun and left some hair loose for dramatic effect. She smoothed down her baby hair and sprayed oil sheen to set it. She freshened up her make-up and headed downstairs to enjoy her last night away.

SINCERE

Sincere returned home to a spotless house. He walked over to the Bose system and connected his cell. He put on his playlist and the first song that came on was *Lil Wayne's Bitches Love Me*. He undressed, hopped in the shower and pondered the songs words and how the lyrics pertained to his life.

Benae – she caught him today and her overly emotional display confirmed just how in love with him she was and confirmed that she wouldn't be going anywhere anytime soon.

Bonita – she's still showing me love even though I'm not with her. She's a true rider and I don't have to worry about her going nowhere either.

Now he could add Melissa. He could tell Melissa was enamored with his good looks and physique. She was the perfect addition. Her schedule brought her to NY regularly enough, but she didn't live here. He told her he had a lady and a son, but she didn't seem to care about the status of that relationship.

He was so fucking horny. He held his dick and stroked it slowly while the hot water pulsated against his skin. It was hard and he could nut in two minutes if he wanted to, but he decided to save it for Melissa. It's not like he would be having a long drawn out lovemaking session with her. It was just hit it and quit it, giving her just enough to make her come back for more.

He threw on a pair of black True Religion jeans, a white Polo shirt and white on white Air Force Ones. He splashed on Creed cologne and called Rick on speaker while he put on his one carat diamond studs, gold chain and watch.

"So, where we headed? I'm about to leave now," Sincere said.

"To this spot in the Bronx. That's where this chick Brandi I met works. She's gonna hook us up with drinks and wings and shit. Then we can head to the club."

"Okay, cool. I'm gonna scoop Melissa. She's in Queens near the airports."

Sincere found parking and strolled ahead of Melissa toward the little hole in the wall. Rick walked over from the opposite side of the lot with the chick that had to Brandi. They gave each other a pound and a half hug before introducing them to their companions for the night. They both eyed the women appreciatively. Both girls dressed to impress for their first date with someone else's man.

"Dayum," Sincere exclaimed when he got a good look at Brandi.

She stepped from behind Rick in sky-high, candy apple, red platform stilettos and a tight, black mini halter dress that showed her dangerous curves. Her waist was small, and her hips and ass were large. Her brown skin and long black weave gave her an exotic look. Rick gave Sincere the nod indicating that Melissa looked good too. She'd worn a short, silver wig and a strapless silver dress with clear and silver heels. Brandi's co-workers led them to a comfortable booth near the back of the restaurant which they reserved for Brandi's party.

"Thanks, Keisha," Brandi said once they were seated. "Can you start us off with a couple of Ciroc shots, some wings and onion rings?"

"Sure, coming right up." Keisha switched away hoping to attract the attention of the two fine guys at the table with her co-worker.

Rick and Sincere noticed and laughed out loud not letting the ladies in on the joke. The foursome ate and drank until they were full, tipsy, and ready to party.

Sincere was feeling Melissa and couldn't wait to slip his dick in her. She let him know that she was not wearing panties under her short dress and that she hadn't had dick in a couple of months and wanted him to break her fast. Sincere was more than down. He tried to think back to the last time he had new pussy and couldn't remember. The last new pussy was Benae and she's over a year now. That's far from new-new. He'd been a good boy for the most part, not counting the times he and Bonita got busy but that was a given, she was his baby moms. Now with Melissa it would be bona fide cheating. He felt guilty for a second but said at least he's not like Rick. He's not married.

"I'll be right back," Melissa whispered to him and slid across the booth to go to the bathroom."

"Okay, sexy, meet me at the car," he said, keeping his eyes focused on her ass as she walked away and thinking about what he was going to do to her in the Reggae Room.

BONITA

"I don't remember the last time I had so much fun!" Bonita shouted from the dance floor while sipping Alize' from a clear plastic cup.

"Yeah, girl, that's my song!" Shakirra yelled back as she squeezed onto the crowded dance floor.

Kendra and her cousins were somewhere on the dance floor getting their groove on as well.

Bonita stood near the wall watching the happy people on the dance floor moving to the pulsing beat. There were a few guys trying to get her attention. She noticed a tall, muscular guy and wanted him to turn her way so she could peep his face. Once he did, she had to do a double take when she saw that it was Rick. She wondered if Kendra told him they were going to be here. While they were at BBQ's, she'd heard Kendra tell Rick they were going to the Lounge. They did go there, but it wasn't poppin' so they left and ended up at Cloud. She looked around for Sincere but didn't see him anywhere.

"Whew, girl I need to go the bathroom and wipe this sweat off my face," a clearly exhausted Kendra said, snapping her out of her thoughts. She followed behind Kendra and her cousins and grabbed

Shakirra on the way. Once inside the bathroom, Bonita had the chance to tell Kendra she saw Rick. "When?" Kendra said very loudly, attracting the attention of everyone in the small bathroom.

"Right before we came in here."

"Why the hell you didn't tell me?" Kendra asked with attitude.

"I just got the chance, too. Did you tell him we were here?"

"Now why would I do that?" Kendra asked sarcastically. "I came here because I always tell him I hate this place because people be having sex in the Reggae room. Are you sure it was Rick?"

"Yes, I'm sure. I looked right at him."

"Did you see Sincere, too?"

"I looked for him, but I didn't see him."

Kendra smirked. "I'm sure his whorish ass is in the Reggae Room."

"Well, let's go see," Shakirra said drunkenly.

The ladies handled their potty business, fixed their hair, and retouched their make-up before heading back into the club. They moved through the crowded bar area and entered the Reggae Room. Immediately, the pulsating hip-hop beat was drowned out by the rhythmic melody of reggae. It was darker and harder to see who was who. The couples were hugged up so tight and grinding so hard it made it extra hard to find someone. Bonita felt anxious. She was really hoping that Rick wouldn't be in here, but she knew from some of the things Sincere told her about Rick that it was a good chance he would be. Somehow the ladies were separated in the near darkness. Bonita found herself standing in front of Sincere as he grinded on a girl's ass. His eyes were closed, and he opened them briefly to make a face indicating how good the ass felt grinding on his hardness.

Bonita stood a little bit closer. "Who she?" Bonita screamed.

Melissa stopped her nasty wind and Sincere's eyes flew open. "Who are you?" Melissa answered.

"I'm his baby mama."

"What you doing here?" Sincere asked. "I thought you were home with Gen."

"Nope, looks like I'm here."

"Shit," Sincere said scanning he room. "Before they could walk away, they heard a commotion on the other side of the small but packed room. They walked over to find Brandi laying on the floor with her naked ass exposed from under her short dress. She tried to get up but only made it to all fours before Kendra literally kicked her ass.

"Get up, bitch! You want to fuck with my man? After I done warned you to stay the fuck away from him!" Kendra bellowed.

The club bouncers rushed through the crowd, grabbed Kendra and proceeded to drag her out of the club. Rick jumped in and told them to get the fuck off his wife. The bouncers were big but not as big as Rick and Sincere was right by his boy's side.

"Aight, man, go head and escort her out," one of the bouncers said.

"No problem, I got her."

"No, you don't. Get off me, Rick! You out here fucking bitches in clubs? That's what you doing?"

"Miss you have to go," the bouncer stated with Authority. "If you don't leave you will be escorted out."

Kendra turned and walked toward the exit.

"I'll get your bag," Bonita offered. Kendra's pocketbook and some of its contents were scattered on the ground.

"I'll go with you, "Shakirra said.

Bonita and Shakirra hurriedly picked up Kendra's things as everyone around them continued to get their party on.

SINCERE

Sincere helped Brandi to her feet and guided her and Melissa out to the main area of the club. "You alright?" he asked Brandi.

"Yeah, I'm okay. I'm just pissed that Rick had his wife come to the same damn club. He knows that bitch can't stand me."

"Rick didn't know she was gonna be here. He wouldn't put you in a position to get fucked up like that."

Brandi rolled her eyes at Sincere. "I have to go fix myself up. You coming with me?" she asked Melissa.

"Yeah, this is some crazy shit," Melissa said following her.

"Y'all wait here. We'll be back!" Sincere yelled.

Melissa waved her hand indicating that she heard him. Sincere headed out of the club trying to figure out what could happen next. How the hell did they let this happen? He stood beside Rick as he apologized to Kendra. She cried while she let Rick and anyone else who wanted to listen know just how much of a nasty ass, piece of shit he was. She grabbed her bag from Bonita as soon as she and Shakirra approached.

"I can't believe you did this!" she yelled at Rick. "Embarrassing me in front of my family."

"I'm sorry," Rick said softly. "Please stop crying, baby. I hate to see you cry." He tried to hug her.

"Get off me," Kendra said through gritted teeth. "Here," she said to her cousin, passing her the keys to her car. "I can't drive, right now."

"Me and Bonita can take an Uber back to Brooklyn," Shakirra offered.

"Y'all don't have to do that," Kendra protested.

"Nah, babe, you go home. Me and Sin will drop them off," Rick said. Kendra cut her eyes at him and got in the passenger seat of her car. "I might as well enjoy the rest of the night," Rick said. "I'm for damn sure not going home to Kendra and her family tonight. Kendra is a force of nature on her own and I don't need her and her reinforcements." He and Sincere laughed.

"That's not funny. You out here cheating and got cold-busted. Now you need to go home and take the consequences," Shakirra chimed in from the back seat of Rick's Tahoe.

"For real," Bonita instigated. "If I were you, I would go home. Staying out will just make it worse."

"Man, shut-up and mind your business," Sincere said half-jokingly. He was glad to see that the buzz he'd had earlier hadn't worn off. "The man said he's not going home, so he's not going home." He turned around in the passenger seat to look both Bonita and Shakirra in the eye, making sure they got the message. To his surprise, they quietly spoke amongst themselves or not at all since it was difficult to do over the loud music.

Rick pulled up in front of the projects, then Shakirra hopped out and yelled, "Thanks, Rick!"

Sincere helped Bonita with the door and told Rick he was going to ride with them on the elevator to make sure they got inside okay. When the elevator stopped on Shakirra's floor they held the door and watched until she entered her apartment and closed the door. When they reached Bonita's floor Sincere held it and watched her slow sashay down the hall.

She stopped before reaching her door and turned to face him, "Why don't you come in for a minute?"

"Nah, you know Rick is waiting downstairs."

"Let him wait with his cheating ass. Looked like you were cheating, too," she said walking towards him.

"I was just dancing. Last time I checked that's not cheating."

"You were dancing pretty close and loving the feel of that girl's ass on your dick. Even in the darkness, I could see it on your face." She smiled at him sexily while retracing her steps back to him. "I can see it on your face now, too." She stroked his dick through his jeans and quickly felt it jump to attention. "Poor baby must not be getting it good at home. Come in for a minute."

Sincere stepped out of the elevator and followed her into the apartment all the while thinking how sexy she looked in her short, tight dress and high heels. As soon as the door closed behind them, she pushed him up against the door and squatted down in front of him.

"Yo! What you doing?" he asked looking down at her unzipping his jeans. She responded by slipping his dick out and sticking it in her mouth. "Oh, shit," he whispered. "That shit feels so good." For some reason the whole time Benae's been out of town he had been feenin' for pussy, head, some sex period. She'd been too busy to have sex the way they used to, and it was like the cat was away and the mouse wanted to play. He quietly enjoyed the A+ head Bonita was giving him and let a load go into her mouth. She licked and sucked him dry.

"Damn, baby, what was that for?" he asked when they were done.

"I saw you had a need and I wanted to fill it. That's what I do."

"Really," Sincere said adjusting himself.

"Apparently, so the way you were all hugged up on that trick at the club."

"You must have been a little hungry yourself, the way you were eating tonight."

"That's right, because I take care of my man and always will. You know I'll always be here to take care of you. I ain't going nowhere." Sincere was slightly stunned. He knew Bonita was a rider, but damn.

"Now go on, before Rick leaves you." Sincere felt a swelling of emotion. "I love you," he said and kissed her lips. He thought he heard her say, "I know," before she closed the door behind him.

CHAPTER 21

KICK YOUR GAME

BENAE

The flight landed so smoothly into LaGuardia Airport that some of the passengers applauded. Benae was one of them. She was in a great mood and excited to be back home. The first-class cabin attendant helped her with her bags as she deplaned. She would have flown coach, but her parents bought her a First-Class ticket as they always did when she traveled to see them.

Walking through the exit doors, she called Sincere to make sure he was there to pick her up. She spotted him standing beside her white Audi and headed over. "Hey, babe." She smiled reaching out to give him a hug and a kiss.

"Hey, how was your trip?" he asked.

Immediately she sensed something was off. His hug was weak, and his kiss was perfunctory. Benae was slightly put off by his behavior. She watched as he put her bags in the trunk and walked around to the passenger side of the car.

"You can drive."

"Oh, that's new," she said sliding behind the wheel and adjusting the seat. "You never let me drive. What's wrong?"

"Nothing babe, I'm just tired."

"Tired from what?" she wanted to know.

"From last night, there was some drama." Benae stayed quiet and waited for him to elaborate. Sincere tilted the chair back further and placed his arm over his eyes and continued, "Long story short, we ran into Kendra and her and Rick got into it."

"Oh, wow! What happened? Why did they argue?"

"I don't feel like getting into all that, right now," he said. Before Benae could protest, Sincere's phone vibrated. "It's Rick," he announced and went on to have a brief conversation that Benae could not decipher. "Rick may stop by later," he said.

Benae was in no mood for company. She just got home and all she wanted to do was catch up with Sincere and spend some quality time with him. "Is Kendra coming, too," she sighed.

"He didn't say but I doubt it. Her peeps are in town."

"Sincere, what is wrong with you? Something is clearly bothering you and it can't be me. I just got home."

"I'm good. Like I told you I'm just tired."

Benae parked across the street from the house. No sooner had she turned the car off, Sincere hopped out and grabbed her bags from the back. He headed toward the door like she wasn't even there. Benae was getting aggravated by his distant behavior but more than that she was hurt. She couldn't understand why he didn't seem to miss her. She followed him upstairs determined not to let her insecurities get the best of her.

"Babe." She stepped up behind him and put her arms around him. "I missed you."

He turned around to face her but didn't meet her gaze. "I missed you, too, let's get in the bed."

Inwardly, Benae smiled. *Oh, that's what it is. I should have known that he wants some lovin'.* She quickly showered and stepped into the bedroom revealing a new black and gold Victoria's Secret panty and bra set and slid into bed beside him. She decided to give him some even though she wasn't ovulating.

"You look nice," he mumbled then held her in his arms and fell asleep.

Benae laid there for a few minutes, her spider senses were on 100. *His ass is never this tired,* she thought looking back at him sleeping with his mouth gaping open.

She eased out of bed and threw on her satin robe. It was only 4:30 in the afternoon and she wasn't tired. As she tied the robe around her waist, she spotted Sincere's cell on the nightstand. She never felt the need to snoop through his phone before but at this moment she felt an overwhelming need to do so. Quietly, she crept over to the nightstand and slipped into the bathroom with the phone in her hand. She entered his birthday. It didn't unlock the phone. She tried Genuwen's birthday and it worked. She scrolled through his outgoing calls but all she saw were some short calls to random people, including Bonita, but nothing that caught her attention. She then scrolled through the texts and once again found nothing to cause concern.

She put the phone back and leaned down to kiss Sincere gently on the forehead. *I love this man,* she thought. *"Why do I keep doubting him?"*

The distant ring of her cell phone broke her from her thoughts. She scampered to the kitchen and pulled her phone from her bag. The number on the display was not recognizable but was somewhat familiar.

"Hello?" she answered.

"Hi Benae, it's Bonita. Did you have a good trip?"

BONITA

"Bonita?" Benae said with attitude, "Is everything okay? Why are you calling my phone?"

"Because I want to talk to you," Bonita said glancing at Shakirra who was by her side. "I thought you should know that while you and Sincere over there playing house, we still see each other, and we are still active. He told me that he is only using you for money and shit because you're obsessed with him."

"Girl, bye, you sound stupid," Benae snapped.

"I sound stupid? We're about to switch places real quick. Why don't you ask him who he was with last night then? I'm sure he told you about everything that went down with Kendra and Rick. We were right there together when it happened. After that he brought me home and the things that went on last night...girl." She laughed. "Mmm, mmm, mmm, I wouldn't be surprised if he couldn't get it up

to give you some welcome home dick." Bonita looked at Shakirra triumphantly and waited for Benae to respond.

"I still don't believe it but if it's true. You are pathetic for knowingly sleeping with someone else's man. When he's made it clear he doesn't want you. Apparently, you're easy pussy, so fucking you don't mean shit."

"Bitch, he was my man first. You the homewrecker!" Bonita shouted.

"But he's my man now!" Benae shouted back. "Stay in your lane, baby mama," she said and hung up the phone.

"That didn't go as planned," Shakirra said, looking at Bonita with a smirk on her face.

Bonita stood up and picked up her half-eaten box of Crown Fried Chicken and fries to throw it in the trash. Benae's words had stung. What had she really gained by sleeping with the father of her child if she was still alone every night and he was in Benae's bed?

"You're not gonna eat that?" Shakirra said grabbing her by the arm and stopping her from throwing away good food.

"No, you can have it," she said tossing the box back on the table. "Anyway," Bonita said leaning against the kitchen sink and facing her friend. "I still got to tell her what's up. She's only prolonging the situation because he'll be back with me cause he's just using her."

Shakirra looked doubtful.

"That's what he told me," Bonita defended.

"I'm sure he did, and he tells her shit about you, too. Now the shit's about to hit the fan since you called her and put it out there. I hope you don't think she gonna just take your word over his and hand him to you on a platter?" Shakirra said in a rare serious tone.

"I know. She over there trying to play it cool, but you know she's tripping, and stressing him out right about now." Bonita laughed. "And I don't care. I know he's not gonna do nothing." The phone rang and vibrated on the table. The screen filled with a family picture of Bonita, Sincere and little Gen.

"I'll put it on speaker. Hello," Bonita answered with a smile in her voice.

"Yo, what's wrong with you?" Sincere's angry voice boomed through the speaker. "Don't be calling here trying to start shit. You know me and you cool, we got a son together but that's it. I've moved on. I don't want no more trouble. Stop calling here with the bullshit. I'm not entertaining it," he said, ending the call before she had a chance to say anything.

Bonita could not believe what she just heard. The anger building up inside her was so intense she let some tears fall out of sheer frustration before grabbing the garbage bag from the can and beating it on the floor.

"What the fuck?" Shakirra muttered.

"I'm gonna call him back," Bonita said walking away from the garbage on the floor. "That cold blooded bastard, I'm fucking sick of him."

"No, he's just gonna ignore you or keep playing the role while he's in front of her. Just wait and get that ass when you see him." Shakirra took her friend in her arms and held her while she cried. She walked away for a moment to grab a handful of napkins for Bonita to wipe her eyes and blow her nose. "You have to calm down. You can't let him get you like this."

"You know what?" Bonita asked removing herself from Shakirra's hold. "Fuck that. Remember Robbie who's always trying to get with me? Well, I'm gonna hook up with him. He's friends with Rick's cousin so I know it will get back to Sincere's dumb ass. We'll see how he likes it when I quote unquote move on, too. Two can play this game."

"Any other time, I would say you were wrong and are just gonna make things worse. But after that stunt he just pulled, you do you. He deserves whatever he gets."

SINCERE

"What the fuck!" Sincere felt like he was dreaming that someone had him down on the ground kicking his ass.

The high-pitched voice of a female is what let him know it was a dream because there was no way a chick would have him down beating the shit out of him.

"Sincere, wake your ass up." It was Benae wailing on him with a mix of fists and opened hand hits to his face and chest.

"What the fuck is wrong with you?" he asked grabbing a hold of both of her wrists.

"What's wrong with me? What's wrong with me?" she screamed.

Sincere was wide-awake now. He had never seen her like this. "Get off me. What the fuck is wrong with you?"

"Your baby mama called my phone."

Aww shit, Sincere thought and lowered his eyes. *Better her than Melissa.* After the appetizer from Bonita, he put it on Melissa so good, he knew she would be calling the next time she was in town.

"She insinuated that you two had sex last night then straight out told me that you are just using me. And that you plan to leave me to go back to her," she said standing in front of him, her robe tied haphazardly around her waist and her chest heaving.

"What!" Sincere exclaimed. "I'm not leaving you, and using you for what?"

"I don't know. You tell me?" He could tell she was furious. "You tell me how she even knew about Rick and Kendra?"

Sincere stood up so that he could look Benae in the eyes and appear truthful while he lied. "We ran into her and Shakirra last night at the club. I didn't know she was there until Rick and Kendra got into it. That's when I found out she was there with Kendra. She's using any little bit of information to get in your head."

"Oh, so now Bonita was there?" Benae said sarcastically.

Sincere took Benae by the shoulders. "Listen to me. Calm down, be reasonable and think for a minute," he said looking deeply into her eyes. "She's just trying to come between us. You know I love you. We been good and she's just trying to mess it up. She's jealous." He could see that his words were having the desired effect as her eyes searched his for the truth. He stared back at her with all the sincerity his name could muster.

Just as he was about to hug her to his chest in triumph, she pulled back and gave him the side eye. "How did she get the number to my cell?"

"I don't know," he said, he really didn't know.

"Call her."

"Nah, I'm not trying to get into all that drama."

"You haven't seen drama yet, but you will if you don't call her, right now. Tell her to leave me the fuck alone."

There was no way out, so he acquiesced and called Bonita rationalizing that she got what she deserved for calling Benae in the first place. "You satisfied now?" he asked after ending the call with Bonita.

"No," Benae said smugly.

"Sure, you're not satisfied?" he asked again, eyeing her sexily.

"No, I'm not." Benae smiled and sat down on the bed with her legs slightly open.

Sincere walked over to her and gently pushed her back on the bed until he was on top of her. He leaned down and kissed her lingeringly. He pulled back and ended the kiss all the while looking into her eyes. He ran his hands slowly across her neck, around her breasts, down her belly and inside of the folds between her legs. Effortlessly her legs fell apart providing him with a clear entrance. He fingered her until her juices began to flow then lowered his head to lick them up.

"You satisfied now..." he asked briefly pausing his feast.

In response, Benae grabbed both sides of his head and pulled his face back into her wetness. Sincere smiled and went back to putting the final touches on ending the argument.

CHAPTER 22

DON'T PUSH ME

BENAE

After receiving some excellent oral sex from her man with no reciprocation, after all he had to have some punishment, Benae was back in love. She got up and started the preparations for an early dinner of smothered chicken, mashed potatoes, and asparagus.

"Hey, babe, it smells good in here," Sincere said lifting the top off the pot with the chicken.

"Yeah, everything will be ready by the time you get back," Benae said wishing he would leave already so that she could get on the phone and bring her girls up to date on the drama.

"Is there enough for Rick? He can use a good dinner. You know he's still staying at his brother's crib until Kendra lets him back in."

"If he was cheating on her she shouldn't let him back in." She stood with her hand on her hip and turned to face him. "I heard what your baby mama said last night, and I am choosing to believe you. But should I ever find out that you are cheating on me, I'm gone. There will be no second chances. You hear me?" she asked seriously.

"Yeah, I hear you," Sincere said squirming a bit. "You don't have nothing to worry about." He kissed her on the forehead.

"Okay. Tell Rick he's welcomed to have dinner with us. His cheating is none of my business and his wife was never nice to me so..." She shrugged.

"A'ight, I'm out," Sincere said quickly leaving the apartment.

She peeked through the blinds and watched as Sincere hopped in his car and pulled off. Benae couldn't wait to talk to Ming. Chrissy was her bestie, but she preferred talking to Ming about issues with Bonita.

"What's up, girl," Ming's warm voice greeted her through the phone.

"Drama with a capital D."

"Rick and Kendra's mess? I already heard about that. Can you believe he was fucking a chick in the club?"

"What?" Benae asked loudly.

"Yup, that's what Tru told me."

"Sincere didn't tell me that. He just said Kendra accused him of cheating. Ugh, I can't believe Rick could be so nasty. No wonder she kicked him out."

"I don't put nothing past a man," Ming stated emphatically.

"Speaking of that, did you know Sincere's baby mama was there last night, too?"

"Yeah, but that ain't nothing. She was just kicking it with Kendra."

"Okay, so let me tell you her version of events." For the next few minutes Benae regaled Ming with all that she heard about the night before.

"She a lying ass," Ming hissed when Benae was done. "You already know that she don't want to move on. I'm not even gonna give her life, but I will tell you this – tighten up the reigns. Sincere got to do what he got to do for the baby but since he's bringing him to y'all house now. Go with him for pick-ups and drop-offs. Send her the message by making your presence known. This chick is not trying to go nowhere, for real."

"Really? I don't even want to see her," Benae said disgusted.

"It's not about that. She needs to be checked. Sincere did his part and you have to do yours. Stop being so damn civilized and letting this chick think she's still that Bitch to your man. The nerve of her calling your phone. You better check her."

Benae laughed. "Alright, I'll do it, but I just hate feeling like I'm in competition for my own man."

"Don't get it twisted," Ming warned. "You are in competition. Don't ever forget that, especially, with a baby mama like her. If anything, you'll get more information from her by seeing her sometimes. Because in most lies there is some truth and you can learn a lot by observing how she acts around him. Plus, you still need to know how she got your number. There are two logical options – one, she got it from Kendra, which I doubt or two she got it from Sincere's phone cause he was comfortable enough to just lay it down. He shouldn't be over there sleeping or taking showers and shit." Benae remained quiet. Ming continued, "Get closer to her in an indirect way and see what you can see. I don't trust her, and I definitely don't trust Kendra's ass."

"That's a lot to think about Ming, but it all makes sense. I'm going to pour myself a glass of wine and get my thoughts together for my conversation with Sincere."

"You do that. Let him and his baby mama know that you are that Bitch."

Benae laughed and shook her head. "Okay, Ming. Will do."

"Let me go, Tru is in there waiting for me to give him some head. He acts like every time he gets out the shower and his peen is clean, I should suck it." Benae laughed again. "But I do it because he usually leaves me some money when I'm done."

"Like you're a whore?" Benae exclaimed.

"Yes," Ming said seductively. "I am his whore. Talk to you later girl," she said and hung up.

"Well, damn," Benae said looking at her phone as the screen went blank.

BONITA

Bonita flashed a dazzling smile and took a sip of her Pina Colada. Robbie sat across from her eating her up with his eyes. She enjoyed his admiration of her and completely played into it. It had been forever since she'd been on a real date and it felt good. Robbie picked her up at her door and escorted her to his old, but still in good condition Honda Accord. She felt like a teenager and talked constantly on the twenty-minute drive to the Red Lobster in Starrett City. As usual for a Saturday night, the place was packed. Robbie steered her to the bar where he was able to find one empty seat. Without hesitation, Robbie offered her the seat and stood beside her. He flagged down the bartender and placed their drink order while they waited for their table. They'd just sat down and Robbie staring at her made her feel sexy and beautiful. She stared back and smiled again. Robbie was a good-looking guy, brown-skinned, tall, well-dressed and decent. The only problem was his chipped front tooth and slightly falsetto voice.

"So, Ms. Grimes, I finally get you out on a date? What made you change your mind after all this time?"

"It's simple. Me and my baby daddy ain't together no more," she said.

"Say word." Robbie smiled brightly. "His loss. You look beautiful and you're wearing the hell out of that dress girl." He laughed.

Yes, I am, she thought.

Bonita was almost back to her pre-baby weight and the low-cut red dress was new. She spent all the *just in case* money Sincere had given her on new clothes and shoes. His dumb ass was so caught up in the head she had given him that night that he forgot to ask for the money back. Then he showed his ass the next day so there was no way he was getting the money back after that. She had forgotten about it, too, but when he left a message asking for it she quickly let him know that it was gone.

"Thank you. It's new. I bought it just for tonight," she purred.

"Oh, yeah, I like that," he said nodding at her appreciatively.

"So, what are you getting?" she asked.

"Admiral's Feast, I always get that. You, can get whatever you want."

Bonita giggled. "Thank you. You're so nice. I think I'll have the shrimp scampi."

Admiral's Feast, shrimp scampi, three pina coladas and three rum and cokes later, the pair headed back to Robbie's car. Once inside, Robbie placed his hand on Bonita's thigh. "So, what you want to do now? It's only ten-thirty. The night is still young."

Bonita rested her head on the headrest and closed her eyes. She could feel the effects of her drinks and it felt so good, she slowly turned to face him and asked, "What you want to do?"

"You mind if we get a room and chill for a couple of hours?" he asked timidly.

"I'm down."

"Okay, cool." He pulled over in front of a liquor store. "I want to pick up a bottle of Henny. What you want?" he asked stepping out of the car.

"Alize' is good. The red one."

"Red is your color girl," he joked and jogged over to the store.

Bonita's phone rang. It was Sincere. *I was wondering when he was gonna call.* They'd spoken since the blow-up but just about the baby. She was determined not to let him know how much he hurt her fronting for his girl. "Hello," she answered making sure her voice sounded low and sexy.

"Hey, what's up?"

"Just hanging out," she said shortly.

"You with Shakirra?"

"Nope, on a date." She smiled to herself as she listened to the silence.

"Oh, you on a date?" he stumbled.

"Yep, moving on like you said."

"Oh, a'ight, you still on that?"

"I'm not on nothing. I'm just living my life."

"Well, go on. Do you," he said with attitude.

"Don't worry, I will." *Fuck him,* she thought disconnecting the call and putting it on silent.

Robbie came back to the car and Bonita leaned over and kissed him on the lips. "Damn, girl, you're making my night."

Walking into the cheap, rent by the hour motel, Bonita felt a strange sense of excitement. Once inside, she took in the drab surroundings, strolled seductively over to the bed, and sat down.

He never took his eyes off her. "Damn, Ma, you sexy as fuck." He practically drooled as Bonita reached down and slowly removed both of her shiny red heels.

Robbie eased down on the bed beside her. She scooted into the middle of the bed and laid down. Robbie rolled on top of her, then began kissing her and feeling her breasts. His rough and unfamiliar touch excited her. She briefly thought of Sincere and his repeated betrayals. Nothing was going to stop her from enjoying this revenge fuck. Robbie rubbed her thighs and hiked her dress up over her hips and fingered her while unzipping his pants.

"You got a condom?" Bonita moaned.

"Yeah, right here." He held up the Trojan packet. "But let me just put it in raw for a minute, baby. I want to feel you. I've been waiting for this for a long time," he pleaded looking intently into her eyes.

"Okay," she whispered. Bonita was so turned on by his attention. "But just for little while. I'm not on the pill and I'm not trying to get pregnant."

"Ooohhh," they both moaned as he entered her. "Shit this some good pussy," Robbie said while kissing and grinding into her.

Bonita gave into the feeling and swiveled her hips in a figure 8 up and down Robbie's pulsating dick. Next thing she knew he had her legs up over his shoulders and was working her out. She felt her own orgasm building and clutched him tightly around the back as they pounded each other towards their ultimate release.

"I knew you were gonna be worth that wait." Robbie smiled at her as she laid in his arms.

"Can you get me something to drink?" she asked softly.

"All we got is the liquor. I didn't think to get a soda or something."

"That's fine. Just pour me some Alize."

He handed her a cupful. As the sweet liquid slid down her throat, she felt high. She was tipsy and she couldn't stop smiling. Robbie was looking at her like he wanted to eat her, so she decided that's what he was going to do. He gulped down two shots of Henny and walked towards her stroking his dick.

"I want some more of that pussy, baby."

"Okay, daddy," she purred. "But you have to eat it first." She leaned back and spread her legs wide.

"Oh, hell yeah," Robbie exclaimed and dove in face first.

"Yes, yes, eat that pussy," she commanded, loving the feeling of being in control. She pushed Robbie's face into her pussy and guided his tongue up and down along her clit, and into her vaginal opening. *This shit feels incredible,* she thought.

She could feel Robbie trying to pull up for air, but she was not going to let him stop. The orgasm that was cresting was hitting her like a wave and she was going to ride it. She ground her pussy into his face with both hands and continued to guide the movement of his head.

"Oh shit, oh shit, oh shittttttttt!" she screamed as she came and came.

Before she could catch her breath, Robbie slid up her body and shoved his dick in her waiting pussy. Once again, she just felt that this was some bomb ass sex. Robbie worked her out holding nothing back. She felt like a rag doll as he twisted and turned her into one incredible position after the next. As she was about to have her fourth orgasm from him slamming into her from behind, she briefly thought of Sincere and how getting sweet revenge was even sweeter than she thought it could be. Keeping that thought, she cried out again in pleasure as she was overcome with that cum that made her legs weak and she collapsed on the bed completely spent.

SINCERE

Sincere sat at the counter of his favorite diner having coffee, eggs, and corn beef hash before heading to work. He scrolled through his social media feed and saw a public plea from Rick to Kendra apologizing and expressing his love for her.

"Damn, Kendra ain't playin,'" Sincere said under his breath.

Rick had been out of the house for almost two months. The same amount of time that Bonita had been giving him the freezing cold shoulder. He really hadn't expected her to take it this far. She knew he was with Benae but they still had their thing going. He wanted to know what she was doing and who she was doing it with. She mentioned she went on some dates with Robbie from around her way, but he knew she wasn't ready to move on sexually especially not with that lame Robbie.

He sipped his coffee and thought about Rick and the drama in his life because he got married before he sowed all his oats. He knew he wasn't ready for that. For the most part he figured he would be content with Benae and Bonita for a while. Thing is he loved them both in different ways. Benae was the love of his life and everything a man could want in a woman. She was beautiful, successful, loving, sexy and easy to get along with. Bonita was the mother of his only son, she adored him, she was sexy, and she was down. He didn't want to choose. He just had to figure out how to get Bonita back on track.

He realized what he needed to do. "Hey, Nita. What's up, baby?" he asked speaking softly into the phone.

"Hey, nothing we're in the bed," she said dryly.

"We who," he asked loudly.

"Me and your son, silly." She giggled.

"Just making sure, since you've been acting so funny."

"You said move on so that's what I'm doing."

"You know I didn't mean it like that," he whined. "You still love me, right?"

"You already know the answer to that, but it doesn't matter."

"It matters a lot. Matter of fact, I want to come and spend the day with you and our son."

"Okay," she said trying to be cool, but he could hear the happiness in her voice.

"I'm working the early shift. I'll come by as soon as I get off."

"Okay fine," she said nonchalantly. "As long as you don't think you're getting some pussy."

"What! I hear you. Love you, girl," he said ending the call. *She must be out of her mind if she thinks I'm not gonna hit that. Enough of this bullshit.*

CHAPTER 23

DIRTY

BENAE

Benae reviewed the slides for a presentation she had to give next week. She made her comments and left the edited document on Candace's desk for her to type up her revisions. Looking at her watch, her timing was perfect. It was 4:55 and she was done for the day. She dialed Chrissy to confirm their plans.

"Hey, girl, we still on for dinner?"

"Yeah, girl, but I'm too tired to cook. I'm in the mood for soul food. I'm gonna stop by Amy Ruth's and get some catfish, whiting, buttered corn, cabbage and pineapple-coconut cake for dessert. How's that sound?" Chrissy asked.

"Sounds good to me. I'll Cash App you for dinner. Since you have everything covered and I can't bring wine."

"Nope, got it covered. Get on the road before the traffic gets too crazy."

"On my way, see you shortly," Benae said closing her office door and heading toward the elevators.

Once she got in her car, she called Sincere to let him know she was stopping by Chrissy's for dinner and that he should pick up something to eat, but he didn't answer so she left a message. By the time she made it through rush hour traffic from downtown Manhattan to Moshulu Parkway in the Bronx it was 6:30. She pulled her Audi A7 behind Chrissy's Lexus in the driveway and sat for a moment admiring the quaint little house. It was so humble and simple that she would have never chosen it for herself, but there was something about it that brought out a longing in her. Underneath it all, it was the love and family inside that made it so much more. She could see the little heads of Marquise and Kye peeking at her through the blinds. She was in no way jealous of her friend, but she wanted this. She wanted a house, a husband and children and she wanted it with Sincere. She stepped out into the chilly November night and waved to the boys.

"Mommy, mommy auntie Benae is here," she could hear them exclaim on the other side of the door.

"Your God son's love them some you," Chrissy said opening the door.

No sooner had she stepped inside the vestibule both boys rushed at her and grabbed her around the waist for two child-sized hugs. "Hey, boys! How are you?" she asked squatting down to talk to them at their level.

Both boys spoke at the same time filling her with stories of Kindergarten and second grade. Benae took a seat at the kitchen table while continuing her conversation with the boys.

"You see mommy's belly? It's getting so big. I hope she has a little girl in there," Benae teased.

"Me too," Marquise chimed in. "I already have a little brother now I want a little sister."

"Me too," Kye copied.

"Here you two," Chrissy said passing the boys paper plates with their dinner. "You can take these in the living room and eat on the coffee table. Don't make a mess!" she yelled after them.

"Okay, your turn," Chrissy said pulling out a paper plate from the stack. "Do you want some of everything?"

"No, I'll do that. You sit down. I can't believe how big your belly is. Last time, I saw you, you were barely showing." Benae started filling her plate.

"If you want wine there's an open bottle of Moscato in the fridge and the Merlot is on the counter."

"Sure, it's okay? I don't have to drink in front of you. I would hate it if someone did it while I was pregnant," Benae said sitting a plate in front of Chrissy.

"Thanks, but it's fine. It hasn't stopped Greg one bit and I make wine spritzers sometimes if the mood hits. So, tell me what's going on. I can tell that something's on your mind. It's not Sincere is it?"

"No, not really. Things between us have been better than ever. Since that last incident with his BM calling me. He's still picking up the baby and bringing him over our house. I feel very good about that."

"I remember you telling me that. How is it having the baby around? Tell the truth," Chrissy warned.

"It's better than I expected it to be. He's such a good baby. He just makes you smile and to see Sincere taking care of him and playing with him it just makes me love him more," she gushed.

"Aww, I'm so happy that things are going so well for you," Chrissy said smiling at Benae.

"Here's what I'm thinking. We will be together two years next Summer. I plan to start the marriage discussions after the holidays, but I really want to get pregnant. You're pregnant, Ming's pregnant, I want to be pregnant, too."

"So, what are you waiting for? If he's gonna marry you, he's still gonna marry you if you have a baby for him," Chrissy insisted.

"That's true, but I don't want to be a baby mama. Ugh."

"Wait a minute Ms. Bougie Givins. Don't forget I was a baby mama before Greg, and I got married. Truth is I'm still a baby mama. I'm the mama of his babies so what?" Chrissy said with mock attitude.

"But you were childhood sweethearts. Everyone knew you and Greg were going to get married."

"Doesn't matter, I ended up marrying my baby daddy. Look at Kendra and Rick, they had their baby first, too. It's not that serious."

"I'll have to think about it and talk to him. I want to see how he feels about everything, but your girl is ready to be a mom."

"Listen you two are going on vacation soon. It's a good time to go for it and see what happens. I'm just saying." Chrissy got up and jogged down the hall to the bathroom. Benae contemplated her friend's suggestion. It wasn't a bad idea.

"Hey," Chrissy said returning. "I'm gonna get some more food. You want something while I'm up?"

"No, I'm good. I was just thinking that we'll be in Jamaica next week for four nights and five days. That's plenty of time to have the talk...and have some unprotected sex." She smiled wickedly at her friend.

"Yes. This is good news. Now our kids will be the same age."

"Calm down, I'm not even pregnant and you're already acting up," she said shaking her head.

"I know, I know wishful thinking. Anyway, it's almost nine. I have to get my boys in bed. They took advantage because you're here."

"Boy, time flies. I thought it was a little after eight. She walked into the living room where the boys were watching *Spiderman* for the umpteenth time. "Hey, guys, I'm leaving, come give me a hug." She kneeled down and absorbed their sweet little hugs and kisses.

"Your phone is vibrating," Chrissy said handing it to her.

"Hey, baby," she said to Sincere.

"Hey, I just got in. The day was crazy there were a lot of emergencies. You on your way home?"

"I am, I was just saying my goodbyes."

"Cool, I want to spend some time with you before I fall asleep but I'm dead ass tired." He yawned.

"You sound it. I'm on my way. Hop in the shower and I'll be home soon."

"Okay, Babe."

By the time she made it home and walked into the bedroom Sincere was already asleep

BONITA

Bonita rolled over in bed and stared at the sky through the open window. She knew in her heart that Sincere wasn't offering her what she wanted. He was still with the next chick and parading her around in the spot that belonged to her. She wasn't going to settle for second place anymore. The plan she was concocting was falling into place. She'd planned to lure him over and seduce him, which was as easy as luring a bird with a crumb. The plan was so scandalous she worried if she could carry it out, but she was desperate and desperate times called for desperate measures. Bonita slid her son to the middle of the bed. She kissed the sleeping baby on the forehead and leaned back to stare at him.

"You deserve to have both of your parents all the time," she choked up and her voice cracked. "And I am going to see to it that you will."

She went into the bathroom to shower and as the warm water ran over her body, she thought about the conversation she recently had with Robbie. He told her to get checked for gonorrhea. Another girl that he was sleeping with unprotected had contracted the STD and passed it onto him. Bonita recently tested positive as well but didn't have the money for the treatment. It hurt her so bad. She cried and cried. Robbie seemed genuinely sorry for infecting her since they had slept together a few more times unprotected, but Bonita was disgusted and told Robbie she didn't want anything to do with him anymore.

Now she was going to purposely pass the nasty STD onto Sincere. She washed between her contaminated legs as she thought about what she was going to do. The way she figured it, Sincere wouldn't know who he got it from. It could be his girlfriend or some other chick he's messing with. I'm probably the last one he'll suspect. Best of all when Benae gets it she will know without a doubt that *her man* ain't the faithful guy he pretends to be.

After the shower, she moved Genuwen to his crib and slathered on Sweet Pea from Bath and Body Works. She sprayed her vajayjay abundantly. She didn't feel different down there, but she wanted to make sure there were no funny smells. She'd already decided not to let him go down on her. She knew he would try since that is one of the ways he liked to make up. Besides, that would just be too foul. She shuddered at the thought. Just to make sure her intentions were clear, she put on thong panties and a tank top. She pinched her nipples so that they were sticking out through the thin fabric and begged to be sucked.

No sooner had she finished primping Sincere was at the door. She opened the door and stood there letting him take all her in. Once he'd had a good look she turned around and walked towards her bedroom. Sincere was on her heels and quickly closed the door behind him, not even bothering to ask about his son as he usually did. She peeked over her shoulder to see his eyes glued to her ass.

Like a bird to crumbs, Bonita thought as she felt his hardness press up against her.

SINCERE

"Don't worry about a thing. Every little thing is gonna be alright," Sincere sang the Bob Marley classic, while stacking their luggage near the door.

"Baby, your singing is awful." Benae laughed.

"...I said don't worry, about a thing..." he continued moving closer to Benae's face and finishing with a kiss on her nose. "I can't wait to get to Jamaica. I need a real get away."

"I know, just think we will be there in a few hours." Benae peeked out of the window as the Uber pulled up. "Babe, the cab is here."

"Alright, one second!" he yelled from the bedroom and pulled his phone from his pocket. "Hey, what's up Nita?"

"Just seeing what's going on with you today."

"We have to go the cab is waiting," Benae said standing in the doorway of the bedroom."

"Okay, I'm coming. I'm just making sure everything is locked up."

"Everything's good, we're on our way to the airport now," Sincere said continuing his conversation.

"What?" Bonita asked with attitude and shock.

"Yeah, we're going to Jamaica today. I thought I told you," he lied.

"Wow, you taking and trips and shit with her. I can't even believe you."

"We'll be back on Monday. I have International service so you can get through if you need to reach me. Alright, kiss Gen for me. I gotta go, the cab is here. Later." He looked at Benae who was listening the whole time.

"What?" he asked.

"Nothing, let's go." Benae grabbed her Gucci carry on and held the door open for Sincere to get the remaining bags.

The direct flight from JFK to Jamaica was on-time and pleasurable. Sincere and Benae were acting like giddy teenagers the way that they kept kissing, smiling at one another, and touching. They reveled in the moment of their first vacation together. Sincere felt particularly good since Benae was cool with flying coach and he could afford to pay for the tickets himself. The package he purchased also included shuttle service from the airport to the Sandals Resort.

He was already feeling good about the island. The warm tropical breeze and clear blue water was soothing to the soul but there was also an undercurrent of sensuality that turned him on. They checked-in into the popular couple's resort and both were impressed with the lush surroundings.

"I can't wait to see our room," she said.

"Yeah, let's go check it out," he said grabbing her hand and leading her toward the elevators.

The bellman had already brought their bags up. They opened the door to a King-sized bed filled with pillows, a big open balcony accessible through the open French doors, a huge bathroom replete with a Jacuzzi tub and a separate seating area. Sincere lead Benae out onto the balcony and stood behind her with his arms around her waist and his chin resting gently on top of her head. He felt her relax into his arms as they took in the beautiful resort and the beach. He felt his emotions stir for her, just by having her by his side in this beautiful paradise.

He turned her around to face him. "You know how much I love you?" he started, looking into her eyes. The look he found there was filled with nothing but love for him. He took in her pretty smile, her brown skin glistening from the heat and her hair blowing softly in the wind and felt an overwhelming desire for her and confirmed, once again, that she was everything he ever wanted in a woman.

"Yes, I know, and I hope you know how very much I love you," she said unaware that she had already told him.

He leaned down to kiss her, and she returned the kiss as deeply as he gave it. He backed her into the room and kept going until her back was against the wall. He pulled her tube top down so that her braless breasts popped out above it. He held one in each hand and took turns licking both until the nipples were plump peaks. She reached down to unbuckle the belt holding up his denim shorts, both fell to the floor and the buckle sounded with a satisfying clank. She massaged his already stiff manhood and took him in her mouth. He watched as she delighted in giving him pleasure. She swirled her tongue around his length and girth stopping only to give the same attention to his balls. She lifted them up and tea bagged him expertly. When he couldn't stand any more, he pushed her up against the wall, lifted up her maxi skirt, moved her thong over to the side and inserted himself into her waiting wetness.

"Damn, you real wet baby," he murmured against her ear.

"Ohhh," they both cried out as he began to plunge into her ferociously.

"Yes, baby," she said clinging to him tighter as he lifted her up forcing her to wrap her legs around him.

"I'm about, I'm about to cum." He grabbed her ass and released a powerful orgasm. Panting and out of breath he walked over to the bed with his pants around his ankles and dropped them both onto the bed. Even though they had just arrived and planned to get out of the room and kick-off their vacation, they both fell asleep - Benae with her breasts sticking out from the top of her dress and the rest of it around her waist. Sincere fell out on his back with his pants still around his ankles. They wanted to get up but the warm tropical breeze from the open balcony doors combined with the air-conditioning and twirling ceiling fan felt too good after the intense love making session to move.

CHAPTER 24

MATRIMONY: I GOT PLANS FOR YOU

BENAE

Benae copped a squat on the beach and watched Sincere speed across the water on a jet ski. She beamed watching him control the powerful machine given that he'd never ridden one and was a bit afraid of the water. Since they had arrived in Jamaica three nights ago, they had been having a blast, especially Sincere. He indulged in every activity offered and together they had won a couple's dance contest. She reminisced on the night before when they'd had the best meal of the visit. They made reservations at one of the many restaurants recommended for authentic Jamaican food. They both had the jerk chicken, rice and peas, coco bread and sorrel. Afterwards they were treated to a live performance from a local band. The sound of the steel drums resonated in her mind. She snapped out of her reverie when she saw Sincere approaching.

"You did great, you were out there looking like a pro," she said standing up to give him a hug and kiss.

"Yo, it's fun, you should try it. I can't believe you're such a scary cat," he teased.

"I know, I just don't feel like it. It's probably all the drinks. All I want to do is lounge and eat."

"So, you just want to chill here at the resort tonight? They're having a toga party that sounds like fun."

"Yeah, that does sound like fun. Tomorrow, sightseeing in town, right? Our last day." She made a sad face.

"That's the plan."

"Okay, well I came down to get my hair braided but I stopped to watch you on the jet ski. I'll be over here for about an hour." She pointed to a spot on the beach under a tree where a woman was sitting and braiding a white girl's hair. "But first I am going to get me a roti and some rum punch."

"In that case, I'll see if anyone wants to play ball."

"Alright then, see you later."

Benae picked up her food, her drink and walked back to the beach to get her hair done. She sat down and told the woman the style she wanted.

"That's a good-looking man you have there, better keep your eye on he," she said with the Jamaican sing-song accent. "Not married," she inquired looking at Benae's bare ring finger.

"Not yet," Benae answered. "We're just going on two years so hopefully soon."

"No babies?"

"No, hopefully soon for that, too."

"Ummm hmmm," the woman responded without speaking and set to the business of braiding.

There was something about her line of questioning and seemingly worldly wisdom that cultivated a sense of urgency within the deepest corner of Benae's soul. Right then and there she said a silent prayer asking God to bless her with a healthy pregnancy and baby. She knew that she was ovulating and was happy when Sincere just thought the extra wetness he was feeling was just her being extremely aroused. The thought of getting pregnant while on this romantic get-away was exciting, memorable, and perfect. They had been having sex at least twice a day. She still worried at times about being pregnant and unmarried but she was more certain than ever that she would marry Sincere so what was the point of waiting. She felt secure that she was doing the right thing after the implied comments by the old hair-braider.

She looked up to see him walking back toward her. He looked so damn good in his swim trunks and bare chest. The sun had kissed his skin giving it a bronze glow.

"Babe you, done yet?" he bellowed from a distance.

"Almost, mon, almost," the hair braider chimed in and they all laughed. "Keep your head still and let me finish up."

Benae smiled up at Sincere sheepishly and shrugged her shoulders indicating that she was helpless. "I guess I'll go back to the room. Hope you're done soon. I miss you."

Benae blew him a kiss before he turned and walked away. *He misses me,* she thought, and she knew exactly what that meant. It was almost like he was trying to get her pregnant too.

SINCERE

Sincere looked at Benae asleep beside him. She was naked and he pulled back the sheet to admire her beautiful body. She lay on her stomach with both arms wrapped around the pillow. Her long, toned legs, round butt and hair falling just beneath her shoulders, gave Sincere thoughts of slipping it in from behind but decided to let her rest. He had been a sexual savage since their arrival. Something about the place made him horny. The fact that she was half naked in everything that she wore didn't help. He completed his admiration of her body, got up and poured himself a glass of Jamaican rum before heading to the balcony to look at the ocean. It was shiny and dark in the moonlight. But it was the sound of the waves hitting the shore that was soothing to his pensive mood.

There were many weddings at the resort during their stay. He had seen the happiness in Benae's eyes each time a bride walked past them or engaged them in conversation. He wanted her to know that joy for herself and he wanted to be the one to give it to her. After almost a year and a half together, he was ready. Benae Alexis Givens was going to be his wife. He took some time to look at rings at some of the jewelry stores on the island while she was getting her hair braided but he decided to wait until they got back to the states to make such an important purchase. He wouldn't be getting the ring she showed him at Tiffany's, but his jeweler would hook him up with something nice. Still he couldn't stop thinking how nice it would be to propose here in Jamaica on their first trip together. It would be memorable, and he could see her keep looking at her left ring finger in disbelief at the huge diamond that adorned it all the way back home.

Briefly, he thought about Bonita. She hadn't called the whole time he'd been away. He took that as a sign that marrying Benae was the right thing to do because even Bonita was falling in line. He stood up and took some pictures of the beach being sure to capture the moonlight as it shone on the water creating millions of individual ripples. Of course, he turned the camera around to face himself and took a few selfies. He walked back into the room and captured a few of Benae sleeping, too, taking the liberty of snapping a few shots of her nude body. He grinned thinking about how mad she was gonna be when he showed them to her, but he didn't care. She was going to be his wife and he could do what he wanted with Mrs. Benae Law. Yeah, he liked the sound of that.

BONITA

The crowded B25 bus struggled through the busy downtown Brooklyn traffic. Bonita sat in a middle seat with Genuwen on her lap, the diaper bag on her left arm and the fold away stroller on her right. She was about to ask the old woman seated next to her to press the button to signal for her stop when the old woman pressed it first. At the next stop Bonita waited impatiently as the old woman propped up her cane and slowly stepped both feet onto each step as she exited the bus. As soon as she was able Bonita rushed out behind her and quickly dropped the diaper bag to the ground. She attempted to click open the flimsy stroller, but it wouldn't open.

"Excuse me, do you need some help?" the old lady inquired.

"No, I got it," Bonita said finally opening the stroller and strapping the baby in.

"You, sure?" the lady asked again.

"Yes, thank you," Bonita said slightly irritated. She picked up the diaper bag and started the walk home.

"Hi grandma, sorry I wasn't here to meet you...wait a minute, 'Nita is that you?" the girl stopped in her tracks to get a better look.

"Renee?" Bonita looked surprised. "How are you?" The two girls embraced tentatively.

"I'm blessed girl. About to go to this revival with my grandmother."

"*Revival?* You!" Bonita laughed out loud. Remembering how scandalous and trifling Renee was known to be back in the day.

"I know what you're thinking, 'Nita but I've found Jesus and he has turned my life around."

"Really," was all Bonita offered.

"Here." Renee handed her a pamphlet about giving your life to the Lord. "Take this and if you feel it in in your heart to join us you are more than welcome. Matter of fact, why don't you give me your number so that we can talk some more and catch up?"

Bonita thought about it for a moment. "How about you give me yours?"

"Sure, no problem. Here's my number and I promise if you call me, I will not lecture you. I just want to tell you how good God has been to me."

"I wasn't thinking that," Bonita lied.

"Either way, I hope to see you or hear from you soon." Renee reached out and gave Bonita a hug and knelt down to say hello to Gen.

Thoughts of her conversation with Renee replayed in her mind as she strolled slowly even though it was cold out. She could see without even really speaking to Renee how much she had changed. She no longer looked like the neighborhood hoe she once was. Her clothes, her make-up, her speech was cleaned up and she looked happy from within. But what was most noticeable was her joy and goodness. It was just there. That blessedness was something Bonita felt was markedly missing in her life and she felt a pining for it. She thought of the nasty act she committed against Sincere and his girlfriend and suddenly felt ashamed, dirty, and evil for what she had done.

She had finally gotten the shot to clear up the gonorrhea and should be completely clear of it now. When she got home, she put Gen down for a nap and sat at the kitchen table confessing her sins out loud to God. She cried her heart out and fervently asked God for forgiveness.

CHAPTER 25

EMOTIONAL

BENAE

It had almost been a month since their trip to Jamaica and Benae was tracking the days since she had missed her period. She couldn't believe that something she had planned for actually worked out the way she wanted it to.

How often does that happen? she thought.

She was now officially three days late and her 26th day cycle appeared each month as though it was set on a schedule. She knew she had to be pregnant but had yet to take a test to confirm it even though there were two test kits sitting in the bathroom cabinet. Today's the day, she said aloud kicking off her shoes and walking into the bathroom. She peed on the stick, sat it on the sink and waited for the results. She washed her hands and could hear her cell ringing from her pocketbook that she had flung onto the sofa. The number on the phone was not one she recognized and for a brief second, she was glad because she really didn't feel like talking to anyone she knew right now.

"Hello," she said.

"Yes, is this Benae Givens?"

"Yes, it is. Whose calling?"

"This is Officer Jackson, I'm calling from Mary Immaculate Hospital to notify you that Sincere Law was in a car accident."

"What? What happened to him? Is he okay?"

"I can't really say ma'am. You can find out more from the hospital directly."

"Fine, I'm on my way," she said ending the call while sliding her feet back into her shoes. Just as she was about to walk out, she remembered the test in the bathroom. Without hesitation she ran back to the bathroom and looked down at the word *Pregnant* on the stick. She said a quick thank you to the Lord and said a prayer that her baby's father was okay as well.

For some reason she was overcome with a desire to call Bonita and let her know that Sincere was in an accident. As she neared the hospital in Queens, she dialed her number. Now that they each had access to each other's phone numbers they sometimes called each other. Bonita would call to check on Gen and if Sincere didn't pick up she would all Benae. One-time Benae called her to ask about dosage of cold medicine when Gen had a cold.

"Hello?"

"Hi, Bonita, it's Benae."

"I can see that."

"Oh." Benae laughed nervously. "I'm calling about Sincere. I just received a call from Mary Immaculate Hospital that he was in a car accident. I just thought you should know."

"Oh, my God. Thanks for telling me." She hung up.

Benae was surprised by her reaction and had envisioned them having a bit more of a conversation. Well, it didn't matter now she had just pulled up at the hospital. Of course, there were no parking spots, so she just parked in an illegal spot and asked for Sincere's room. She was relieved to find out that he was not in surgery. The elevator up to the 4th floor seemed to take forever. Benae tapped her foot impatiently until the doors opened. She hurried over to the reception desk and gave Sincere's name again.

"Oh, hello," the perky nurse said. "Bonita, right?"

"No, I'm Benae," Benae said with attitude for days.

"Oh, so sorry, it's just that I spoke to someone named Bonita on the phone and she sounded so concerned I thought you were her."

Benae took a deep breath and rolled her eyes. "Well, I'm not, now where is Sincere Law?"

"He's in room four-eleven. He's fine they are just keeping him for observation."

Benae walked away from her and strutted down the hallway toward Sincere's room. When she walked in, he was on the phone.

"No, I'm good. I'm telling you the accident was crazy but I'm good. Don't worry, don't worry. Me too," he looked up and saw Benae. "I got to go," he said ending the call.

Benae pulled herself together although she felt very hurt that he was on the phone with Bonita and may have just told her he loved her. What else does *"me too"* mean at the end of a call? Before she could ask him anything.

Sincere offered up information. "Hey, that was 'Nita. She told me you called and told her what happened to me. That was nice of you," he said smiling at her. "Come here." She couldn't bring herself to give him the hug he was expecting.

Instead, of going over to him she sat beside him on the bed out of arm's reach. "Baby, I'm so glad you're okay. You're completely fine nothing is broken or anything?" she asked. "Tell me what happened."

"I had just got off work and I came out here to meet my man at the Coliseum who had the hook up on some Jordan's. I'm coming off the Grand Central Parkway when this motherfucker in a Suburban rammed into me and caused me to go up on the sidewalk and slam into the front yard of this house. The only thing that slowed me down and stopped me was the brick and metal gate. From there I must've been knocked out or something because next thing I remember was them asking me questions and putting me in the ambulance."

"Did you have on your seatbelt?" she asked knowing that many times he drove without it. He looked at her sheepishly and answered, "No. That's why my head hit the windshield and knocked me out."

"It's okay, baby," she said standing up to grab him in her arms. "The important thing is that you're okay. I don't know what I would do if I lose you. I love you so much."

"I love you, too." She looked at him with tears in her eyes.

"Bae, what's wrong? Why you so emotional?" he asked smiling and shaking his head at her. "I promise you I'm okay."

The best answer to that question was that she was completely overwhelmed at the moment. She was trying not to think of what could have happened to him and what her life would be like if she lost him. Only to be met with hearing the end of his conversation with Bonita and the fact that she was always intertwined in their lives somehow.

All of that would take too long to explain, so she gave the other plausible explanation. "Maybe it's because I'm pregnant."

SINCERE

Sincere awakened to a dark room with no light or sounds which was unusual because even with the blackout curtains, the light from the living room or kitchen usually crept down the hall and peeked into the bedroom. He wondered if Benae had gone out to the store or something. He pulled himself up and swung his legs over the side of the bed, that's when he saw the light coming from under the bathroom door. Without calling out to her, he got up and barged into the bathroom to find Benae sitting at her make-up table crying.

"Babe, what's the matter?" he asked from the doorway.

"Nothing," she said quickly wiping her tears away with the wad of tissue she held in her hand. "How are you feeling. How's your head?" she asked standing and inspecting him.

"I'm good. Now tell me why you're crying."

"Alright, I'll tell you," she said heading out of the bathroom. "Let's go sit at the table. I need some water." She poured them both a glass of water and leaned against the counter while Sincere took a seat at the table.

"Okay," she started. "Bonita calls my phone looking for you when she can't reach you on your phone." Sincere rubbed his forehead and continued listening. "It's not so much an issue that she called me but it's just that she's *always* there. She's *always* around. Just like yesterday, I let her know you were in an accident and by the time I got to the hospital they thought I was her because she'd talked them on the phone. When I finally made it to your room, you're on the phone with her. I was so irritated by it all, but I didn't say anything because you were the priority at that moment." Sincere frowned briefly but quickly straightened up his face before she noticed. "And that's the thing that's got me so upset," she said tearing up again. "I'm pregnant and I feel like she's going to just overshadow everything. I don't want to share you as much as I apparently have too. It's like I'm with both of you. I understand you and Genuwen are a package deal but what the fuck is she? Why is she always in our lives? The only thing I should be concerned about right now is having a healthy baby, but I am so irritated with her," Benae said pacing back in forth.

"Come here," he said indicating that she take a seat on his lap. "Listen, I understand everything you're saying but I do feel that some of those pregnancy hormones are kicking in already," he said tickling her belly and making her laugh. "Seriously, though, I will do whatever I have to do to make you happy. I do check in with her just to make sure my son is good but all the extra stuff we can make changes and dial it back. Okay?"

She turned to him and nodded. "So, you're happy we're having a baby? We really didn't get a chance to talk about it."

"It wasn't in my plan just yet, but yeah, I'm happy. Are you? You sounded a little unsure just now."

"Are you crazy do you know how bad I wanted to get pregnant? Chrissy and Ming being pregnant was just like flaunting it in my face. I am very happy."

He picked her up and kissed her nose. "I know what else would make you feel better."

"I can think of at least three things but what do you have in mind?" she asked.

He could tell she thought it was something sexual, but he was thinking on a whole other level. "I think you would feel a lot better if I put a ring on it." He chuckled at the look of absolute surprise on

Benae's face. Her mouth was hanging open. "Say something, before you start catching flies."

"Are you serious? Do not play with me about this," she said sternly as she stared at him.

"I was thinking about it since we were in Jamaica. It was the most perfect experience I ever had with a woman and it showed me that you are the one. I was gonna ask you on our last night there, but I wanted to wait until I got the ring but now that you're carrying my child, there's no reason to wait."

"I don't know what to say," she said, tearing up.

"There's nothing for you to say, right now. We can go to my jeweler in the diamond district to pick out the ring this weekend," he said hugging her to his chest.

She looked up at him and he wiped the tears from her eyes. "Thank you," she said through her tears. "You are making me so happy. I love you so much." She started bawling.

He held her tighter. "You don't seem happy," he joked. "Stop crying."

"I can't." She gave a little laugh.

"You need to relax. I'll run you a bath and you can just chill for a bit."

"Okay," she said and followed him back into the bathroom.

"While you relax, I'm gonna head out for a bit."

"Are you sure you're up to it?" she asked settling into the tub.

"I'm fine. I coulda came home yesterday."

"Where are you going?"

"I have to stop by my job and fill out some paperwork. Then I'm gonna stop and see Gen for a minute. If you want, I can bring home dinner, so you don't have to worry about that."

"Okay," she said closing her eyes and sliding down in the tub so that her head rested on the edge of the tub.

"Here," he said placing her bath pillow behind her head. "I'm gonna go take a shower in the other bathroom so I won't disturb you."

"You can use the shower in here. I don't mind."

"No, this is your time," he said dimming the light.

He kissed her on the forehead and walked into the bedroom to find something to wear. He noticed how settled and relaxed Benae became after he mentioned getting her a ring. He hoped getting engaged would bring the much-needed peace to his household and his life that he was looking for. Plus, he had plans to clean up his act and be the man and husband she deserved. No more fucking other women, no more lying. He had dreams of being a good husband and father and he was going to live up to that.

BONITA

Bonita ended her call with Renee. The two had kept in touch since the day that they had reunited at the bus stop. She was a bit surprised when she caught her own reflection in the mirror and saw that she was smiling. The conversation was so uplifting. They talked about God and what His presence meant to her. Renee had devoted her life to God and Bonita felt a longing to do the same, at least some day. She wasn't sure if she was ready now, but she knew she needed to go to church and pray to be forgiven for knowingly passing on a disease, even if it was treatable and even if she felt the two parties involved deserved it for causing her so much pain. She was so happy because Renee invited her to get Gen christened at her church. Her mom had asked her many times about getting him christened, but at that time she was in no hurry to do it. Now she wanted to get it done as soon as possible.

"Let me call Sin and see when he is available on a Sunday so that we can get this thing scheduled," she said to herself. She called his cell but didn't get an answer. "Well, since Ms. Benae doesn't hesitate to call my phone when she feels like it, I guess I will return the favor."

"Hello," Benae answered sounding a bit confused.

"Hi, is Sincere around? I tried calling his cell, but he didn't pick up."

"No, he's not," Benae said shortly.

"Well, is he ho...I mean is he out of the hospital?"

"Yes."

"Tell him to call me. It's sort of important."

"Is Gen, okay? Otherwise, I would rather you leave him a message and not call my phone."

"He's fine, but what's the problem with me calling you. You just called me yesterday."

"Yes, I did Bonita. It was an emergency but trust me I will not be doing it again. Just don't get into the habit of calling me when you can't reach him."

The nerve of this heifer, Bonita thought. She was about to say this bitch, but she caught herself and corrected her thoughts to remove the curse word.

"And another thing," Benae continued. "When I informed you of Sincere's accident yesterday, it wasn't for you to call the hospital. That's what I am here for."

"Excuse me but I am his son's mother and I can check up on my son's father if I want to. I didn't want to wait to get the information second hand from you if I could call the hospital and find out for myself."

"Speaking of baby mother's, I'm pregnant. So, I'll be his baby mama for as long as it takes me to plan our wedding and become his wife."

"I don't believe that. He wouldn't do that to me," Bonita said secure in her conviction.

"Believe what you want. I'll let him know you called," Benae said ending the call.

She has to be lying. She's just mad about yesterday, Bonita thought. *But what if it's true? It can't be. After all that Sincere has put me through, he would not go out and start another family.* Then it dawned on her that she may be pregnant with gonorrhea. It's been a few weeks since she'd infected Sincere. Could they have already found out and gotten it cured or are they still unaware? Is it possible that she didn't pass it on after all? There was really no way for her to find out without giving herself away as the culprit. All she could do now is pray on it. As much as she couldn't stand the thought of Sincere having a baby with someone else, she was pro-life and wouldn't be able to live with the fact that her dirty deed harmed an innocent baby.

CHAPTER 26

CONGRATULATIONS

BENAE

Benae laughed to herself as she set up three-way call with Chrissy and Ming. They were right she couldn't hold water. They were the first ones to know about her pregnancy and now about her proposal, ring-less though it was.

"Ming you were right," Benae said before anyone had the chance to exchange hellos.

"I'm not playing no guessing games with your ass," Ming threated. "Tell us what happened."

"It could only be one thing," Chrissy interjected. "She told him about the baby, and he said he wants to get married."

"Yes, but even a little bit better. He said he was thinking of proposing while we were in Jamaica, but he wanted to get the ring first. He decided to tell me after I told him about the baby."

"I knew it. That man loves you. He ain't stupid. He knows he has to put a ring on it with you," Ming said.

"Congratulations, girl!" Chrissy yelled. "I am so happy for you my love. Okay, we have to start going over some dates and making plans. First date, due date, when is it again?"

"August twenty-third."

"Okay, so working backward from the twenty-third we can plan the shower. Are you trying to have a wedding before or after the baby?"

"Definitely, before, preferably before I start showing."

"Well, I can be your wedding planner. I have nothing but free time and good taste," Ming said seriously.

"I am sure you would be an awesome planner," Benae lied. She and Ming would not have the same vision of a tasteful affair.

"Besides, I am about to call Rhonda and let her know her only child is getting married. She will have the wedding planned in no time."

"That's true, "Chrissy added. "Well, keep us posted. Hopefully, she'll let us do the shower."

"She will once I tell her that's what I want," Benae said confidently.

"Spoiled brat," Ming chided.

"Well, I am only child so...oh, and before I let you go, guess who called me earlier?" Before they could answer she continued, "Bonita. She called me looking for Sincere after she couldn't reach him on his phone. It was funny the timing of her call because I had just got finished telling Sincere that I felt that she was in our lives too much and then she calls. I told her not to call my phone unless it was an emergency. She got an attitude and pulled her baby mama card. That is when I shut it down. I told her I was pregnant and that Sincere and I were getting married."

"What she say?" Chrissy and Ming asked in unison.

"She said she didn't believe me and that he wouldn't do that to her."

"She's really delusional," Chrissy said.

"I'm glad you told her. But how do you think Sin will feel when she tells him?" Ming asked.

"I told him I told her. He didn't mind at all."

"Very good sign," Ming said.

"Okay, ladies, I am going to lay down and relax a bit. It's been a long day," Benae yawned.

"Oh, not that you asked Benae, but me and the baby are doing fine," Ming said sarcastically.

"Same here." Chrissy laughed.

"I'm sorry," Benae said. "It's just that I always have something going on. I am very happy that all four of you are doing well."

"I'm just messing with you. It's all love," Ming said.

"Goodnight, ladies."

"Goodnight."

SINCERE

It felt good to be in a bar surrounded by big screen TVs, the smell of beer, buffalo wings and French fries in the air. Best of all Sincere couldn't remember the last time he felt so relaxed, maybe even happy. Kicking back with his brother and his homie was just what he needed.

"Damn these wings are good," Tru said licking his fingers.

"Stop eating like a Viking and use a napkin, bruh," Sincere said, tossing a stack of napkins his way..

"We ain't using those," Rick chimed in sucking sauce from his fingers.

"Yo' Benae is rubbing off on you man. Talking about use a napkin, fuck outta here," Tru snarled.

"Go on and eat then. I'm glad we were able to get together, man. I'm good but I got a lot of shit on my mind," Sincere said turning the mood serious.

"Talk," Rick said.

"Well, first of all Benae is pregnant."

"For real dog? That's what's up," Rick said. "I know she's happy as hell."

"She happier than a whore in Boys town." Tru laughed.

"I wasn't expecting to be, but I'm happy, too." He pulled out one of the sonogram pictures and proudly showed them the first image of his second child."

"So, when is she due?" Tru asked using his pinky to get a better view of the picture on the table.

"She's six weeks. The baby is due August twenty-third."

"So, you just walking around with the ultrasound?" Rick joked.

"Yeah, I had it in my wallet since her first appointment. The real news is I just got back from the Diamond District, I put money down on a ring. You know my man Jacob is gonna add some bling here and there so that her ring is one of a kind. I gotta call her pops and everything but I basically already asked her to marry me."

"Yooo!" Tru exclaimed.

"I can't believe this," Rick said. "Congratulations man!"

"Thanks. I can tell already that rings change things man." He laughed.

"They definitely do, especially in the beginning," Rick added.

"She trying to put the rush on me. She wants to have the wedding and everything before she starts showing. I thought we would be engaged at least year."

"Damn," Tru said.

"I know and I ain't even finished yet," Sincere continued. "So, Benae told 'Nita that she was pregnant and that we were getting married before I got the chance to tell her. So, she came at me hot threatening what she was going to do if it was true. She said she would put me on child support, make me get visitation to see my son and she said she's celibate and I'm cut off."

"That sound like some shit Kendra would do," Rick said shaking his head in sympathy.

"That's why I can't stand her ass. None of that shit is necessary," Tru said with a scowl on his face.

"That's the same thing I said, but it didn't change nothing. So, I have to figure out how to fix this."

"You think Bonita is for real?" Rick asked.

"To an extent, I just have to figure out how to get her back on board,"

"I don't envy you," Tru said. "It's hard enough trying to please one woman and you have to try to please two. That's too much damn work. When I fuck around, I let 'em know up front it's just sex. Don't be calling my girl, don't be posting shit on social media, none of that," Tru said emphatically.

"It is a lot of work. That's why I just decided to get married and simplify this shit. I didn't expect Bonita to go in on me like that. Benae fucked it up. She knew what she was doing when she told her, but 'Nita called her on some being annoying shit and she got more than she planned for. Crazy thing is I just went through this with Benae she was going off about me talking to Bonita too much and feeling like she was too much in our lives. The ring talk shut that down real quick. What can I do to keep Bonita happy, too?"

"Lie," Tru said. Rick and Sincere laughed. "Works for me all the time."

"I ain't saying shit. Things just getting back on track with Kendra and I'm staying on my Ps and Qs. Matter of fact, I need another drink while you try to figure this one out," Rick said.

Tru dipped two fries into a small cup of mayonnaise then into the ketchup he had squirted in the corner of the basket of fries. "The way I see it," he said chewing. "You have to use a delay tactic and tell Bonita that you're not sure the baby is yours and that you decided not to get married."

Sincere and Rick locked eyes and shrugged. The idea wasn't half bad.

"Or you can try the classic Stevie J. move and get Bonita a ring, too." They all had a good laugh at the classic Love and Hip-Hop scene.

"You know what, this just might work," Sincere said. "Now let me eat my food. I been talking so damn much, shit is cold."

"One last thing, you heard from Melissa?" Rick asked.

"Funny you should ask. She's coming into town tonight. Perfect timing, too, 'Nita cut me off, Benae is tired." So much for trying to be a good man, he said lifting his Heineken and toasting to his boys.

BONITA

Bonita sat on a bench right outside the door of her building. It was hovering around the forty-degree mark but no wind chill factor. Genuwen sat in his stroller asleep with a plastic stroller cover shielding him from the cold. Bonita sat with her crossed leg swinging back and forth. She couldn't wait for Sincere to pull up. She had a lot to say and he wasn't going to like any of it. As if on cue, she saw his car pull into an empty space in front of her building. The love she felt as she watched him stride toward her could not be denied. It wasn't the first time she'd wished that she didn't love him like she did.

"Hey, 'Nita," he said walking over to her and clearly waiting for her to stand up and give him a kiss. When she didn't, he picked up his son and lifted him up over his head. The little boy squealed and laughed as his dad lifted him a few more times. "So, what's going on? "Why you sitting outside in the cold?' he asked her, holding Gen in his arms.

"As if you give a fuck."

"What?" Sincere looked surprised.

"You tell me. Is she really pregnant for you? Our son will be a year-old next month and you have another one on the way with someone else. What are you thinking?" She looked at him with disgust.

"First of all, don't come at me like that. It wasn't like it was planned or nothing..."

"Oh, so it's true," she interrupted. "Wow."

"Maybe it is, maybe it's not. I just saw the test on the stick. It's not like she been to the doctor or nothing."

"Yeah, that's probably the same game you ran on her when I told you I was pregnant." Sincere sat down and remained quiet.

"Wow, I am so tired of you hurting me. I really am," she said solemnly.

"'Nita, I am not trying to hurt you. I'm still here for you whenever and whatever you need me for. I'm good to you. I respect you and you know I'll always have love for you. If you stop looking at what we had, you'll be alright."

"Don't you miss what we had? I do."

"I do, too. I do miss it, but things have changed, especially now." He turned to face her his facial expression serious. Her mind and her heart raced trying to figure out what he was about to say.

"I want you to hear it from me before anyone else. I asked Benae to marry me."

She closed her eyes and shook her head no. Before she could stop them, tears sprang to her eyes but this time she wasn't hurt, she was angry. "You know what, congratulations. I hope you're happy and all that good shit but know this – God does not like ugly and karma will bite you in the butt because what you are doing to me is so wrong."

"How it is wrong? I'm still here with you. You still have me like you want and I have what I want. What's wrong that? Let's be real, you knew I was with someone else. I didn't hide that from you. It was your decision to try to keep us going."

"I really can't believe what I'm hearing, right now. You were still coming around telling me you love me and still having sex with me. So, what did you expect me to do?" she yelled as she stood up to stare down at him.

"Yo' keep your voice down. And yes, I did those things and I expected exactly what I got from you because you love me. I'm not about to let the next dude be here with my son and you know that," he said earnestly.

"You are really something else. Your arrogance is unbelievable! Go head, Mr. Have his cake and eat it too..."

"What's the point of having cake if you can't eat it?"

"You keep doing what you do but I'm definitely making some changes, too." She sat back down and crossed her legs. "First thing tomorrow, I'm putting you on child support." He tried to interrupt, but she held up her hand and shook her head no. "Hold up. If you want to take your son to your house, you are going to need a visitation order for that. I figured since you have another baby on the way, I need to make sure me and mine is good." The look on Sincere's face was too funny.

He was pissed and trying hard to maintain.

Gen cried out and reached for her, seeming to want to comfort his hurting mother and get away from the man causing her pain.

"Hey, big boy," she cooed taking her son in her arms.

"'Nita, all that is not necessary, nothings gonna change," he pleaded.

"That's not the point. I'm doing this for me, and some things are gonna change. Like I've been telling you, I started going to church and I'm celibate. So, there will be no more fornicating with you."

Sincere chuckled and flashed that smile that melted her heart. "We'll see about that."

"Ah, no we won't. You have to respect me, or I will tell your fiancé." She rolled her eyes at the word fiancé.

"Be like that then, fuck it."

"Don't curse around him," she said holding her baby protectively.

"Don't tell me what to do. Come on, Gen, let's go," he said trying to pull his son from his mother's arms.

"I told you, you need a visitation order."

"Come on 'Nita, you see he wants to come with me."

Little Genuwen was reaching for his dad and it would break her heart to see her son crying for his dad knowing she would be the reason for his tears. Reluctantly, she handed him to his father. "Okay, he can go this time, but don't think I'm playing. I want a documented visitation order so that I can have scheduled days off to live my life, too." Again, she saw the flash of anger and irritation in his eyes, but he didn't say anything.

"I'll bring him back tomorrow about five or six."

"Make that seven." She smiled sweetly. "Bye, baby, see you later," she said giving her son a kiss.

Without giving Sincere a second glance, she headed in the opposite direction of her building with no particular destination in mind. She just didn't want him to see her going back in the house.

"You need a ride somewhere?" he yelled after her.

"No, I'm good," she said adding a little switch to her walk because she knew his eyes were on her wondering if he was losing her, and everything she had always been to him.

CHAPTER 27

BURN

BENAE

Benae closed her office door and laid her head down on her desk. The past few days she hadn't been feeling well. She figured it was par for the course since she was expecting a baby, but she just felt weird. The worst thing was she was having trouble peeing. It felt like her bladder was full, but the pee trickled out after she tried to force it out. It was getting worse, she never felt like her bladder was empty. She decided it was time to call Dr. Cassidy and dialed her direct on her cell.

"Hi, Dr. Cassidy."

"Hello, Benae, is everything okay?" her Dr. asked her voice full of concern.

"No, I'm having trouble urinating. I feel like I can't empty my bladder."

"I know," Dr. Cassidy's voice was pensive. "I was going to give you a call today about your results of you pre-natal testing. We screen you for all STDs and you tested positive for gonorrhea."

"What! There's no way?"

"Yes."

"But I've only been with my fiancé," Benae protested. Dr. Cassidy remained silent, which allowed Benae to come to the only other conclusion. "I knew it, I knew something was going to happen. Everything was just too perfect," she cried. "What's going to happen to my baby."

"The baby should be fine. You need to get to the nearest emergency room to get a shot of antibiotics. I'm in my Westchester office today. The issue you are having with urination will clear up once the antibiotic is administered."

"I'll go now. Thank you, doctor."

"You're welcome and I'm so sorry this happened to you."

"Me too," Benae said hanging up the phone and crying hard into her hands. As she started to catch her breath and wipe away her tears, there was a tentative knock at the door. Candace poked her head in. "Hey, is everything okay?"

"No, I'm not feeling well. I have to go the emergency room, right now."

"I'm so sorry," Candace said. "I'll cancel your meetings for the rest of the day. Is there anything else you need?"

"Yes," she said checking her face in the mirror and touching up her make-up. "I'll be working from home the rest of the week. I won't be in. Also, can you call Sincere and tell him I'm on my way to Long Island College Hospital and for him to meet me there. I can't talk to him, right now."

"Okay, I'll go make the calls but first do you want a bottled water?"

"Make the calls, I can grab a water on my way out. Thank you so much. I promise I'll give you a call tomorrow with any news," Benae lied.

The walk to the elevator and through the lobby felt surreal. It was impossible to believe that the man she loved, trusted and whose child she was carrying, was not only cheating on her but had infected her with a STD. The emotions running through her were too many to name. *Sincere is cheating on me and though I had my suspicions, I never really believed that he would cheat on me. Not once,* she thought. It wasn't with Bonita because she would have told me the first chance she got." She stepped into one of the corporate cars waiting outside.

"Where to Miss?" the driver asked.

"To LIC, please," she managed.

As expected, her phone rang and a picture of Sincere's smiling face appeared. Her energy seemed to leave her body, she curled up and laid down on the seat before answering.

"Hello," she whispered.

"Baby, it's me. I'm on my way. Why didn't you call me?" She didn't respond. "Benae did something happen with the baby?"

"The baby is fine at least for now." She hung up. He called back but she didn't answer.

"We're here Miss," the driver indicated.

Benae was thankful that the driver just drove and didn't inquire about her or try to keep a conversation going. She dragged herself into a seated position and handed the driver her corporate card. She'd pay the company back when she submitted her expenses. She told the driver thank you and stepped out of the car. An EMT truck was parked haphazardly near the emergency room entrance and she knew it had to be Sincere. His co-worker that drove him there was pulling out. Sincere was at the triage desk.

"Why'd you hang up on me? What's going on?" he asked anxiously.

She ignored him and spoke directly to the woman behind the desk. "I am six weeks pregnant and my gynecologist informed me that I have contracted gonorrhea and I need to get a shot of antibiotics. I am also having a hard time urinating and I have to go really bad, right now. It feels like my bladder is going to burst."

Sincere was talking but she wasn't paying attention to what he was saying. She was still too upset to face him. A Nurse came over and guided Benae to a cot and curtained it off. She gave Benae a hospital gown to change into and told her she would be right back with a catheter. Those words were music to Benae's ears, she had to pee so bad it hurt. Sincere helped get her into the robe but decided not to keep trying to talk to her.

Once the catheter was inserted Benae relieved her full bladder. "Oh, God, that feels so much better." She breathed.

Not being able to pee when her bladder was full was a horrible feeling and one, she wouldn't wish on her worst enemy. Now that she was comfortable, she was finally able to deal with Sincere. "So, you're a cheater?"

"No, I'm not cheating on you. What you talking about?"

"You heard me tell the nurse that I have gonorrhea. You do know that that is a sexually transmitted disease, right?" she asked condescendingly.

"I don't have an STD so I don't know what you're talking about."

"What? So how the hell did I get it, Sincere? I for sure didn't cheat on you," she whispered angrily so that the patients on either side of the curtain couldn't hear her.

"I didn't cheat on you either. So, I don't know what to say."

"Are you serious, right now? You think I cheated on you?"

"All I know is I don't have it."

"What!" Benae shouted incredulously. "How do you know you don't have it? You haven't been tested."

The nurse reappeared. "Ms. Givens you will need to undergo a gynecological exam before the antibiotic can be administered. You sir..." She turned to Sincere. "Will need to get a shot as well if you have had sexual contact with her."

"He gave it to me, don't make it sound like I infected him," Benae was losing control and yelled loud enough to quiet some of the conversations in the busy ward.

"Well, since you were diagnosed, and he has had sexual contact with you. He will need to get a shot regardless of who infected who." She looked at Benae with disdain and once again turned her attention to Sincere. "You will need to get checked in so we can get you to see the doctor, too," she said ushering Sincere through the curtain.

Once again Benae was in shock. Why was he treating her so cold when he had to know that she did not cheat on him? She balled up and silently cried into the paper pillow realizing that the life she had so recently gotten accustomed to was already over. There was no way in hell she was marrying Sincere even if he still wanted to. She couldn't even see herself being with him anymore after the way he had just treated her. She definitely wasn't going to have this baby. It was bad enough she was pregnant and unwed, but she was not about to be a single mother or a baby mama. No way, not Benae Alexis Givens.

SINCERE

The general doctor on call came through and administered the antibiotic shot with minimal eye contact and conversation. It was fine with Sincere because he definitely wasn't in a conversational mood either. He asked the flirtatious nurse if Benae was done yet.

"No, she's asleep. We're still waiting for the gynecologist."

"Can you ask her to give me a call when she wakes up?"

The nurse gave him a judgmental look that said, *You just gonna leave her here like that?*

Sincere added to his statement, "I got to go back to work to get my car and then I'll come back for her. After all of this, she'd prefer the car to a cab."

"Well, she shouldn't be here long enough for all of that. You might want to wait."

Now she was getting on his nerves. "Can you give her the message or not?"

"I can," she said smiling at him helpfully again.

"Thank you," he said quickly making his way to the elevators. He sat in the Uber trying to make sense of everything. *Benae is pregnant with my baby, has motherfucking gonorrhea and she's saying she got it from me. That's just blowing my mind right now,* he thought.

It's possible he could have passed it onto her but he honest to God didn't have any symptoms at all. The last time he had sex with Melissa was a long time ago, prior to the other night. He always wrapped it up and he was 100% sure 'Nita was fucking with no one else. Benae gave him no reason to think she would cheat on him, except her high sex drive. He never believed she would cheat, but she's the one with the STD. Maybe she got it from her ex that she fucked the day we met. To be honest he never felt he was good enough for Benae and maybe she felt the same way and was stepping out with one of those corny corporate dudes.

I really can't see that," he said aloud.

The whole situation was so unexpected and upsetting. He wanted to talk to Rick, Tru or even Dad but after picking up his car he found himself headed to Bonita's. He wanted to see his son and ask Bonita straight out if she had anything even though he knew she would be offended and that she didn't have it.

"Hey, Sincere, it seems like I haven't seen you in a minute," Ms. Lucille said opening the door.

The smell of old fried food hit him in the face. He made a mental note to tell 'Nita not to be giving Gen all that fried food. Her and her mother fried all the time.

"Hey, Ms. Lucille. How you doing?"

"I'm alright," she said slowly walking back to her chair in front of the TV in the living room.

"Da, da," Gen called to him. "Hey, little man," Sincere crooned and scooped up his son.

Bonita stepped out of her bedroom in blue tank top and red sweatpants. He could tell by her face and messy hair that she was asleep. "What you doing here?"

"I need to talk to you real quick." He carried Gen with him into her room and took a seat on the bed. "I need you to be honest with me, right now. Don't get all upset, there's a reason why I am about to ask you what I'm asking."

"Okay," she said

"Did you have to go see your GYN for anything? Were you having any problems or issues down there?"

For a minute her face looked shocked and scared but quickly changed to a frown and she started to shake her head. "No, why you asking me that?"

"I have my reasons," Sincere said softly.

"No, you can't do that. Tell me why."

"You, sure, everything good? No problems down there at all?"

"Everything is good. Why? What's going on?" she insisted.

"You been sleeping with anybody else?"

She looked at him like his question irritated her. "No, Sincere. You already know. I am not having sex with you or with anyone else. Is that why you're asking?"

Before he could respond his cell phone rang. He pried the phone away from Gen who was playing with it. "Hello,"

"I'm getting ready to leave the hospital where are you?" Benae's weak voice came through the phone.

"Oh, they told me you were still waiting to see the doctor, so I went to get my car. I'm on my way back now."

"I still can't see why you just left me like that. You're treating me horribly and you know I didn't cheat on you."

"I really don't know what to think. This whole situation is fucked up. I don't want to talk about it, right now."

"I'll take Uber home," she said and hung up.

"I got to go, I just wanted to stop by and see my son for a minute."

"Alright, see you later," Bonita said closing the door behind him.

He was glad that Benae didn't want him to pick her up. He still didn't know what to say to her. The traffic was light since it was an hour and a half before rush hour. Thankfully, he was able to get home, park the car and walk to the promenade to think. He needed more time to process his thoughts and feelings towards the woman he had planned to marry.

BONITA

"Oh, my God," Bonita said running both hands over her face. "It happened. It really happened. I can't believe it." The feelings of guilt and shame she previously had disappeared as she realized that the plan was working.

She scooped Genuwen up and sat him back in the living room with his grandmother. "Ma, I'll be right back, I'm going downstairs to Shakirra's real quick."

"Okay," Ms. Lucille said glancing at Genuwen who happily playing with his fingers.

She took the stairs and knocked on Shakirra's door.

"To what do I owe the honor? You hardly ever come down here anymore," Shakirra said as Bonita walked through the door.

"Shut up I have to tell you something."

"Before you get started, you want something to eat? I'm about to make fish."

"No, I'm good," Bonita said a little annoyed. "Remember when I was seeing Robbie? I told you we had sex a few times. What I didn't tell you was he gave me gonorrhea."

Instead of interrupting, Shakirra paused seasoning the fish and waited patiently for her to continue. That's how she always was when listening to good tea.

"So, Robbie told me and apologized and everything, but it took me a minute to get it treated. I didn't know if it was covered under Medicaid and it took forever to get an appointment at the clinic. So, while I was still infected, I had sex with Sincere on purpose. I wanted him to get it so he could pass it on to his girlfriend and she'd leave him for cheating. But guess what? He thinks she gave it to him."

"Whaaattt?" escaped Shakirra's lips.

"Yes! She called while he was at my house. Apparently, he left her in the hospital and came to my house. He said he wanted to see the baby, but he asked me if everything was good down there and if I had any reason to go to see my GYN. I said no."

"How you know he believed you?"

"I know because I can tell. Look at the facts. His girl is in the hospital with an STD and carrying his baby but where is he at? Here with me. If he thought I gave it to him, he would not come over here. He definitely wouldn't have left her at the hospital."

"Damn, all of this is fucked up," Shakirra exclaimed.

"It is. I didn't expect for him to think he got it from her. I thought it was going to be the other way around and I didn't know she was pregnant then. I feel sorta bad about that part," Bonita said softly.

"No need to feel bad now, what's done is done. And to make you feel better remember when she didn't give a shit about what you were going through when you were pregnant. As the saying goes, karma is a bitch."

"You're right, what's done is done. Now I just have to see how this plays out."

"No matter how it plays out, you definitely exposed a problem in their relationship, but you never know they might work it out. After all, they are about to get married," Shakirra rationalized. "Think about how many times you forgave him for cheating yourself. As far as we know this is his first offense with her."

"I didn't think about that, but what about the fact that he thinks she gave it to him. I must be the only other chick he's fuckin' with it coming down to just me and her," Bonita said.

"And how you know that?"

"It's just a feeling. I don't think he would ask me at all if there was someone else in the picture."

"That's possible but maybe he wears protection with the other chicks." Shakirra shrugged. "Well keep me posted," Shakirra said dropping the battered fish into the hot oil.

"Okay, I'll call you later." As she waited for the elevator, she pulled out her cell. She was so tempted to call Benae and tell her what she knew. *That would really piss her off,* she thought. By the time she exited on her floor, she'd already put her phone back in her pocket. For some reason she felt a bit of sympathy for her rival and didn't want to cause any more harm than she already had.

CHAPTER 28

IS THIS THE END

BENAE

Ming and Benae walked down the street holding hands. Benae's eyes were slightly swollen from crying and her overall disposition was solemn. Holding her hand was the best comfort Ming could think too offer. They stopped just outside of the Women's Care center and Ming tried one last time to convince Benae to keep her baby.

"You know I don't think that you've thought this through. You're acting out of hurt feelings and disappointment. You're being selfish and not being fair to anyone especially that baby."

Benae sighed deeply before responding, "Ming, we've been over this and over this. My mind is made up. I asked you here today for support not lectures. And how are you going to tell me about my decision when you've made the same one before."

"That's why I'm telling you to think about it. It's not something you get over easily."

"Neither is getting over a broken heart, a broken engagement and broken dreams with the man you love. I don't want this reminder. I still want the fairy tale and I have to start over with a clean slate. I'm sorry that you don't agree with me but that's the way it is."

"But your baby will give you all of that. You will still get to be a Law."

Benae looked at Ming like she was crazy. "I don't care about that and I don't want a baby to be the glue that holds my marriage together. Do you not see how Sincere treats the woman that had his child? I couldn't deal with being treated that way. I refuse to put myself in that position. I want better for me and from the way he

286

acted about the STD, I saw a completely different side of him. He is totally capable of treating me like a piece of shit, and I want no part of that. So, are you coming in with me or not?" Benae asked hotly.

Ming raised her eyebrow at Benae. "I don't know who you think you're talking too, but I'll give you a pass. Come on let's go."

After the procedure Ming took Benae for a bite to eat before dropping her off at home.

"Thanks for being here Ming and I'm sorry for going off on you." She smiled at her friend.

"Girl, no need for apologies. I'm just sad, I wanted my little niece or nephew." She pouted and leaned in for a hug. Looking over Ming's shoulder Benae spotted Sincere's car parked across the street.

"What is Sincere doing home?" she asked rhetorically.

"Shit, I bet Tru told him."

Benae couldn't believe what she was hearing. "Of course, he did if you told Tru!"

"Well, don't get mad at me again. I needed someone to talk to, too"

"Alright it doesn't matter now anyway," Benae said getting out of the car. "I'll talk to you later."

When she walked through the door, Sincere was sitting on the sofa in the semi-darkness. The day was overcast giving the room a gray, dreary feel. He sat with his legs apart, elbows on his thighs and his head in his hands.

"Is it true?' he asked without looking up at her.

She sat on the sofa beside him. "Yes."

"Why?" He looked at her with genuine pain in his eyes.

The sadness she saw there surprised and hurt her to see that she had hurt him. She was not expecting that. "Uhm, things were not the same between us after the STD issue. You never admitted that you gave it to me which meant you believed I cheated on you. No matter how many times I said that you never admitted it. It's okay. I am not asking you to, but I know I never cheated, and I can't be with a man that thinks that way about me."

"You should have been a little more patient, Benae. At first, I did feel confused about the situation and was gonna take my lies to the grave. The truth is I'm the one who cheated. I should have told you the truth from the beginning and I'm sorry." He looked her in her eyes.

The way she felt about it was that his apology was coming way too late. He's just now admitting to something that she knew from the beginning. "I hope your apology makes you feel better because it means nothing to me. You're not telling me anything I didn't already know. I smelled pussy on your face one night, but that's neither here nor there. The bigger issue is how you treated me and left me when I was at my lowest. That's what led me to abort our baby and end our relationship."

He sat up surprised registering across his face.

"You know what's really fucked up?" she continued, "The way you treated me like I was a liar and a cheater. You left me in the hospital alone when I was worried about the health of the baby and potential damage to my body. Do you know how it feels to not be able to pee? Wouldn't you worry about that? Of course, you would. You showed me that you didn't give a damn about the baby or me. You left us and I can't forgive or forget that." She stood up slowly and walked towards the bedroom but stopped in her tracks. "Let me ask you a question," she said turning around to face him. "Was the person you cheated with, Bonita?"

"Yeah."

"Was she the only one?"

"Yeah."

"Hmph, well apparently you weren't the only one she was fucking. Nasty bitch." Benae walked into the bedroom. "You can sleep in the guest room tonight, but I expect you to be out of here by the end of the week," she said calmly and slammed the door.

Benae was fuming and too mad to even cry. More than that, she was both physically and emotionally exhausted. Not bothering to wash her face or brush her teeth, she locked the bedroom door, pulled off her jeans and got in the bed. After tossing and turning for a few minutes she got up and poured a glass of water from the bathroom faucet. She popped two Ambien and laid back down. Sincere had taken enough from her, he wasn't robbing her of the good night's sleep she desperately needed.

SINCERE

Things had gotten out of control so quickly, Sincere didn't have time to think. Today was it. The day that Benae wanted him out and he hadn't made any plans to go. By now, he thought that she would have calmed down and saw how unreasonable she was being. But before she left for work this morning, she made it clear that she wanted him gone before she got home. Too be *"nice"* she said she was going to Chrissy's to give him time to get his things after work. His only two options came down to staying with his parents or Tru and Ming neither were where he wanted to go. In fact, he didn't want to leave period. He loved Benae and their life together. It was only at this moment that he realized how badly he had fucked up. None of the other women he'd dealt with had ever broken-up with him and there was no way Benae would be the exception. Realizing she just needed more time he swung his legs over the side of the couch and sat up.

"Once she comes home and sees all my stuff gone, she'll see that she made a mistake," he said.

He threw his clothes and personal items into a suitcase, two duffle bags and a garbage bag, and he was done packing. Considering everything that was going on they had never gotten around to get new furniture for the living room, so everything was hers. The only thing left was Meth's bed, big bag of food and his dishes. To his surprise he was able to fit it all into the car with a spot to spare for Meth on the passenger side backseat. He pulled off the Bruckner Expressway and headed to the KFC drive-thru on the corner.

"Yeah, let me get a three-piece original recipe, potato wedges, coleslaw and a Pepsi."

"Does that complete your order?" a sexy voice inquired.

"Yes" Sincere said briefly, pulling up to see if the voice matched the face. *Damn, she through, not at all what I was expecting. So much for a little distraction tonight,* he thought.

Using the spare key, he entered his dad's house with his bags and his dog and set up in the guest room. He just threw the bags in the room and didn't bother to unpack. Meth walked around the familiar house and sat in the spot where his bowls usually were when he was there.

"Alright, Meth I got the message." Moving slowly Sincere poured some hard food and water into Meth's bowls. He opened the fridge and looked in. "Nothing, just like I figured," he said peering into the empty refrigerator. "Good thing I picked something up." After he ate and took a nap, he woke up restless and ready to find something to do.

"Hello."

"Sup, 'Nita, what you doing?" he asked.

"Just about to feed your son and give him a bath."

"Hold off on that, I'm gonna come do it."

"What?"

"Just listen, I'll be there in about a half hour."

"I can save bath time for you, but this boy is ready to eat," she insisted.

"Okay, save me bath time and I can read to him."

"Oh, so you have permission to see your son at my house now?"

"Yeah something like that. You need anything?"

"No, we're fine."

"Alright then, later." Seeing his son was always a guaranteed way to pick him up when he was feeling down.

BONITA

Something was definitely up with Sincere. They hadn't spoken much since he came by to ask about her sexual health status. Now he just wants to pop up and be daddy over here. No matter the reason she decided to look good for the visit. So, she put on one of her new wigs, threw on some leggings and crop top. Gen had already been fed and was entertaining himself with his toys while periodically looking up to laugh at Sponge Bob's high-pitched voice. This gave her time to straighten the place up a bit. As soon as she was done, there was the familiar knock at the door.

"Hey, you," she said obviously happy to see him.

"Hey, what's up," he said looking her up and down quickly. He leaned down for a kiss, but she turned her head. She was determined to keep her vow of celibacy not just to further her walk with God but to make Sincere miss what he had. After her rejection he moved onto the reason for his visit and picked up his son. Bonita sat on her bed and watched TV while her two favorite guys indulged in the longest bath ever. Once he finished bathing his son, Sincere got him ready for bed and sat in the rocking chair in his room to read him a story from his Dr. Seuss collection. After about an hour, he emerged from the room and informed Bonita that Genuwen was asleep.

"Well, thank you for putting him to bed and everything tonight. It was nice."

"It was. I love spending time with him. He's growing up so fast and I want to be here for everything."

"I know you do, you already know that's what I want, too." Changing tactics, she said, "What's going on with you? You haven't been yourself in a while."

"There's a lot going on. Nothing that I want to talk about though," he said dismissively while grabbing the remote and settling himself comfortably on her bed pillows. He kicked one of his sneakers off with his foot and was about to kick off the other one when she stopped him. "What are you doing?"

"Chillin' watching TV with you," he said picking up the remote.

"Uhm Hmm," Bonita said knowing full well what chilling and watching TV had turned into many times in the past. That was not going to be the case tonight. "Sincere, you came over and spent time with your son now he's asleep. There's no reason for you to be chilling here with me. Go home to your girl, I mean your fiancée. I am not playing this game with you no more. If I'm not good enough to marry, then get out the way and don't block me from the man that wants to love me and treat me right."

"But I never said I didn't love you. I never said that."

"I know you didn't, and you won't but it's the second part that's the problem. You don't treat me right and you never did. Funny thing is, I didn't truly see it until I saw how different you were with this chick, you're with now. You showed me a side of you that I didn't think existed. Now that I see that you do know how to treat a woman, there is no way that I am going back to the way things were with us."

Sincere sat up and looked at her intently. It felt like it was the first time he was really seeing her. "So, what you saying?"

"I'm saying that we'll always be friends and I will always love you but that's it. I'm celibate, I'm in the church and I'm good with that."

"I hear that," he said standing up and preparing to leave making it clear to Bonita that she was right to assume that he wanted to have sex. "Well, the winds of change are definitely blowing," he joked.

"Yes, they are," she agreed. "Hey, wait a minute I'll walk out with you," she said slipping her feet in her shoes and throwing on a jacket. Silently they waited for the elevator, when it arrived, Bonita opened her arms for a hug.

They embraced warmly and parted when Bonita's cell rang. "Talk to you later, she said as she answered the phone without looking at the caller ID.

"Hello, Bonita." Not wanting to believe her ears, Bonita pulled the phone away from her ear and looked at the screen, sure enough it was Benae. Curiously, Bonita responded, "Hey, what's up?"

"I want to talk to you for a minute, woman to woman, if I may."

"Shoot," Bonita said while locking the door and heading to back to her bedroom.

"First off I want to apologize to you. Even though Sincere clearly lied to me and told me he was no longer involved with you, the fact that you were carrying his baby should have been enough for me to know better. The problem was by the time he told me about the pregnancy, we were together for about six months and I had already developed strong feelings for him and he convinced me that his feelings for me were the same. My real reason for calling is to let you know that Sincere confessed to sleeping with you. So, you were telling the truth all along." They both sat silently, each taking in the breadth of Benae's statement. "I also wanted you to know, if you don't already, that I called everything off...the engagement, the wedding and the relationship. So, he's all yours."

"What!" Bonita was instantly ecstatic. All she could muster was, "Does Sincere know?"

"Of course, he knows, I asked him to be out of my place today and he abided by my wishes. Why is he there?"

"No, he just left but he didn't say anything about y'all breaking up."

"I'm sure he has his reasons for that. At any rate, I could never remain with a man that has shown me such disrespect. It's bad enough that I did the one thing I never thought I would do in my life, and that is share a man. Whether you want to admit it or not that is what we were doing. We both knew about the other yet we both decided to stay with him thinking we could one up the other until one of us gave him up. Sadly, the only person that was winning in that scenario was Sincere Law."

Bonita thought about it a moment and realized that she was right. They had been sharing Sincere and she was even more to blame than Benae. "You know what, you're right. You're one hundred percent, right. So, I owe you an apology, too. Because even though he was mine first and I am the mother of his child. It's not like I didn't know about you. I knew he was your man at the time, and I kept messing with him because I wanted him. I was so busy trying to take him from you that I did some things I'm not proud of and I'm sorry for that." That's as far as she was going to apologize for purposely spreading the STD.

"Thanks for that. I appreciate our conversation. I'll miss little Genuwen. He's an awesome little boy. I wish you well. Take care," Benae said, finality in her voice.

"You, too and I want you to know that Sincere isn't winning. He's losing two women who really loved him," Bonita said. Without missing a beat, she called Shakirra. "Girl you won't believe this. Sincere's girlfriend called here telling me they broke up and that I can have him. You know I don't believe a word she said."

"No way!" Shakirra shouted.

"Can you come up? If not, I'm coming down. We need to figure out my next move."

EPILOGUE

SINCERE

It's almost been two years since his break-up with Benae but he simply could not get her out of his mind. Although he had decided that it was in his best interest to marry Bonita since she had gotten pregnant with his second child, he often wondered what life would have been like if things didn't get so messed up with Benae. He and Bonita had a good life she was as loving and devoted as he knew she would be, but after a year of marriage something was already missing. He was there out of obligation for his kids more than anything else. She was taking classes before she got pregnant and still wasn't working so all of the bills were on him and he felt a little resentment at her lack of partnership in that area. He busted his ass to get them a nice three-bedroom apartment in a decent area of Brooklyn and she just took it all for granted. The bond he had with Bonita was still there, but it was different, he wanted more than just a bond. Now that he had a taste of better that is what he craved and that is why he found himself parked outside of Benae's apartment. It wasn't the first time he'd done it, but this time he was going to talk to her. He needed to see her. Ringing the bell to the apartment that he used to have the keys to, hurt.

"Who is it," Benae asked through the newly installed security system that allowed her to see who was there before she responded.

"Sincere." There was some hesitation before he heard a buzz allowing him entry into the building. He opened the door to see her standing at the top of the stairs. He envisioned running up the stairs and into her arms, but the look on her face told him otherwise.

"Hey, what are you doing here?" she asked concerned.

Heading towards her he said," I was in the area and I decided to stop by. I haven't seen you in a minute and you changed your number."

"Come in," she said standing aside to let him pass. "I know. I had to break away from you. I couldn't just talk to you like we were old friends. I needed time to get myself together."

"I understand. The time apart was needed."

"I heard you married Bonita," she said glancing at the gold band on his ring finger.

"Yeah, I did," he answered sheepishly.

"So, Ming was right. She told me she heard that you were going to marry her, but I didn't think much of it. She stopped speaking to me once she saw that I was not going to become a Law. I was useless to her at that point." She chuckled. "You want something to eat? I was about to order takeout."

He laughed. "So, I see you still don't do too much cooking."

"Nope, I did the most when I was with you. Now I order delivery or eat at Chrissy's."

"Yeah, I'll stay to grab a bite and catch up with you." He smiled.

They sat and talked until late into the evening reminiscing about good times and bad but laughing at it all. Stretching and yawning, Benae said, "You need to get going. I have work in the morning and I'm sure you do, too."

"Yeah, I do. Before I go, let me get your number?" he asked.

"What do you need my number for?"

"To keep in touch with you. I care and I want to check in on you from time to time." He looked at the skepticism on her face.

"Okay," she said reciting her number as she walked toward the door and held it open. He wanted to kiss her but knew better than to attempt it. At least he had opened the door to possibly being around and who knew where that could lead.

After getting in his car, he called her to make sure she gave him her real number.

"Hello?"

"Hey, it's me. Just making sure you gave me your number." He laughed.

Benae laughed, too. "You're so silly."

"Benae," he said softly. "You have a man or seeing someone?"

"No, not that it's any of your business."

He brightened. "You have my number, too. Don't be a stranger."

"Goodnight, Sincere," she said ending the call.

He turned on his car and headed uptown to Melissa's new apartment. They had been seeing a lot more of each other over the past few months and she had even relocated to New York to be closer to him. If he could get Benae back he would kick Melissa to the curb. She was a great replacement, but she wanted to much. She had a fly apartment in Queens and a great career, but she had caught feelings and was trying to lock him down even though she knew he was married.

BONITA

Bonita looked around her charming little apartment filled with pictures of her, Sincere, Genuwen and Sinthia. Her favorite photo of all was the one of them on their wedding day. It sat in a large crystal frame in the center of the wall unit. Now that she had her boy and her girl, things could not be better. It didn't take too long for Sincere to put a ring on it once she stopped giving up the nookie. He kept trying to get her to give in, but she was steadfast in her resolve to remain celibate and never wavered. Next thing she knew, he asked for her hand in marriage on the same day that she had overheard him tell Rick that it was *"cheaper to keep her."* She didn't care about his reasons as long as they got married. During the engagement period she decided that it was okay to resume a sexual relationship with him since they were getting married.

Now she was a stay-at-home mom and loved taking care of her family, including Meth. The church and her family were her life and she was very content. In fact, she thought of Shakirra and her battles with Joe, Kendra and the drama she'd been through with Rick and was sure they were jealous of her perfect marriage to Sincere. He had given her everything she wanted.

The only thing that put a damper on her happiness was the fact that Sincere didn't seem to be too happy. He was often distant, mean and stayed out a lot. Trying not to be a nag, she didn't complain about it but showed her displeasure by not speaking to him and refusing sex. More than once it had crossed her mind that he was still messing around with his ex. She lied and told Benae she was done with Sincere.

Maybe she had lied to me, too, Bonita thought.

Determined to find out what was going on, she crept into the bedroom where Sincere laid asleep across the bed and cautiously pulled his cell phone from beside him. Scrolling through his contacts, recent calls and texts she saw that she called someone named Mel a lot but didn't pay it no mind. Another number that stood out was assigned to Bags.

"Bags," she said aloud. She recalled a day when she and Shakirra had laughed at Miss High and Mighty's poor initials. "This negro thinks he's slick, he told me they were no longer in contact." Entering *67 she dialed the number.

"Hello," Benae answered.

"Hello, can I please speak to Benae Givens?" Bonita asked disguising her voice.

"Yes, this is she."

Bonita quickly disconnected the call. Tears sprang to her eyes she was so mad. *How could she do this to me? She called and told me that she was going to leave him alone, but she didn't.* Furious, Bonita called back, once again blocking the number.

"Hello?"

"Leave my husband alone!" she yelled. "He's my husband now."

She heard laughter on the other end of the phone. "I don't bother your husband. Unlike, you I don't mess around with other women's men, much less their husbands."

"You heard what I said leave my husband alone! What is wrong with you? Why can't you find your own man?" Bonita yelled.

"Bonita, when I told you I was done with Sincere, I meant it. You married him." She laughed. "So, don't get mad if you're where he's at but I'm where he wants to be," she said, reciting the Lil Kim lyric. "Don't call me again."

"Bitch!" Bonita yelled and realized the call was disconnected.

Before she realized what was happening, Sincere snatched the phone away from her. "What the hell you doing?" he yelled at her.

"Calling the ex-girlfriend, you said you weren't in contact with!" she yelled back on the verge of tears.

"What's the problem?" he asked annoyed.

"The problem is I don't want you talking to her. There's no reason for you to be in contact with her."

"There's no reason for you to be going through my phone either but you do it." He walked into the bedroom and slammed the door. Bonita walked to the bathroom and watched her reflection in the mirror as tears flowed. Through her tears she could hear Sincere talking on the phone.

"Hey, sorry about that, I have to apologize because all that is unnecessary. I promise you won't get any more calls like that, alright? Cool. Talk to you later."

That motherfucker had the nerve to call and apologize to her? "God I am trying to be strong, but this man is pushing me past my limits. Please help me God before I hurt him," she cried out through her tears.

"You ain't gonna hurt nobody. Come here," he said opening the bathroom door and hugging her.

She knew she shouldn't, but she let him hold her and kiss her tear streaked cheeks. Closing her eyes, she pretended that their marriage was perfect, and she was the only woman he wanted.

BENAE

"Wow," Benae said through her laughter.

After all this time away from both Sincere and Bonita they both pop up within days of each other. It really was hysterical. After parting ways with Sincere, Benae relied heavily on her parents and Chrissy to help her get over him. The loss was so severe that she had taken a leave of absence from work and moved in with her parents in DC. They let her mourn in peace and only bothered her to ask if she wanted or needed anything. Initially, she stayed in bed all day with the drapes closed, only coming out when notified that food was available. Slowly, she joined her parents at the dinner table and the next day for breakfast. Rhonda was able to talk her into getting her hair and nails done and Benae started to feel like herself again. After six weeks of hiding out, she felt well enough to go home and face life without the man she loved. As promised, Chrissy was at the airport to pick her up when she returned. If Benae wasn't ready to go home alone, Chrissy and Greg had extended their home to her for as long as she needed. Benae joked that that would get old real quick and politely declined. Over the next couple of weeks, she threw out any reminders of Sincere...cards, perfume, photos, ticket stubs, and certain items of clothing. The only thing she kept was jewelry. She figured she could pawn it, but never got around to doing it.

As the pain in her heart subsided, she returned to work, applied for a promotion, and got it. She requested a new phone number when she transferred to her new role. Thanks to the extra money she made, she splurged on a Disney Cruise for Chrissy's kids, Marquise, Kye, and the new edition Cristina. She threw in tickets for Greg and Chrissy for good measure. They were in the lobby of the Residence Inn Cape Canaveral Cocoa Beach waiting to board the ship when Bonita's call came in.

"Why is she still calling you?" Chrissy inquired.

"I have no idea. I just feel that karma is a bitch. She continued a relationship with him knowing full well that I was with him. Now she's worried that I am going to do the same thing to her. Oh, I could if I wanted to too. Sincere would definitely be down for that, but I'm not interested. I really feel like I dodged a bullet."

"Clearly, you did. They deserve each other," Chrissy said.

"Hey, Greg. How you doing man?" a tall, chocolate complexioned man with well-trimmed facial hair and deep voice asked.

"Lance, what's up my man?" Greg answered standing up to shake the man's hand.

"We're about to go on a Disney cruise. This is my wife Chrissy and her friend Benae. This is my colleague, Lance Marshall."

"Hello, nice to meet you ladies." His gaze resting on Benae as he spoke. "Yeah, I just came back from the cruise."

"Really, I didn't think you had any kids," Greg said.

"I don't. It was a family reunion. I think I was the only one there unmarried and childless." He laughed once again glancing at Benae.

"Well, if I were there, I would be a part of the unmarried, childless club as well," Benae piped in.

"Is that right?" he inquired.

"That's right." She smiled at him.

"How much time do you guys have before boarding," he asked.

"About an hour," Chrissy and Benae answered.

"Well, that should be enough time for one drink," he said singling out Benae.

"Sure, the bar is over there." She pointed.

"Promise, I'll have her back well before boarding time." He held Benae at the small of her back and guided her towards the bar.

Taking a seat at the bar, Lance asked, "So, what's your poison?"

"Kettle One and cranberry with a twist of lime."

"That's a solid drink," he complimented. "Since we don't have too much time, do you mind if I get your number so I can get in touch with you when you get back?"

"I would like nothing more," she said sexily and put her hand out for his phone. As she added her name and number to his contacts, she thought, *There is life after Sincere.* She smiled at the man she was sure was going to make her forget all about him. *After all, third time's the charm, right?*

CPSIA information can be obtained
at www.ICGtesting.com
Printed in the USA
LVHW052014271220
675097LV00012B/1429

9 798690 504595